Black Bear

Also by Aly Monroe

The Maze of Cadiz
Washington Shadow
Icelight

Aly Monroe

Black Bear

JOHN MURRAY

FT

First published in Great Britain in 2013 by John Murray (Publishers)
An Hachette UK Company

1

© Aly Monroe 2013

A CIP catalogue record for this title is available from the British Library

Hardback ISBN 978-1-84854-486-4
Trade paperback ISBN 978-1-84854-487-1
Ebook ISBN 978-1-84854-492-5

Typeset in Sabon MT by Servis Filmsetting Ltd, Stockport, Cheshire

Printed and bound by Clays Ltd

John Murray policy is to use papers that are natural, renewable and recyclable
products and made from wood grown in sustainable forests. The logging and
manufacturing processes are expected to conform to the environmental
regulations of the country of origin.

John Murray (Publishers)
338 Euston Road
London NW1 3BH

www.johnmurray.co.uk

To J.S.D.
born 11 November 1918

COTTON HAD no grasp of where he was and no notion of how he had got there. He could not even tell whether his eyes were shut or he was trapped somewhere dark enough to make no difference. What he did begin to feel was a very heavy weight pressing on the right side of his head. It felt flat, like the flange of a sizeable I-beam. It was squeezing his skull.

The few words of response that came to his mind were slow and insecure, as if they were not certain what form they should take, however simple. Though he had not moved, the pain in his head abruptly shifted, became something bulb-shaped pulsing at the base of his neck. His tongue felt dry as if it had not moved for a long time. His mind appeared to have whole sections missing, and what was left, apart from a few sparks of alarm, was as lively as dried, old dregs.

'Have I been in a – have I been in an—?'

The letters that came to him formed *accent*. He winced, partly at the excruciating pain in his head. He meant *accident*. He knew the word. But he could not see how to get at it. With each throb the pain wiped part of it out.

Cotton had regained consciousness before. As a child of about eight at the dentist he had been given gas for the

extraction of a milk tooth. And about fifteen years later, in Sicily, after the shock wave from an explosion had flung him against a jeep. From both he remembered a light spinning sensation before he recovered his senses. They had all come back in a bright rush – not like this. As if on cue, his mind saw a spin of blue sky and white clouds, but the wrong way round. He was leaving them, dropping back not rising up. The clouds fractured and turned black.

Cotton slumped into unconsciousness again.

'Can you hear me? Colonel Cotton? Can you hear me?'

Cotton tried to answer but he heard a sound he did not recognize as anything to do with his intent to say 'yes'. He was not sure he had really managed to speak, only that something like a moan had reverberated in his skull. The bones in his head felt brittle and light, somewhere between dried-out honeycomb and crumbling leaves. The image made him feel like retching.

'How are you feeling?' said the voice. The voice was American and male. There was nothing at all familiar about it. Cotton could not understand the question. He could not get a grip on it. He recognized the words but could not run them together to make sense. Though his heart was already beating very fast, he felt it quicken. He could barely breathe.

'Can you hear me, sir?' the voice repeated.

Cotton made a big effort. 'Yes,' he said. This sounded to him more like a growl than a word.

'Good. Good.' The man was speaking very slowly and carefully. 'Tell me now. How are you feeling?'

Cotton didn't know what to say. He could not get past the pain and the nausea.

'I guess you're feeling pretty rough,' suggested the voice.

Cotton tried again. 'Have I been in a crash?' He sounded to himself like a profoundly deaf person speaking.

'Is that what you think?'

'I don't know.'

'You're having problems remembering.'

'Yes.'

'What can you remember, sir?'

'I've been unconscious. Haven't I?'

'In a manner of speaking.'

Cotton considered the man's reply. None of this made any sense. He could remember nothing. He could find nothing to remember.

'Is there a problem?' said the voice.

'I'm thinking.'

But the truth was Cotton wasn't thinking much at all. His mind felt gruesomely tenderized, but he had no recall of the blows that had tenderized it.

Somebody he could not identify had once said to him, 'Are you actually capable of panic?'

'I was always taught panic was of no use,' he had replied. 'You have to think. There are times you can think pretty fast.'

Cotton couldn't move and he couldn't see. And, despite his scudding pulse, he could barely think. Was he blind? Paralysed?

He breathed in as deeply as he could. From somewhere in the dark he recalled, as a very small child,

3

looking over the top of his cot as his Mexican nanny approached. She was smiling and talking to him but he could not hear what she was saying. In his mind, he held up his arms to be lifted.

'What are you doing?' said the voice.

'Remembering something,' he said.

'Of what happened to you?'

'Long ago.'

'That's good too,' said the voice. 'I mean it. That'll do. Can you tell me about it?'

Cotton felt another wave of nausea. 'Am I blind?' he said.

'No, you have a cover over your eyes to protect them. You may be having acute problems with your sense of balance. You have to trust me, Colonel Cotton. I need your collaboration. Try to keep talking. Tell me about the memory you just had. Is it still there? Can you recall it?'

Cotton understood the bit about balance. He thought about landing craft yawing in a swell. But that wasn't right. This was worse; a sensation that he was on the verge of falling out of the space that contained him. The space was egg-shaped but the egg was fragile. He recalled someone telling him an egg was the most efficient aerodynamic shape. He had no idea if that was true, nor what good it did him. This shape was prone to shifts and lurches.

The more he engaged with the voice the more conscious he became of how many separate bits of him hurt. His joints, for example, felt as if somebody had gone mad with a small, shiny hammer, the kind doctors use to test reflexes but had used like a weapon on him. Had

4

he been badly burnt? 'Something when I was very young, that's all.'

'Tell me.'

'It's before I can even speak. I'm watching my *ama* come to pick me up out of the cot.'

'Ama? What's that word?'

'Nurse,' said Cotton. 'Nanny. In Mexico.'

'Can you recall her name?'

'Consuelo.'

'Right,' said the voice. Cotton was aware the speaker had turned his head towards someone else. 'That makes sense, right? *Consuelo* means "consolation". Isn't that the case?'

Almost instantly Cotton felt a surge of utter distress, as if he had just received the most heartbreaking news possible – but all from the notion that the other man was misunderstanding. It wasn't the translation of Consuelo's name that mattered; it was Consuelo herself. Why was he so abject and alarmed that he might be misleading a doctor?

'It's quite a common name.'

'Oh, I'm sure it is. I'm not doubting that, Colonel Cotton. Not at all.'

Cotton confirmed the man was calling him by his old rank. 'Who am I speaking to?'

'My name is Dr Sanford.'

'Are you a proper doctor?'

'What do you mean?'

'You're not a psychiatrist?'

'No, I'm not,' said Dr Sanford. 'Are you telling me you've had a bad experience?'

5

'Not me.' Cotton thought he was falling asleep again, but he was prevented from doing so by someone speaking. It took him some time to appreciate that the fluent, peremptory, sneering voice he was hearing was coming from him.

'But it was quite exceptionally difficult to avoid an impression of the psychiatrists involved in our war effort as combining the qualities of both Uriah Heep and Torquemada. The abject alacrity with which they kowtowed to funding and authority was most striking. Almost as much as the speed with which they dispatched the soldiers they were supposed to be helping. Is "shirker" a recognized term in psychiatry? I once saw one of these people call a sergeant that. The man had no skin on his lower legs but presumably the psychiatrist couldn't look down past the table he was sitting behind.'

Dr Sanford laughed. 'Well now! Where did that come from?' he said.

Cotton had no idea. It had been like listening to someone else, a bitter, vindictive someone else – like the second master at his old school, who insisted on being addressed as *padre*. Or possibly, it seemed to Cotton, like a certain kind of interrogator.

'Let me reassure you, Colonel Cotton. You have no need to worry. I'm a physician, a neurologist. Are you in a position right now to know what that means?'

'You deal with epilepsy, Parkinson's, cerebral palsy . . .'

'None of those is your case, Colonel. But I'm sure you know that sometimes we have to use symptoms to trace

back. This conversation is in the nature of an investigation.'

'Of what?'

'Your condition. Right now your eyes are covered because light is extremely painful for you. Do you remember that? It's not too strong to say you were in agony. You said it was like having rusty hat pins stuck into your eyes.'

Rusty hat pins? It seemed a bizarre, far-fetched simile to Cotton. 'I don't remember.' Immediately, however, Cotton felt himself cringe. He felt frightened of having the surface of his eyes scratched by flecks of rust. The flecks floated in the liquid between his lids and his eyeballs, and the damned things were spinning, rather leisurely, like blotched, metallic sores. What the hell was the matter with him? Why was he worried about rust when a hat pin in his eyeball would certainly have blinded and very likely killed him directly? Where was his sense of depth?

'That's why I am asking you about memories,' continued the doctor. 'We want to see how much you can join up, as it were.'

'Are you telling me I'm brain-damaged?'

'Honestly? We don't know yet. But you are doing extraordinarily well so far, let me assure you.'

'Was I in an acci—?' It wasn't that Cotton couldn't say the word; he couldn't even find it.

'An accident? You were found unconscious in a doorway in Centre Street, about a block down from Police Headquarters.'

'Where's that?'

'Little Italy.'

Cotton heard 'Lillillily'. 'Lill—?'

'Colonel Cotton! Colonel Cotton!'

Cotton came back with a grunt of protest. 'What?'

'Italy,' said the doctor. 'You were found in Little Italy. New York. Have you got that?'

'Yes.'

'Good. You were found in a doorway. When I saw you for the first time you were having convulsions. We didn't have an easy time. At one stage you went into shock.'

'What is wrong with me?'

'You've had an influx of drugs in your system, Colonel. We are pretty sure we know what the main drugs were but we don't quite know how much you got.'

'What are you saying?'

'Well, for example, we found substantial traces of scopolamine in your blood. And there was mescaline in your urine.'

Cotton heard the words but they vanished immediately. 'Say those again.'

'All right. You may have heard of mescaline. Or perhaps you've heard of peyote? Oh, that has a link with Mexico, doesn't it? Peyote's another word for mescaline.'

'Yes.'

'Tell me.'

'Peyote. It's a hallucinogenic.'

'It doesn't cause what we would call true hallucinations.'

'I see. More like symphonies and harmonies, an

8

intense feeling of oneness with the colour and petals of a rose?' It was that sarcastic voice again. It made Cotton feel sick, as if he had swallowed a ventriloquist's act and couldn't get rid of it.

'That's correct,' said Dr Sanford. 'And how about nightshade? Scopolamine is derived from nightshade.'

'Deadly?'

'There are variations and non-lethal doses. We suspect you've also had sodium amytal, but that is harder to sort out from other barbiturates. Do you know what that is?'

To his own surprise Cotton heard himself speak, quietly, as himself. 'Yes,' he said. 'The Germans invented it. They wanted it to be a truth drug.'

'Good. What we are doing is clearing you out. I'm afraid this has meant more drugs. And we've been monitoring your heart and, in particular, your kidneys. That's the physical side. On your mind we are less able to work because we can't monitor it so well. Do you understand what I am saying? I need your help. We need to communicate.'

'Right,' said Cotton. 'I feel tied down.'

'You are,' said Dr Sanford's voice. 'You've had convulsions. Do you remember I said that? They were violent but we got them down in intensity and frequency and in the last twenty-four hours you've had no attacks whatsoever. I assure you, however, that even three days ago, they were still violent enough to cause you quite severe injury. We had to ensure you didn't bite your tongue. But we've been reducing the sedation and you really are holding up pretty well.'

'I don't remember any convulsions.'

9

'That's not a problem. I wouldn't expect you to remember any. OK?'

'No,' said Cotton. He sighed. '*Mierda.*'

'You remember Spanish?'

'I think so.'

'Say something.'

'*Estoy jodido.*'

'What does that mean?'

Cotton felt enormously tired, as if each word he had spoken had been bruising his brain and he simply had no more space left for any more bruises. He could see a kind of kaleidoscopic fracturing of colours under his eyelids. These broken bits began to spin and melt into a single colour. It was a repulsive shade of urine and tangerine.

'He's screwed,' said another American voice, one that Cotton had not heard. 'He says he's screwed.'

If he had been able to, Cotton would have nodded. The translation was just right enough. He passed out again on a feeling almost like relief.

2

COTTON WAS woken by tugging. The tugging turned into twitching. He felt himself start, as if he had been given a small electrical shock.

'What's the date?' he said.

'Oh, my,' said an American female voice. 'He's awake. Get Dr Sanford, would you?'

'What's the date?'

'Wednesday, June 18, 1947,' said the woman. 'I am sorry, sir. Did we hurt you with the drip?'

Cotton was sure this meant something but was not at all clear what.

'How long? How long have I been here?'

'Colonel Cotton, you've been here for thirteen days. You weren't really supposed to wake up properly until tomorrow.'

Cotton did not know what to say to this. That was nearly two weeks, a fortnight. He tried to count. That took him back to the 5th of June, which still did not mean anything. He heard the door open.

'Well now! How are you feeling today?' said Dr Sanford.

Cotton felt relief. He understood the question.

'In less pain,' he said. 'Confused. Or ignorant.'

Dr Sanford laughed. 'Good,' he said. 'You're

reacting well! I am going to check your pulse. Is that OK?'

'Yes,' said Cotton. He felt something vague on his wrist. He presumed he should translate the feeling into seeing the doctor's fingers. He waited. He saw nothing.

'Seventy-five,' said Dr Sanford. 'What were you before?'

'Lower,' said Cotton. 'About sixty.'

'Oh, seventy-five is acceptable for now, let me tell you.'

'I can't smell.'

'Right. You're very likely dehydrated. We'll tackle that. How's your sense of touch?'

'Dull. Distant but with twitches.'

'OK. Hearing?'

'That's relatively sharp. At least, I think it is.'

In the dark, Cotton understood he was waiting to 'jump' back into himself. But he could not. He could not raise a sense of a self to jump back into. He had no impression of a flood of memories waiting to be summoned up. In Sicily, though injured, he had had adrenalin to help him react. Here there was nothing. He still had no idea how he had got there, could recall nothing of the last weeks. He was clear that he was in the US but could not even remember how he had arrived there. He decided on a plane, but could find no detail to back the decision. He added engine drone, tried to look around the cabin, but started getting that tunnel vision again. He did not mean that. He was looking down a tube and the tube was tightening.

'I don't know,' he said.

'Yes, Colonel Cotton. That's why I am here.'

'I don't know what I am.'

There was a pause. He could hear a pen moving quickly on paper. Then another male voice spoke.

'Hell,' it drawled. 'Does this stuff turn them metaphysical?'

There was a noise Cotton somehow heard as sneezing. Dr Sanford did not approve of the interruption. Cotton had heard the other voice before but wasn't sure when.

'Where do you want to start?' said Dr Sanford.

Cotton's skin had started to prickle. He was not sure if he was cold or was trying to sweat.

'My name is Peter Cotton.'

'Right! Where do you live?'

'Wilbraham Place.'

'OK. Where's that?'

'Off Sloane Street.'

'You're not talking of New York.'

'London.'

'Where do you live here? In Manhattan?'

Cotton waited. Nothing whatsoever occurred to him. He couldn't recall a door or a window, let alone a building or a number.

'Don't worry, Colonel Cotton. You're going to find you have acute recent or short-term memory loss.'

'*Lagunas*,' said Cotton.

'What's that?'

'Lagoons. Roundish empty things.'

He heard someone write.

13

'We say "lacunae",' said Sanford. 'But I think you'll find the emptiness a little more consistent than just gaps. How old are you?'

'I'm twenty-eight.'

'Can you remember your birth date?'

'Yes. I was born on 20th February 1919.'

'Good. Are you married?'

Up to now Cotton had been able to answer promptly, without thinking. Now he frowned. Embarrassed, he could only see a few trite curves of female flesh held by some very thin, gauzy material. 'No, I'm not.'

'Why do you pause?'

'I was engaged. I've been engaged. First to Emmeline Gilbert, then to Katherine Ward. Emmeline died in a bombing raid in 1943. Katherine died in a motor car accident in 1945.'

Dr Sanford's voice turned grave. 'Colonel Cotton. Are you quite sure about that?'

Cotton wondered. 'Yes,' he decided. What he found dispiriting and absurd was that he could recall neither Emmeline's nor Katherine's face – each had been reduced to a blank with one simplified feature; eyes for Emmeline, lips for Katherine. He couldn't put the faces in profile. To his shame, both women resembled round balloons defined by a single projection. These balloons were drifting past him. Cotton had never been tearful, but here again he could have wept. A moment later, he saw the balloons had burst and that their insides were flecked with spittle.

'Oh, not fucking slobber,' he said. He had no idea what he meant but somehow it fitted his suspicion that

14

he would have to build up his memory out of small, childishly simple tokens.

'Colonel?' said Dr Sanford. 'You just keep going, all right? There's no pressure. You take your time. Can you remember arriving in the US?'

'No.'

'All right. Would you know *why* you came to the US?'

'For the United Nations.'

Cotton remembered something here all right, somebody saying, 'We want Intelligence mixed in with the fucking cement. We want Intelligence in there from the foundations up.'

'Yes, for the United Nations.'

'Right! So were you at the Sperry plant? At Lake Success?' This meant nothing to Cotton. 'You do know the old gyroscope plant is the organization's temporary headquarters?'

'I don't know what you're talking about.'

'OK. Let's see. Do you know if you are based in Long Island or Manhattan?'

'Manhattan,' said Cotton. 'I think. Wait. East River? Turtle Bay?'

'That's where the building will be.'

'Right,' said Cotton. He sighed. He had thought the building was there already. He looked for something he definitely did know. 'I have a sister. She lives in Manhattan and Long Island. Joan and her husband have a large house on Centre Island, overlooking Oyster Bay.'

'Can you tell me more about her?'

'Yes. She married an American called Todd Buchanan. They have three children. Emily, Halliday and Foster.'

15

'Good. What about your parents?'

'What?' This was ghastly, like one of those dreams in which you are bereft of answers. 'I think my mother's dead.'

'You think?'

Cotton waited. All he could manage was a miserable lack, expressed as a draining, almost sucking sensation, of where his mother should have been. Again he had to resist a powerful urge to weep.

'I'm sure.'

'Your father?'

'I don't think he's dead.'

'You're not certain?'

'No,' said Cotton. 'He's not dead. But he has a heart condition.'

'OK,' said Dr Sanford. 'Am I right? Would you prefer to stop for now?'

'Yes,' said Cotton. 'I think I would.'

The doctor had said short-term memory loss. Not remembering whether his parents were alive or dead didn't strike Cotton as being other than miserably and thoroughly confused. It made him feel wretched and guilty. He breathed in and, even though his eyes were covered, he squeezed them shut.

'Colonel Cotton, you've had a cocktail of drugs. You do understand that?'

'A cocktail? What do you mean? Like a Manhattan?'

He heard the smile in Dr Sanford's voice. 'Make that a brandy Manhattan and mix it with a Death in the Afternoon, that's absinthe and champagne, and then add . . . I don't know, a—'

'Chupacabra?' Cotton offered.

'Good,' said Dr Sanford. 'This is remarkably positive, Colonel Cotton. What is a chupacabra?'

'I really have no idea,' said Cotton. 'It's got tequila in it, certainly, but after that . . . perhaps some Tabasco sauce?'

'I meant the creature.'

'That's just a mythical bloodsucker, a kind of vampire, I suppose. No charm or garlic, though. It's an animal.'

'Did you pick that for any reason?'

'I don't follow.'

'Are you conscious of nightmares you've had? A sensation of invasion? Possibly being the victim of something akin to a vampire?'

'No,' said Cotton. 'I don't remember anything like that. I can hardly remember cocktail names. I don't drink them.'

'OK. You can recall nothing of what's happened to you? It's just a blank.'

'It's a dark blank,' said Cotton. 'Sometimes I get – I don't know – volcanic colours, and egg yolks and stained glass. When will you uncover my eyes?'

'Not yet,' said Dr Sanford. 'Let me tell you why. I want you to understand more of what you've been through. Do you remember I told you something of scopolamine?'

'Scopolamine,' said Cotton. He was pleased he could say the word. And something stirred. 'Isn't that used to combat travel sickness?'

'Yes!' said the doctor. 'Though that's only one of its uses. I also told you about mescaline.'

17

'Yes,' said Cotton. 'It can cause hallucinations, or at least very heightened perceptions.'

'Good. How about sodium amytal?'

'It's a barbiturate. Some people believe it's a truth drug.'

'Excellent. Colonel, you've had a cocktail of all these drugs. Do you understand what I am saying? You've been used – though I don't want to alarm you or be overly dramatic – as a kind of human cocktail shaker.'

Cotton felt no alarm whatsoever. 'Are you saying this is a hangover?'

'OK,' said Dr Sanford. 'Something like that. But rather more. You've got more than a headache.'

'Right,' said Cotton. 'I'm confused.' Something had snagged in Cotton's mind. It did not make obvious sense.

'Go on, go on.'

'I remember, at least I think I do, that John Maynard Keynes was on sodium amytal in late 1945, a few months before he died. In Washington he would put ice packs over his heart and take capsules of sodium amytal.'

'Oh, that's wonderful,' said Dr Sanford. 'You see, Colonel, our problem is about the scale of things; the dose, if you like, and the very different reactions of different people in different conditions. Lord Keynes was prescribed sodium amytal in an effort to keep his heart rate up.'

Cotton wasn't sure. He remembered his own heart-beat had certainly been fast enough to blur the pulse. He heard himself emit a kind of giggle. 'It didn't work on Keynes as a truth drug now, did it?'

'It wasn't meant to,' said Dr Sanford. 'Keynes would have taken capsules, you see, with a period of action of about forty to forty-five minutes. You've a grand heart, Colonel, but I did have to take action to slow it down.' There was a slight pause. 'You were injected. Directly into the vein. In very much larger quantities. Lord Keynes' capsules were used to sustain an old life a little longer. In your case, as a fit young man, your physical and psychological integrity was placed under very considerable strain by this cocktail.'

There was a pause. Cotton registered the words well enough but the significance of them escaped him. For the first time he had a suspicion this lack of understanding was partly his decision.

'Tell me about my eyes,' he said.

'Then we're talking mostly about scopolamine. It's fairly commonly used, in very small doses, by ophthalmologists, usually to dilate the pupil or to paralyse the eye-focusing muscle. Both are useful, of course, in the treatment of disorders of the eye. It can also be used, as you've said, to quell travel or motion sickness. That is a tiny dose. The dosage is, however, absolutely critical. During the war, never under ideal circumstances, a number of mistakes were made. They gave scopolamine to paratroopers on D-Day and the dose was large enough to put a few of them out of action. I mean by that that they were unable to jump with any guarantee they knew what they were doing. A couple lost even the most immediate sense of knowing that they were in an aircraft and wearing a parachute.'

'They were useless but potentially dangerous?'

'Yes. It's probable the dosage given was not just meant to quell motion sickness but had the additional aim of calming them and reducing their stress levels. Did you know scopolamine is also sometimes used in childbirth?'

Cotton had some difficulty moving from parachutes to labour wards.

'The drug doesn't actually suppress the mother's stress and pain,' said Dr Sanford. 'What scopolamine does is suppress the *memory* of it. And in conjunction with morphine, even the pain part is reduced.'

'I'm rotten at remembering pain,' said Cotton. 'I feel the pain all right, but I can't recall it, even a short time afterwards. I'm not sure. Is it even possible to remember pain exactly?'

'What do you mean?'

'This drug suppresses the memory of the pain, but not the pain at the time. Is that right?'

'Right. As far as we know, scopolamine blocks the medium temporal lobe of the brain. That's the lobe that is thought to control certain kinds of memory, behaviour and some spatial tasks. This blocking effect has even allowed some to drive a vehicle perfectly competently but to retain no memory of what they have done. That's why scopolamine is becoming quite popular in obstetrics. They call what it does "twilight sleep". The patient is able to respond to the instruction "push", for example, without the fear and upset that can accompany childbirth. In the war, I guess the idea was that the paratroopers would be able to act but without the strain and personal sense of risk that jumping into enemy-occupied

territory can cause. You know how fraught parachute invasions can be.'

Cotton suddenly found some sense of smell was returning. It was very brief and came with a strong feeling of mistrust and involved the smell of blood and mothballs.

'Rip and sew,' he said.

'Colonel Cotton?'

'I don't understand,' said Cotton. He was telling the truth. He had difficulty retaining parachutists so chose women in labour. 'If morphine removes the pain, why do you need scopolamine to suppress the memory of it?'

'Oh, that's all about timing and low doses,' said Dr Sanford. 'The morphine is only really used towards the end of labour. I don't know, Colonel, but unless you are with the Stoics or believe pain to be ennobling and are happy to deny relief to others, I think you have to recognize that some of those mothers are pretty grateful for an easier time than their own mothers had.'

'What's the effect on the child?'

'That's why the doses are low. By the time you get to the morphine the child is just minutes away from having the umbilical cord snipped.'

'Good. You've got the doses just right for mothers in labour. Are they still giving it to parachutists after what happened on D-Day?'

There was a pause. 'I understand you're an educated man, Colonel.'

'I don't feel educated.'

'What did you study at university?' asked Dr Sanford.

'Economics,' said Cotton. 'It encourages a certain lack

of trust in our ability to measure precisely and indeed as to cause and effect.'

'But I guess it still has a large element of trial and error, as you find out what works and what doesn't.'

'Of course. But there are other considerations. An economist might ask if the convenience of the labour ward staff hadn't, however subtly or even unconsciously, led to an increase in the use of scopolamine. A groggy mother is hardly going to protest.'

Dr Sanford laughed. 'Were you always this cynical?'

'It's not cynical. It's a down-to-earth view of why things actually get done. Sometimes parachutes don't open. But the chances of a good landing are better if the paratrooper remembers he is in the air.'

Cotton paused. He could recall nothing of what he had just said and did not know if it made any sense. 'I'm tired,' he said and fell asleep. The fall was not long, no longer than a thumb brushing a rush of silk.

3

ONE UNSETTLING problem for Cotton – it had the feel of a horde of diminutive caterpillars walking on his skin – was that he never knew for how long he had just slept. Minutes? Hours? A day?

'You OK?' said Dr Sanford.

'Opium,' said Cotton. He had remembered someone telling him that fifteen minutes of opium-induced sleep could feel like eight hours.

'Opiates?' said Dr Sanford. 'No, sir. Not in your case. How are you feeling?'

Cotton listened to himself. The pain in his head now throbbed with his pulse. But it was less demanding. 'All right.'

'Good. You understand you have a drip and other tubes?'

'Yes.'

'We're going to take them out. And then take the straps off you. OK?'

'Yes.'

'Tell me if you feel any discomfort.'

There was a deal of fiddling Cotton couldn't feel very well. Then there was a sharpness in his right arm. It felt like a cut.

'What's that?' he said.

'It's all right, Colonel. Nobody's putting anything into you. It's been some time, though, and the vein gets . . . well, a little flaccid and soggy. OK? Nurse!'

Cotton smelt a whiff of surgical spirit a fraction before the sting. Someone pressed down on his arm.

'OK. We're there,' said Dr Sanford. 'In a moment you'll be able to move but I don't want anything sudden. You just lie there. Flex your fingers. Stretch your legs. But keep doing that until I say.'

'All right.'

'Can I ask you some more questions?'

'Of course.' Cotton flexed his hands, raised his forearms.

'Good man!' said the doctor. 'Don't worry if the questions seem strange.'

Cotton grunted. He raised his shoulders. 'Have you had flying sensations?' asked Dr Sanford.

'If I have, I certainly can't remember them.'

'Now *that's* supposed to be more like him.' It was that other voice again.

The doctor sounded irritated at the interruption.'You may have had visions. They may even have suggested religious or metaphysical perceptions. Lights, looking up, the impression of some kind of altar, perhaps someone powerful and safe, maybe with an aura around the head.'

'No,' said Cotton. 'Nothing like that.'

'OK,' said Dr Sanford. Cotton thought he sounded disappointed.

Cotton's hearing was becoming sharper. He heard Dr Sanford consult his notes. The paper sounded thick and

expensive, of the kind that could cut if you weren't careful.

'Did you dream of animals? Perhaps you even saw yourself as one. They tend to be quite grand and powerful. Like an eagle? A lion, perhaps. Or maybe a bear?'

'No.'

'But you've seen something.'

'You know those things – it's a sort of tube – shit!' he said.

'Keep trying, Colonel.'

Cotton exhaled. He raised his legs. 'It's like a telescope. But it has coloured crystals inside.' Cotton stopped. He lowered his legs. Someone sighed.

'The colours shift.'

'They're above you?'

'I don't know. They feel very close. Then they collapse.'

There was a pause. 'What is that?' asked the doctor.

Cotton had the sensation he was substituting vomit with a grunt.

'A kaleidoscope,' said Cotton.

'Well done!'

Cotton said nothing. Unbidden, he had what felt like a memory rather than an impression of a powerful shape barrelling out of the darkness. This developed and expanded into the image of a bear in a dappled clearing. The bear was tearing at a fallen tree to get at a bees' nest. Though infuriated by the stings, the bear remained intent and greedy. Its claws tore at the mix of larvae and honey. The muscles of the bear made the fur shake and go the wrong way.

Cotton frowned. He was confident that he knew nothing about bears. He had been to zoos as a child. Perhaps this was from a film documentary he could not remember. What was clear, however, was that he did not identify with the bear on any level. What disturbed him more was that he was so promptly and dumbly suggestible.

'All right, Colonel Cotton?'

'Yes,' said Cotton. 'I'm all right.'

He did not feel all right. He knew the word 'kaleidoscope' wasn't the one he was after. He was beginning to realize that an accurate representation of what had happened was presently lost on him, but that versions, whether true or not, would be of interest to others. He began to be cautious.

'Are you with us, Colonel?' said Dr Sanford.

'When do I get to speak to other people?'

There was a pause. 'I think maybe we should take off the covers on your eyes first. Do you feel up to that?'

'In theory.'

'That's good,' said Dr Sanford. 'I have here a pair of Ray-Ban Aviator sunglasses. Do you know what those are?'

'Protection for pilots' eyes when they're above the clouds.'

'Yes. The shape of them is called teardrop, to give you a bigger area of protection, but the characteristic we are interested in is that they only transmit about twenty per cent of incoming light. They also filter out infrared and ultraviolet rays. Is that clear?'

'Yes.'

'When we take off the eye bandages you should not feel intense discomfort. But we'll get the sunglasses on as quickly as we can. OK? As far as I know the effects of the scopolamine should be much reduced now, after so long, but if you consider scopolamine has a half-life of three days . . .'

'What's half-life?'

'Basically it's the time it takes for the drug to be eliminated from the body. So after six days it's twenty-five per cent, after nine it's twelve and a half, and so on. You understand? You've been here for longer but, especially when other drugs are involved, it's a complex calculation.'

'I understand,' said Cotton. 'I still have a little left in my system.'

'I was going to suggest we did one eye, then the other.'

'No,' said Cotton. 'Let's just get this done, unless you think that's unwise.'

Dr Sanford did not reply but Cotton understood he was, at least, a little nervous. It made him feel better.

There was a brief, flaring magnesium-bright white flash when the doctor took off the binding, even though Cotton squeezed his eyes shut. His eyes watered. He counted to ten. It was uncomfortable but it was not painful. He relaxed his eyelids a little. The watering slowed and stopped. He nodded.

'All right. Stay still if you can.'

Cotton felt the sunglasses going on. He breathed in. He opened his left eye just a crack. The result was not bad; he was aware of something grey as the North Sea

in front of him, then became aware he was shivering. He felt a hand on his shoulder.

'We have air conditioning,' said Dr Sanford. 'That might explain the chill you feel.' Cotton thought this a decidedly generous explanation. He was reasonably content with shock. There was a pause. 'Concentrate on something else. Tell me if you feel your heart rate has increased a great deal.'

Cotton listened. He closed his eyes again and his heart settled down. He opened both eyes a fraction. The right lid fluttered. Then he opened them a little more. His eyes stung but did not water. His heartbeat did not increase. But it reminded him of drumsticks hitting taut drum skin in two time. He concentrated on trying to hear the gap between the beats. His teeth chattered.

'How's that?' said Dr Sanford.

Cotton swallowed. 'Not bad.' He tilted his head. He could see a band of light grey interrupted by two spots – partly white for the doctor, completely white for a nurse. There was nobody else there.

'Good!' said the doctor. 'There's no need to rush. Open your eyes right up when you feel comfortable, but not before.'

'There's no window here,' said Cotton.

'That's correct. We'll get you to a comfortable room very shortly. In here you are in artificial light and it's pretty low. In any case, we'll screen the windows in your new room. I can assure you of that.'

'Where am I? I know I'm in New York. Just tell me where.'

'Of course. You're in the Upper East Side of Manhattan

in a clinic named after a lady philanthropist, the late Barbara Stuyvesant Ogden. We are in East 76th Street. The very well-known Lenox Hill Hospital is a block away, should we need them. The Ogden Clinic is exclusively for veterans, Colonel.'

'Is this a US government facility?'

'No, no. As I said, it's a private clinic,' said Dr Sanford, 'and our benefactress left us pretty well funded. We do of course have a relationship with the War Department – as you'd expect given the nature of our work with veterans – but that's mostly in the line of laundry and catering facilities and some auxiliary staff when required. We also get laboratory and scientific help from Cornell University and additional financial assistance from the Carnegie Foundation.'

Cotton opened his eyes wider and looked about. He could just see he was in a narrow, high-ceilinged room. The walls were of the same silver-grey colour as the cloth they used for blimps. I'm in some kind of balloon, he thought.

'What colour are the walls?' he asked.

'A kind of grey,' said Dr Sanford.

'Is this a psychiatric hospital?'

Dr Sanford spoke patiently. 'No, Colonel, this is a neurological trauma clinic. We do have some similar facilities, however. Because Colonel, let me repeat – when I first saw you, you were having convulsions. We did not know then what problems you had. The possibility that you were having what is called a psychotic episode existed and that influenced our decision to put you in this room.'

Cotton blinked, put a finger under the sunglasses and wiped his right eye. It helped him see that the nearest wall had buttons in it, that the walls were padded. He shivered again.

'We didn't want you to hurt yourself, Colonel, that's all it is. We also think of the safety of our own staff. What do you say? Come on, you don't belong here. We'll have you out and in the kind of hospital room you'll recognize in no time.'

Cotton turned his attention to Dr Sanford. He could not focus on him at first as anything other than a vague, patchy figure sitting beside the bed. Cotton squinted at his face but found the doctor's glasses were troublesome – they removed the eyes behind and set off angles and twists.

'Your spectacles,' he said. 'They're—'

'Of course,' said Dr Sanford. He took them off and held them out. From about a foot Cotton could see they were bifocals.

'Benjamin Franklin's invention,' said Dr Sanford.

'Yes,' said Cotton. 'Thank you.'

'I'll put them on again,' said Dr Sanford.

Now he understood the arrangement, Cotton could see Sanford's eyes. Even though he registered only briefly that they were a soft grey-blue, he didn't mind when they darkened. He could see the man who had been treating him but understood that a certain strange, sleek, seal-like quality to the doctor was due to his own eyes. He thought Dr Sanford was about fifty, with a slightly heavy face. Cotton could make out his hair had a centre parting; the front looked absolutely white while the rest

30

was still dark. He was wearing a bow tie. It had spots. It took Cotton a moment to make out the spots were red and the background blue rather than the other way round. Then he wasn't sure again. He blinked. Colours were a problem.

'Who else knows I'm here?' said Cotton.

Dr Sanford nodded briefly and cleared his throat. 'We were informed that there was another angle, as it were, almost immediately. Our own intelligence services and yours have since taken what I'll call a general interest – mostly to check on the progress of your recovery.'

'Because we're allies, of course.'

'Colonel?'

Cotton tried to shake his head. That hurt. 'How about that normal room?' he said.

'Why, of course. You may feel – I don't know, pretty weak or underpowered. You've not been using your muscles for some days now. Let's get you a wheelchair. Nurse!'

The nurse went out and Cotton began getting himself upright. He was in a metal cot with shallow sides. He used the side bars to sit up. He didn't feel particularly confident about his position or the strength of his arms and legs. The sides of the cot were lowered. Cotton paused, then swung round. He swayed and Dr Sanford steadied him.

'Take it easy. The dizziness will go away.'

Cotton waited. When his head cleared his legs started to prickle. He nodded.

'Give it time.'

The prickling ceased and his legs felt heavy. He

31

decided to try standing. For a moment he could not feel anything; he may have rocked, but then there was more prickling in his legs, thighs, calves, feet. He had his hands firmly gripping the lowered side of the bed. He lifted his left foot and didn't stamp it so much as let it down to the floor again. The prickling sensation became a little more intense and then faded. He could feel quite well up to the balls of his feet but his toes were something else, as if they existed as a lack that ached in a melting sort of way.

'Colonel Cotton!' said the nurse. 'Sit! Sit!'

Cotton let himself fall into the wheelchair. 'Why do you keep calling me by my old rank?'

'Because this is a clinic exclusively for veterans, sir.'

'OK!' said Dr Sanford. 'You go with the nurse, get comfortable and then we'll move this on. What do you say?'

Cotton's head was swimming. He breathed in, then nodded. 'Yes,' he said. 'Why not?'

He was wheeled to an elevator by the nurse. He saw he was on the second floor. Inside the elevator, she pushed a button saying 7.

As soon as the elevator started up Cotton felt his stomach clutch as if he were in an aeroplane that had abruptly lost height. It was absurd – the elevator was a demure trundler – but it got a sound out of him.

'Are you OK, sir?'

'Yes, thank you,' said Cotton and breathed out. He was aware the elevator was very slow and steady and that it arrived on 7 with a gentle, airy stop. It still jolted him.

The nurse wheeled him along a corridor and then into a white room. The venetian blinds were almost closed. Cotton had an impression of very thin stripes. These tilted and made him feel sick. He was feeling sick in a stationary wheelchair.

Cotton looked around the room. It was large and L-shaped because the square was broken by a bathroom. It had two windows screened by the blinds. In the short part of the L, behind a foldable screen, was a hospital bed with a metal and glass table on either side. The one nearest the window had a telephone. In the long part of the L was a small sofa, two chairs and a low coffee table. Beside the right-hand window but facing a windowless wall was a table-cum-desk and a metal and canvas chair. The walls and the blinds and the bed were varieties of white but the sofa looked darker, was maybe a pale green. The chairs were even darker, perhaps blue.

'Your closet is here,' said the nurse.

Between the bathroom door and the corner to the bed was what Cotton thought of as a wardrobe in the wall.

'Thank you.'

She opened it. There were hangers inside but nothing else.

'Do you know what happened to the clothes I was wearing?'

'Oh, Colonel,' said the nurse as if the matter were tragic, 'I think they were beyond hope, you know. Do you want to get into bed now?'

'Can I sit here for a while?'

'Of course, sir. I'll be back shortly.'

Cotton sat in the wheelchair. After a while, breathing out after almost every movement, he contrived to turn the wheels in a full circle, each shift as long as the first joint of his thumb. At least he could do that. He wiped his eyes again and could see that the door to his room had a stout spring about shin high so that it always shut. The bathroom door was wide enough for the wheelchair. Moving forward was worse than turning. He was not sure whether he was about to vomit or fall. He managed to get into the bathroom with minimum use of his eyes. He saw he had been given a toothbrush, toothpaste and soap. All had been stamped 'US Navy'. The towels had the clinic's name on them. He had the powerful impression he was about to fall out of the wheelchair and did not want to hit his head on the bathroom tiles. To leave, he had to reverse.

Cotton's biggest problem was a sensation that he was tilting to the right. At first he thought it was solely because of the windows. But when he turned round he understood it wasn't. This left him with two unnerving sensations. One was that the floor tilted and that he was in danger of sliding downwards to be chuted out of the windows. In the other direction, he would be caught by the swing door. Cotton had never liked heights. The door business, however, was novel.

The nurse pushed in. She was carrying a tray with a carafe of water on it, of the kind that has the glass as the cover for the neck.

'Oh, you're having orientation problems, sir. OK. Let's get you into bed.'

It took a moment for Cotton to understand what she

had said but he managed a smile. 'Thank you,' he said. He felt – it was almost a swoon – that it was exceptionally kind of her to speak to him like that. She helped him into bed.

Though the room was air-conditioned, Cotton saw a slow-spinning roof fan that wasn't there. He shut his eyes and hoped the whoosh would stop.

4

WHEN COTTON opened his eyes the next morning, he felt, just for an instant, much brighter, much sharper, much more himself. But then the light dulled, presented itself as a whitish mass like risen dough. He struggled up and put on the Ray-Bans.

There was a nurse in the room. He saw, with gratitude, that she had already put a glass of orange juice on his bedside table. He reached out for it – and found his fingers closed on nothing. He peered at the bedside table. There was a ring mark left over from another glass. He put his hand out and touched it. It looked almost crusty but he could not feel it.

'I'm so sorry,' said the nurse. 'I'll have that attended to directly.'

'No, no. It's all right. You've brought breakfast for me.'

'Yes, of course. I'll put it on the table over here.'

'Thank you.'

Cotton watched carefully, his attention fixed on the tray she put down. He was having trouble with the colours but was pretty sure there was orange juice there. The problem was that his eyes were not registering the whole volume of the juice contained in the glass. He raised the sunglasses. In the juice glass it was as if

someone had barely whisked an egg – there was something yellowish-orange but it contained globules and streaks of clear, slightly green glair. Whatever else was wrong with him, the link between his eyes and his brain was definitely ragged. And what of the brain itself? He knew the brain could 'see' or at least provide from memory what someone expected to see. But his brain did not seem able to register what his eyes saw beyond something like a hasty sketch. What was so difficult about registering liquid in a glass?

'Do you need help getting out of bed, sir?'

'No, thank you,' said Cotton. 'I'm just going to do this at my own speed, all right?'

Cotton pulled back the bedclothes and swung his legs to the side. He put his feet in the slippers provided and stood up. He felt absurdly weak but got into the dressing-gown issued. His feet had some sensation but only enough to indicate he had an untrustworthy relationship with what he remembered of them. They were as uncertain as narrow, somehow boneless flippers attached to his legs. Cotton lifted one knee, then the other. There was a slight, dull tingle in his feet. He raised one foot and took a step. He wasn't sure why, but he then decided to shuffle.

He had moved about a yard when he remembered that on the birthday before he had travelled from Mexico to England to be schooled, at age eight, he had received a clockwork toy. It was a painted tin landscape that involved a tiny mountain, a tunnel and a train that did not have wheels but softish, white bristles like some sort of diminutive nail-brush. When wound up, the track

itself shook and the train shuffled forward on those hairs. It was far smoother at shuffling than he was.

He got to the table with the breakfast tray on it and dropped into the chair. In front of him was a substantial American breakfast comprising about half a pint of orange juice, toast, coffee and, under a metal cover, scrambled eggs, bacon and hash browns.

He drank some orange juice and realized that as well as not yet being able to trust even primary colours, he had also been reduced to primary tastes and sensations – sweetness, bitterness, sourness and saltiness. He found the orange juice was simply cold and sour, and the coffee hot but bitter; the toast was crunch and nothing else, and the only difference his tongue could register in the rest of the meal was in the texture – eggs between fluff and mush acquiring a tepid kind of crust; brittle, cold bacon smelling rather than tasting of salt; and lumpy hash browns that reduced to a tasteless paste in his mouth. He swallowed, then put down the knife and fork. He had no appetite.

When two nurses came in to tidy up, Cotton retreated to the bathroom. In the bathroom were handles to grip. He gripped. The light was not brilliant and he took off his sunglasses. He thought he was focusing well enough but his face looked lopsided in the mirror, as if it had slid down a little on the right side. Was that the effect of his beard? He realized he was half wincing, half squinting at his reflection. He had dark purple patches under his eyes. He looked down at the backs of his hands, brought them closer to his eyes, and saw that they were covered in tiny, very bright red spots. He closed his eyes and lowered his

hands. He stepped out of his pyjamas and got under the shower.

The hot water was pleasant. When he used the soap, he smelt no perfume. It was just something warm and sudsy. Alarmingly, he could feel rather than see that he had lost weight. His forearms felt as fragile as wishbones, his ribs thin and very spare and the skin on his thighs was slack. Was his sense of touch as unreliable as his sight? He concentrated on using shampoo on his head and beard.

He got out and patted himself down with a towel. Shaving equipment had been provided, but his hands felt too weak and his beard was too long and untidy for him to risk it. He combed his wet hair, then stared at himself. One of his cheeks bulged, old and greyish, like a weathered tennis ball. He tried to touch it, but it wasn't there. He closed his eyes, opened them again, and winced. The mirror had taken on the sluggishness of wet grey glue. The reflection of his flesh came back as some sort of white wax. He peered at the back of his hands again. Now, the spots did not look red but russet. He realized he wasn't swimming through colour blindness but mostly in and out of it, as if he couldn't, in colour terms, manage contact, maintain the reds as reds, get the blues to cohere.

He turned away from the mirror and picked up the talcum powder. He used a lot, but only enough to make him sneeze, not to smell. It did, however, make putting on his pyjamas much smoother. Feeling like a patchwork of powder and damp, Cotton put on his Ray-Bans again.

'Bet you're feeling fresher,' said the nurse when he came out.

Cotton tried a smile. 'Yes, thank you.'

'You've hardly touched breakfast. Are you sure you've had enough?'

'Yes.'

'More coffee, sir?'

'No, thank you.'

'Radio?'

'No, thanks. You're very kind but I think I'll just sit for a little.'

'Sure thing,' said the nurse.

Cotton sat. He realized that getting out of bed and having a shower had left him exhausted. He didn't really have a reaction to this. It wasn't that he was out of breath, just that he had no strength at all, as if his muscles had been left with nothing in them. He stretched out his legs and raised his feet but could only hold them up for a few seconds. Next he flexed his fingers, first slowly, then faster, as if he had a circulation problem. Again, after a short time he stopped because his fingers ached. It reminded him of the ache he experienced sometimes from the fingers he had broken. Here they all ached. Despite the air conditioning, he felt as if he was trying to sweat. The stuff on his forehead felt more greasy than wet. Almost immediately he started shivering.

'Shit,' he said. He got up, rewrapped his dressing-gown and sat down again. He breathed in as slowly and as long as he could, then let the air out of his lungs in a rush. He did this several times. But he still felt he was falling asleep again. It wasn't just that his eyelids felt

40

heavy. His entire forehead felt as if it were sliding down to cover his eyes.

Cotton clapped his hands to ward off sleep and tried to concentrate. He could, more or less, identify three things. The first was that he was suffering from something he decided to call sedation sickness, which involved a failure to grasp what he was looking at. The second was that he wasn't shivering so much as trembling as a result of something beyond temperature. The third was that he could feel no sort of strength that he could rely on.

He tried. Despite a tendency to sway and feel he was about to black out, he stood up several times. He succeeded in lifting himself by pressing down on the arms of his chair and pushing up. He managed to do that twice. He got hold of the pad of paper and pencil provided and attempted to draw squares. After a while he tried to put circles in the squares. This took him way back to his time at Miss Lupita Montez and her *kindergarten moderno* in Mexico City. *A Pedro le cuesta escribir sin salirse de los cuadritos* – Peter has problems fitting his writing into the squares of the exercise book. *Mi mama es buena.* My mother is good. *Mi mama es muy buena.* My mother is very good. There was *letra de molde,* or printing, and there was *cursiva,* or joined-up, cursive writing. Cotton thought he had always preferred the flow of cursive handwriting to the round pegs in square holes business. On reflection, he couldn't even tell if that was true.

Dr Sanford pushed into his room carrying a food tray.

'I didn't eat breakfast that long ago,' said Cotton.

41

'You didn't eat,' said Dr Sanford. 'You barely even picked. To me your breakfast was as a poem, Colonel. One bite of toast, minimal disturbance of the hash browns and the scrambled egg, and a single bite of bacon. What's the problem? Don't you feel hungry?'

Cotton didn't know. 'It was the taste,' he said, 'or the lack of it.'

Dr Sanford gave him a look as if he were being a picky child.

Cotton shook his head. 'I went to an English boarding-school,' he said. 'It doesn't make you choosy about diet.'

'OK,' said Dr Sanford. 'But we have to get you eating, get your strength up. You've lost a lot of weight, maybe twenty pounds, in a very short time. We want to get your digestive system working and back to normal. OK? So let's eat.'

The hospital kitchen had prepared creamed chicken, mashed potato and a purée that contained sweetcorn. The chicken did have taste – to Cotton, like rancid butter – the potato registered as nothing much more than paste and warmth, but the purée contrived to mingle the smell of starch and bad breath. Cotton thought of it as a ghastly version of baby food.

Dr Sanford frowned. 'You don't look happy. Are you about to gag?'

Cotton shook his head. He was, in a sluggish, almost sedate and absent-minded way, beginning to panic. He wondered whether the various changes in his reactions to being alive might not just last, but, in the case of his taste buds, be permanent.

42

He blinked. With extraordinary and abrupt clarity, he was quite certain that if this were the case, he would kill himself with dispatch and discretion.

Dr Sanford was looking at him. 'Along with feelings of dullness you may have surges of what I'll call high drama that don't feel at all dramatic,' he said.

Cotton frowned, then nodded. 'Big gestures?'

'Something like that.'

'I'll try to bear that in mind.'

The doctor laughed. 'Good,' he said. 'Most of us have the illusion, possibly delusion, that we have balanced minds. Or at least we recognize when a balance we relied on is disturbed.'

'I'm not really a steak man,' said Cotton, but—'

'Rare?'

'Please.'

Dr Sanford picked up the telephone and rang through. 'We have a soldier here who needs a rare steak. Pronto.' He sounded pretty pleased.

Cotton was aware that this would be the third meal provided and he had better eat it. He twitched. He understood he had been trying to please again.

Dr Sanford smiled and sat back. Cotton had never seen anyone quite so healthy-looking, despite his age and tendency to plumpness. 'Have you ever heard of a condition called gustatory auditory synaesthesia?'

Cotton closed his eyes. 'Hang on,' he said. 'Yes, that would be a link between sounds and tastes.'

'You've got it! It's not always auditory. I mean, I've had a patient who reacted to written words too.'

'Give me an example.'

'He said the word "vanilla" tasted like celery. I had a woman patient who said the name Brian smelt of urine and Alan of drains.'

'Really?' said Cotton.

'You've got to admit it's fascinating! I mean "marble" tasted like tobacco for the vanilla–celery man. He said the word "blue" was like sour milk.'

Cotton could not, in fact, remember the smell of vanilla. He could invoke something of the lift he associated with the scent of vanilla, but it vanished into a space that seemed resolutely stale. 'You're serious?'

'Oh yes! It's not a frequent condition. But let's be honest, this is the kind of psychological nudge we can all relate to. Imagine the crowd of tastes as you read! Extraordinary!'

Cotton raised his eyebrows. Presumably Dr Sanford would get to his point.

'There are also people who identify letters of the alphabet with certain colours. What colour does A give you?'

'I'm more in greys and whites at present, for just about anything. Sometimes there are small spots of colour but they turn grey, then the greys filter out, leave white as the sediment sinks.'

'Good,' said Dr Sanford. 'How about that kaleidoscope you saw. What were the colours?'

'I'm not sure now.' Cotton closed his eyes. 'A sort of burnt-orange. A mint-green. And a blue . . . I don't know the word. Deep glass-blue?'

'Deep-sea-blue glass?'

'Maybe.'

'Good. Strong colours are good. You've got them in your head but not yet in your eyes, you see?'

Cotton wasn't sure he knew what this meant. 'All right,' he said.

When the steak arrived he cut off a piece and ate. There was a moment, from the heat and the juice, when he thought he'd found something. Almost immediately afterwards he found himself chewing what tasted like a mix of fat and cardboard.

'Better, eh?' said Dr Sanford.

Cotton smiled and nodded.

'You get that down you,' said Dr Sanford, 'and we'll have a talk. What do you say?'

Cotton tried to keep him happy. 'Yes,' he said.

'I kind of knew you'd be a blood man,' said Dr Sanford. He clapped Cotton on the shoulder and left. Cotton chewed on. He found he got on better if he did not breathe through the nose. His stomach grumbled and gurgled. He chewed on till there was only a strip of fat left on the plate. Only a second or two after putting down his fork, Cotton was asleep in his chair.

Cotton opened his eyes. He could see a white shape, or rather white shapes moving in front of him. They were round, almost like starch-coloured bubbles or globes. He blinked. The smaller, plumper nurse was wearing white shoes, white stockings, white uniform and a white cap, somewhere between a coif and a waitress's hat. Her cap reminded him of the detachable celluloid collars he had worn at school, except that this was much longer and twisted into something like a

starched origami headdress. She resembled a strange, white maggot.

'A good steak and you're eyeing up the nurses, eh?' said Dr Sanford.

Cotton was less embarrassed than unclear. 'How long have I been asleep?'

Dr Sanford laughed. 'Not long. I was here half an hour ago.'

'Right. I'm sorry if I've offended you,' he said to the nurse.

She smiled. 'It's not a problem, sir.' He began to think of her as Nurse Plum.

'Cheer up!' said Dr Sanford. 'You're showing interest. I wish some of my other patients were.'

Cotton nodded. He had had no interest in the nurse other than as a shape that looked both bizarre and vulnerable. A man in overalls came in carrying a gleaming wooden box. At the front it had a section let into the wood and covered with material like a radio.

'This is a Brush BK-401 tape recorder,' said Dr Sanford. 'It's pretty well three hundred dollars. We're going to tape some of our sessions, OK? Build up a record of your progress.'

Cotton felt slow and wary but unable to react.

'I need a moment,' he said.

'That's not a problem, Colonel. Take your time.'

Without knowing why, Cotton suddenly remembered being under friendly fire in Sicily in 1943. Some distance out to sea, an American warship had been a couple of hundred yards short of its target as the landing craft went in. The first salvo of shells hit the beach. The beach

46

was sandy, and here, in the Ogden Clinic, Cotton saw an explosion ahead and to his right. He knew this was false. In Sicily, he had been thrown some distance by a shell that had come down slightly behind and to the side of him, and he had landed against a jeep. In other words the shell had landed south-east of him and he had been sent north-west. From five to a little before eleven on the clock. The real shell had killed two men, taken the legs of a third and wounded several more. The shell he saw in the hospital caused a burst of flame and flying sand, but no one was there. It left a particularly smooth, even hole in the beach, like a sand trap the *hormiga león* or ant lion builds. He looked up. 'All right,' he said.

'Ready? Good.' Dr Sanford turned on the recorder. 'Now,' he said, 'I suppose some of this may be feeling something of a brave new world for you.'

'I hadn't noticed anything particularly brave about it, and it doesn't feel so new. But it does have something of a twist. You know the expression "not all there"? I have the impression I'm not all here.'

Dr Sanford nodded. 'We'll get things joined up again. Can you count backwards?'

'Why would I want to do that?'

'To help us.'

'Ten, nine, eight, seven . . .'

'OK. What I am doing is going through a checklist. For example, the literature says scopolamine can cause something like temporary senile dementia or Alzheimer's. Have you heard of Alzheimer's?'

'No.'

'It's a condition that can afflict the old but is

sometimes seen in relatively young people, in their forties. It's a terrible condition. It erases the mind, as it were.'

'These patients can't count backwards?'

'It's one of the things we test. Like what day it is and so on.'

'I've no idea what day it is.'

Dr Sanford smiled. 'I hardly know myself,' he said. 'That's not a problem. You know where you are.'

'You said the Ogden Clinic in New York.'

'Exactly. Who's the president?'

'Harry S. Truman.'

'I should probably have said who's the prime minister of Great Britain?'

'Clement Attlee.'

'OK. Colonel, you have no idea how well you're doing.'

'That's correct,' said Cotton.

Sanford smiled. 'Good,' he said. 'Now I want to reassure you, Colonel. You haven't received physical damage of any note. You don't appear to have been tortured, raped, anything in the gruesome tradition of inquisitions. You have some bruises. Some are from the convulsions, but you have others that show you were gripped at the wrists and upper arm and there are marks that may show your ankles were tied. Whoever was injecting you was not perhaps the most skilled at the job, but let's be honest, we get that kind of thing in hospitals. Sometimes veins are hard to find.'

Dr Sanford pointed. It took Cotton a couple of seconds to understand. He pulled up his pyjama sleeve.

On the inside of Cotton's left elbow was a patch as big as a coaster that looked like some cross between a cactus and a purple rose. It was the first time Cotton had seen it. He couldn't believe he had missed it.

'Now that you've seen it, does it hurt? It sometimes takes a visual connection to feel something.'

Cotton stared and then touched the rose. At most the area felt like a dry, somehow flabby sponge.

'No,' he said. 'I don't know that there's even an itch there.'

'Does it make you think of anything?'

'No.'

'No need to worry. We'll put some more antiseptic on it,' said Dr Sanford. 'And a dressing. What do you say?'

'Yes, why not?'

'Good! Colonel, I've said before that I need your help. Do you understand? We can't, after all, put a dressing on the brain. It's a lot more complex and, frankly, we don't know very much about how the brain works. Would you accept that?'

'Yes,' said Cotton.

'We do know the brain is to some degree protected. Have you heard of the haematoencephalic barrier? Maybe the blood–brain barrier? They're the same thing. The barrier protects against most bacterial infections. Not all, though. You've heard of meningitis?'

Cotton nodded.

'Good. There are also some drugs that can get through that barrier. Scopolamine is one.' He paused. 'Do you know that in some parts of the world it's called "the

devil's breath" or "zombie powder"? It's been given all kinds of amazing, not to say incredible, properties.'

'Are you telling me it's a superstition as well as a drug?'

'That's it! Frankly that's one of the reasons people use expressions like "zombie state" – though they say the patient is quite capable of performing quite complex tasks, just that they don't know or appreciate what they are doing.'

'Have you seen this?'

'No, I haven't. I do know that high doses, a gram of scopolamine say, can stop a heart and I have seen some of our paratroopers, with far less than that dose, seriously affected but not showing signs of any incompetence.'

Cotton nodded. 'Let me see if I have this right. There's a possibility scopolamine might have rendered me ... unwitting. But able to perform tasks I can't recall. Though you're not sure. Sodium amytal may have encouraged me to behave rather like a confessional but not necessarily accurate drunk. The mescaline gave it all a heightened perspective. Is that what you're saying?'

Sanford smiled. 'Well, that'll certainly do for now, Colonel.'

Cotton shrugged. 'All right. What do you want to know?'

'Can I ask you *not* to edit now? I mean, just let your immediate reactions speak. Don't stop and consider.'

Cotton shrugged again. 'I can try,' he said.

'Good. Can you remember what you first felt when you heard of truth drugs? Or truth serum?'

'No,' said Cotton.

'Take it easy. Relax. Let your mind go blank.'

Cotton closed his eyes, exhaled and relaxed. 'Coco,' he said.

'I'm sorry?'

'That's really "I should coco". My mother used to say that. It meant—'

'I know what it means. It's ironic, even sarcastic, agreement.'

'Yes. *Coco* is also the Spanish for "bogeyman".'

'You've just equated truth drugs with a figure used to frighten children. Have I got that right?'

Cotton shrugged. 'All I meant was what kind of person believes a chemical can make people spout truth? What kind of person fears he can be made to tell the truth because he has been injected with a drug?'

Dr Sanford frowned. 'The truth here would be a specific piece of information.'

'But the drugged person still has to know what is wanted. Have you ever tried to get the car keys from a drunk? Given all the side effects, wouldn't a drugged person have difficulty identifying and appreciating what that true piece of information is? If the drugs have made him wretched and miserable, he might well collaborate with his interrogators in the same way someone being tortured will, just to get it to stop.'

Dr Sanford looked doubtful. 'Wasn't there,' he said, 'a case of a Britisher being given the wrong information about the invasion of Europe? He cracked.'

'And misled the Nazis. Surely that's my point. The poor man believed what he had been told and it had been

impressed on him not to reveal it. The Nazis believed torture could obtain hidden information. So they believed him when he could no longer resist. Were drugs used on him?'

Dr Sanford shook his head. 'I don't know. You're suggesting sodium amytal?'

'I have no idea.'

'Did you know that during the Battle of the Bulge those with battle fatigue were given sodium amytal to get them back in action? The men called the pills Blue 88s because they were blue in colour. The 88 was a truly impressive piece of German artillery. The pill flattened them, let them sleep. They had to be watched because, although they were in a profound sleep, they were prone to screaming, writhing, awful facial expressions you couldn't quite believe. The idea was it was cathartic; they'd get rid of what they'd seen.' Dr Sanford shook his head. 'It worked for some. Some of the men went back to fight, others . . . weren't in charge of themselves, that was the phrase.'

'This is the same stuff that is being used as a truth drug? Are we back to dosages?'

'Oh, no, no. We've moved on. And quite fast. Since the war some doctors have tried a technique called abreaction. It's an effort to make the patient relive traumatic experiences under the influence of barbiturates. To wipe the slate, as it were. There is also narcosis or deep-sleep treatment. This is sometimes combined with electroshock therapy; the idea again is to clear traumatic experiences from the brain. The technique is called cerebral lavage.'

Cotton nodded. His ex-boss, Ayrtoun, had, before his spectacularly abrupt breakdown, always claimed that when unpleasant, nasty or embarrassing things had to be named, English speakers much preferred to couch them in French. 'Words like "covert", "surveillance", "clandestine", even "espionage". The sneaky or shabby things,' Ayrtoun had said. Cotton remembered this because the last time he had heard of Ayrtoun, he had been told he had volunteered for electroshock therapy. In Canada, thought Cotton. While 'cerebral' was a Latin-rooted form of English, 'lavage' was pure French. But there was a simpler name.

'That's called brainwashing.'

'Oh I'm not sure it is,' said Dr Sanford. 'Surely brainwashing refers to the intolerable pressure put on people, as at the Soviet show trials, so that they abjure themselves, become their own prosecuting counsel. Cerebral lavage is attempting to remove a trauma. Its aim is completely different. It is about enabling someone to recover from a trauma, not traumatize them into total submission.'

From somewhere, Cotton recalled reading a British report on the Soviet show trials. Its point was that the Soviet authorities 'had eschewed drugs' because they had found other techniques, 'chiefly keeping the defendants awake day after day', perfectly suited to reducing the accused to 'abject and reliable compliance'. Cotton blinked. He could remember that, but he had no means of tracing it.

'Cerebral lavage has been used to cure drug addicts,' said Sanford.

'Successfully?'

'Sometimes, I understand.'

Cotton was not aware that his face had moved, but Dr Sanford reacted as if he had flinched.

'No, no! Nothing like that has been done to you. Our approach was, *faute de mieux*, to sedate you while the drugs worked out of your body.'

'You didn't want to wash away any memories.'

'It was a purely clinical decision, Colonel, aimed at getting the best possible result for you.'

Cotton considered. 'All right,' he said.

'Colonel,' said Dr Sanford, 'have you ever been hypnotized?'

'Not as far as I know.'

'Ah!' The doctor laughed. 'Yes, yes, I see what you mean. Would you be prepared to undergo hypnosis?'

'No.'

'But why not?' said Dr Sanford. He sounded very surprised. 'Is it the idea of someone else controlling you that upsets you?'

'I hadn't got that far. You said hypnosis and I instantly thought no.'

'But if I said hypnosis might help you?'

'I'm sorry, Doctor. I am not going to be hypnotized.'

'I am suggesting, Colonel Cotton—'

'That I may not be conscious of things that might help my treatment. I understand that. I don't think however that the effect of the drugs used on me will translate neatly into language and images after a session of hypnosis.'

'Is that your belief?'

'No,' said Cotton, 'it's my opinion. I can't really say I've made a decision based on that opinion or that the opinion is an informed one. This is much more basic. Now I have some control back, I don't want to give any up again.'

Dr Sanford clapped his hand to the back of his head. 'I don't think you quite grasp, Colonel, what it is we are trying to do!'

'What is it?'

'Discover what happened to you. To find out why and how you are coming out of this in the way you are. To find potential problems. Colonel, I have to be honest. I just haven't had an opportunity like this before. You remember the Blue 88s? I have some experience of their various effects. They can be most distressing to watch. I once saw a soldier break his jaw on his own knees. He bit through his tongue. He was trying to assume a foetal position but with very considerable strength. It was like trying to deal with an impossibly hard knot.'

Cotton nodded. He felt notionally sympathetic but resolutely uninvolved.

'From your point of view hypnosis might help, you know. I'd certainly give you feedback. I mean, it's been found that under the influence of sodium amytal a subject can be given what is called a false memory. The subject believes the memory but it has been, as it were, implanted. That makes it not so much a truth drug as a kind of Trojan horse. The subject believes the memory and considers it to be true.'

Cotton thought he was mulling over what Sanford had said. It wasn't until he started speaking that he

55

realized the cutting voice he had heard in himself after regaining consciousness had come back.

'I see. And how exactly is this done? How is the memory implanted? Is it a verbal suggestion? A lot of repetition? Is it visual? A photograph? And how do they know, given the vagaries of a drug-affected memory, that the implant will reappear accurately when they want?'

Dr Sanford sighed and made a face. 'I understand a subject can be accused of something – his condition will take it from there. A drug like sodium amytal affects the emotions, removes our usual safeguards and inhibitions. It can also encourage a degree of fantasy, as it were.'

'Are you saying sodium amytal encourages self-accusation and can stimulate a story to make the charge more convincing? Is that legally usable?'

'I don't know what the legal situation is.'

'Do you think I have false memories?'

'That's not my point, Colonel Cotton. The mind records far more than we are conscious of. That's why I suggested hypnotism.'

Cotton nodded. 'I've got bits of me missing, Doctor. I want to get them back. I don't wish to be delayed doing so. I am perfectly willing to cooperate, but I want to get out of here. That's my priority. It may not be yours, but unless you can convince me I'm a danger to myself and to others, I'll stick to it. On the whole, I think that's fair. Don't you? At present I have no short-term memories at all, not good, bad or self-accusatory.' He looked up. 'How do they stop the scopolamine rubbing out what they have implanted?'

'It's a suggestion rather than a theory that this kind of thing can be done.'

'That has to be tested. By hypnosis rather than hypothesis. Is that ideal?'

Dr Sanford sounded tired. 'Hypnosis was never an ideal.'

The Brush tape recorder began to make a flicking noise. The tape had run out.

5

THE NEXT morning when Cotton opened his eyes, he saw a male orderly dressed in white standing with his back to him. He was hunched and was going through Cotton's belongings.

It wasn't until he remembered he had no belongings to search that he realized the orderly was not there. Despite that, he continued to watch. The orderly started to turn and Cotton waited for a backwards look worthy of Nosferatu, but this figment had a regular, quite handsome face, almost like a doll's.

'Oh, bugger,' Cotton said to himself. He asked himself to remember for future mornings *not* to open his eyes when he woke. He should keep them closed and allow a few minutes for anything dreamlike to dissipate. It was worth a try at least. The hallucination had given him a sensation of displacement as if he were a spinning top that had been flicked. That wasn't quite right. Shit.

'How are we feeling today?' said the nurse as she pushed in with his breakfast tray. 'This morning you're having oatmeal, an omelette and a fruit cup. OK?'

Cotton ate it all, pleased that none of the foods had much taste to begin with.

After breakfast, he showered and managed to trim

his beard a little. His hand was still too shaky to shave. Around ten, Dr Sanford arrived with a nurse and a wheelchair.

'I want to show you something,' he said. 'You want to walk?'

'Of course.'

'Good. But we'll take the wheelchair just in case. It's only a few floors. We'll take the elevator.'

Cotton put on his dressing-gown and went with him. He realized that the grip he had to use to keep his slippers on was helping. As the elevator trundled softly down, Sanford smiled uncomfortably.

'I'm afraid the staff call the floors by names. Fifth is Eternity, fourth is Purgatory and third is Limbo.'

They were going to Limbo. Cotton nodded. Presumably Sanford meant that in the Ogden Clinic there was no Heaven.

On the third floor the corridor was lit as for night. At one end a burly man in Navy whites sat behind a desk with a reading light on it. He had a stick on the desk as well as the *Saturday Evening Post*, and was reading papers marked 'PO1'.

Dr Sanford signed a paper on a clipboard and after his signature wrote *plus FP*. He told Cotton that 'FP' meant 'fellow patient'.

He took Cotton along the central corridor to a grey-painted door with the number 308 stencilled on it. The door had a sliding hatch through which people in the corridor could look in. Sanford opened the hatch, glanced in and stepped back.

'Take a look,' he said.

Cotton did. Sitting on the bed, perfectly still, was a man of about his age. His legs were apart, he was slightly hunched, his hands were clasped and his mouth was open. The man's eyes were open but gave no sign of seeing anything.

'His name is Martin Hall. On June 7, 1944 he was a lieutenant in the 325th Glider Infantry Regiment. They gave him scopolamine like they did everyone else. Somewhere over the English Channel he went berserk, something you can't do in a glider. So his men knocked him on the head to quiet him down. Later they knocked him out again, this time with a rifle butt and no helmet. The glider crashed and there was a lot of confusion. Lieutenant Hall was found near the glider about two days later with a fractured skull and a broken jaw. That was three years ago. We consider him to be long term. He has no memory of his past, his parents or where he's from. He finds it difficult to speak and has to be spoon-fed. He has to wear diapers. In a flailing sort of way, he can be violent. We're not sure why. But he's absolutely clear about one thing.'

'What's that?'

Dr Sanford made a face and then knocked quietly on the door. The ex-paratrooper immediately stiffened and spoke very clearly.

'Put that bayonet down!' he snapped. 'Don't you know it's dangerous, soldier?'

Cotton waited. There was no more. The lieutenant slowly sank into his previous position, hands clasped, mouth open.

'And that's it,' said Dr Sanford. 'That's the clearest

thing he ever says. He's probably just wet himself, possibly more.'

Cotton looked round at Dr Sanford. 'Not a popular lieutenant?'

'Pernickety, we heard.'

Cotton nodded. 'I'm very sorry for him and his family,' he said, 'but why are you showing me this poor man?'

'Three reasons. One, to illustrate to you some of the work we face. Two, to suggest to you that I don't regard you as our typical patient. The third thing is to make you think. This poor guy can't do anything, Colonel. But he can come up with the same words again and again, clearly expressed, clearly enunciated. All he needs is someone to knock on the door.'

Cotton nodded. 'If you're suggesting I've been much luckier than Lieutenant Hall here, I accept, of course. I also know he can't have this kind of conversation with you. I'm more responsive, if that's what you're saying, and I'm much better than I was even a couple of days ago.' Cotton held up his hand. 'Are you telling me you've been lucky to get me so soon? If you had seen the lieutenant earlier—'

'Oh, that's good and probably true. But it wasn't my main point.'

'It's not that implant idea, is it? Someone knocks on my door and I start spouting state secrets I was never privy to?'

Dr Sanford laughed. 'No. I was just passing that on.'

'And I'm very grateful, Doctor. And if I haven't thanked you for looking after me before, let me—'

'Colonel! Colonel, that's not necessary.' Dr Sanford paused and peered at him. 'Are you being ironic? I mean, are you playing with me?'

'No,' said Cotton, 'I'm not. Would you close the hatch?'

'Right,' said Dr Sanford. He shut off the view to Lieutenant Hall.

'Do I have a real choice about the hypnosis? Or is this something I have to do, a test I have to pass before I can be pronounced fit?'

Dr Sanford blinked. 'I always place medical concerns over any others. I will not oblige you to undergo hypnosis.'

'Good. I will collaborate, Doctor, but may I suggest we think again how this is done?'

Cotton was abruptly very tired. He thought he was about to fall over. He asked for the wheelchair.

Dr Sanford looked at him. 'What's the problem?'

'I feel exhausted.'

Cotton dropped into the wheelchair.

Back in his room, Cotton had an absurd dream. A string of sausages was cooking in a frying pan. The sausages began to spit, then caught fire. From the side, someone poured what looked like white petals into the frying pan. Long after the flames had died the white stuff kept falling, as if sand had been replaced by snow in a clock.

Cotton woke, irritated, and sat up. In Spain he had liked small chorizo sausages called *cantimpalitos*, but he had never had a taste for British bangers. He was not a

Freudian. He did not know what the white stuff was. It wasn't sand from a bucket provided to put out fires. This was much softer than grit, more like fatty snow.

He got up but realized he was still having problems tilting away from the windows. He groaned and sat down. As far as he was aware, he was like everybody else; his memory functioned at various levels, one being association. His problem was that while he saw the images, the association required a lot of puzzling. He frowned. The white stuff in the dream could be soap flakes. He thought. Sausages and soap?

He raised his eyes to the ceiling. The name that came to mind was Ayrtoun, his ex-boss. Why? Advertising. Before he had joined propaganda and misdirection during the war, Ayrtoun had worked in advertising. He had sold sausages and soap. Cotton could not remember who had told him that, but did remember that Ayrtoun had had the nickname Rikki-Tikki-Tavi. Ah yes. It had been Cotton's very first boss, D, who had told him. Rikki-Tikki-Tavi is a mongoose, named by Rudyard Kipling, that kills a family of cobras threatening the pet's human family.

Cotton closed his eyes and thought. He knew Ayrtoun's nickname was not just about the speed of the mongoose's snap and its tenacity. But what was it?

'Bugger,' he said, partly in the hope he would dislodge something. He tried raising his eyes to the ceiling again, but that didn't work either.

He got up. He decided to leave sausages, soap and Rikki-Tikki-Tavi for a while.

*

After a lunch of fried chicken, string beans and potatoes, Dr Sanford came to see him again and started the Brush tape recorder. 'I'm going to give you a long list of questions. It is important you answer them truthfully.'

'Why do think I wouldn't?'

'Colonel, I don't know you. But I guess you are used to what I'll call a certain command of yourself and of others.' Dr Sanford sat down. 'As far as I can tell, you are pretty well balanced. But certain things you notice about yourself now and in the near future may embarrass you. You could even find them humiliating. And you may, entirely understandably, want to suppress them. These may range from, let's say, frequent urination to sudden surges of fear. Of course, I don't know what these things may be.'

'I understand. Reactions I'm not accustomed to.'

'Right. I want you to write them down. Think of them as not being you. There's no call to feel weak or bereft. Do you understand?'

Cotton smiled. 'Yes.'

'Colonel Cotton, I am regarded as a highly trained professional. There are times I feel like a fraud, largely because I really do understand just how little we know about how the brain and the mind work. For example, I know something about the drugs you were given but I know very little about how they interact, if indeed they do. So I am kind of obliged to approach this from an almost philosophical point of view. It's not something I'm happy with, but that's what we've got. Understood?'

'I think so,' said Cotton. Dr Sanford nodded. 'Thank you. My apologies if I've pressed.'

'As my sense of balance improves, my mind see-saws more.'

Dr Sanford nodded. 'Do you have an overriding mood – or are we talking of uncertainty?'

'I often have a longing to be alone.'

'OK. How strong is this longing?'

'Bad headache strong. There's another, a very thoroughgoing indifference, which sometimes feels like contempt.'

'Who for?'

Cotton frowned. 'I think I'm included.'

'Would you call this self-loathing? A feeling of unworthiness?'

Cotton shook his head. 'Just somebody I'd prefer not to meet.'

'Do you feel somebody has tried to take you over?'

'No, I feel very tediously pestered.'

'Do you think you're depressed?'

'I don't know. I'm certainly slow, certainly flat. There's an element of waiting for something to appear on the blackboard so I'll know what the subject is.'

'I meant by depression what your former prime minister called Black Dog, an overpowering melancholy just short of despair.'

Cotton shrugged. He wondered if Dr Sanford was trying to relate to an Englishman. He didn't really understand 'melancholy' or 'despair'. 'Black Dog' made him think of pirates. For some reason he could not imagine a dog. He could manage a bear, however.

'I'm not suggesting any depression hasn't been chemically induced. Are you OK, Colonel?'

Cotton blinked. 'Could I *do* something?'

'But of course!'

Dr Sanford gave Cotton some puzzles of a kind he had never seen before. They were made of smooth, bright, extraordinarily light metal. Some were like three-dimensional jigsaws. Others were beautiful, with air and metal knots. All were about putting together or taking apart. Cotton was not conscious of thinking. He had to peer, but he did them mostly by touch and without difficulty.

'Why are you doing that?' said Dr Sanford. 'You turn the puzzle, you know. You do everything leaning a little to the left.'

'Ah,' said Cotton. 'I've had a fear of falling to my right.'

'I didn't know that.'

Dr Sanford got up and looked at him. 'Did you see better with your left eye before this?'

'I'm not aware of it.'

'You're right-handed?'

'Yes. But I usually kick with my left foot.'

Dr Sanford nodded, sat down again and made notes.

'Do you know what this tilt means?' said Cotton.

'No,' said Dr Sanford. 'Can we try something else?'

Dr Sanford gave Cotton some sheets of paper. The Rorschach blots Cotton handed back at once.

'Not now,' he said. But then, flicking through the sheets, Cotton's attention was caught by some letters. They spelt NOLPAD. He had no idea what that was.

'I'm sorry,' said Dr Sanford. 'Those are just anagrams.'

'I don't know what it is,' said Cotton. He squinted, kept thinking the word should begin with an *al* but couldn't find one.

'Poland,' said Dr Sanford. 'How about that one?'

It spelt MAYRENG.

'Oh, that's Germany,' said Cotton. 'It's a name that impresses for obvious reasons. But I think if you'd given me Bulgaria, for example, I'd have been lost. With Poland, I tried to get it started with *al*.'

'Why would that be?'

'I don't know. There are a lot of Spanish words that begin with *al*, like *almohada*, *alcochofa*, *alcornoque*, the Arab words, like *algebra*.'

'Are you telling me Spanish is your mother tongue?'

'I've probably got two mother tongues. I learnt them side by side.'

'But do you think Spanish might be your *emotional* mother tongue?'

The air conditioning buzzed and the tape recorder hummed.

'Doctor, I have no real knowledge of the extent to which speakers are subjects of the languages they speak. I speak two, I use them.'

'When did you stop living in a foreign country?'

'When I went to school. I found England rather foreign too.'

'At what age was that?'

'I was eight. I went to boarding-school.'

'What was that like?'

'I was pretty lucky. I was reasonable at sports. And I

67

saw immediately that unhappiness and self-pity led to bullying. What are you trying to find out?'

'Reasons why you're doing well now. There's the brain and its chemistry – and there's the mind the drugs work on.'

Cotton nodded and smiled. 'I get spells, like now, when I have red or blue spots in front of my eyes. They're shuttling about through grey.'

'Ah, the ophthalmologist says there's little point in seeing you yet, not until your eyes settle down.'

'My taste buds are on strike too.'

'Thank you,' said Dr Sanford. 'This has been a useful session. You're free to have visitors now.'

'I dreamt of a mongoose this morning,' said Cotton. 'You mentioned animals?'

'I'm sorry?'

'It's a quick, sharp-toothed carnivore that is famous for killing snakes. It can kill rats too, though someone once told me terriers were quicker with rats.'

Dr Sanford blinked. 'OK. Were you frightened?'

'No. It's the first time I've been aware I was dreaming.'

'Right,' said Dr Sanford. He paused. 'Do you know what a lucid dream is?'

'I'm guessing it doesn't mean "clear".'

'It's a dream in which you are aware you are dreaming and can even exercise a degree of control about what happens.'

'I see.' It was only then that Cotton realized that while he had been sincere when he mentioned the mongoose, it had not in fact been part of the dream.

Dr Sanford wrote down *lucid dream* on the notepad. 'That's fine. That's fine. I'm putting down what we'll call considerations, OK?'

'What's the difference between a lucid dream and a hallucination?'

'Quite a lot.' Dr Sanford sighed. 'Years ago people used the term "visions". Since there could be a religious element there sometimes, scientists moved on. Now "hallucinations" is looking inadequate for the various kinds of fictive visuals people can be prone to.'

'Fictive visuals,' said Cotton, mostly to himself.

Dr Sanford wrote down the word 'Lilliput'. He held it up. 'There's a condition that afflicts some people with macular degeneration, Charles Bonnet syndrome, it's called. It's not an indication of mental problems. But sufferers see things and people that aren't there. The thing is, they usually see them as very small. That's what the Lilliput is for.'

'OK,' said Cotton. 'If I imagine very small things I note it down. Am I likely to get this degeneration?'

'Not yet anyway. Frankly we'll have to wait until the ophthalmologist decides to see you to find out the state of your eyes. But I want everything you can give me, no matter how trivial it might appear. Not just physically. It could be something very brief, something just odd.'

'All right.'

Dr Sanford was busy writing again. 'I mentioned "false memories" before. But the term also means a memory you may recall, possibly in great detail, but when you think about it, you realize the events could not have taken place.'

Cotton nodded. He said he thought false memories were commonplace. People elided, used photographs and memories of being told something and saw themselves being somewhere they had not been, but all most convincingly.

Dr Sanford nodded. 'Yes, you should put everything down. That's the kind of thing. I'm particularly interested to know when and if you are controlling your visuals.'

Cotton smiled. 'Good,' he said. He had just remembered where the Rikki-Tikki-Tavi nickname had come from. Geoffrey Ayrtoun had had something to do with the 'Tavi' – the Tavistock Clinic and the more recent Tavistock Institute. The first had been founded to help trauma patients after World War One; the second had a much wider brief looking at behavioural patterns in individuals and groups, and had a powerful influence on government in World War Two.

6

ABOUT TWO hours later a nurse came into his
room.

'Colonel Cotton,' she said. She beamed. 'You've got a
visitor!'

Cotton was on his guard at once. Or at least he was
until he saw his sister Joan at the door. She was dressed
in a black long-skirted outfit and hat, fit really for any
formal occasion from a funeral to a sombre afternoon
party.

'It's lovely to see you,' he said.

'You can see in here? In sunglasses?' Joan moved
towards him slowly, put one arm round his neck and
sighed into his ear.

'Dear God, Peter.'

'Shh,' he said. 'I'm getting better. Really.'

She drew back and looked at him very closely. He
couldn't read her expression but thought of anxiety and
pity.

'Please sit,' he said.

Joan kept looking at him. 'Is this about Sicily? Have
you had a breakdown?'

'Who told you that?'

Joan hissed. 'Jesus Christ! We haven't been told anything at all, Peter! Nothing clear but all long-windedly

and in the most mellifluous and respectful of tones.' She shrugged. 'But given all the delay and the discretion and the very particular address, we rather thought—'

'What? What kind of place do you think this is?'

'The Ogden Clinic's supposed to be for very, very seriously damaged veterans, Peter. That's its reputation. The security at the door is very tight. And once you get through, you see a motto in the entrance hall – "Making Heroes Whole Again". The rumour is that quite a few rooms for heroes have soundproofing.'

Cotton nodded. 'That's interesting. Thanks. That's useful.'

'Not to me! What's going on?'

'I'm recovering. All right?'

'Are you talking psychologically?'

Cotton shook his head very briefly. 'No. Physiological. A bad reaction to some drugs. It happens. My heart rate began galloping, I got delirious – they tell me my reaction was one of the bad ones.'

'A reaction to what?'

Cotton felt tired, of lying mostly. It wasn't that he wanted to confess; it felt more like an utter boredom with pretence. It made him feel sick, as if he wanted to open his arms and be filleted like a fish. He took a breath. 'You know I got rather badly cut in the thigh by a razor earlier this year? A stitch started to open, there was a little discharge, so I went to have it seen to. The doctor injected a local anaesthetic, stitched it up and then injected a little adrenalin and an antibiotic. They think it's possible the combination of things was responsible for what appears to have been some kind of seizure, but

they're honest enough to say they don't really know what caused me to react like that.'

Cotton had been so intent on his story that he didn't see that his sister had stopped listening until he reached the word 'honest'. She leant over from her seat and stroked his face.

'Your beard is horrible. You look like John the Baptist. And you've lost your looks.'

'All of them?'

She sighed. 'I've never seen you look scrawny before.'

'I've lost weight,' said Cotton. 'But I'm eating now.'

Joan shook her head.

'We told Pop something, not much. Like you with me, really. Except even less. I can't imagine it's doing him any good at all.'

'Have you tried to get him to come over?'

Joan started weeping. There was no sob, no noise, no crumpled face, just a few tears coming down her cheeks. 'He's not going to come. I really don't know why.' She turned and reached for a handkerchief.

'He's frightened of dying away from home. I'll write him a letter.'

Joan sniffed and put away her handkerchief. 'Why the hell can't you telephone?'

'Yes, of course I could. I'll ask if they can arrange that.'

'What's going to happen?'

'I'll leave here. I don't know when. In a week or ten days, perhaps. I then plan to go off for a holiday, read, walk, get myself back into shape and start in the autumn.'

'You can do that with us in Oyster Bay!'

'No, I can't,' said Cotton. 'Much as I love you all, I hate yachts and I'd rather not be pestered by your charming but noisy children. And from what you say, they may find my appearance frightening.'

'How bad are you?'

'I was pretty bad, I think. Apparently I went into shock at one stage. But now my sense of balance is much better, I'm beginning to taste what I eat and I've started noticing the nurses are women rather than strange white shapes.'

'You could be serious.'

'I am.' He smiled. 'I am *feeling* lots better. Physically I'm still a little shaky but otherwise I'm feeling pretty relieved. If I were really ill, I'd tell you. You know I would.'

Joan did not smile. 'This is my second visit to the Ogden Clinic,' she said. 'The first time I came here, I wasn't allowed to see you. But you were apparently trussed up like a mummy. The only difference I think is that the mummy's nose and mouth aren't displayed. You had some kind of gag between your teeth. You went into a kind of shaking fit and the man who told me this was asked to leave. That was about June 12th. I was brought here by someone called Hornby from your office.'

Behind the Ray-Bans, Cotton closed his eyes for a moment. 'What did he tell you?'

'That you'd had a bad reaction to some drugs but they weren't sure how it was going to play out. They were trying to get you – "safe" was the word used.'

74

'I see,' said Cotton. He looked at his sister. 'Can I ask you some questions? They may sound decidedly silly.'

'Such as?'

'Do you have a calendar of some sort?'

Joan shrugged. 'Would my pocket diary do? I've got it here.'

She got it out of her handbag and gave it to him. He flipped through to the end of May. He saw she had noted his arrival.

'What's the matter?'

'I have what the doctor calls short-term memory loss. I can't remember very much of the last few weeks. Your diary says I arrived on the 26th of May?'

'Yes. Why?'

'How did I arrive? How did I get across the Atlantic?'

'You flew! You were late, stuck in Newfoundland till the weather cleared. Don't you know this?'

'No. That's what I'm saying. For a time of about three weeks I cannot recall who I was, where I was ... anything. What did I do after I arrived?'

Joan registered only the slightest of pauses. 'You stayed with us, of course. On the 27th and 28th you went to your office. Oh, on the 29th we certainly went shopping – you were looking for summer clothes. On the 30th you spent the whole day at your office and took us out to dinner in the evening. On Saturday 31st you moved to a short-stay apartment in Waverly Place you took initially for a month with an option on a second while you had an agent look for something more long term. That was the last we heard of you. We didn't hear from you on June 1st, but then that was a Sunday. I called you

at your office on the Monday but they said you hadn't come in. By Tuesday 3rd your office wasn't answering any questions. On the sixth we were told you had been taken ill.'

'I can't remember anything of that. What the doctor calls memory loss may be short but it's complete. I have no memory of any of it. Absolutely none.'

Joan blinked; she tilted her head at him. 'Sometimes when you speak you sound like someone else.'

Cotton nodded. 'I even sound like someone else to myself sometimes.'

She frowned. 'You don't sound agitated.'

'I'm too slow to be agitated.'

'How honest are you being?'

'As honest as I can. I've had a bad reaction to some drugs. Laid low doesn't quite meet the case. But I'm getting better. And if the British sent me here, well, they're trying and, perhaps, even spending some money. Though they're evidently keeping me safely tucked away.'

Joan looked at him. 'Mummy used to tell me there were two types of men. Reliable men. And rats. I used to think you were reliable.'

'I don't know what to say,' said Cotton. 'Sick men are probably all rats, but I am certainly not trying to be one.'

'When I came here first I was told your chances of recovery had increased. They were no longer fighting for your life but they didn't yet know whether or not your heart and kidneys had suffered long-term damage.'

'Yes,' said Cotton.

'I was told they were keeping you sedated for quite a few more days to give you a better chance.'

76

'Thanks.'

'For what?'

'Telling me.'

Joan rolled her eyes.

'Can't you at least telephone your father?' said Joan. She took hold of one his hands. 'I'll come back, Peter. Is there anything I can bring? Do you need anything?'

'No, I don't think so,' said Cotton. 'But then my memory is very poor. Come on, these things sometimes happen.'

'Really?' said his sister. She stood up. 'You're the only person I know they happen to. You're supposed to be an economist. You're supposed to be a civil servant.'

Cotton nodded. He couldn't think of anything else to do. The nurse saw his sister out.

Cotton shook his head. He had never considered himself a shirker. But he was asleep within a couple of minutes of his sister leaving.

When he woke he felt wretched. He shook his head and thought about dates. He could see the numbers but found it hard to deal with them. He worked out, however, that between 31 May and 5 June someone had been pumping drugs into him. Who and why were beyond him. He did not know whether this was down to reluctance or a desire for more and better time.

'You have meatloaf this evening,' said Nurse Plum. 'You get this down you, Colonel.'

The meatloaf came with onions, carrots and mashed potato. Dessert was syrupy peaches with some sort of creamy accoutrement. Cotton chomped obediently.

7

COTTON ARRANGED to telephone his father in England the next day, Saturday, 21 June. The call was booked for 9 a.m. in New York, 2 p.m. in England. Cotton dreaded explaining his state, but found that his father was not only anxious that he be well, but insisted on it. He did this with a kind of shout, as if very conscious they were far apart, and that he had to encourage his voice along the cable under the Atlantic.

'Peter!'

'Yes.'

'You're in hospital!'

'Yes.'

'But you're all right, aren't you? That's good. That's what I wanted.'

'Yes, I'm much better. How about you?'

'My ankles are a bit swollen. I could pop off, I suppose, at any time. The strange thing is that after that awful winter we've now got rather a hot summer. The doctor tells me I shouldn't forget to drink.'

'Of course not.'

'But the water may settle round my ankles.'

It took a moment for Cotton to understand this really was what his father had said.

'Yes, but it's very important you keep yourself hydrated.'

'Oh yes. I say, you are all right, aren't you?'

'Yes. I've got to convalesce for a bit, that's all.'

'Good! I told Joanie she was worrying too much.'

The telephone conversation, the crackles and the clicks, battered Cotton. I have no stamina, he thought, just before he fell asleep in his chair. He knew he had said this before and was getting tired of it. Like the word 'shit'.

A small, plump, elderly lady was peering into his face.

'Are you there, hon?'

'Yes. I'm here.' Cotton had no idea who she was. Had he forgotten her? She was not dressed in any medical capacity but was wearing a dark purple suit and a small hat with a wobbling, forward-placed feather, also dyed purple. Cotton stared back for a moment. He noticed there were some specks of glitter on the feather. For some reason, that detail made him think he wasn't hallucinating. He smiled as best he could.

'OK!' she said. 'Now what do you say, young man? Feeling up to reading today?'

Cotton stared. She had a peculiarly plangent nasal tone to her voice.

'Reading what?'

'I'm the library lady, hon. Marian Leibowitz. I come Tuesday, Thursday and Saturday. I've got all the latest bestsellers for you. I really have. We have a deal with the publishers for you vets, you see.'

'That's impressive,' said Cotton. 'The thing is, I'm not really up on bestsellers just now.'

'OK,' said Marian Leibowitz. 'I'm getting there. I'm getting a picture of you. You're English, right? Maybe more of a belles-lettres kind of guy?' Something occurred to her. 'Or maybe you're strictly non-fiction.'

Cotton felt himself beginning to get alarmed. He thought Mrs Leibowitz would go on and on. The name of a writer came to mind.

'Do you have anything by Rex Stout?'

'I most certainly do! His latest won't be out till October. But I've certainly got his last. Just one sec.'

Mrs Leibowitz went off. Cotton breathed out. Abruptly he remembered that Rex Stout wasn't popular with the FBI. What he couldn't remember was how he knew that.

'Here you are,' said Marian Leibowitz. '*Silent Speaker* is from last year. This other one is from a couple of years back. *Not Quite Dead Enough*. It's really two short novels.'

Cotton smiled. 'That's very kind. Thank you very much,' he said.

'See you later,' she said. 'Oh, do you want a bagel?'

'A what?'

'A bagel. I do books but I bring some bagels too. Feed the mind, but let's not forget the body.'

'No thank you. The books are fine.'

'Then have a bookmark instead,' she said and handed him over a piece of stiff card shaped like a paper-knife. Running down the blade there was some writing: *Our admiration is so given to dead martyrs that we have little time left for living heroes – Elbert Hubbard.*

Heroes again – like the motto at the entrance to the

clinic Joan had mentioned. Cotton smiled and thanked her.

'Oh, you'll make it,' she said. 'I can always tell. Enjoy your reading.'

When Marian Leibowitz had left Cotton looked at the two books she had brought. *Not Quite Dead Enough* had an orchid-cum-grenade on the cover. *Silent Speaker* showed a brimful wine glass of clear liquid, a row of carnations or similar and a line of small establishment faces. Mrs Leibowitz had reminded him of one of those stock characters in Mexican films he had seen as a child – *costumbrista*, they called them, the Spanish word for tradition and types. He breathed in. He realized he could smell something – a mix of elderberry and lavender, perhaps? That was how his late aunt had smelt. What was that word? 'Atomizer'! It sent out a short-lived little cloud of drops that dissipated after a few seconds.

Cotton picked up *Silent Speaker* and opened it, but found he couldn't even see the print on the pages – the stuff resembled black flecks in murky water. He concentrated. At least this gave him something relatively simple to fight. It took him about five minutes, but by fixing on two words, he managed to identify them as 'monkey wrench'. It had been used to beat an important man to death.

'How are you doing with the reading?' said Dr Sanford when he came in. 'Not bad, right? Marvellous lady, don't you think? Marian Leibowitz?'

Cotton nodded.

'She's wonderfully charitable with her time as well as her money,' said Dr Sanford. He smiled. 'There's

someone else here to see you. A Mr Terence Hornby. He's from your people.'

Cotton reacted slowly, as if his eyeballs were sticking in their sockets. His sister had mentioned the name but Cotton had been unable to link it to anyone. 'All right,' he said. He put down the book. 'Show him in.'

But the man meant nothing to Cotton either. He was a slight, slim but rather plump-faced or small-featured person with a large forehead in his early to mid thirties. There was something wrong with his hair. Somehow it didn't fit properly. It took Cotton a little while to grasp that Hornby was doing what he could so as not to look too bald from the front. From other angles there simply wasn't enough hair to pretend with. From the side, with a wall light behind, Hornby looked as if he was wearing something between an Alice band and a sparse ferret's tail. And though he was neatly dressed, his trousers pressed and his shoes polished, his shirt had come adrift from his waistband and he had stuffed it back in. Cotton saw that Hornby's scalp had beads of sweat. His neck looked oddly soft, not exactly like a woman's, more like a timid thyroid condition.

'Very nice to see you again,' said Hornby. He withdrew a handkerchief from his sleeve and dabbed at his upper lip.

Cotton noted the 'again'. He frowned. It wasn't that he remembered anything of Hornby himself, but he suddenly associated the man or his name with two things. The first of these was 'small beer'. Cotton was fairly sure he didn't mean 'unimportant'.

The second association was more difficult. Why had

he suddenly thought of the name Byron? Byron's *Don Juan* had been Cotton's codebook in Cadiz in 1944. But it wasn't to do with that. Nor, on the face of it, did it have anything to do with the man sitting across from him. Hornby remained just a slightly untidy presence called Hornby. There was nothing at all Byronic about him. Then Cotton noticed that Hornby's hands and – he checked – his feet were tiny. Cotton wondered whether or not he was seeing accurately – had he fattened the poor man's neck? Had he grafted these little entities on to the real man's arms and legs? He did remember that Byron had been very proud of his own small hands and feet.

'I say,' said Hornby. 'Does he always stare like this?'

'Shh,' said Dr Sanford. 'Colonel Cotton is perfectly able to hear you. What he's doing now is trying to place you. It's not as easy for him as you might think.'

Pleased, Cotton nodded. Dr Sanford had done his job for him. Hornby sat, uncomfortably twiddling his hat. Those hands remained disproportionally small, almost mousy. Cotton blinked. He had the sensation, not unpleasant, that things were moving in extraordinarily slow motion.

'Doctor,' said Cotton, 'will you accompany us? I think I may need some help. By all means turn your recorder on, if you think it would be a good idea.'

Hornby stopped turning his hat and made a tutting noise. 'I really don't think that will be necessary. Of course I suppose there's an official element to this, but I'm also making a friendly visit, you know, on behalf of the entire office to check on how you are.'

'You see?' said Cotton. 'If you stay, Doctor, you may learn more of the difficulties I'm having distinguishing formal and informal.' He turned towards Hornby. 'My sister says I've lost whatever looks I ever had.'

Hornby essayed a cautious smile. It looked decidedly uncomfortable. Cotton nodded. That smile was probably about the same in relation to a genuine smile as small beer was to beer with alcohol in it. Small beer was weak, sometimes with a little bran and molasses to add substance and sweetness. He frowned. The point about small beer was that it had been boiled, and so had often been drunk in the past instead of water, to avoid infection. He sighed. Yes, that would be the British position. A certain decorous hygiene.

'I take it,' said Cotton, 'you've come to argue, with some degree of deference towards our host country, for discretion and resignation from me?'

Hornby looked puzzled and possibly even hurt. 'Well there is a larger context. Of course. We had rather hoped that you might already have a grasp of that, but I do appreciate that your present position may make it all seem rather hard to understand. The fact is, we're dealing with a delicate matter. As you yourself pointed out, we're guests in this country at a difficult time, a time of considerable suspicions, necessary checks and so forth. We are, as it were, the junior partner in the alliance. Security's what we deal in, after all. Checks have to be made.'

Cotton turned to Dr Sanford. 'Did you understand any of that?'

In fact, Cotton thought they probably all did. Hornby

seemed to be suggesting that one of the numerous American intelligence agencies had been responsible for Cotton's condition, and that this was probably the result of his being 'checked'.

Cotton pushed the Ray-Bans further up his nose. He frowned. He wondered if Hornby had memorized something and then got it wrong or had bits missing.

'I see,' he said. 'Now you talk of checks and suspicions, Mr Hornby, but I understand an element of experiment was also involved. I was kidnapped, wasn't I? Or have I got that wrong?'

'No,' said Hornby, 'not kidnapped. Kidnap is about a ransom, isn't it? There's been none of that here.'

'All right,' said Cotton. 'Have you got an alternative word for my removal to a place I never wanted to go for treatment I never wanted to have?'

'Well, I suppose something like *sequestered* would be one of the present front-runners.'

'I see,' said Cotton. 'Is there a front-runner for whoever sequestered me? It's all right. Dr Sanford has already heard a great deal.'

'I won't listen,' said Dr Sanford.

'Thank you,' said Cotton. He nodded at Hornby. Hornby leant forward and dropped his voice.

'We have considerable doubts about whether the Soviets were involved.'

'No evidence whatsoever they were?'

Hornby shook his head. 'No.'

'And, I take it, whoever was, was not part of our services?'

Hornby looked surprised. 'Absolutely not!'

Cotton held up his hand to tell Dr Sanford that if he cared to listen, he could. He sat back and stared at his visitor. He was still trying to place him. He didn't think this was the man who had told him the new UN building would be a great opportunity to ensure intelligence work was inbuilt from the foundations up.

But was it Hornby who had told him about Trygve Lie, the Norwegian 'compromise candidate' who had been chosen to be the first secretary general of the UN? Cotton remembered that it was pronounced Trig-va Lee but couldn't actually recall Hornby saying it. Foreign secretary in exile with the Norwegian king in Britain during the war, Trygve Lie was being paid twenty thousand tax-free dollars to sugar the compromise. Cotton remembered somebody telling him that the United Nations was a milk cow and that it would be milked; that Lie had accepted a 'stupid piece of flattery' and that the tax-free salaries and services and privileges would inevitably lead to corruption. Had that been Hornby?

Cotton heard a grating noise. Dr Sanford was peering at him. 'You're grinding your teeth, Colonel,' he said.

'We don't want to be rash,' said Hornby.

'And what name is the front-runner to describe events after I was sequestered?' said Cotton.

Hornby's eyebrows rose.

'Colonel,' said Dr Sanford.

Cotton breathed in. He nodded. 'It's all right,' he said. He looked at Hornby.

'You'll be backing me?'

'Of course!' said Hornby. 'As much as we can.'

'Very well,' said Cotton. He could barely get his

mouth to move, but he recognized that the British were being British. Any backing would be abject and uselessly prim.

'He tires pretty quick,' said Dr Sanford.

'Oh, I understand perfectly,' said Hornby. 'I do. He's been through a very great deal.' He got up. Cotton felt himself sliding into sleep. The last thing he heard was from Hornby. 'I don't know about you, Doctor, but on the whole I think it's gone rather well, don't you think?'

After Hornby had gone Dr Sanford came back to see Cotton.

'You need a break,' he said. 'It's Sunday tomorrow. I won't be in. You take it easy. We'll talk on Monday, OK?'

Cotton nodded. 'Yes. That's a good idea.'

On Sunday morning Cotton woke up in bed and forgot to keep his eyes closed. Beyond his feet stood a smiling man in a dog collar.

Cotton narrowed his eyes. 'What do you want?' he said.

The figure spoke. 'I'm here to ask if I can be of any assistance, in any way, of course, not just the spiritual.'

Beside him was a nurse Cotton recognized.

'Please get this buffoon out of here,' said Cotton.

'Colonel!' said the nurse.

'Oh, he'll understand,' said Cotton. 'It's his job to understand. I don't want to see an Anglican priest.'

'Are you saying you're not an Episcopalian or Anglican?'

'No, I'm not,' said Cotton. 'I'm English, but it's not the same.'

'I'm so sorry,' said the priest. 'Really! Perhaps if you gave me your denomination I could—'

'No,' said Cotton. 'For pity's sake, man! The denomination doesn't matter. You all get to be pious about making a material living out of a power nobody can see. I've only been drugged; I haven't been converted. Is that clear enough?'

'It's quite all right, my dear,' said the priest to the nurse. 'I don't have a problem. God be with you, Colonel.'

Some time later, breakfasted and sitting on a chair, Cotton realized that he had little idea of what time it was. He remembered, from Sherlock Holmes, the phrase 'to fall into a brown study'. At age eight or whenever he had read the story, Cotton had found the phrase strange, akin to the fall into a rabbit hole. It was then explained to him that it meant a, possibly dull or depressed, spell of reverie. He had still found the word 'brown' difficult to fit. It was too brackish. He had a moustached master at prep school, always in brown tweeds. Whenever he was asked a question he considered worthy, he would 'knock out' his pipe, unscrew the mouthpiece and then allow a very thick brown dribble of saliva and tobacco tar to join what was in his capacious ashtray before he discussed the intricacies of the ablative form in Latin.

Sundays at boarding-school – a very slow stream of time; a chilly version of the lagoons he had read about in books like *Coral Island*. Instead of a hot, bright sun,

he had had a smoky, brown fire in the common room before evensong.

Cotton remembered a conversation with his sister Joan.

'You've cut off, you know. One of your more attractive characteristics was your apparent interest in other people. You were reasonably kind, looked like you were paying them some attention.'

'I'm sorry. I feel as if I'm in a curiously genteel but powerful sea swell. The swell is long but fairly flat. I can see the shore. But the swell is taking me away from the land and there's too much glare from the sun on the sea.'

'Dear God! You're remembering Yucatan. You were about five.'

'What are you talking about?'

'You got swept out to sea! You didn't make a sound, you know. It wasn't until Mummy looked up that anyone knew what was happening. A very muscular little lifeguard with a rope around his waist plunged in and you were rescued. Let's say there was a bit of parental flutter. But you! You were rather touchy about it, behaved as if you'd been interrupted from something important.'

Cotton shook his head. 'I really don't remember anything of that.'

Joan smiled. 'You see?'

In his room in the Ogden Clinic Cotton tried to focus. There were two main difficulties. He could not work out when he had had this conversation with Joan. The other, rather grander problem was that he had no recall of the Yucatan peninsula and could not believe they had

89

undertaken the arduous journey to such an isolated place in the twenties.

Cotton had talked of *lagunas* or lagoons with Dr Sanford to describe gaps in his memory. This Yucatan business seemed to him compensation, as if his mind were furnishing stories to replace gaps, but which were actually no more than dramatized representations of his reaction to the drugs, a response to his inability to register what had happened to him.

Cotton blinked. The Ogden Clinic had something of the feel of an English boarding-school Sunday, an imposed hush and lack of traffic. It made some sense. Sundays at school had been very sedate lagoons encountered each week but rather depressingly circumscribed. Cotton sighed. His progress now was not consistent and it was not clear.

He did not, of course, trust Hornby. More depressingly, he knew he could not now trust himself.

8

O N MONDAY morning Cotton picked up the telephone and met the telephonist.

'My instructions are to screen incoming calls, sir, and to check with the medical staff about outgoing calls.'

Cotton had had no incoming calls. He wasn't sure if that meant there had been none or whether they had been turned away.

'Thank you very much. You've been very helpful.'

When Dr Sanford came on his morning rounds, he asked Cotton about 'the incident with the priest'.

Cotton listened to himself and felt no sense of apology. 'I woke up,' he said, 'and saw him and his dog collar. I never asked for a priest. Never even thought of it.'

'The poor man was only asking if you needed anything, you know.'

'But he wouldn't have done that unless he had both the permission and the authority to do so. '

Dr Sanford nodded. 'Right. I take your point. You don't find you are agreeing with everyone, no matter what they say? In fact, the reverse and quite aggressively?'

'Thank you, Doctor. I'd really like to be out of here by Friday. That's the 27th of June.'

'I don't know if that is realistic.'

'Clinically?'

'I have no other yardstick, Colonel.'

'I want to re-engage with the world, Doctor. That's what I want. This morning I tried to telephone my sister, see about clothes and my normal toothpaste and so on. I found the telephonist charming but clear I wasn't allowed to.'

'I'll see to it,' said Dr Sanford. He paused. 'What have you got against the toothpaste here?'

'That it's not my usual.'

'You don't think it contains anything untoward, do you?'

Cotton had some difficulty getting his teeth apart, as if something had magnetized them.

'I see!' he said. 'That's what you mean by paranoia? No. It's just a question of taste. Mine has more peppermint in it.'

He smiled without parting his lips and, as he breathed in through his nose, he smelt something. 'The toothpaste I'm after is American!'

'I'm sorry?'

'Yes! The British stuff I brought was rather rough and plain. This one was a tube. Wait. I bought it near Waverly Place!'

'You're getting recent memories back?'

Cotton held up his left hand. 'The assistant offered me ... Ipana toothpaste, Listerine toothpaste and, yes, Pepsodent with irium. What is that, by the way? Irium?'

Dr Sanford shook his head. 'It'll just be some fancy name for something inexpensive. Do you have other memories?'

'I'm still in the drugstore,' said Cotton.

'OK,' said Dr Sanford. 'Can you remember the assistant? Are we talking about a man? A girl?'

Cotton had been staring ahead. Now he closed his eyes. He thought of a glazed bread roll, frowned, but from that association, via the shape of the girl's hair, he saw her again. She had a square, rather heavy jaw, wore deep-red lipstick and was chewing gum. Her dark hair was parted in the middle and then rolled up high on either side in a way that reminded him of seventeenth-century wigs.

He opened his eyes again. 'I think she was very conscious of fashion.'

That might have been the Saturday, thought Cotton. He looked at Dr Sanford. 'I'm pretty sure I bought the Pepsodent.' Saturday had been the 31st of May.

Dr Sanford smiled and nodded. 'That's good.'

'Yes,' said Cotton. 'But the thing is, I have a memory of the taste of the toothpaste.'

'Good,' said Dr Sanford again. 'What does that mean?'

Cotton tried to work out what it meant, then slapped his hand on his own forehead. He sighed. He made a mental note to ask his sister what toothpaste he had used when he was staying with her in the days before.

'Shit,' said Cotton. He looked up. 'Why was I brought here and not to a normal hospital like Lenox Hill?'

Dr Sanford blinked. 'I don't know,' he said. 'You arrived here in an ambulance. This may surprise you, but I respond to immediate demands on my skills, without demur or, forgive me, the considerations of people who work in intelligence.'

93

'Tell them I'm ready.'

'Colonel Cotton, it's not like that.'

'Oh yes it is!' said Cotton. 'Trust me. I've trusted you, haven't I? Apart from hypnosis I've been a lamb, surely? Now it's time for me to talk to people in intelligence. All you have to do is mention it outside this room.'

'Are you angry?' said Dr Sanford. 'Is this rage?'

Cotton frowned. 'I have no feeling of rage,' he said. 'Or at least, it's ahead of me.'

'What do you mean?'

'From what you say, there seems to be a gap between what I say and anything I feel. I don't feel anything much at all.'

Dr Sanford used his fingers to stroke his nose and briefly block his nostrils.

'You're at the next stage,' he said. 'Perfectly understandable. As you recover you're going to be very angry about who did this to you. Do you feel betrayed?'

Cotton frowned. 'No,' he said. 'It's not a word that applies here.'

'Why do you think that?'

'Because I don't know yet. I do know somebody put drugs into me. That's the best I can do for now.'

Dr Sanford scratched his head just above the right ear.

'OK. Do you think we can manage this next part, Colonel?'

'What's that?'

'It's more tricky. It deals with context.'

Cotton shook his head. 'Most of the time I have the sensation of parrying your questions. There's not much

thought behind it, just a desire to keep the questions at bay. If I'm not fighting, I feel I have no defences.'

'Oh, this is very good,' said Dr Sanford. 'How are you on personality?'

Cotton stared. 'As opposed to character or psychology?'

'It's up to you.'

Cotton held up a hand. 'Give me a moment. Ah, yes, I read David Hume on this. We're a bundle of sensations, a process. We make choices, develop patterns but any entity like personality is pushing it. I've seen brave men stressed. That wasn't about personality. It wasn't about character. It was the odds they were facing, sometimes overwhelming.'

'You're a sceptic, then.'

'No,' said Cotton, 'I'm uncertain.'

Dr Sanford smiled. 'OK,' he said. 'But I'm still going to ask you to be patient, to step back a little. May I speak a little more generally?'

'Go ahead.'

'Right now, every summer, we have terrible outbreaks of polio. It's our modern-day plague. People live in fear that their children will be struck down, either die or end up crippled. Researchers are trying to come up with a solution and they are doing so in lots of different ways. But there are risks involved. And when you're dealing with children, some of the fear of the polio becomes fear of the researchers.'

'You're using young people as guinea pigs or lab rats.'

'There isn't really a choice. But the thing is, no

researcher can know with absolute certainty what the effects of what he comes up with will be.'

Cotton nodded. 'You run the risk of causing horrible problems rather than finding a cure.'

Dr Sanford shook his head. 'There is no cure for polio, Colonel. What there may be is a vaccine. But before you get one, you have to test it. There have to be clinical trials – first on those who've already suffered polio. Until you give the vaccine, you don't know whether or not it made them worse. It sounds like the most awful cruelty.'

'Trial involves error, yes.'

'Exactly,' said Dr Sanford. 'I'm trying to explain why so much of medical endeavour is a sort of trade-off. People want to keep their children safe but they're unhappy about the potential costs to some individuals.'

'All right,' said Cotton. 'I understand that. But I can't see the link between a possible vaccine for polio and what's happened to me.'

'There isn't one,' said Dr Sanford. 'What I'm saying is that we live in a culture that experiments, Colonel. I'm not for a moment justifying your unfortunate experience. But, you know, some people have actually put themselves forward, volunteered that is, for the kind of thing you've been through.'

Cotton did not reply immediately.

'Did they know what they were volunteering for? Were they told what cure they were contributing to?'

Dr Sanford looked pained. 'Colonel, I'm just trying to convey to you the reality we live in.'

'Dr Sanford,' said Cotton. 'Will you answer a question for me?'

'I'll certainly try.'

'Do you believe a doctor was in charge of the drug experiment carried out on me?'

Dr Sanford twitched. He was careful about his words. 'I'd like to think not,' he said, 'but I can't be sure.'

'That's fine,' said Cotton. 'Would you agree that my case is complicated by a problem that has to do with the nature of intelligence services?'

'I don't know anything about that,' said Dr Sanford.

'It's beyond your remit.'

'Yes it is! I'd have had a much easier time if I had been given a clear indication of the drugs and quantities you were given.' Dr Sanford frowned. 'You have no recall whatsoever of anything to do with it?'

'None. I'm a little anxious about inventing something.'

'What do you mean?'

'Finding things merely to fill in the gap. Did someone put something in a drink? Was I knocked out in a dark corridor? You know the kind of thing. God, I've even thought someone might have drugged my toothpaste.'

'OK,' said Dr Sanford. 'I don't want you to misunderstand me.'

'That's all right. Will I get an American Hornby?'

'Sorry?'

'Someone to check on me from your side?'

'I don't know,' said Dr Sanford.

Cotton wanted to write some notes. Is Sanford unhappy, and if so, how much? Has he complained to

anyone about having a drugged foreign intelligence officer dumped in his clinic? Has he been given something in return for his treating me? Where are the tapes going? Is he reporting to someone? And just how much, if at all, is he involved in other experiments with these drugs? But Cotton did not want to leave any traces of how he was thinking beyond what was on the tapes. He spent some time repeating the questions to himself in silence. There were six questions. He gave each finger of his left hand a question and kept Sanford's possible involvement to himself.

A little after, he fell asleep.

When he woke, his thumb immediately started pressing on each of the fingers in turn. Cotton thought that at least some of his short-term memory was returning. He just needed to keep insisting.

Dr Sanford came in and stood by his bed. He looked a little uncomfortable. 'I've come to find out whether or not you'd be prepared to see someone.'

'Who are we talking about?'

'A Mr Sam Hoberman. He said you'd know who he was.'

Cotton nodded. 'Yes, I do.'

Cotton had met Hoberman and a man called Bill Dawes in Washington in late 1945. They had met at FBI headquarters and exchanged information that had embarrassed Geoffrey Ayrtoun, Cotton's boss at the time. British analysts had misidentified a Soviet agent and failed to pick up that the agent was in charge of Barabbas, the codename for the policy of exterminating

defectors from the USSR then living in America. Cotton had never been sure whether or not the agent had later been killed out of embarrassment or policy.

'I'll be delighted to see him.'

Dr Sanford insisted. 'Are you sure? I don't know anything about Mr Hoberman but, well, you may want another couple of days before you see him.'

'No,' said Cotton. 'Tell him I look forward to our meeting.'

Dr Sanford sighed. 'He said he could be here by eleven this morning.'

'Splendid,' said Cotton.

Cotton recalled Sam Hoberman as a considered, quiet professional who somehow looked as if he always wore a suit and polished shoes, even to mow a lawn, and who spoke as if carefully knotting a slippery tie. He had found Hoberman admirably contained and polite in an impersonal sort of way. Despite himself, Cotton felt relief. He smiled. He had never thought of the FBI as being a source of relief before.

At eleven, Dr Sanford showed Sam Hoberman into Cotton's room. Hoberman took off his hat and Cotton held out his hand. Hoberman shook it.

'Mr Hoberman. Nice to see you again. I hope you're well.'

'Very well, thank you, Colonel,' said Hoberman.

'Do you wish me to stay?' said Dr Sanford.

Cotton thought he probably expected a positive answer.

'No, thank you, Dr Sanford.' He looked at Hoberman. 'Please sit. Dr Sanford accompanied me when Terence

99

Hornby came to see me. He sometimes records conversations for medical reasons.'

Hoberman considered this.

'I'd prefer it if that wasn't done in this instance,' he said.

'Then I'll get back to my duties, gentlemen. When you're finished, would you ring the nurse's bell?'

'Thank you, Doctor,' said Hoberman.

Hoberman waited till Sanford had left, then looked around the room. He did this without hurry and with some care.

'I'm sorry,' said Cotton. 'Would you like some hospital coffee or anything?'

Hoberman shook his head but did not interrupt his examination.

'The blinds are because of the scopolamine?'

'Light-sensitive eyes, certainly. Would you be happier if I removed my sunglasses?'

Hoberman looked very slightly surprised. 'That's not necessary, Colonel.' From a side pocket he withdrew a notepad and from his jacket a propelling pencil, and sat down. 'Do you mind?' he asked.

'Not at all.'

'What do you know?' said Hoberman.

'I'm told I was found in a doorway in Centre Street on the morning of the 5th of June. Until the 18th of June I was kept comatose here; apparently I was prone to convulsions. The sedation was reduced; I woke up. I was then confused and very light-sensitive. What the doctor calls my short-term memory was non-existent. I still have no recall whatsoever of what happened. As far as I

can work out, my drug course started either on the 1st or the 2nd of June.'

Cotton saw that Hoberman used Gregg shorthand to write down what he said verbatim.

'Do you know what was injected into you?'

'I don't. According to the doctor there was the scopolamine you've mentioned, sodium amytal and mescaline.'

Hoberman looked up. 'How do you know it wasn't the Soviets?'

'I don't. I have however had a visit from Mr Terence Hornby, a colleague, suggesting I not get too excited or vindictive about what happened. There's also where I am. I imagine foreign nationals found having convulsions in a doorway in Centre Street are not normally whisked off to the Ogden Clinic for American veterans. For those deemed to be a serious security risk, I imagine there might be somewhere even more private.'

Hoberman gave no reaction that Cotton could see but did take time before he spoke again.

'How well are you now?'

'Well enough to think that if anyone is going to try the Soviet sympathizer or unreliable angle on me, they are being cautious or at least taking their time. Dr Sanford has mentioned the possibility of an "implant" – a suggestion or instruction I don't know about. I don't know why he did that.'

Hoberman nodded. 'You really have no idea of how you were taken?'

'None. I have dispiritingly few memories of the days

even preceding my arrival in New York. Are you based here now?'

Hoberman shook his head.

'Still in Washington?'

Hoberman did not reply. Instead, he asked a question.

'This may be to ask too much. Have you been involved with anything like truth serums for your own government?'

'No,' said Cotton. 'My understanding is I was sent here for the United Nations.'

Hoberman looked up. 'You don't know for sure?'

'I don't want to mislead you. I have no memories of what happened to me. My impressions are not secure – except that I'm here, of course. Apart from Mr Hornby and my sister I've seen no one.'

Hoberman nodded. 'Oh, I can understand an element of caution,' he said. 'Have you thought about what you're going to do?'

'When I get out, I plan to rest. I can't say when and where, but that's what I'm going to do.'

Hoberman turned to a new page. 'Have you had any contact with Geoffrey Ayrtoun?'

'Ayrtoun? No. I last saw him earlier this year in Paris before his abrupt resignation.'

'His wife died.'

'So I heard.'

'All right, Colonel Cotton. You've been pretty straight. Thanks for that. I'm not in a position to promise any-thing but . . . well, if you want to talk about anything in the future, if you remember anything, we'd be pretty

interested to find out what you recall and your take on that. You understand I can't say any more? Is that fair?'

It took Cotton a moment to catch on. It was not that Hoberman didn't know or didn't have his suspicions. He was prevented from communicating them by intelligence protocol.

'It's very fair. Thank you.'

Sam Hoberman did not really indulge in smiles, but Cotton saw a minor twitch of his lips.

'Given your circumstances, Colonel, I'm truly obliged to you,' he said and got up. Cotton rang the bell. A nurse came to let Sam Hoberman out of the clinic. Dr Sanford came shortly afterwards.

'How do you feel?' he said.

'Fine,' said Cotton. 'It was good to see Mr Hoberman again. He's with the FBI.'

'Washington?'

'I don't think he made a special trip to see me,' said Cotton. He smiled. He believed the FBI was, in his case as in many more, tracking the other American agencies and that Hoberman had, in consequence and always in the protocol, confirmed that those who had put Cotton in the Ogden Clinic belonged at least to a department in one of those other American agencies.

It had not occurred to Cotton before that Ayrtoun's breakdown earlier in the year might not have been entirely due to his workload and the death of his wife. Hoberman had not suggested anything chemical, but Cotton thought he had touched on the possibility. Cotton was encouraged, not so much by the quality of his thoughts, but by managing to think at all.

9

COTTON DECIDED to ask for help from the nurses.

'What kind of help?'

'A haircut and a shave, if that's possible.'

'Of course, Colonel, we'll get right on it.'

For some reason Cotton expected a man to do this. But it was the little nurse he thought of as Miss Plum who came to attend to him. The sounds were of starch and water, scissors and comb. Then Miss Plum tackled his beard. First she cut with scissors, then she used a cut-throat razor with a white handle and pulled on parts of his face.

'Now wad your tongue, Colonel. Upper lip.'

On reflection, Cotton thought he did quite well not having an erection for so long. But her belly pressing into his shoulder and her reaching across and turning his head towards her breasts proved irresistible.

Miss Plum said nothing but Dr Sanford, when he came in, felt obliged to comment.

'No, no, that's good,' he said. 'The libido can be quite badly affected by these drugs.'

Cotton saw the doctor was more embarrassed than he was.

'The libido or the blood flow?' he asked.

Dr Sanford looked uncomfortable. 'The drugs can cause, as it were, a distraction.'

Miss Plum had finished shaving him. She patted his face, checking for bristles. 'I'm going to put some cream on your face,' she said. 'Colonel, you're looking kinda dried out.'

Bit by bit, Cotton concentrated on recovering simple actions. The next day he shaved himself with the small safety razor provided. He went too high and nicked himself just under the right eye socket. There was a pause and then startlingly bright blood appeared. Cotton took a small piece of tissue and dabbed. He was delighted by the colour of the blood, and when he saw it turn the sort of blue he associated with woodlice in England he felt encouraged. His eyes were definitely getting better and he began to feel a physical sort of clarity and cleanliness. And a certain lightness. He did not try dancing but certainly smiled at the possibility.

That morning at breakfast he also found he could smell better. His taste buds were still lagging but he registered the hot, sweet fat of a sausage and bacon and the tartness of a grilled tomato for longer than he had previously managed. He felt cheered.

'I'm missing garlic,' he said. 'And maybe black pepper.'

Nurse Plum tweaked the blinds so that they sent fatter lines of light into the room.

'Sorry, Colonel. We don't provide garlic at the Ogden.'

'No, I'm sorry. I was talking to myself.'

'Oh, that's OK,' said Miss Plum. 'You go right ahead.'

*

When Dr Sanford came in, Cotton told him he thought his vision was improving. He was wheeled off to a tall, big-boned old ophthalmologist on the first floor. The ophthalmologist stubbed out a cigarette and shone a light in his eyes.

'Is that uncomfortable?'

'Uncomfortable's the wrong word.'

The ophthalmologist smiled. 'Do you have a better word for me?'

'Awkward.'

'Something that might help me?'

'Bright but fuzzy.'

'That's OK. What was your vision before? Pretty near twenty-twenty?'

'Something like that,' said Cotton. 'I've never worn glasses. Now my long vision isn't very good. And, as I say, things can get fuzzy at short distances.'

'Can you read?'

'I can see the letters very well now. I couldn't before.'

'OK. I'd recommend you keep wearing those fancy sunglasses, certainly for a while and certainly while you work on your long-term vision. How were you as a shot in the service? Good at four hundred, five hundred yards?'

'I wasn't bad in 1942.'

'You practise at that. Line up shots. Your lead eye is the left, isn't it?'

'Yes.'

'Give the right a good workout too. You've got to get those muscles back in order. Anything else bothering you?'

'Colours. I see them quite well for a second and then

they go grey-blue, grey-white . . . though sometimes I get a fairly revolting purple. Earlier I had red or blue spots that went grey. The spots have faded.'

'Yes,' said the ophthalmologist. 'These spots were like a kind of mist or shadow?'

'Yes.'

'I don't think we have to look far for a reason.' He thought very briefly. 'Your eyes were given a battering. Your pupils were fixed open, then you had them rolling about, then maybe paralysed again. But I think your eyes will make a pretty full recovery. You should recover most of your colour vision bit by bit. Watch out for green and orange. When you've got those, you're fine. When are you due back to work?'

'September I hope.'

'Can I check him out then?'

'Yes,' said Dr Sanford. 'But we'll do it downtown in my rooms.'

'Your office will send me a reminder.'

'Yes.'

'Long-term military man?' said Cotton when he was being wheeled back to his room.

Dr Sanford smiled. 'That's pretty fair. He's good, though. I've had another request for people to visit you.'

'That's fine. When will that be?'

'I told them you'd be available now. We'll get you back to your room and comfortable and have them come up.'

When they arrived, Cotton was intrigued to see that there were three of them. He identified one as a lawyer

or counsel type; a bald, serious-looking man in his forties with a briefcase. The short, thin man Cotton identified immediately as an interrogator in Intelligence. There was also a red-faced blond fellow in the naval uniform of a lieutenant-commander.

'Dr Sanford, do I know any of these people? Have I met them before?'

'I don't believe you have, Colonel. Gentlemen, would you care to introduce yourselves?'

The Navy man identified himself as a Claiborne Lockhart, the lawyer as Eric Gaynes and the thin, little man said his name was Bob Yeager. As soon as Yeager spoke, Cotton recognized his voice as belonging to the other man he had heard when he had come out of sedation and in and out of consciousness.

'Are you all right with that?' asked Dr Sanford. 'I'll stay, if you wish.'

'There's no need for that,' said Gaynes. 'I'm sure the Colonel would appreciate discretion. Colonel?'

Cotton thought of discretion without representation but nodded as amiably as he could. He then remembered something.

'I don't think you said who you represented, gentlemen.'

'In general terms we're all involved with Un-American Activities, Colonel,' said Gaynes, 'but in different capacities. Lieutenant-Commander Lockhart is from the Department of the Navy, Mr Yeager works for one of our intelligence agencies and I myself am a lawyer assisting the Committee itself.'

Cotton nodded. 'Thank you, gentlemen. I'm Peter

Cotton, sent by British Intelligence to New York to report on the establishment of the United Nations Organization and how that may affect British interests, and I have a special brief on decolonization. My background has been in Intelligence since 1944, and as you probably know, I was in Washington from September to December of 1945. From the beginning of 1946 to May 1947 I worked at the British Colonial Intelligence Service in London.' Cotton smiled. 'As you can see, I am not American.'

'We're allies,' said Gaynes, 'in the same struggle against Soviet imperialism.'

'Indeed we are.'

Gaynes looked round and stared at Dr Sanford. Sanford left. Gaynes wrote something down. Cotton thought it looked like the time.

'Would you like me to remove my sunglasses?' he asked. 'I understand some people find it upsetting not to see my eyes.'

'That won't be necessary,' said Yeager. 'Colonel, are you conscious of what's happened to you?'

'Only partially. And some of that is hearsay. I understand from Dr Sanford that I was injected with a number of drugs which, according to him, included scopolamine, sodium amytal and mescaline. I can say that they certainly altered my view of the world, not always pleasantly. But I have no idea who administered these substances. Dr Sanford tells me, and I can certainly vouch for it, that I've suffered acute short-term memory loss; he says that's probably from the scopolamine. He tells me that it's used in much smaller doses to reduce any unpleasant

109

memories in childbirth. I have no memory at all of who was responsible for administering the drugs to me or my capture or any of the circumstances that led up to it. I don't even remember arriving in the USA.'

Gaynes looked up. 'Have you any reason to suspect you may have fallen into the hands of the Soviets?'

'None whatsoever.'

'How can you possibly say that?' said Yeager.

'Partly from what I've been told. And partly from examination of the circumstances. The only way that could have happened is if the Soviets had made a catastrophic mistake.'

'Would you like to explain yourself?'

'I think it's clear,' said Cotton. 'If the Soviets had been trying to kill me, there are so many easier, quicker methods.'

'What if their aims had been different?'

'In what sense?'

'To make an example of you. To compromise you.'

'If you mean that they wanted to make me doubtful to my own side and to you, surely there are methods that don't include short-term memory loss and confusion? It seems very complicated for something that could have been done so much more easily.'

'How?'

Cotton shrugged. 'Just by giving my name to a double agent. Mentioning me in coded messages they knew you'd get. Simply by being apparently careless.'

Yeager paused.

'What if they had been trying to implant something in you?'

'Dr Sanford mentioned that. But if that were the case they have made rather a hash of it. I'm here in the Ogden Clinic, having been abandoned in a doorway. They'd have drawn attention to the possibility.'

'You've met Soviets,' said Yeager.

'Yes, I have.'

'You've met Oleg Cherkesov,' said Yeager.

'Yes, last February. I had lunch with him at a restaurant called Simpson's in the Strand in London. I was doing my job.' Cotton shrugged. 'I filed a report on the meeting. I have no doubt that if Cherkesov had made a mistake, he'd have eliminated me, not abandoned me in a doorway. He talked to me of practising on your own.'

'What did he mean?'

'I took him to mean that their purges on their own citizens had made them particularly ruthless and unforgiving towards others. If Cherkesov had been in charge of this, I'd have been found dead or not found at all.'

'What's your own theory?' said Yeager. 'You must have one.'

'I don't have a theory,' said Cotton. 'Partly because right now I'm in no state to develop one. I do know that my own side has asked me to be calm and reasonable – and get better. They haven't provided an explanation, but again, Terence Hornby told me he doubted that the Soviets were involved. I don't think you appreciate quite how shaky I am. I'm not rushing anything, and certainly not rushing to conclusions.'

Lieutenant-Commander Lockhart reacted for the first time. Cotton thought he looked startled, incredulous and suspicious. He applied more Englishness.

'I've been in Intelligence for some years,' he said. 'The first thing I learnt was not to be hasty. You remember that when your eyes are painfully light-sensitive, your sense of taste has given up the ghost and you find print difficult both to see and to interpret.'

'You also met a Soviet agent called Slonim,' said Yeager.

'Yes, in Washington in 1945,' said Cotton. 'Our analysts had failed to pick up that he was actually Arkady Musin, in charge of Barabbas, the operation to eliminate Soviet defectors of any kind. Slonim, or Musin, died later, as I'm sure you know. An apparent heart attack, possibly due to altitude. Again, if the Soviets had wanted revenge for that, they would surely have killed me.'

'You were working for Geoffrey Ayrtoun at that time?'

'Yes. He had a breakdown later, earlier this year when his wife died. I believe he's no longer employed by His Majesty's Government. Gentlemen, I don't want to rush you. But one effect of my treatment is a marked drop in stamina. I tend to fall asleep after the effort of quite routine conversations. If you have more questions, I'd get them in now.'

'Have you had any contact with Mr Ayrtoun since his resignation?'

'None whatsoever. Why would I?'

'Are you aware that he himself has been undergoing quite radical therapy?'

Cotton shrugged. 'I heard only that he had submitted himself to electric shocks, in the hope of alleviating his depression. I have no idea if any treatment he had was

successful. I don't know where he is. The last time I heard – and my source may or may not have been reliable – he was in Canada.'

'A British dominion,' said Yeager.

Cotton frowned. 'I've met Canadian economists but not many Canadian Intelligence people.'

'No?' said Yeager. 'Well, they're doing a lot of work on barbiturates and electroshocks at one of their universities. Perhaps you may want to look more closely at where Mr Ayrtoun is. Would you say you'd both had a breakdown?'

Cotton was struck but not surprised at how clumsy this was. But Gaynes positively started. He did not approve of Yeager's tactic. Cotton shrugged. In the end he thought Yeager had a point. There was also the suddenness of Ayrtoun's resignation. Had that made the Americans suspicious of Ayrtoun? He'd check when he was in a position to check.

'No,' said Cotton. 'Somebody may have tried to break me down but I don't think that's the same as having a breakdown. Do you? And in either case it's not clear it was successful.'

'What are you thinking of doing when you get out of here?' said Lockhart.

Cotton sighed, raised his sunglasses and rubbed his eyes. 'I'd like to rest, Commander. Rest up and recover, preferably away from New York, somewhere quiet. My aim is to get well enough to start work in September and to concentrate on the United Nations. It's one thing at a time. Physically, I'm rather weak. Mentally, I am still pretty slow.'

'Do you think you're going to make it?' said Yeager.

'There's that too,' said Cotton. 'I don't know that the medical staff here are overly optimistic.'

Yeager had not finished. 'Do you speak Russian?' he said.

'No,' said Cotton. 'Oh, I can ask the time.'

Yeager shrugged. 'They'd have been perfectly able to ask you any questions in English.'

'I dare say,' said Cotton. 'But I don't remember any questions from anybody.'

'Then you have no idea of what you may have said.'

'That's it exactly,' said Cotton, 'always given that someone was trying to get me to say something in the first place. Have you heard anything, Mr Yeager?'

But that was it. Gaynes nodded. The meeting was over.

On the whole, Cotton was pleased. Three visitors said something. A number of agencies and groups had evidently taken an interest in his case. He thought it likely then that no one had yet made a drastic decision on his future. Was that true? He didn't trust his own thoughts enough to be sure.

'How did that go?' said Dr Sanford.

'I don't know,' said Cotton. He felt, however, a curious tripping sensation in his heart and a certain light-headedness. His heart was registering a degree of fear. His mind, with what justification he did not know, was not.

'You look like you could use a nap,' said Sanford.

'I could.'

Cotton frowned. He now felt surprised and suspicious they had given him such an easy time.

'Are you OK?' said Sanford.

Cotton nodded. The visit had left him depressed. Was this because of his meetings with the Russians? Why had they asked about Ayrtoun? It occurred to him that he might unwittingly have condemned himself somehow. Gaynes had looked like a real lawyer and would be able to turn anything he had said.

Later, Cotton had his first visit from a petty officer first class called Tully, who described himself as a 'physio'. He had a boxer's nose and square-knuckled hands and wore his hair so short he provided another test for Cotton's vision – he still could not make out if the man was bald or not. Tully put Cotton through some simple exercises with a mixture of respect, strength and watchfulness. There was nothing more demanding than some stretching, some sit-ups, press-ups and some running on the spot. In the morning session everything was in fives. In the afternoon, in tens. So that meant five press-ups went to ten, and running on the spot went from fifty thumps of Cotton's left leg to a hundred.

'How do you feel, sir? We don't want to overstrain that heart but I think we could up this. Two hundred tomorrow? Twenty press-ups?'

'That would be about my limit.'

'Then you stop at the slightest sign of difficulty. Agreed?'

'Agreed.'

Cotton found two hundred much harder than he expected. Whether or not in anticipation of what was to

follow, he began to sweat a great deal before he had even finished the previous day's target.

'Do you want to stop?'

'No,' said Cotton. He kept going. He felt decidedly light-headed. His pulse was bouncing about, with an odd staccato riff. He thought this was about every fifty steps but couldn't keep count and had to rely on POFC Tully to call out the numbers.

He dropped into a chair when he had finished. He blinked. He had never been a great sweater before. Here he saw that even his forearms were beaded. The sweat looked slightly yellow to him. He looked up.

POFC Tully was frowning. 'Maybe we've gone too fast,' he said.

Cotton shook his head. 'No, we haven't.' He had to admit the sweating felt good, like some sort of relief.

'I'd better consult,' said Tully. 'I was told to watch for heart strain.'

Cotton shook his head and remembered to smile. 'No,' he said. 'We'll stick at this in the afternoon.' He looked up. 'Otherwise it's hardly worth going on. Agreed?'

'You could try taking it a little gentler, sir.'

Cotton nodded. He had no intention of taking it gentler.

When Dr Sanford came in, he gave him a fat artist's pad and some coloured pencils.

'What's this for?'

'Have you heard of automatic writing?'

'Yes. I read something about that. I believe the poet

W. B. Yeats was a fan. I can't remember whether or not he used his non-writing hand. As far as I understand it, he wanted to quash the edited, rational side of himself and let the irrational free to flow. But I'm not sure he didn't think other voices were involved, though I can't remember whether he thought they were other beings speaking through him or potential characters for his plays.'

'Do you like his poetry?'

'As a matter of fact, I do. At least I think I do.'

'But you don't approve of automatic writing?'

Cotton shrugged. 'It reminds me of séances. Writing and a lack of control don't really go together, do they? Is this your way round hypnosis?'

Dr Sanford smiled. 'Not exactly. What I want you to do when you leave here is to take this pad and these pencils.'

'Is that going to be soon?'

'Hold up there,' said Dr Sanford. 'I want to be clear. Yes, I do want you to suspend your critical, edited side, however weird you think this is. Just draw what comes to mind. You've heard of the mind's eye?'

'I have. But I don't draw, you know. I don't even doodle.'

'No? What do you do?'

'When listening to a boring speaker?' Cotton shrugged. 'I keep one ear open. The rest of me checks things. What have I got to do? Have I forgotten to get something?'

'What do you mean, "get something"?'

'Milk,' said Cotton. 'Do I need to buy some milk?'

Dr Sanford looked almost admiringly at him. 'You do

play close to your chest,' he said. 'But that's not what I have in mind. I am not asking you to turn into an old master, I'm just asking you to take out the pad and let your pencil run. Don't think, just let that point mark the paper.'

Cotton nodded. 'Is the idea that things will float up in my mind, go down my arm and produce a version of the image that floated up? How reliable is that?'

'I really don't know. You haven't drawn anything so far.' Dr Sanford smiled. 'All I am asking is that you relax and mark paper in whatever colour you like.'

'Can I write a word?'

'What do you mean?'

'I don't know. If I see a parrot can I skip drawing the bird and write the word?'

'OK, Colonel.' Dr Sanford paused. 'Are we on for this? You'll do it?'

'Yes,' said Cotton.

'It's important,' said Dr Sanford. 'My experience encourages me to think that if problems aren't solved pretty quickly, they lead on – and cause more problems. Do you understand me?'

Cotton smiled. 'Yes. But I'm no Picasso.'

Dr Sanford shook his head. 'I've got to insist. You really must not overestimate yourself. You certainly shouldn't try to conform to some standard of strength. Because you've done pretty well does not mean you will be free in the future of all kinds of stuff. You might find yourself abruptly unable to function. You may have nightmares. You may have episodes that you don't recall and begin to worry what you've been doing.'

Cotton nodded. He did not actually believe this – or at least not in the way Dr Sanford said it. But he nodded. 'I understand,' he said. 'I'll go softly-softly.'

From this, Cotton thought he must have passed those Un-American Committee people's meeting. In other words, they did not consider him an urgent threat, either from what had happened to him or from his potential reaction. They probably did not think he was capable of much anyway. Perhaps they wanted to see what he would do.

'When can I leave?'

Dr Sanford shrugged. 'It's your call, I suppose.'

'All right. Could I aim for tomorrow?'

'We'll take some more blood from you first. And you have to continue with the exercise programme – Tully will give you the information – and you've got to think of us as still collaborating. Record things; keep a diary. I'll follow up. I'll continue your prescription of one pill.'

'Which one?'

'It's called a stabilizer. It's been helping you even out the ups and downs.'

'Really?'

'Yes, it has. Believe me. It will help until I see you again. OK? I need you to take it. You need to take it.'

Cotton nodded. If that was the price of getting out of the Ogden Clinic, so be it.

10

O N HIS discharge from the Ogden Clinic, Cotton
received his keys and wallet – which had been
found on him intact. Joan had brought him some clothes
that were a size, possibly two, too big and loose for him.

'I should have thought,' she had said.

'It's my fault,' said Cotton.

Dressed, he looked pinched and frail, an impression
not helped by the clinic's insistence he leave the premises
in a wheelchair.

A nurse wheeled him down to the entrance hall. He
read the hopeful motto Joan had mentioned, and got up.

'May I walk out?'

'Of course.'

Cotton was moved to Todd and Joan's apartment by
a chauffeur-driven limousine, a new Lincoln of a colour
he thought was Burgundy. His send-off from the clinic
was formal. He shook hands with his nurses – Sister
Janet Kowolski, Nurse Beryl Oates and Miss Plum, who
turned out to be called Helen Belisle. He was tucked into
the back of this presidential-type vehicle as if precious
to the future of mankind. He tried to be graceful in his
gratitude but was relieved when the Lincoln pulled
away. It was the first time he had not felt on display for
a long while.

Todd and Joan had an apartment at 25 Central Park West, a block-sized art deco building with twin towers rising some thirty floors above ground. When he had been in the US before, in 1945, Cotton had learnt of Classic Eights and Sixes, referring to the number of rooms in New York apartments. Todd and Joan had twelve rooms – as well as the large house in Oyster Bay.

It may have been the change from hospital to domestic lighting, but Cotton thought Joan and Todd looked hideously uncomfortable – as if he were the younger brother getting into scrapes. Was he oversensitive? He thought probably not.

'I want to send something to the staff at the Clinic,' he said. 'There were three nurses who looked after me. Sister Kowolski and Nurses Oates and Belisle. Flowers and chocolates?'

'If you want to,' said Joan.

Todd nodded. 'Sure,' he said. 'Do you have plans, Peter?'

'Can I check back with you? And can I use your telephone?'

'Of course,' said Todd.

Cotton wanted somewhere to hole up. He telephoned Hornby and said he was out of the Ogden Clinic and was going on leave.

'Strictly speaking, you are not due for leave until you have served eighteen months.'

'Unless you are holding me to hospital time for the last of those, I have done them. Just to make this clear, I am taking at least two months.'

There was a pause.

'What are you actually thinking of doing?' said Hornby.

'Going somewhere quiet.'

'In the States?'

'Yes. I haven't decided where yet. Do you want me to tell you?'

'When you know, old boy.'

Cotton told Joan and Todd that he was now on leave and his plans were to go away somewhere quiet.

'You'll need some more clothes in any case,' said Joan.

'Yes.' Cotton paused. He wasn't sure. 'Wouldn't I have ordered some when I arrived at the end of May?'

'Where did you go?'

Cotton could not remember. 'You probably told me where to go.'

'You've no names?'

'I don't remember any.'

Joan went away and used the telephone.

'I've found you. We'll go tomorrow. You ordered a sports coat, two pairs of trousers and six shirts from Brooks Brothers. In Madison Avenue. They're waiting for you.'

Cotton nodded. He had no memory of the order or the shop.

'You're going to need more than that, though,' said Joan. 'A lightweight summer suit, for example. Perhaps one in cotton corduroy? And what would you say to seersucker?'

'I don't remember what seersucker is. Why do I think of milk and sugar?'

'Because that's what seersucker means, Peter. In Persian, I think.'

Cotton stared at her. 'Wouldn't that attract insects and then curdle?'

Joan looked at him. 'Are you OK? You look like you are going to keel over.'

'Really?' Cotton put both hands on the side of the armchair and gripped. He tried a smile.

Todd and Joan had already sent their children to Oyster Bay. Cotton was acutely aware he was probably embarrassing and potentially alarming.

'I want to get away,' he repeated. 'Spend the summer somewhere quiet.'

'Do you have any place in mind?' said Todd.

'I haven't got very much in mind at all, Todd. I just want somewhere quiet where I can rest and get better.'

'OK.' Todd nodded. 'Leave it with me.'

Joan smiled. 'You should also think of autumn,' she said. 'You'll need clothes for the other seasons. Tonight I am giving you watermelon, coq au vin and Mexican rice pudding.'

'Lovely,' said Cotton. He tried but could not recall the taste of any of these foods. In the event they tasted thin, salty thick and sweet thick.

Cotton spent a tedious night in an over-pretty guest-room. He kept waking up. Having been desperate to get away from the place, he had to admit he missed the seclusion of the clinic. There had been noises there too

123

but also a sort of reassuring thrum of plant under the hush. Here in Todd and Joan's apartment he felt somehow thinner and more exposed. The bedroom was relatively narrow and the ceiling low; it reminded him of an office with a bed instead of a desk. Around three, he had to tackle the window business, the sense that floors sloped down and would send him sliding out. He pulled back the curtains and looked out over Central Park. There were many lights in the distance. They were still slightly fuzzy. He squinted. He put on his Ray-Bans, then took them off. The lights had become fuzzier. He grunted. Below him, he could hear traffic. He was happy with that. He knew he had been looked after and that now he had to adapt and fit in to not being a patient.

He still could not sleep, so he picked up the *New Yorker* magazine. The cover showed a fat recreational fisherman in waders disappointed that he had caught only a tiddler. Downstream, behind a rock, hidden from the fisherman but clear to the viewer, a bear was pawfishing from the bank, surrounded by a glut of large fish, possibly salmon.

Cotton spent a long time looking at the illustration. He couldn't understand it. Was this a joke? Some wistful reflection for anglers with all their equipment that they knew nothing about catching fish compared to a bear? Or was it ridiculing anglers? He wasn't even sure when salmon went upstream to spawn. In Scotland, he thought, salmon began spawning around November. Presumably they started upstream before then. He was also aware that bears in North America relied on salmon to pack on

weight before the winter. That probably meant the fish started upstream in the summer. In which case the angler in the illustration, standing in fast water, would have noticed the fish, which the bear was catching in the pool, leaping upstream. The date of the *New Yorker* was June 21, 1947. It cost 20 cents.

He never did open the magazine. Around five in the morning he dozed off.

By six he was in the shower. He shaved, took his prescribed medication and dressed. He was determined to reassure his sister and brother-in-law but was not sure how to do it.

At breakfast he chose porridge – it never had much taste anyway – and found things had moved on.

'Do you know where Narragansett is, Peter?' said Todd.

'Rhode Island?'

'Yes. Just across the bay from Newport.'

Cotton frowned. 'Isn't that rather grand and social? Astors and people like that with mansions and yachts?'

'No, no, no. Newport's still fancy, but Narragansett was popular a long time ago. I think almost all the big hotels were torn down around 1920. It should be quiet. A place to rest up. It's pretty easy-going I think and it has some pleasant beaches. What do you think?'

'You have somewhere in mind?'

'Yes,' said Todd. 'I have a kind of aunt. I think she's really a cousin a generation up. She paints. She could give you what she calls her guest-cottage and could provide meals if you wanted. She has a library like

125

a barn. She's – well, let's say Eleanor concentrates a lot on her painting.'

'What does she paint?'

'Seabirds,' said Joan without enthusiasm. 'Cormorants in particular.'

'Her work is somewhere between naïve and surrealist,' said Todd.

'Black bird on red rock,' said Joan. 'House with blue windows in the distance behind. Yellow sky.'

'Is she a professional artist?'

Joan made a face. 'I think we could call her generous-spirited – she often gives her paintings as presents.'

Cotton nodded. 'All right. How do I get there?'

'There's a train, but I'd recommend you drive,' said Todd. 'Are you up for that?'

'Yes,' said Cotton.

'Good. Hire a car, then. I'd guess it's what – about four hours' drive?'

'Should you really be driving?' said Joan.

'Apparently that's one of the things I can do in my sleep. How many miles?'

Todd thought. 'A hundred and eightyish, I guess. Take the coast road.'

Cotton looked at his sister. She nodded.

'Today we're going to do some clothes shopping,' she said. 'We've got to get you a proper wardrobe. Here we have four seasons, you know. We'll finish summer and plan for fall. And we should check on the agent who was looking for an apartment for you. I suggested somewhere between East 40th and East 57th.'

'I don't know New York.'

'That'll be good for the Rockefeller Center and the new building in Turtle Bay.'

'All right.'

Todd smiled. 'I'll see you two for dinner. Do you feel like going out, Peter?'

Cotton smiled back. 'Yes, why not?'

There were calls to be made to Oyster Bay and the children. Cotton took the opportunity to go back to his room and rest. He sat on the dinky chair and tried to exude fatigue, get rid of it. He even bent towards the air-conditioning unit to help blow his tiredness away.

Around ten, Cotton and Joan took the elevator downstairs and the doorman beckoned a taxi.

'I wanted to ask you about clothes in Britain,' said Joan.

'People wear what's available to buy and what they've got left.'

'Is that why Pop doesn't come?'

'I don't know. You're saying shabby gives a certain shame to victory?'

Joan frowned. 'He's too proud.'

'Well, he's spent his life taking care and being in control. Darning socks and underwear is something of a problem for him.'

'But it's so silly, Peter – and so unnecessary!'

'Just what the hell do you think rationing really is?' said Cotton. He had not even registered that he was irritated before he spoke and it wasn't until he looked across that he recognized he had said anything to upset his sister.

There was silence until they reached Brooks Brothers.

'I'm sorry,' said Joan. 'I don't know what Pop's been through.'

'No,' said Cotton. 'It's not your fault. I'm the one who should apologize. Sorry.'

Joan smiled. 'It's OK,' she said. 'Shall we go shopping now?'

Cotton was genuinely interested in what America had to offer. He presumed he had been in the shop before but had no recall of it. He found clothes for men had become what Joan described as 'fulsome'. They used a lot of cloth; suits were often double-breasted, with wide trousers and wide lapels. More intriguing to Cotton were what shops called 'sports clothes'.

'What is that?' asked Cotton, pointing at a shirt that reminded him of wallpaper, madder and cream flowers, pineapple yellow and green foliage.

'Those are Hawaiian shirts,' said Joan.

'We prefer the expression *Aloha Attire*,' said the prissy person attending them.

'Do you have this kind of thing without the flowers or the colours?'

'But of course, sir.'

Cotton was most surprised by the swimming shorts.

From the Jantzen Sunclothes collection there was a model called Beach Boy made of Oxford cloth and with a buttoned coin pocket; the background colours were raw linen and dull sepia but with green splodges that turned out to be guitars, pineapples and conch shells.

Cotton wondered who on earth would wear that, but then realized some Americans would.

He stuck to navy blue and dark green. He also got new underwear in 'Sea-Island cotton', socks and a couple of short-sleeved shirts.

'Todd and I are going to give you a couple of suits, OK? Belated birthday presents.'

Cotton shook his head. 'You've done enough and I have to watch my budget.'

'You're going to need a black tie. After all, we're going out this evening.'

'It's one thing being a poor relative—'

'Knicker elastic,' said Joan. Caught by surprise, Cotton laughed. As children, they had had this expression to mean something they didn't like. 'There is nothing worse than soggy knicker elastic,' Joan had announced when she was about ten and had been afflicted by the condition at a friend's birthday party. The phrase had stuck as a kind of private shorthand for something not worth bothering about.

Cotton breathed in.

'What are you smelling?' said Joan.

'Newness.'

She smiled. 'Good. That's the spirit.'

Later in the afternoon, Cotton visited his bank. In the evening he took Todd and Joan out. They went to the Bar Room at 21 and it took Joan very little time to worry that Todd's desire to show Cotton 'a genuine New York institution' was a mistake. Cotton paused when he saw the miniature models of jockeys outside. Inside, despite the discreet service, it was very noisy, a place to

be seen. There was a very loud party nearby, with lots of 'glad handing' and back slapping. A drunk lady leant back too hard and, exposing some very long teeth, forgave herself with a delighted shriek.

Joan leant over and whispered to her brother. 'Are you OK? What do you think?'

'They have what look like toy flies on the ceiling.'

Joan started and looked up. The Bar Room had toys, a lot of planes, pinned to an already low ceiling. Cotton smiled. 'I'm all right,' he said. 'I don't want to be mean, but it's a bit like the Day of the Dead in Mexico for those who have money.'

'Have the sirloin,' said Todd. 'I can really recommend it.'

Cotton smiled. He filtered out the noise and concentrated on his sister and Todd. He needed help in remembering who got what at tipping time, but he thought the dinner had gone well. He felt amiable but decidedly dull. And he much preferred being treated as a non-patient.

Later, in bed, he began reading and found he could immediately and vividly understand what was written. The novel was *Under the Volcano* by Malcolm Lowry. His sister had bought it earlier that year simply because of its Mexican background. She had not liked it. 'The Soak's Obtuse Self-Justification' was her alternative title. Cotton was more favourably impressed. He liked the heightened sense of a pained and confused consciousness at work in the words. The main character lived near Cuernavaca, a place he and Joan had both been to as children, and the place the Soviet Oleg

130

Cherkesov had told Cotton he had once dreamt of retiring to. None of them would have recognized the drunken Consul's version. Cotton wondered if a copy could be got to Moscow.

He fell asleep and slept for seven hours straight. It was the first time he had done that for as long as he could remember. As soon as he woke, he tried to recall what he had read. He found that he could and was more interested in that than in any similarities between the Consul's drunkenness and his own confusion after the drugs. He got up and did the exercises he had done with POFC Tully, then showered and shaved. He began to think he wasn't doing that badly.

After breakfast Cotton learnt that Todd's cousin had been what he called 'amenable'.

'She'll take your cheque when you arrive,' said Todd.

Cotton went for a walk in Central Park. His clothes that had needed alteration were beginning to arrive. He tried them on. He made a list of things he needed. It began with *suitcase*. He wrote to his father.

At dinner at home that evening – Todd and Joan were going to the theatre – he discussed when he should go to Narragansett.

'How about this Friday morning?' said Todd.

'You mean on July 4th?' said Joan. 'Yes. Why not? Peter?'

Today was Tuesday, 1 July. That left him a few days to get organized. Cotton nodded. 'Friday's fine. Tomorrow I'll deal with my office.'

After they had gone, Cotton sat and looked out of the windows and across the park. He liked the view but he

wanted to get away. He was asleep in bed before Joan and Todd returned.

The next day, Terence Hornby suggested they meet in a café on 52nd Street near the jazz clubs. Cotton arrived first, looked at some of the famous jazz names like Jimmy Ryan's Bar and the Three Deuces in daylight, then went into the air-conditioned café and ordered coffee and iced water.

'What a climate this is,' said Hornby when he arrived. 'I shouldn't have walked.'

He took off his hat and used a handkerchief to wipe his face. While Hornby drank a glass of chilled water, Cotton took off his sunglasses. What he thought of as Hornby's Alice band of hair had collapsed into some wet tendrils and stray upward curls. Hornby crunched ice.

'I'm off on Friday,' said Cotton.

'I'm hoping to get a few days in August,' said Hornby. 'I'd like to go to Maine. Have you been there?'

Cotton shook his head and gave Hornby a sheet of paper with his Narragansett address on it. 'I'll be here until the 1st of September.'

'Your leave hasn't gone down too well in London,' said Hornby.

'I didn't think it would,' said Cotton. 'Do they think I'm ready for work now?'

'No, I said that you needed to convalesce. Do you know anybody in Narragansett?'

'What do you mean?'

'Well, have you any friends or chums there? Acquaintances?'

'No.'

Hornby frowned. 'Wouldn't Newport have been better? Lots of people go there.'

'I'm going for what I hope is a lot of quiet,' said Cotton.

'I see.' Hornby made a face. 'I think you might be very seriously quiet, if you understand me.'

'That's perfect,' said Cotton. 'Are you speaking from experience?'

'No, no' said Hornby. He shook his head and looked up. 'You know, I'm thinking of taking up a pipe.'

Cotton wasn't sure he had heard correctly. 'A pipe?' He shrugged. 'All right.'

Hornby frowned. 'I say,' he said, 'you're not holding my visit to the clinic against me, are you? I drew the short straw, as it were.'

'No,' said Cotton. 'After you, I saw the FBI and some others. My understanding is that someone from around the American side was responsible.'

Hornby made a face. 'That still leaves a lot of options.'

'I've ruled out the FBI.'

'Yes,' said Hornby. 'You're probably right about that.'

'What do you do?' said Cotton.

'I'm in Counter-Intelligence,' said Hornby. 'But I get other jobs. You're a level or two above me.'

'I see,' said Cotton. 'How long have you been in?'

'Just since the end of the war. I was in Military Intelligence before. Booby traps really. Now things are less physical. My speciality is dirty tricks, you see. Well, how to combat them.'

133

'Good,' said Cotton. 'Has this been a dirty trick?'

'Not in the usual sense of the term,' Hornby said. 'It looks more like a punt, a sort of try it and see. I don't know what the motives or aims were, though.'

Cotton smiled, paid, and Hornby offered his hand. Cotton shook it. It was indeed very small, presumably good, thought Cotton, for dealing with physical booby traps.

Cotton went next to Waverly Place. Having paid the cab, he looked around. There was a pharmacy on the corner of 6th Avenue. He looked in but he had no memory of it and could see no assistant even remotely like the girl with the thick lipstick he had remembered selling him Pepsodent toothpaste with irium. Besides, his memory had had the feel of old polished wood and cabinets: this pharmacy was altogether brighter and smelt of talc, sugar and antiseptic. He remembered nothing of having been there before. He walked on, let himself into the building and took off his Ray-Bans, but he still could not understand how he had taken an apartment in such a dingy, dark place. He took the elevator to the third floor and looked for 3G along narrow, barely lit corridors. He paused. Would this have been a good place to grab hold of him? He thought it probably was, though the corridor was hardly wide enough to allow two people to stand abreast.

Sticking fairly close to the wall and then peering, he made out 3F on a door. 3G was at the end of the corridor and he ran his fingers over the letter to make sure he had the right apartment.

Cotton took out his keys, opened the door and pushed

in. He found that, at the end of May, he had taken a small penumbral place with what was called the kitchen rather smaller than the bathroom. There was a living room with a small dining table and two chairs, and a sofa and an armchair, both with side tables and lamps with parchment shades with small green fringes on them. On one wall there was an undistinguished painting of a seashore somewhere. Through a door was the bedroom. There was a double bed bare to the mattress, a bedside table and the same parchment and fringe lamp. Against one wall was a narrow wardrobe. He opened it. There was nothing inside except two wire hangers.

Cotton went back to the living room. The kitchen was a sort of alcove that could be shut off by louvre doors. When he opened them, a cockroach on the counter paused and waved its antennae at him. He blew at it. The antennae paused, then worked again. Without haste the cockroach turned and disappeared into a crack between the counter and the wall.

There was nothing in the bathroom except a faded smell of bleach. Cotton somehow felt disappointed there was no toothpaste. He looked around the living room again. Even for someone not particularly interested in stylish accommodation, it looked like a poor choice. Had he been so down in late May that he had thought somewhere as depressing as this was just the thing?

He frowned and looked around him. He had never seen the place before. This was not possible. It appeared he had not even begun moving in. At least, none of his things were here. What did that mean? That he had run into drug experimentation earlier than he thought?

Cotton had one last absurd try at remembering. He worked the front door back and forward, trying to dislodge a memory. None came. He closed the door, shuffled down the corridor and took the elevator down to the lobby.

There was still nobody there, but there was a bell. Cotton rang it. After a few seconds an elderly, unshaven man came out.

'What do you want?'

'I want to return some keys. They're for 3G.'

The old man shrugged. 'This should have been done before.'

'The apartment was taken for a month.'

'So? Keys are keys, right?' The old man looked at his book. 'Did you say 3G? I've had problems with that one.'

'What kind of problems?'

'It was cleared out. Nobody told me anything.'

'Who cleared it out?'

'I don't know! Somebody took it on. Somebody cleared it out.'

'When you say "cleared out", what do you mean?'

'I don't know. There's nothing there now.'

'These are the keys. Do I have to sign anything?'

'Why would you?'

'I took the place on.'

'It got signed off.'

'When did that happen?'

The old man looked at his book. 'June 4,' he said. 'I wasn't here. It must have been done in the evening.'

Cotton saw someone had signed 'P. J. B. Cotton'

136

without any effort to imitate his signature. He took out a dollar and offered it to the old man.

'What's this for, exactly?'

'It's a thank you.'

The old man put a finger on it but did not bring it towards him. 'OK,' he said. 'Is there trouble?'

'None at all,' said Cotton.

He turned and walked out. While he waited for a taxi he considered. Whoever had got hold of him had first removed his keys, cleared out the apartment and then returned the keys to him before his Centre Street experience. Why had they bothered?

Cotton saw a taxi and raised his arm. The cab screeched and pulled up.

Whoever it was had got rid of all his clothes as well. The clothes had been British, some even pre-war and well worn. As he got into the cab Cotton felt not quite reborn but certainly as if he were starting again. One thing he had to do was pick an apartment with more light.

He gave the driver the house agent's office address. Within an hour he was looking at an apartment in Sutton Place. It had the virtue of being painted in white, but the ceilings seemed low to Cotton, and the rooms on the narrow side. There were two bedrooms and bathrooms at the back. The kitchen was smallish but was a separate room. There was a tiny, even dinky dining room off it, just enough for a small round table and four chairs. Cotton couldn't tell if the panelling was real and painted or just painted. The living room, however, in the words of the agent, was 'positively gracious'.

'It's nearly twenty-three feet long. Yes, that is an

air-conditioning unit. And look, sir. You even have views of the East River. Splendid, isn't it?'

Cotton looked out. He understood 'views' came as a plural because the view was broken up by other buildings. He didn't think the East River that splendid.

'That's the 59th Street Bridge, sir.'

'I'll need a second visit.'

'Sir?'

'I always take my sister's advice on this kind of thing. She's better at it.'

The next morning Cotton woke tired. He arranged a hire car for Friday and then took Joan to see the apartment at 10.30. Cotton was aware he needed to fix up somewhere to live from September but was immediately more anxious to see how his memory was functioning. Not that well, he thought.

He had somehow missed how bulky the red-brick building was at 14 Sutton Place South. According to the agent there were fifteen storeys and ninety-three apartments. Cotton would have called it revival Georgian from the outside.

'Built in 1929. It's a full service building, sir.'

He had also missed that the apartment was described as having '4.5' rooms. He wondered what the point five referred to, but didn't ask.

But Joan was pleased. 'How big is the floor area?'

'About two thousand square feet,' said the agent.

'This'll do you nicely,' she said and squeezed Cotton's arm. 'Make the second bedroom your study.' She smiled. 'It is kind of British, don't you think?'

'What do you mean?'

She pointed at the plain chimney piece. 'Now I don't mean Norman Shaw,' she said. 'He was sort of Gothic. I know. Lutyens! It reminds me of Lutyens!'

Cotton blinked. He could see nothing of either architect there. He thought it more like Georgian cottage colonial, way above street level.

'Really?' he said.

Joan leant towards him.

'It's a good area. It's convenient for you. It's pretty quiet. It looks like a well-managed block. You could do a lot worse, you know. New York isn't easy.'

'All right.'

Joan turned to the agent. 'I have,' she said 'a worry about closet space.'

They went off to look at the bedrooms again. Cotton sat by the window. Nothing about the place struck him as being a potential home. That did not particularly worry him. He felt too tired to worry about anything except that he might fall asleep. He cleared his throat and widened his eyes. An image came to him of one of the keys to 3G that he had handed back in Waverly Place. In his mind the key looked much brighter and brassier than it really had. Was he compensating? Brightening things up to help his memory? He wondered if perhaps the point about a false memory or an implant was that the subject scurried to embellish it.

'Are you all right, Peter?'

He got up. 'Yes, I am.'

'We've arranged to increase your closet space before you move in.'

'Good,' said Cotton. He wasn't sure what she was talking about.

There was quite a long pause.

'What do you think? Are you going to take it?' said Joan.

Cotton took a moment to understand that 'it' referred to the apartment. 'Yes,' he said. 'Yes, I will.'

Joan agreed then that he would take the apartment from the beginning of September for an initial period of six months, with an option to extend. The agent would have the contract drawn up and sent round to Joan's apartment for Cotton to sign at his leisure. Cotton gave his office address and Joan gave the agent her card.

'You could look just a little more excited,' she said. 'For New York this is a good, spacious apartment.'

Cotton smiled. 'Thank you,' he said. 'I know. But I just need some rest before September.'

'What's the problem?'

'I have one day on, two off.'

Joan laughed. 'Nap,' she said. 'That's what Todd does.'

Cotton remembered what his lucid, dreamlike sister had said about his being wafted out to sea in Yucatan. He still couldn't remember any such incident but now he had a comfortable sensation, as if he was re-experiencing the feel of it, an indifference to the future so thoroughgoing he would have been alarmed if he had been able to engage with any sense of anxiety or had the sense that he mattered in any way even to himself. He smiled.

140

'What?'

'I don't know which drug it is, but it's a beauty,' he said.

Around 9.30 on Friday morning, Cotton signed for an automobile from Hertz Drive-Ur-Self he had taken until just after Labor Day. He had said a two-door model was fine but the Buick Sedanette or Roadmaster still looked very large. It was definitely post-war, an expansive eighteen feet long and six and a half feet wide, with a streamlined roof that curved in one long line down to the base of the trunk. It had a wide, slightly toothy grille at the front, an eight-cylinder engine with what the car company called 'the reliable Fireball Dynaflash system', and a three-speed manual gearbox. The colour of the automobile was called Sequoia cream. His sister was horrified.

'You can hardly call this blending in!'

'Surely it is. It is not quite garish, is it?'

His sister made a face. 'It's like cream of chicken soup – or anaemic *crema inglesa*!'

It wasn't until he had got to school in England at age eight that Cotton had found out what Mexicans had been trying to invoke. There was little resemblance between what they called *crema inglesa* and the stuff the English called custard, and he had much preferred the Mexican version. Cotton smiled.

'You don't actually care about this kind of thing, do you?' said Joan.

'The colour of a hire car? No.'

'If you have any problems, any misgivings, anything

141

at all, just get in and drive to us in Centre Island. Right?' said Todd.

'Right.'

His sister embraced him. He felt the tackle in her hug. She held on and spoke firmly. 'You've *got* to get out of this!'

'Isn't that what I'm doing?'

'No! I mean the whole murky, dispiriting business. You're putting yourself in danger all the time. We're not at war any more!'

'I know, I do.'

'Then don't risk any more damage! How many stitches have you had this year? And then a spell in the Ogden Clinic! God, there's still six months of the year to go!'

'The next two are about rest,' he said.

Joan stepped back and shook her head. 'You're an economist, Peter. It may be boring, but nobody puts economists into the Ogden! Accept a little tedium. Survive!'

'I haven't really found it *that* exciting,' he said. He smiled. 'Give my love to the children.' He shook Todd's hand, then kissed his sister on the cheek. 'You have a good summer.'

11

A T TEN, Cotton rumbled out of New York City. He
was determined to be in no hurry and Manhattan
was easy, the streets clear of the normal hustle for the
Independence Day holiday. The Buick was big, he was
glad to be alone and he soon fitted in with the slightly
fat, decidedly forgiving, well-oiled mechanics of the car.
There were more people but still little vehicular traffic
in Harlem.

Once he had passed housing blocks that looked like
dour brown slabs of layer cake, he turned towards New
England and was delighted the trees started so soon and
so thick. Cotton liked the green. It had a dense, sappy
quality unmatched in England. He did not really know
which was American elm, white ash or one of the varieties of oaks, but liked the chlorophyll-tinged reflections
on the windscreen. From time to time he had a glimpse
of the sea and Long Island. He had not really appreciated
before how flat Long Island was.

Cotton had planned to stop for lunch in New Haven,
but finding it scruffier, rustier and more industrial than
he had imagined, he drove on and ate crab cakes and
grilled swordfish at a white clapboard place towards
Groton, almost on the bank of a creek or inlet. There
was a large family gathering inside, so Cotton sat outside

where he was the only customer. Across the water the trees were a thick mass of green.

'Do you know what kind of tree that is?'

The waitress, a chubby girl with peroxide hair, said she'd ask.

'Thank you. Could you give me garlic with the swordfish?'

'Not a problem. Do you want it rubbed – or chopped?'

'Chopped, please. I don't mind if it's a little brown.'

'Are you serious? Have you thought of a little chilli pepper instead?'

Cotton wasn't sure why, but he found this conversation – the chef even came out to tell him the trees were 'just regular elm. But that one there is Northern catalpa' – a proper welcome to America. Before he ate, sipping ice-cold water, he wrote a couple of thank-you notes.

Dear Hoberman
Many thanks for coming to see me in the Ogden Clinic.

I am on my way to Narragansett, RI for two months' rest and recuperation.

With luck I should be back at work after Labor Day.

Best wishes
Peter Cotton

His food arrived all together. He thought the chilli pepper went better with the crab cakes than the swordfish. The garlic tasted almost sweet, like burnt pears.

The other note was to his sister and Todd in Oyster

Bay, thanking them for all their kindness and help. He was aware his writing had changed. It looked a little slacker, was less controlled than before, as if he were more anxious about keeping his pen moving than in making the words clear. After he had eaten he ordered coffee and sat looking out over the inlet. There was an old-fashioned black caulked boat by a jetty. A brown pelican flew in and settled by the prow.

A while after he woke up. The waitress and the chef were looking at him.

'Are you OK, sir?'

'How long have I been asleep?'

'Twenty minutes, maybe. We couldn't wake you.'

Cotton nodded and smiled. 'Sorry, I didn't get much sleep last night.'

'Are you OK to drive?'

'Yes, I am.'

'Because you kind of slumped, you know?' said the waitress.

Cotton stood up, paid, tipped too much and smiled again. He asked them for a bottle of water and they agreed that was a good idea.

'Because of this heat,' said the waitress.

Cotton realized he had parked badly. The Buick was hot to touch. He was supposed to know these things. He opened both doors and wound down both windows. He drank some chilled water, got in, closed the doors and put the car in gear. The breeze on the road was not refreshing exactly but at least it moved his shirt and hair.

A few miles on he suddenly had a powerful urge to close his eyes, accelerate and turn the steering wheel

towards the roadside trees. He pulled over. He was having a repeat of the low-key desire for melodramatic action he had experienced in the clinic. He had never liked theatre and at school had resolutely avoided appearing in plays, on one occasion successfully wangling his way from a lead part to an extra lord down to a set painter. He had been responsible for a lot of trees in the Forest of Arden in *As You Like It* in November 1935.

'You OK? You got a breakdown there?'

Cotton looked at the driver who had pulled up beside him. For a moment he wasn't sure if he'd seen him before. He blinked. 'Just taking a break. Thank you.'

Cotton breathed in and let his mind go blank. He restarted the Buick, pulled his shirt free from his back, drank some already lukewarm water but then thought of something: he certainly wasn't behaving like a zombie or an efficient if unconscious scopolamine driver. He felt much more actively flustered and unsure. It wasn't much, but it did. He realized he'd have to watch out for a witless desire to kill himself. He looked backwards and pulled out on to the road again. That had been a lot of garlic.

Cotton had always found driving boring but here he concentrated. He got to Ocean Road in Narragansett at about five in the afternoon, without incident but with two more stops to get something to drink and, on the last stop, to change his shirt.

Todd's relative was called Eleanor Ramsden. A grey-haired, squat, robust-looking old lady, she told him she was sixty-four and had been a widow for twenty-one years. 'Garrett passed in 1926. This was our summer

home but now I use it all year round. My father gave it to us as a wedding gift in 1904.' She called it 'a carriage house' but Cotton was not sure if this meant it was in the style of a carriage house or really had been one. To his eye the house looked more like an Essex barn – or two linked Essex barns. Each roof was a kind of Dutch hexagon and everything was wood. One barn was the library Todd had mentioned where Eleanor had also set up her easel, the bookshelves coming up to the beginning of the crossbeams. There was no ceiling. The view continued up to the underside of the roofing. The floor was cobbles and to one side there was a huge Swedish-type stove.

'I don't read much now,' said Eleanor, 'but you're welcome to browse all you want. There are over ten thousand volumes in here. Garrett was quite the collector. A bibliophile, you know?'

The other barn was her house. That had two floors and what she called a porch facing the ocean, like a long verandah.

His own accommodation, the guest-cottage, also had a hexagonal roof, and was tucked away at the edge of the plot about thirty yards from the house, screened by shrubs and trees. It was small and on one floor, rather like a railway carriage, and consisted of a living room that gave on to a corridor that contained a kitchenette and a bathroom and then widened again into a bedroom. There was a roof fan in the living room and the bedroom.

Everything was of wood. The floor, the walls, the ceilings and the rather Arts and Crafts furniture. Outside,

the place had a small, weathered deck about twelve by twelve with a balustrade. There was a short tree-lined view towards the sea. It framed some sort of stunted pine that leant the way of the prevailing wind.

He handed over his cheque and offered to take Eleanor to supper. She accepted at once, although she said she had to clean herself up. She showed him her hands with apparent pride. They were swollen with arthritis and as grubby as a worker's.

Cotton unpacked, washed and changed. He found Eleanor waiting for him by the Buick. She had put on a dress and a hat and had added cologne to the smell of turpentine. Her stockings had rucked at her ankles.

'This swanky car yours?' she said, when he had started the engine. 'We'll take a right first.'

Cotton put the Buick into motion. 'It's a hire car,' he said. 'Joan and Todd hate the colour.'

'Well, they would. But they have a point. What do you do?'

'I'm over here for the United Nations,' Cotton replied.

'Yeah? You don't look like a diplomat,' said Eleanor. 'Though I mean that as a compliment. You don't have that constrained look.'

Cotton smiled. 'Most of the real diplomats come after the planning stage.'

'Right. So how come you get such long holidays, Mr Cotton?'

'Oh, I had a flare-up of something old and I'm now recuperating from some treatment I had to combat that. That gave me a month off. The other month is because I haven't had any leave for three years.'

Ocean Road finally lived up to its name and swung down towards the shoreline.

'You were in the war?'

'Yes.'

'You were wounded?'

Cotton did not reply.

Eleanor Ramsden glanced at him and sighed. 'We have some pretty messed-up young men round here. Bits of them are missing.'

'I'm not in that class,' said Cotton.

'Good,' said Eleanor, pointing to the left. 'Turn in here. We're going to the Inn.'

Cotton had expected something relatively small, but this American Inn was a very sizeable shingle structure with a couple of tall, stone chimneys and creepers on the pentagonal bulge at the angle of an L-shape. It was fronted by bright bedded-out plants, quite a lot of them yellow, and had yellow drapes and sun screens on the windows facing the ocean. There were bits of stone-work, small retaining walls and a thing Cotton had to avoid when parking that looked more like a wishing well than a gazebo.

'This is where illicit love used to come,' she said, 'around the turn of the century.'

'Really?' said Cotton.

She laughed. 'You're thinking it's pretty staid-looking now, aren't you? That's what happens. Your Lothario becomes a valetudinarian.'

Cotton looked round. Somebody had spent time putting plants, mostly yellow and purple, in a narrow bed behind the walls. So close to the Atlantic, it struck

149

him as optimistic as much as labour intensive. He opened the door for Eleanor.

'You want to try the spinach,' she said.

'All right.'

Inside, Cotton found they were two of a total of five diners. Eleanor ordered her spinach and then striped bass.

'With the bass add a couple of scallops,' she told the waiter. 'You know how I like them.'

Cotton went along with her choice. Eleanor was not a drinker.

'Water will do me just fine,' she said. She turned and considered the other diners.

'I don't know for sure,' she said, 'but I certainly feel the second youngest here.'

Cotton considered a very old man in what looked like some sort of yachting uniform. His manicured hands had a pronounced shake.

They were offered rolls. Eleanor took one and broke it open. It was warm enough to steam.

'I just like to see they're paying attention. I don't eat it.'

Cotton nodded. He drank some cold water.

'May I ask how old you are, Peter?' asked Eleanor.

'Of course. I'm twenty-eight.' Cotton put down the glass.

'And you're not married?'

'I'm sorry?'

'Well, a man of your age!'

'Oh, I see. I was going to get married but she died in a car accident. In December '45. In fact I was going to get

married in 1943 but that girl died too. She was killed by a bomb. Or perhaps a V1. What the British called a doodlebug.'

Eleanor closed one eye on him. 'You're not teasing me?'

Cotton shook his head. 'No,' he said.

Eleanor winced but quite demurely. 'My. You people had a rough time.'

'The British?' Cotton shrugged. He kept to himself that the second death had been that of an American in Washington DC after the war.

Eleanor nodded and decided it was time to look up and out towards the ocean. She smiled. 'What do you think of that? Isn't that just a wonderful view? That's what people come for.'

Cotton looked. He wasn't so sure. 'It reminds me of the view at sea. I don't know why but in Britain you don't get that sense of empty space that you do here.'

'I'm guessing you're not much of a sailor?'

'Not at all.'

Cotton looked around him. There was something grandiose and high-ceilinged about the place but also something cottagey, as if the architect had wanted to invoke a simpler life while reminding the patrons they were important.

'It was swank but folksy,' said Eleanor. 'Now it's a little tired, but my, they do use a lot of polish here. And they've most certainly refreshed the soft furnishings.'

Cotton smiled. She was right.

Her spinach turned out to be accompanied by crisp little bits of ham.

'I didn't used to eat like this when Garrett was alive,' she said. 'This is down to Felismina.'

'Who's Felismina?'

Eleanor looked surprised. 'My housekeeper. Portuguese. From Warren. We've got a lot of Portuguese in Rhode Island. They've been coming over for years for the fishing. Felismina got a Portuguese divorce, you know.'

'I don't know what a Portuguese divorce is.'

'No? Well, she couldn't have children, you see, and they didn't have enough money to buy one of those Catholic divorces. They call them . . . annulments. That's the word, annulments. So she got out of the way and let her husband have a big family in sin. Been with me twenty years. If you want, she'll cook for you.'

'No, thank you,' said Cotton. 'I'm all right. But I need to get some supplies.'

'There's a place nearby. We can do that after.'

'Thank you. Todd and Joan tell me you're an artist.'

She gave him a double-take. 'It's a pastime. I like the squish of the paint. I don't have the talent to learn from the masters, you know, so I just express myself.'

The fish and scallops were cooked in what Cotton thought of as *a la plancha*, on a dry grill or griddle. After the Ogden Clinic everything tasted quite salty. Cotton didn't mind. It gave him the impression that, if not quite life, he was at least getting some iodine.

After eating, they drove to a grocery store. For Cotton's taste, it was a little on the pioneering side, wood walls and wood shelves, but it came equipped with a number of noisy freezers.

'You have an icebox in the guest-cottage,' said Eleanor.

Cotton did not plan to cook much. He bought some coffee, oats, milk and fruit, including a watermelon and some strawberries.

'That's not enough,' said Eleanor. 'Get some ham or something. And some beers and soda. We have good lettuce here. You'll need olive oil. And get some bread.'

Cotton did as she suggested.

'Have you heard?' said Eleanor as they were driving back. 'We have a bear in the vicinity.'

'A bear? Is that common?'

'It happens. They can be destructive and you don't want to meet one.'

'What kind of bear are we talking about?'

She blinked at him. 'A black bear. That's what we have here.'

'Do they come near the coast?'

'Why wouldn't they? Mind you, they do tend to be young males. They get disorientated, you know, keeping out of bigger males' territories and their noses picking up all kinds of sweet smells. So don't leave food outside. If you do, you might get woken by something rootling about. Don't go outside, just make a loud noise. That usually moves them on.'

'OK, I'll remember that. Thanks,' said Cotton.

'You're welcome, Peter.'

In the guest-cottage, Cotton put away his groceries. The icebox was on a counter with a handle on it like that of a butcher's cold-room door but with not that much

space in it. He went to bed about eleven. The bed was quite hard; he lay in the dark for a while. All he could hear was a soft whoop from the ceiling fan. He closed his eyes.

Cotton woke suddenly. He was sweating. He had been dreaming and had seen himself huddled in a doorway having a fit. He lay thinking for a moment and decided that this was about the information the doctor had given him rather than a genuine memory. It made him acutely aware he had holes in his memory, as if an unpractised potter had been working at soft clay and left holes and depressions before the maltreated vessel had been fired. His dream had shown him as a down-and-out, unshaven, dirty, his knees pulled up. For some reason, he remembered some knuckledusters he had once seen. He frowned. Did this reflect a desire for revenge, a version of what had happened to him? Or was it really about the holes for the fingers, the holes in his memory? He was clear that the sleep had not refreshed him. He felt he had been sandbagged and quite a lot of the sand had got into his bloodstream.

He got up and drank some water. He opened the icebox and brought his face towards the cold leaking out of it. He closed his eyes – and was privy to an unpleasant little scene. From the outside corner of each eye, he saw two shapes move into focus to present a single image of an old man with palsy sitting on some fairly grand stone steps. Cotton stayed still and watched. The man's shins were covered in sores. From somewhere, the director of this little misery introduced a gold coin. The coin was placed beside a sore; Cotton somehow understood this

was a test. If the sore was as big as the coin, the old man would be given help.

Cotton winced. He opened his eyes, shut the icebox door and started to make some coffee. He could trace the old man with palsy. He had had a spot where he used to sit outside the library his mother went to in the 1920s. It hadn't been a particularly grand library. He didn't know where the grand stone steps came from. Nor could he recall anything to do with the size of sores matching a gold coin. He finished making the coffee, got a cup and saucer out of the cupboard, then cut himself a slice of watermelon and put everything on a tray. The sun was just above the horizon.

He took the tray out on the deck. A young but very self-possessed little girl was sitting there having some kind of diminutive early morning tea party. She had red hair – not carrot top, but a deep reddish-brown – and a lot of freckles. The freckles looked dark against creamy skin. Her eyes were brown. She looked up at him.

'Who are you?' she asked.

'I'm Peter,' he said.

'OK,' she said and went back to her party.

Cotton put the tray down. He watched her for a moment. He was pretty sure she was real. 'Who are you?'

Surprised, she looked up. 'I'm Susan.'

'Nice to meet you, Susan. Where do you live?'

'Next door.'

'Do you come here every morning?'

'No,' she said. But then she thought about it. 'Most mornings I do.'

A voice nearby spoke. 'Who are you speaking to, Susan?'

'I'm speaking to Peter.'

'Who's Peter?'

Cotton spoke up. 'Peter is staying in Eleanor's guest-cottage,' he said.

There was a pause, then a rustle and a young woman appeared. She was in her late twenties, very pale, with the kind of skin that looked almost translucent under the trees, like some greenish by-product of milk. Was it called rennet? She stepped forward. Her hair was the colour of dried ginger and she looked flustered or uncomfortable, possibly both, and was plucking at her pale yellow, buttoned dress as if being bitten. It took Cotton a blink or two to understand she was worried the dress was too thin, though he was a long way from considering her underwear, its condition or what it concealed.

'I'm so awfully sorry, sir,' she said. 'Is my daughter bothering you?'

'Not at all. My name's Peter Cotton. I'm very slightly related to Eleanor. My sister's husband is some sort of cousin, I think.'

'Sally Ingram,' she said.

'Delighted to meet you. I'm staying in the guest-cottage until Labor Day.'

'Well I certainly hope you enjoy your vacation,' said Sally Ingram. 'Susan, you mustn't bother Mr Cotton. Come along now.'

'It's all right,' said Cotton. He smiled. 'She can have all the tea parties she wants on the deck.'

The child had watched this exchange as something that did not concern her. She squinted up at him.

'Can you swim?' said Susan. 'I mean . . . *really*.'

'Yes,' said Cotton. 'I can swim.'

'You could take me to the beach, then?'

'Susan!' Her mother sounded more shocked than reproving.

'My mom can't swim and my dad is dead.'

'I see,' said Cotton. 'In that case, will you let me think about it? Let's see. Have you got a bathing costume?'

'Swimsuit,' said Sally Ingram.

'Right. Do you burn easily, Susan?'

'Yes.'

'Me too.'

'I have a hat,' said the little girl. 'And my mom has calamine lotion.'

'Good,' said Cotton. 'Will you let me get settled in? And then maybe tomorrow—'

They were interrupted by Eleanor. 'Oh, you've met.' She sounded disappointed. 'Sally's late husband's grandmother and I were dear friends for thirty years. She passed about six years ago.'

'Peter's going to take me swimming tomorrow,' said Susan.

'Is he now? Well, I might come along.' She looked up. 'Now do you need anything, Peter?'

'No. I'm fine, thank you.'

'Sleep well?'

'Yes, thank you. And you?'

'Oh, yes. It's the Narragansett air, you see. It's what we call good sleeping air.'

Cotton smiled politely.

'Peter's here to rest,' said Eleanor. She had brought a small pile of books. She handed them over and started turning away. 'Now, if you want anything from the library, Peter, there's no need to ask. You just walk up and take what you want.'

'Thank you very much,' said Cotton.

He watched Eleanor go to her house and Sally and Susan Ingram go to theirs. He wasn't entirely sure whether Eleanor had come to rescue him or join in. In either case, a quiet life in Narragansett had something touchy or nervous about it so far. He sat down and bit into the watermelon. It was no longer cold. He shrugged and munched on. The great thing about watermelon was that it never had much taste anyway. It was refreshment with pips.

Eleanor had brought him five books – Marcus Aurelius, Nathaniel Hawthorne, Edgar Allan Poe, Henry David Thoreau and Henry James.

He had a look at the Hawthorne – something called *Tanglewood Tales* – reread enough pages of what had once been his codebook, Henry James' *The Ambassadors*, to remember again the middle-aged American hero suffering from 'prostration' and the sensation of freedom he felt in Liverpool and Chester – but then read one of the Poe stories through to the end. It was about someone being walled up in Spain. Partly because of the humidity in Narragansett, Cotton did not find it convincing. But the morning's reading had done him some good. He stood up and looked around him. He thought that perhaps this was just what he needed.

He decided to look for somewhere to have lunch and got into the Buick. As he drove, he thought that summer 1947 must be an especially poor season for popular songs, judging by the melodies blasting from other cars and from the diners and restaurants. They were all simple and unmemorable and ranged from the sentimental, like 'Peg O' My Heart' – 'Wait a second,' said Eleanor later, 'I remember that; it was popular round about 1914' – or Frank Sinatra's 'Mam'selle' – 'A small café our rendezvous, mam'selle, the violins were warm and sweet like you, mam'selle' – to jokey, novelty things like Perry Como's 'Chi-baba, Chi-baba'.

In the end, Cotton decided to try the 515 Diner on Narragansett Avenue between Carswell and Beach Streets. Stranded behind a small stretch of lawn, with a couple of tables with umbrellas in front, it was a painted-wood train engine and carriages, the kitchen in the 'engine', the diner in the carriages. He asked for clam chowder but had to ask the waitress to explain the difference between the New England and the Manhattan chowders.

'One's got milk,' said the waitress, 'one's got tomato.'

He chose tomato – the Manhattan – and clam cakes. The cakes were deep-fried and, to his taste, seemed mostly cake. He asked for coffee.

'Milk with that?'

'Please.'

Cotton found out he had ordered a coffee milk – coffee syrup with warm milk poured on to it. He made a mental note to avoid that in future.

It was quite late by the time he left. The only other car

parked in front of the diner – a black Ford coupé – was also getting ready to leave, and pulled out on to the road after him.

Back in the guest-cottage, he spent the afternoon reading more of Henry James but felt exhausted by ten and got into bed. This time, he slept eight hours straight without any sense of dream or difference.

12

WHEN COTTON woke next morning, he drank about a litre of water. At eleven o'clock he drove Susan Ingram and Eleanor to Scarborough Beach, Eleanor's choice. The beach was located between two scruffy-looking low bluffs backed by a curve of telegraph poles, not one of which was quite vertical. A couple of them looked as if they were being held up by the wires. There was enough white sand scattered on the road for the sound of the Buick to change to half soft crackle, half small hail.

'This isn't a good swimming beach,' said Susan.

'Can you swim?' said Eleanor.

'No.'

'Then it's a good beach.'

Eleanor put lotion on Susan. She had no experience of children and Susan swayed every time the old lady dabbed. Cotton wore his blue trunks.

Susan was staring at him. 'Mister, why do you have that scar?'

On his right thigh, Cotton had what he thought of as a 'Karloff scar', after Boris Karloff's role as Frankenstein's monster. It was about eight inches long and was bracketed by marks where the stitches had been, like a vertical version of his youngest nephew's drawing of horizontal

teeth. The cut itself had become a smooth, narrow, squid-white colour with a thin, wavering fringe of red and purple. Towards his knee, the cut-throat razor had jerked; it made the whole scar into a sort of correction mark tick. The stitching there was less obvious because the cut had not been so deep. He didn't get time to reply.

'When he was little he asked too many questions,' said Eleanor briskly. 'Scars like that can fly. You want to watch out that one doesn't fly over to you.'

The small girl looked at Eleanor, her incomprehension complete but ungrudging.

'I'm just going to test the water,' said Cotton.

'Good,' said Eleanor. 'I like a cautious man. But are you going to keep those sunglasses on? They make you look kinda snooty. And maybe a little shifty. You know?'

Cotton laughed, gave her the glasses and took off his shirt. He walked down to the sea. In the bright light his eyes were watering, but he could see Susan was quite right. This was not a swimming beach. The water looked shallow and he did not think a nearly five-year-old would enjoy the surf.

The sea was chilly rather than cold but he had no hint of difficulty when he began walking in. It wasn't until the water was up to his thighs that black shapes abruptly started to flutter at the outer sides of his eyes. Instantly his vision became tunnelled and he thought he was about to fall over. In fact, he was standing quite still while the surf washed against him. He had the absurd notion that the tunnel was trying to pull him over and that if he

didn't give in, he'd break his neck. He held his breath. What was this? A swoon?

Some sort of instinct kicked in. He fell forward and put his head under the water. For a moment he did not know where he was. Then he thought he might be trying to hide. At least his eyes were closed. He realized he could not sigh and hold his breath at the same time. He stood up, keeping his eyes closed till the water ran off him and he had pushed back his hair. Then he opened them and squinted at the blue sky and sparkling sea. He smiled and let his eyes water. It did occur to him to wonder if he had had to deal with water treatment as well as scopolamine. He had heard of people being thrust into cold water and held down. But he was confident enough to surprise himself. He felt sure that had not happened to him.

Cotton breathed in, turned and walked out of the water and up the beach. He was trembling slightly.

Eleanor was looking at him. 'What's the matter with your eyes?' she said. 'You look like you're weeping.'

'The sunglasses aren't an affectation,' said Cotton.

'Why didn't you say?' said Eleanor. She thrust them back at him. He put them on and smiled. 'And what are those things on your body?' she said. Eleanor winced. 'Is that what shrapnel does?'

Cotton looked down. The chill of the sea had brought out the colour in the bruises acquired before and during his stay in the Ogden Clinic. He looked mottled. He shook his head.

'Well?' said Susan.

'The water's lovely,' said Cotton. 'Do you want to try?'

As an answer she held out her hand. He took it and they walked down the beach towards the water. As they drew close, Susan slowed right down.

'We could paddle first, you know,' said Cotton.

She did not look entirely convinced.

'You see those bubbles creeping up the beach. They tickle your toes. Do you want to try?'

Susan made a face. 'OK.'

They moved. Susan went up on tiptoe with several yards still to go.

'The water looks good, doesn't it?'

Susan came to a stop. Cotton looked down. As he did so a speck of surf looped up and landed on her nose. Her hand was out of his like silk and she shot off up the beach at a curious hunch, hands out to her sides, running from the hips, until she realized she was running towards Eleanor. She stopped and looked from one to the other of both the adults accompanying her, unable to decide. Cotton smiled and held out a hand.

'It's OK,' he said. 'It really is.'

They made some progress. After a time, by lifting her up in his arms and going into the water, she claimed she quite liked the water on her feet, 'but not all the time'. An attempt to go up to her knees resulted in a loosening of a small fistful of his chest hair.

They agreed sandcastles would be a much better bet. As Susan dug and patted sand into her tin bucket, Eleanor held out her hands.

'Isn't this beautiful? I don't paint much outdoors, you know. In summer there's all these people. And in winter it's cold.'

Cotton nodded. 'Why isn't her mother here?'

'Sally's doing a course.' Eleanor smiled. 'You can have a free day tomorrow.'

The next day, 7 July, Cotton decided to drive the other way, towards Narragansett Pier. Narragansett had a lot of holes – scruffy plots that had previously had a building but no longer did. About the only big hotel left was the Massasoit up on Mathewson Street. Cotton went past the Inn to take a closer look at the Towers. These consisted of two pairs of round granite towers linked by a central, galleried section that straddled the entire coast road. There was something of a displaced French chateau about them, but apparently this was only the overscaled porte-cochère and all that remained of the original casino built by Stanford White's firm, which had burnt down in 1900.

'Fire didn't even start in the Towers. Started in the Rockingham Hotel. But the wind caught the flames and brought them over. The casino was mostly shingles, you see. They burn fast and hot when they're dry. They kept rebuilding, but, well . . .'

Cotton was having breakfast in the Coastguard House, which had recently been turned into a restaurant. He looked round. The Towers now had something in common with the old man who was speaking to him. He was scrawny and unshaven, with rheumy eyes, and was dressed in a pale green shirt, raw linen coloured waistcoat and clip-on bow tie in butterscotch with milk chocolate spots. His hat was what Cotton thought of as a Glengarry but of much thinner material and without a

toorie. 'There are plans for the Towers, you know, but we'll have to see,' said the old man. Cotton smiled. He saw that beside him, tied with string, the man had what he called his 'own personalized collection of tin advertisements' for 'Hassan', 'Mecca', 'Fatima' and 'American Beauty'. He explained they were the brand names of cigarettes, before the taste for Turkish leaf 'fell off' during the First War and 'Camel started packs of twenty cigarettes'.

They were interrupted by a busty little waitress. 'Is he pestering you?' she said to Cotton, but she did not wait for a reply. 'Now come on, Frank, you know you're not allowed. If you come in here, you've got to buy something.' She looked at Cotton.

'Would you like some coffee?' said Cotton. 'A muffin?'

'Coffee's fine,' said Frank. 'Much obliged.'

The old man trembled and lit a Sweet Cap cigarette. 'My wife passed. Died on the fifth operation, if you know what I mean. It was expensive. I have a married daughter in Maine. She's pretty pissed with me. I have a licence to sell stuff on the beach. But I guess I drink.'

Cotton nodded. The old man's coffee arrived and he suddenly remembered he should be cheerful.

'Narragansett really was something,' he said. 'Used to have *two* railway stations here. Fifty years ago, you couldn't move for people.'

Cotton nodded. He called the waitress. She was smiling and he saw that her cheeks were round too. 'Thank you,' he said.

'You're welcome, sir.'

He paid, said goodbye and left. By the door he had to

step round a kind of tray that contained nuts, candy and a few packs of cigarettes. Perhaps he found the old man more depressing than he thought. When he looked up at the Towers again, they looked more like a ruin. He got back into the Buick and drove off, but as he drove he noticed a wooden sign in front of something he had at first taken for a private house. It was so discreet he had missed the name – Ocean View Café. He made a mental note to investigate further.

The guest-cottage had a mailbox. Sitting on top of it was something like a blackbird, except that the colours tended to purple as well as black. It had bright yellow eyes and did not seem bothered by his presence. He learnt it was called a grackle. It would make a chucking sound but then follow it with a noise between chalk squeaking on a blackboard and an old hinge that needed oil. That was when he learnt the bird perched on the box when he had had a delivery. When he moved to open the box, the grackle shifted to the deck railing and watched him. Inside was a painting by Susan Ingram. Her mother had printed *Dear Mr Cotton, Thank you so much for taking me to the beach. We both appreciate your kindness. Love, Susan.* The painting was a splodge of blue with a yellow sun. He pinned it up in the kitchen.

On Tuesday, 8 July the weather turned what Eleanor called 'most unseasonal'. It was blustery and wet and the temperature dropped several degrees. Cotton didn't mind at all. There was no early morning tea party. He closed the windows and doors and tried several writers. He gave up on Thoreau but read a few more stories by

Edgar Allan Poe, written in a pseudo-rational style that struck him as a precursor of that used in the Ogden Clinic. He quite liked Poe's *William Wilson*, a twist on the doppelgänger, mostly for its overwrought Gothic style and all those words beginning with *un* – 'unparalleled infamy', 'unspeakable misery', 'unpardonable crime'. It did occur to him that, let alone two personalities, he had barely recovered one.

That reminded him to look at the drawing pad Dr Sanford had given him. He got a pencil and opened the pad. But nothing occurred to him, either consciously or not. No image appeared automatically. He shrugged and in his other notebook recorded the few experiences, or what his late aunt would have called 'turns', that he could recall – the tunnel vision episode at the beach; the figures palsied or with a coin-sized sore he had seen by the fridge. If he was getting better, it was a slow business. He still wasn't thinking sharply or fast.

Later, while rereading James' *The Ambassadors*, he came across a carefully described act of betrayal. He stopped reading and considered. Dr Sanford had asked him if he felt betrayed. He still wasn't sure that he had ever quite known what the word meant or how it would apply to him. In the book, the betrayal was more about a promise asked for that had been broken. At one level that was what happens to unreasonable demands. Someone is let down. Cotton shook his head. He had not asked for anything.

He considered the notion that he had not been important as a person or individual but only as a convenient subject for kidnap and experimentation. But he made little progress with that, apart from thinking there might

be people fluttering on the edges of the tunnel vision that sometimes squeezed in on him. He could not identify them.

For a time he sat. He could only think he was unresponsive, possibly indifferent, certainly stupid. Was that the lingering effect of the drugs? A failure to defend himself? Or was he joining in on a view of his own disposability? He shrugged. There had obviously been people who had administered the drugs. He just had no faces for them, nothing he could think of as real.

A little later he decided to go shopping and stock up rather better than he had been doing. He'd cook himself a meal. He'd concentrate on simple things.

In the rain, on his way back, Cotton took a distracted detour. There were very few cars on the road and he drove slowly. Since there was no sun, he took off his sunglasses but found his eyes watered, almost as if they were being set off by the drops of water hitting the windshield. He pulled over, stopped the car and wiped his eyes. The rain was squalling and he could hear and feel the gusts of wind. He stretched and looked around. To his right, he saw a house being built; three men were trying to tackle the roof. They wore things like fishermen's capes that flapped in the wind, and were pinning down roof shingles as fast as they could.

One of the men reminded him of something he had seen four years before on a beach in Sicily. He had recovered consciousness and had seen Sergeant Bruce on his knees in the sand, head down, apparently hammering the middle knuckle of his right hand into the centre of his cupped left palm.

Here, on a Narragansett roof, one of the builders seemed to be doing something similar, but with a real nail and a hammer, the hammer head rushing towards the cupped hand. Cotton frowned and tried to make sense of it. In Sicily, he had found out Bruce had had the skin stripped from his shins and was trying not to scream. Cotton stared at the builder on the roof. He felt queasy. He wondered if he was hallucinating. He looked away, put on his Ray-Bans and started the Buick again.

As Cotton pulled away, the hammer man raised a hand at him in acknowledgement. Maybe someone else the man knew had a car that colour, but what caught Cotton's eye was that the man appeared to have not so much a hand as a stump. Or was that due to raindrops on the side window? He peered. In Britain, he might have thought the man's gesture was ironic. Here, in New England, he raised his own hand in acknowledgement.

He went back to the guest-cottage and wrote in Dr Sanford's notebook. *Not sure if I have removed some-one's fingers or they really were missing. I suppose I could have been misled by the curves in a raindrop.* He made a face. It was a tad poetic, but he left it.

Speak roughly to your little boy
And beat him when he sneezes!
He only does it to annoy,
Because he knows it teases!

Cotton blinked. He couldn't really be reconstructing himself from childhood up, like water in a

rain-gauge. And he certainly wasn't part of *Alice in Wonderland*.

The next day was Wednesday the 9th of July. He checked out the Ocean View Café. He had found what he was looking for. There was a glazed, pillared green porch that ran the length of the place and was rounded at one end. In the round part there was a group of elderly men. Cotton chose a small table three pillars down.

One of the things Cotton had learnt to enjoy about America in 1945 had been the direct, unaffected way people took things on. He watched how the waitress 'worked' her clients with gusto. Her name was Carla, she was eighteen and even on the first day Cotton knew she was going to study at Rhode Island College in the fall and that winter in Narragansett was economically tough. By 10 July, she had his orange juice and coffee on the table before he had quite sat down and was pitching eggs Benedict and some 'terrific smoked salmon' and offering him the *Boston Globe* or *Providence Journal* to read.

Eleanor wanted to know where he was going in the mornings. He told her.

'You're becoming an honorary old man,' said Eleanor. 'You'll be playing pinochle next.'

'I particularly like the fact that that there's no music.'

'Are you serious?'

'Yes, I am.'

'Oh,' said Eleanor. She blinked. 'You know one of your princesses is getting married?'

Cotton tried but failed to think who this might be.

'Her name is Elizabeth,' said Eleanor. 'It was

171

announced yesterday. She's marrying a Lieutenant Philip Mountbatten.'

Cotton nodded. 'Good,' he said.

'But don't you know about this kind of thing?'

'No.'

'This girl is going to be your queen.'

'When this king dies, yes. The last one abdicated. His brother stepped in. There's a line of succession, basically a long queue of people, most perfectly able to wave and smile and open Parliament. It's not like the President.'

'Well I know that!' Eleanor sounded a little put out. 'Would you be able to take Susan to the beach tomorrow?'

'I think so,' said Cotton.

'Sally's doing courses so she can get a job,' said Eleanor. 'Her husband was a pilot. He went down somewhere in the Pacific.'

On Friday, 11 July Susan arrived at 7 a.m. carrying a small bucket, a small spade and a large towel. She was wearing a hat and a kind of shift dress over her swimsuit. Cotton put her in the back seat of the Buick and they drove to the Ocean Café and had breakfast.

'You're Susan, right?' said Carla. 'I'm Carla.'

'Do you have French toast?' said Susan.

'What do you say?'

'Please.'

'Then of course we have French toast. Thank you for your order.'

After breakfast they drove on a little, parked and went down to Narragansett Town Beach. On the half-mile of

whitish sand there were still few people but quite a lot of
seabirds. Cotton was not good at American wildlife.

'What are those called?' he asked Susan. 'The little
white ones?'

'What do you call them?'

'They look like plovers,' said Cotton.

'That's what we say, too. I'm going to make a sandcastle. I can't swim now because I've just had
breakfast.'

Cotton nodded. 'Are you thinking of swimming?'

'Not yet anyway.'

Cotton settled down and read for a while and Susan
got busy with her bucket and spade. The beach began to
fill up. Cotton saw that Americans were like the English
in this respect. They sat in areas. Spanish speakers
tended to gather together in one place and leave a stretch
of sand free, not occupy it at intervals.

Around eleven Susan called to him.

'Mister!'

'Call me Peter, Susan.'

'I'm getting thirsty doing this, you know.'

'Do you want a drink?'

'Can I have a cabinet?'

Cotton had no idea what she meant.

'Can you get it yourself if I give you the money?'

'No. They don't let you take the glass away.'

Cotton took her for what turned out to be a vanilla
milkshake.

Back on the beach, Susan went to put wet sand in her
bucket. Cotton took off his shirt and began reading.
After a time he closed his eyes and listened to the surf.

'Did they put a pin in there?'

Cotton opened his eyes and looked up. The stocky young man speaking to him was dressed in khaki trousers, a white singlet and an open dark blue overshirt. He had very dark hair, probably floppy but kept in place by gleaming hair oil. He looked somehow familiar. As Cotton took off his Ray-Bans and stood up, he saw that the man was missing fingers, either wholly or in part, on both hands. The left hand had been reduced to three knuckle stubs and two, including the small finger, a joint longer. He had retained fingernails on the index and middle finger of his right hand but had lost the remaining fingers and the nail joint of his thumb.

'In your leg,' said the man. 'Did they put a pin in your leg?'

'No,' said Cotton. 'Do you have one?'

'Got a metal plate and three screws in the left thighbone. What were you in?'

'British Infantry. Argyll and Sutherland Highlanders. How about you?'

'94th Infantry Division. Light field gunner.' With almost no movement but very effectively, the man mimed cradling a shell, then nodded and looked at the sea. 'Officer?'

Cotton nodded. 'Only in the war.'

'Moving here?'

'No,' said Cotton, 'I've come from London. I'll be based in New York.' They were interrupted by Susan being nosey. 'This is Susan, my new friend and current neighbour.'

'Hi there. Your mom's Sally, right?'

174

'Yes, she is. Mrs Sally Ingram.'

'And I'm Joe Samms,' said the man and smiled.

The girl stayed still, suddenly smiled, then shot off down the sand waving her spade like some sort of wand.

Joe Samms did not move. 'I went to school with her dad, you know.'

'I understand his plane went down in the Pacific.'

'That's what they say.'

Cotton glanced at Joe Samms. Was this sympathy or disbelief? Or was he simply using a few words to occupy his side of the dialogue?

'Did you know him well?' asked Cotton.

'Well, sorta,' said Joe Samms. 'Did they open you up again? That scar looks angry.'

Cotton glanced down. 'It's from February this year.'

Joe Samms frowned. 'You have a quaint way with words.' he said. 'I guess that's just the English, right?'

'Probably.'

'You here for long?'

'Until Labor Day. Do you know Eleanor Ramsden?'

'Oh, yeah.'

'I'm in her guest-cottage.'

'So that's the neighbour thing.'

'With Susan? Yes. Her mother asked me to take her to the beach.'

'She's doing a course,' said Joe Samms.

'Yes,' said Cotton. 'Are you having a break too?'

'No, no,' said Joe Samms. 'I'm working but waiting.'

'For what?'

'Delivery.' Even Joe Samms thought this reply was on

the sparse side. 'Building a house up there. Waiting for more shingles. We're just a three-house firm, twice over.'

'What does that mean?'

'We start one, we're building one, we're finishing one. Just that we're doing that twice but over quite an area, you know. We take in Wakefield and Kingston too. It's only my father and me and a couple of guys each.'

'Is business good?'

Joe Samms thought about it. 'I guess we're not complaining. The GI Bill's been good for us. And what they call Family Formation.'

Cotton nodded. 'Good,' he said, 'I'm very glad to hear it.'

'OK!' said Joe Samms. 'Where did you get wounded?'

'Sicily.'

'Yeah,' said Joe Samms. He nodded. 'We got a *lot* of Italians here in Rhode Island.' He said *eyetalians*.

'Where were you?' said Cotton.

'I was in England, for a short spell you know.' He shook his head. 'Wasn't so bad. Place called Dorset. Shipped to Europe, September 8, 1944. Got this on September 27. In Brittany. Kinda confusing. People here sometimes think I mean Britain, but it's in France.'

Joe Samms glanced back at the coast road. 'OK,' he said. 'I usually go for a beer after work. Just up there on the Kingston Road. It's not fancy but they do pretty good stuffies. You can't miss it. Looks like an old barn. Everybody calls it Marty's.'

'Thank you,' said Cotton. 'My name's Peter Cotton.'

'Pete, right? We're both crocked.' He laughed. 'I'll be seeing you.'

Joe Samms walked. He didn't have a limp. It was more of a swing of the leg with the plate and screws in it. Within a few strides Cotton heard him yelling at someone in a truck. 'You're late, Luigi! What the hell—!'

'Who *was* that?' said Susan Ingram.

'A rather nice man,' said Cotton.

'He hasn't got a lot of fingers.'

'That's because he was brave.'

'OK,' said Susan. 'I need some water wings. To help me swim.'

'Do you know where there's a water-wing shop?'

'Are you crazy, mister?'

Cotton smiled. 'I think we'll have to make enquiries, then.'

The girl blinked. 'Can you help me make the sandcastle?'

'Happy to oblige.'

Around one, Cotton took Susan home to find her mother on the deck of the guest-cottage. Sally Ingram was wearing an outfit in grey with brown and red stripes that did not suit her colouring. She was wearing a lot more make-up and perfume than Cotton had previously seen or smelt. Reluctantly he took this to mean she was presenting herself again in a way she thought more fitting.

'I'm so awfully grateful, Peter – but somehow I feel like I'm taking advantage of you.'

'Not at all,' said Cotton. 'Besides, I have the impression Eleanor doesn't want me to be entirely unoccupied.'

Sally Ingram's face moved too much as she smiled. 'But it's still *most* kind of you.'

Cotton found her version of good manners grated.

'Would you like to have something to drink? I have some beer. I may even have a Coca-Cola.'

'No, no. Beer's fine.'

Cotton went inside and got the beers from the icebox. Susan was already playing with her tea things.

'I understand you're taking a course,' he said.

'Well I need employment. Susan's father died in the war, you know.'

'Yes, Eleanor told me. Where was that?'

'He died in the Pacific.' She took a sip of cold beer. 'Oh, that's very refreshing. I'm afraid I don't know the circumstances or even where. That's been harder than I thought, you know. No grave, no place.' She looked up. 'I don't know if you understand me.'

Cotton nodded. 'When was this?'

'When Susan was eighteen months old. February 1944. All I know is that the operation had something to do with the Eniwetok Atoll. That's part of the Marshall Islands.'

'Remote?'

'They're just very small specks on a map. Thousands of miles away. They never found his body.' She gave a pained little shrug. 'We had a memorial service and put up a plaque.' She shook her head. 'Now I don't know.'

'What?'

'We got married in July 1941, way before Pearl Harbor, you know. His grandma had left him the house. That was one of the reasons we felt we could, you know?

178

The thing now is I don't know that Susan and I can afford to stay here. It needs a lot of work.'

'Are you thinking of selling?'

'I really don't know. What's sure is I don't have the cash to do it up for a quick sale, you know. And I have to think of Susan.'

'Did you work before you were married?'

'I was a teacher but then, you know, I got married. Married women aren't allowed to teach now. The widow thing complicates it. It's not clear I can go back. So I've been taking courses. Shorthand, typing, some legal terminology. If I can't go back to teaching, I'm thinking of being a legal secretary. I have an interview in September. But that's in Providence. That makes it difficult to manage Susan and the commute.' She looked up. 'I feel bad because I'm losing him, you know. I can't help it. He's becoming fainter.'

Cotton nodded. 'That's natural. I was going to marry a girl called Emmeline, but she was killed in a bombing raid. Mostly I remember her laughing now.'

Sally Ingram stared at Cotton; then shook her head. 'No,' she said. 'My husband was kinda serious.'

'Had you known him long?'

'Oh sure, all our lives really.' She frowned. 'There's a thing I don't understand. Men really don't like to talk about the war, do they?'

'Well, we tend to be struck dumb by decency because we've survived. We also know we were lucky but it had very little to do with us.'

For a moment Cotton thought he had done that part reasonably well. Then he remembered again how

179

unimaginative and short of generosity he was. He winced, tried to recall what he had said in case anything might have hurt her.

He saw she was staring at him with an intent but almost puzzled practicality; he grew aware that she was, whether consciously or not, trying to line up her body with his.

She smiled and stayed quite still. Whatever he had said had been dismissed. But here again the smile irritated him. It struck him as patient, passive and far too plaintive.

'I really should get going,' she said. She downed most of the beer and got up.

Cotton got up too. 'I'm sorry,' he said.

'Don't be. We all have to make do with what we're given.'

She smiled absently again. 'Susan, come along now.'

Cotton watched them go. He was aware that Sally Ingram had not so far mentioned her dead husband's name.

He went into the guest-cottage and took a shower and changed. Then he walked up towards the Buick. From the barn she used as a studio, Eleanor beckoned him. She was dressed in overalls he associated with train drivers and had tied a bandana on her head to protect her hair from paint.

'I used to have a smock but I got too messy,' she said. 'You want to be careful.'

'What are we talking about?'

'Our neighbour.'

'I don't understand.'

'Haven't you seen the way she looks at you?'

'Sally?' Cotton shook his head. 'No. Joan once told me there is a character in some movies who's just called "the man". He's as much a shadow as a person, a sort of prop with legs, who opens doors and speaks when the script requires him to speak. He's interchangeable, not important in himself.'

'You're not a movie star.'

'Of course I'm not. But I fill in the space for a man. She was just telling me she's a widow. Sally may look at me but that's largely because her husband's suit doesn't fit me. She asks me questions. All of them are really about her husband. She doesn't even properly know where or how he died. And she doesn't really have anyone new to talk to about it. So she speaks to someone who was a soldier. But my greatest attraction is that I'm a foreign visitor who speaks English, I can take her daughter to the beach and I leave on Labor Day.'

'What's to stop her taking you for him?'

'Apart from herself, Eleanor? I'd say there was reality, a house that needs repairs and a daughter who calls me mister, mostly.'

'Susan could be looking for a dad.'

'She doesn't remember having one.'

Eleanor frowned. 'There are summer romances, you know. I mean, what would you do if she threw herself at you?'

'I'm certainly not expecting her to. But I'd be very polite and very respectful.'

Eleanor shook her head. Suddenly she smiled. 'She might not want that,' she said.

'Oh come on, Eleanor,' said Cotton. 'I'm a passing novelty, not that important, even as a possibility.'

'Oh my,' said Eleanor. 'A modest man. That's attractive, you see.'

Cotton felt bored and frustrated. He must have shown he was.

'Hey,' said Eleanor. 'All I mean is, just don't take advantage of her.'

'You've just said. I'd be a gentleman, Eleanor.'

Eleanor frowned. 'Don't you find her attractive?'

Cotton avoided the question. 'She's got a child and I have you for a chaperone.'

Eleanor looked slightly sheepish. 'I have been kinda enjoying it,' she said and laughed. 'You'll have to forgive me. Not that much happens here.'

Cotton nodded. 'If you do speak to her, tell her I have my own problems. And of course that she already has a local and very keen admirer.'

For the first time he saw Eleanor really shocked. 'Who are you talking about?'

'His name's Joe Samms. He's a builder.'

'I know who Joe Samms is! Don't be ridiculous.'

'He checked me out as soon as I took Susan to the beach.'

'Are you serious?'

'Yes, I am.'

Eleanor looked pained. 'But don't you find her at all attractive?'

'Eleanor, I'm going to start work at the United Nations in six weeks.'

Eleanor laughed. 'Well, if you put it like that, I guess

182

you're fine and dandy. But there's nothing wrong with a bit of neighbourliness.'

'What does that mean?'

'Take them out. Enjoy yourself.'

'Weren't you just saying I should be careful?'

'Felismina will babysit. She's always looking for extra money. I don't know why, you know. I treat her well.'

'What is this about, Eleanor?'

'Sally's not having an easy time, you know. I'm just talking about taking her to the movies or something. She needs to get out more.'

'Don't you go to the movies?'

'I'll pay for the babysitting.'

Cotton closed his eyes. He found Sally – and here Eleanor – oversweet and somehow fizzy, like sherbet on his nerves. Had Eleanor been testing him? Reassuring herself that he really was a gentleman? But then again, she had definitely not liked the sound of Joe Samms' interest. He opened his eyes and took off the Ray-Bans.

'Will you make it clear beforehand that I am only being neighbourly?'

Eleanor laughed. 'You know it's usually the girl who thinks she's in danger?' She laughed again and shook her head at him. 'OK. I'll talk to her. '

'Thanks,' said Cotton. He put the Ray-Bans back on and walked to the Buick.

13

THE NEXT day, Cotton started a routine. He'd get up about six, do the exercises on the chart POFC Tully had given him, say hello to Susan on the deck and drive to the beach. He'd swim a couple of hundred yards, then drive back, rinse out his trunks, hang them up, shower, shave and go for breakfast. He'd eat spinach omelette, a fruit salad or tomatoes, scrambled eggs and roast peppers. There was also what Carla called 'eggs Benny', with salmon or ham. He'd then read a paper or news magazine over coffee.

On 14 July, stepping into the Ocean View Café, he saw someone who did not look like a local resident or a tourist. The man was young and dressed as for a business meeting, in a suit and tie. He was sitting at Cotton's usual table.

'Your friend's waiting for you,' said Carla.

The young man gave Cotton what looked like a sympathetic smirk. Cotton sat down. He ordered breakfast.

'What are you going to have, my friend?' he said.

'Just coffee,' said the young man. 'Mr Hoberman doesn't like us putting on weight.'

Cotton waited for Carla to leave. 'Is this a threat?'

'The reverse.'

'I see.' Cotton paused. 'Are we being watched?'

'Mr Hoberman's intention is that we be seen together.'

Cotton nodded. 'All right. What is it you want?'

The young man gave Cotton a folder. It contained a couple of sheets of paper on the effects of scopolamine. Cotton knew most of it. He noted that one effect of the drug was so-called 'desert mouth', a mouth so dry some subjects could not even speak enough to give up any information. 'Desert mouth' helped in certain surgical interventions in the throat and mouth.

Cotton had also not known that the first legally approved use of the drug in the US had been as far back as 1922. It had been used to *clear* two accused men. The doctor had claimed scopolamine did not allow the subject to invent a lie and the judge had accepted this. Whoever had written the pages then added: *The judge did not say the subject would tell the truth.*

'Do you want, from your experience, to make any comments?'

'No,' said Cotton. He handed the folder back. 'How much danger am I in?'

'Mr Hoberman advises extreme vigilance.'

'I wouldn't expect him to say anything else. Will you answer some questions?'

'That depends.'

'The FBI has an interest in truth drugs?'

'All the agencies have. You can't not have an interest, sir.'

'How many agencies are there? With their own departments and politics?' Cotton thought the latest count was around seventeen.

The young man said nothing.

'Any ideas on why I wasn't killed?'

The young man looked surprised. 'We surmise they didn't think you'd survive.'

'Bad medical advice?'

'I wouldn't know, sir. Before I came here, Mr Hoberman said you'd understand this business wasn't about stupidity but about power.'

Cotton nodded. 'All right. Tell Mr Hoberman I appreciate that.'

'Sir?'

Cotton could see Carla approaching with a tray.

'What's your name?'

'Raymond Reeves, sir.'

'Mr Reeves will take his coffee to go,' said Cotton.

'Sure thing.'

When Carla had left, Cotton smiled. 'Are you going to stay here?'

'I'm due back in New York today.'

'Good. Have a safe trip.'

'Who was that?' said Carla when Raymond Reeves of the FBI had left.

'Insurance man,' said Cotton.

'That explains the clothes,' said Carla.

Cotton sat for a moment. He now felt sure that if something happened to him the FBI would make enquiries. If it suited them, of course.

When he got up and walked to his car he looked around. He could see no sign whatever he was being watched.

*

On 15 July he read that the pound sterling was now con- vertible. One pound could be exchanged for 4.20 US dollars. On 16 July the papers reported there had been a run on the pound. Investors, the *ProJo* reported, considered that the pound sterling was worth 'no more than three dollars'. Cotton was surprised at their generosity. He'd have gone for a figure of about 2.10. The paper said it was not yet known what action the British government would take. Cotton shook his head. He thought any action the British took would be, to use one of his mother's favourite expressions, 'farting against thunder'. Still, Cotton was pleased he had not committed himself to a long rental agreement in New York; there was always the possibility the British would be realistic and devalue and that he was about to have his income halved.

The second girl Cotton had wanted to marry, an American called Katherine Ward, had once asked him: 'But don't you trust your own government?' Cotton had laughed out loud before he realized she was serious. 'I have difficulty trusting my own judgement, let alone my government's actions. It's not fair. I do appreciate that. But it's not entirely extrapolation either.'

Katherine had laughed. 'Do you trust me?'

'Absolutely.'

Now, in the Ocean View Café in Narragansett, looking out over a startlingly blue Atlantic, Cotton knew his reply had been as much prompt as genuine. He shook his head. He recognized shame, the sort that comes from stupidity and innocence recalled and reconstituted. He resented that the hiatus caused by the drugs

187

had induced in him a review, not a very competent or even coherent review, of his past behaviour. He asked himself if his readiness to dedicate himself to two very different women had not been wretchedly unfair on them. Would he have been a good husband? He surprised himself. He thought he probably would – observant, even dedicated. In Narragansett, he just didn't know why. He looked out of the window. He could not see that anyone was watching him. Had Hoberman's man Reeves been a little premature? Or was the interested party being lackadaisical?

'You want fruit salad now?' said Carla.

'Do you have oatmeal?'

'Sure. Do you want it with extras?'

On 17 July he took Eleanor, Sally and Susan to see an unseasonal movie matinee, *Miracle on 34th Street*, and enjoyed the air conditioning very much indeed.

'You're losing that broiled look,' Eleanor told him. 'That's a tan.'

A couple of days later he accompanied Sally to an evening showing of *Lady in the Lake*. The cinema car park backed on to a bank of the Saugatucket River and Sally suggested they walk a little.

'You know, I used to adore Robert Montgomery,' she said.

'And now?'

'He's getting old. Looks a little seedy. And those camera angles!'

They strolled. He was aware she was not quite beside him, may have been remembering. He suspected she had

returned to a time before marriage, to about fifteen or sixteen. Possibly in the same place by the river.

'What did you think of the woman?' she said.

'I saw she's called Audrey Totter. She is extraordinarily good at curling her lip.'

Sally laughed.

'A tough talker. That's how she makes her living. Talking tough and curling her lip.'

He saw she was blushing.

'She's not a big star, though, is she?'

'No,' said Sally. 'I guess you could say she's a stalwart of B-movies.'

Cotton glanced at her but saw no sign that Sally Ingram was being mean.

Cotton played 'the man', escorted her back to the Buick, opened the door for her and saw her safely seated.

'Thank you,' she said.

'I was enjoying myself too, you know.'

'It's just that I've been out of things for a while, if you know what I mean . . .'

Cotton drove her home and then drove Felismina the very short distance to Eleanor's house. Felismina was not looking too happy.

'Are you all right?' he asked.

'Why shouldn't I be all right? Yeah. I'm fine. She interferes.'

'Eleanor?'

Felismina nodded. She glanced at him. 'When she gets excited her paintings change.'

'I'm sorry?'

'She's using a lot of red now. You want to take a look.'

Cotton nodded. 'All right. I'll do that.' The next day he strolled up to the barn. Eleanor wasn't actually painting. She appeared to be shuffling her canvases. Each one – and there were a lot – had a drape of sacking cloth. Those still drying were turned to the wall. He found out she was having 'an arranging day'.

'I give some as presents,' she said. 'But you've got to match them up, you know. Get the right subject for the right person.'

Eleanor showed him some. She had begun quite traditionally but sometime in the twenties, after her husband's death, had entirely changed her approach, from brush stroke to subject, from colour to perspective, the one very much brighter, the other flattened. Cotton wasn't sure what the word was. 'Naïf'? 'Elementary surrealism'? There were slight Gothic elements. Some of those figures were between man and bird, feather and cloak, a monkish, hooded look. Almost every painting included a building. But no person was ever shown as having features or a face.

'Show him what you're working on now,' said Felismina.

Initially reluctant, Eleanor revealed two paintings-in-progress. 'I just love lighthouses,' she said.

Cotton looked at them. Apart from the colours, they were almost identical. In one, a dark blue lighthouse rose from surf-battered rocks to be finished off with a red cap. In the other, the shaft of the lighthouse was primrose yellow but the cap remained red.

Felismina raised her eyes to the underside of the barn roof.

'I'm trying to convey the sheer strength of these things,' said Eleanor, 'but without trickery. I'm not sure about that kind of yellow.'

Cotton nodded slowly.

'So how did your evening go?' she said.

Cotton ignored the question.

Eleanor laughed. 'You've really come for more books, haven't you?'

Whatever Garrett Ramsden had been, his tastes were traditional and what Eleanor called 'pretty highbrow'. His library was heavily weighted towards the classics and was accompanied by cobwebs and, just below the Ps – Plato, Pliny, Plautus – a mouse so dried out it resembled a furry leaf.

'Garrett just loved reading,' said Eleanor. 'No, he needed to read. He'd come here in the summer and just eat up the books as if he had been starved the whole working year. He'd sit on the porch with a jug of something cold. That's when I started painting, you know. I never saw him happier than when he was reading – just out there.'

'What was his profession?'

'He was a contract lawyer for the Boston office of the bank. You know, the same one Todd works for.'

Cotton left the barn with translations of the Odyssey, Horace, Catullus and Ovid.

Eleanor approved. 'Garrett always said nothing changes except change.'

Cotton nodded. He couldn't think of anything else to do.

Back in the guest-cottage, he took out the artist's pad Dr Sanford had given him, but decided against opening it.

That night he had an unpleasant nightmare. Lines of ants were marching through his veins and he was desperate to keep them apart, the nightmare being that the ants might meet and fight in a seething ball in his chest. They were biting him. Or was that the sting of acid?

Cotton woke. He breathed out. The nightmare was a fairly crude transposition of invasion by drugs and possibly the risk to his heart Dr Sanford had mentioned. A little later he found himself staring at the stabilizer pills he had poured into the toilet. He blinked, then flushed and went directly back to bed to sleep.

On Friday the 25th he decided to see Joe Samms. Marty's really did look like an old wooden barn. Long before, it had been painted a deep red, but weathering had worn down the colour and contributed patches of grey and grain. When he went in, Cotton met years of smells; deep-fried food, tobacco and spilt beer.

Cotton took off his Ray-Bans. There was no need whatever for them. The interior remained dark. The brightest thing had an art deco church window glow – that turned out to be a Wurlitzer jukebox called 'the bubbler'. The record playing was Fats Waller's 'Your Feet's Too Big!' Cotton smiled.

'What can I get you?' said a waitress.

'Is Joe Samms here?'

The waitress weighed around 300 pounds but did not rise much above five feet. When she raised her hand to

point towards Joe's booth, her underarm did not shake. It swung.

'Joe!'

Cotton knew it was Joe Samms because he raised a hand to a low-level light and waggled what fingers he had. 'Thank you.'

'My job, sweet pea. Bring you a beer directly.'

Cotton slid in opposite Joe Samms.

'Glad you could make it,' said Joe.

The waitress thumped down a bottle of beer and uncapped it.

'You want squid rings? Fries? Stuffies?' said Joe.

'The beer's fine,' said Cotton.

'This the Englishman?' said the waitress. 'The English are cheap, right? I'll tell Virgil.'

'She likes you,' said Joe Samms.

Cotton smiled. 'Who's Virgil?'

'Her husband. He cooks. Marianne waits.'

'And Marty?'

Joe Samms shook his head. 'Don't know. Guess he could have been an owner or two before. But Virgil and Marianne have been here as long as I can remember. How's the vacation going?'

'Well, I came for the quiet and it's been quiet enough. The rest part has been more difficult.'

'Yeah. Your leg.'

'Sorry?'

'Mine gets brittle in winter – that figures. But this humidity makes me think I've got rust on the bone.'

Cotton nodded. 'I've been taking Susan and Sally out. Just to the cinema.'

'Yeah,' said Joe Samms and nodded back. 'That's the easy part.'

Cotton did not understand.

'Well, I mean you're being neighbourly. You're not asking more.' He looked up. 'You got a girlfriend back home?'

'No.' Cotton was beginning to understand that Joe felt a link between them, though Cotton had never thought of himself as obviously injured.

Joe Samms gave him a 'there you go' shrug. He smiled. 'My mom says I'm not pretty but I'm not dead, you know?'

'You won't know if you don't try.'

'Girl called me a cripple once, said I was insulting her by asking.'

'Come on. Sally wouldn't do anything like that.'

'OK,' said Joe Samms. He smiled. It was a soft smile and Cotton understood that better. He nodded and Joe Samms immediately started on another subject. It involved the name Galilee 'about six miles away. Didn't you know Galilee was the tuna capital of the world?'

'No, I didn't.'

'Sure it is! There's a ferry there to Block Island, too.'

'Right.'

Joe Samms smiled with genuine delight. 'Round about the third week in August it's football season,' he said. 'You get over a hundred four-man teams in the Rhode Island Tuna Derby.'

'A football is?'

'Mostly bluefin. There's skipjack there too, though.' He smiled and shook his head. 'Oh, it's something. Way bigger than a man, some of them. I mean, some of those

194

tuna fish come in way over five hundred pounds dead weight. I used to fish before the war, you know, just kid's stuff. Thirty-pounders. What do you say? We could make a day of it and watch them.'

Cotton smiled. 'I'd love to.'

Joe Samms lifted his bottle of beer and they chinked glass again. Because of his fingers, he swung the bottle from the neck. It was a firm strike.

'Then that's what we'll do!'

On 28 July Cotton took Eleanor, Sally and Susan to Rocky Point Amusement Park, round Greenwich Bay by Warwick. The odd thing to Cotton was that it was not open to the public. Having been flattened in the hurricane of 1938 and delayed by the war, it was being rebuilt and was due to start operations in 1948.

Cotton was not sure why they had gone. It didn't look like the kind of thing that Eleanor would have visited before, but perhaps she wanted to show him that Rhode Island had large attractions. Or the extent to which America catered for the masses.

Eleanor had arranged a guided tour to show them what it would be like when it was finished. To Cotton, there was something of a military camp about the place. Areas were clearly marked out. There were a lot of concrete strips in the ground. Most of these were foundations for what his Scottish mother had called 'dollie-mollies' – stalls and basic fairground attractions which were not yet there. Permanent structures, like the base for the Ferris wheel or the track for a miniature railway, were there but remained incomplete; there was no big wheel

and no train on the track. But the pillions for a cable car called the Skyliner were up and something called a flume was well advanced.

'It used to be called the Russian Toboggan,' said Eleanor. 'For the rushin', you know.' Cotton thought of her as in pre-Revolution, music-hall mood.

The guide explained that the flume would rush through salt water. 'You see, it's been dug out and cemented already.'

They also saw plans and drawings for the Rocky Point Shore Dining Hall due for 1949 – a huge, hangar-like place that would have 2,500 place settings. Each diner, according to the guide, would have 'eight square feet of space' and an industrial production of 'very reasonably priced' food. They were planning the same menu as pre-war: clam cakes, chowder, Bermuda onions, green olives, cucumbers, white and brown bread, steamed clams, baked fish, French fries, corn on the cob, a whole boiled lobster and Indian pudding.

'What do you think of that?' said Eleanor. 'One dollar fifty for adults; eighty cents for children.'

'Impressive,' said Cotton. 'I don't know what a Bermuda onion is.'

'It's sweet.'

'And Indian pudding?'

'Looks awful, tastes great. Do you make it, Sally?'

Sally shook her head.

'I'll see what Felismina can do,' said Eleanor.

Eleanor was beaming. Cotton wondered how many lobsters they got through if each diner got a lobster and the amusement park was open from mid May to

September. That was something like a quarter of a million lobsters.

'Oh, on a big day we'll cater for ten thousand diners,' said the guide.

'Do you have this kind of thing in England?' said Eleanor.

'I don't think so,' said Cotton. 'There are fairs but they move around. And there's a place called Blackpool but I've never been there.'

'You're not a cotton candy type of guy?'

Cotton considered Eleanor. They had come a long way for her to make that joke.

'I think we call it candy floss,' he said.

Eleanor laughed. 'Susan, there'll be all kinds of rides and things. Ghost trains, Bluebeard's Palace, a roller-coaster.' She laughed again and said she remembered Konyati's Fun House. 'That's mirrors, you know, that make you small as a mouse or big as an elephant.'

Susan looked more bemused than impressed.

'When was that?' said Sally.

'When I was six. Susan will be that age next year.'

Absently, Cotton smiled, but something had caught his eye. Way over by the wire fencing he could see a black Ford coupé. It was a common car but Cotton had seen rather too many of these – or perhaps the same one – several times recently. The realization was sudden. He was grinding his teeth.

Eleanor was staring at him. 'What's the matter with you?' she said.

Cotton turned and looked at her. For a long, black-flecked moment, he couldn't remember who she was.

When he was at Cambridge, Cotton had played as goalkeeper in his college soccer team. One cold, muddy day in November 1939 the ball had come out of the mist, landed with a splat just past the penalty spot and skittered towards him across the mud. He had fallen on it.

As he started to get up, he had heard quick boot-sucking sounds and a moment later someone had started kicking him in the ribs. The kicker was a very short, furiously intent young man with coarse blond hair that looked almost bleached. Warding his attacker off with one arm, Cotton had got up and found himself surrounded by the other team's players.

'Now don't hurt Billy,' someone said.

'Isn't he the one kicking me?'

'You mustn't hurt Billy. You mustn't!'

Cotton had certainly been frowning but did not think he had ever looked like kicking or punching back. Evidently, from the anxious expression on their faces, this had not been clear to those around him. About a minute later, Billy's friends had informed him that he was heir to money and a title 'and absolutely as bright as the Duke of Windsor'. Billy himself said nothing but turned in a tight-arsed, matador sort of way and made a dusting gesture with his hands, as if he had just achieved something. But Billy had a lot of very loyal, even sycophantic friends, including the referee, who decided that a dropped ball would be 'fairer all round'.

Here in Rocky Point, Cotton saw that Eleanor had already taken an alarmed step backwards and had started to blink.

'It's all right,' he said quickly. 'Of course it is.' He remembered to raise his eyebrows and try a smile. 'What would you all say to something to eat?'

'I'd like funnel cakes,' said Susan. 'Have I had funnel cakes? I like the name.'

The guide spoke up. 'Oh, we haven't got anything cooking yet, but I reckon we have some treats available for you. This way.'

He led them to some promotional material in a shed-cum-shop. Susan got a balloon and an oversized pencil with *Rocky Point Amusement Park* on them. Cotton saw a Steven kaleidoscope called 'The Snowflake'. He picked it up and looked. No, the kaleidoscope was not a good comparison with what he had seen in the Ogden Clinic. He had forgotten the look of smooth, coloured crystals tumbling and clicking into new patterns. These patterns were indeed like snowflakes, but regular and candy-coloured, they had no sense of fracture or distortion.

'Those can be dangerous, you know,' said Eleanor. 'If she walks with it and bumps into something she could get a black eye – or worse. Get her some Lifesavers and I'll settle for that butterfinger there.'

Cotton smiled. 'Of course.' He put the kaleidoscope back and bought what she asked. Sally didn't have anything. 'I'm watching my diet,' she said.

'Are you enjoying yourself?' Cotton asked Eleanor.

She glanced at him. 'Sure I am,' she said wryly. 'You know Rocky Point started a century ago? 1847. What were the English doing then?'

Cotton shrugged. 'Nothing like this,' he said. He did

then recall that the Great Exhibition had been in 1851, but let that go.

'In 1877 President Rutherford B. Hayes stood where we are and took the first presidential telephone call from Alexander Graham Bell in Providence.'

'I certainly didn't know that,' said Cotton. 'Impressive.'

Eleanor did not look so much as mollified, more as if she had evened things up.

As they left, Cotton looked around, but could see no sign of the black Ford coupé.

That evening Cotton went again to Marty's for a beer.

'So where've you been?' said Joe Samms.

'Rocky Point.'

'The amusement park?' Joe adopted a radiophonic sort of voice. 'Rhode Island in a nutshell.' He frowned. 'But they're still building it, right?'

'Yes. Eleanor wanted to see the progress. We took Sally and Susan.'

Joe Samms nodded. 'Yeah. Sally's getting out more.'

'It's mostly Eleanor's idea.'

'That figures.'

'Does it?'

'My mom says a woman needs three years to get over a bereavement.'

Cotton blinked. He could think of several he'd met who had moved on a great deal sooner.

'Sally's done three years.'

'Yes, she has. And a little more.'

Joe made a face that somehow included a smile. 'It's

tricky, you know. I don't want to give her the wrong impression.'

'What would that be?'

'You know.'

Actually Cotton didn't. He was not sure whether Joe regarded Sally as very delicate or was very shy himself – or both.

'Come round for a beer some time,' he said. 'You could bump into each other.'

Joe nodded. 'Yeah,' he said without sounding convinced. 'What about you?'

'What about me?'

'Don't the English look for love?'

Cotton smiled. 'Of course. It's just I've had a little too much attention from one source recently.'

'Clingy?'

'Possessive.'

'That happens. You want squid rings?'

'Sally's looking up,' said Cotton. 'I think she's beginning to look ahead. She's thinking of a job, she's got Susan, she's beginning to move on. Don't leave it too long, Joe.'

Joe Samms nodded. 'Yup, you're right. I know you are. Do you want those squid rings?'

'I'll get them. Do you want another beer?'

Life in Narragansett was reminding Cotton of the small town gossip of a Jane Austen novel – which one was it? – that spoke of 'a neighbourhood of voluntary intelligence agents'. It wasn't *Sense and Sensibility*. It wasn't *Persuasion*.

'Sure,' said Joe. 'Maybe a little chilli with the squid?'

14

AROUND 5.30 IN the morning Cotton got up to drink water. He then sat on the edge of the bed and let the ceiling fan disturb the air around his body. He may even, though sitting up, have slept a little.

The next he knew he was fully but calmly awake, something that had not happened for some time. He was pretty sure he had been woken by a rifle shot. He saw it was ten past seven. The rifle fired again, dull crack and fizz peeling off into echo but interrupted by the bullet hitting something the size of a man, but denser-sounding than human flesh. The shooter was no more than twenty yards away to his left, in Sally Ingram's garden.

Cotton pulled on a pair of trousers and a shirt and went outside to the deck, still buttoning his flies. He heard a car door slam and some confused voices.

'Did he get him?'

The rifle bolt worked again. The next shot was very close to, possibly touching the target. That sound was short, fat, dead, still in the Ingrams' garden but thirty to forty yards closer to the sea.

Behind him he heard scuffling. Eleanor and Felismina, both in housecoats and slippers, Felismina with rags in her hair, scuttled past and made for the gap between the

properties that Susan Ingram used for to her morning tea parties. Eleanor went by, waving an arm.

'Men needed,' she called.

Cotton smiled. The small girl's tea things remained as they were. Cotton stepped off the deck and ducked through into the excitement.

He was impressed so many people were already there. The police hadn't used their sirens and there were five troopers. There were a number of neighbours. One trooper was holding a Springfield M1903A4, a US Army sniper's rifle with sights. He was looking flushed with discomfort. Cotton guessed he was waiting for someone to tell him he had done the right thing. In the absence of his chief, the people around tried to set his mind at rest.

The young black bear looked like a coarse, hairy blob of about 120 pounds. The last shot had split the skull. The other two had been to the belly and just above the front shoulder.

'Last time I saw one of these,' said Eleanor, 'the fur was rippling like wind on the sea.'

'When was that?'

'I don't know – 1921? Garrett was still alive.'

There was no hint of wind. But an early fly had arrived to buzz and circle the blood on the black bear's head. Cotton felt something round his scarred leg. He looked down at Susan Ingram.

'Are you all right?'

'I was kinda scared,' she said. He could feel her damp breath on his leg. She looked up. 'Did they have to kill him?'

'Best thing,' said Eleanor.

Cotton lifted Susan up. She put her head on his shoulder.

'I heard it by the garbage bins,' said Sally Ingram. 'So I looked out, saw him and called it in.'

'What do they do with it now?' said the portly little male neighbour from the other side of Sally Ingram's house. He was wearing a red paisley robe, mono-grammed slippers and, from the red marks on his forehead, looked to have been wearing a hairnet.

'I don't know,' said the shooter. 'I really don't. I guess they'll take it away.'

Susan Ingram looked up. She half stroked, half scratched Cotton's cheek. 'You haven't shaved,' she said.

'I will,' said Cotton.

'The British,' said Eleanor, 'use bearskin for hats. They call them busbies.'

'Or bearskins,' said Cotton.

'What's the difference?'

'Bearskins are higher,' said Cotton. 'You know about lifts, when men add height to their shoes? Bearskins add height to the head.'

'You do have a way of expressing yourself,' said Eleanor. 'When do they wear busbies?'

'I think that might be on horseback.'

Cotton turned. The girl giggled. Behind the police cars, he saw two men in suits and hats checking out what was going on. They were standing beside a black Ford Sedan coupé. They were some way from the Rocky Point Amusement Park. The police chief was arriving. The two men got back into their car. Cotton saw that the

police chief had come with a photographer and that things were about to start flashing. The Ford took off.

Cotton realized that he had begun rocking his shoulders. It wasn't just that he was reassuring a nearly five-year-old. He could hear a pipe tune in his head – 'Black Bear'. A skirl of raucous simplicity, it was usually played at quite a lick, when Highland Regiments were marching back to barracks. The British march with stiff shoulders but Cotton remembered how, with this tune, adapted from a hornpipe jig for a dancing bear, the soldiers' shoulders would begin to roll and when the tune stepped up the men, all together, would roar 'Hey!'

Cotton could not stop himself. He grinned. In an absurd sort of way he felt not so much as himself again, but in some way home.

Eleanor was staring at him. 'What's gotten into you?' she said.

Cotton shook his head and leant over. 'I'm fine, Eleanor. Thank you for asking.'

When the tarpaulin arrived to put over the bear, Cotton put Susan down, went back to the guest-cottage, showered, shaved, dressed and drove to the Ocean View Café for breakfast.

'No bear steaks today,' said Carla.

After breakfast Cotton turned the Buick and drove north along the Boston Neck Road towards Wickford. He glanced behind him several times, to check the following cars.

Wickford looked to him very like clapboard English, similar to coastal villages he had seen while training in

Colchester in Essex, except Essex had been muddy and far less hot. In a drugstore called Earnshaws, Cotton bought some postcards and stamps and sent one each to his father and his sister. He wrote: *Narragansett is so wonderfully quiet I have come to Wickford for the day. Not entirely sure Wickford isn't quieter. Love Peter.*

In Earnshaws, an assistant told him of an 'absolutely beautiful' small church interior nearby and of the Wickford Lobster Hatchery. Cotton missed the church but found the hatchery about half a mile off Main Street. It was a clapboard building on a pier with a single-storey extension on something that looked like a pontoon bridge but turned out to be 'house-boats' that supported 'scrim bags'. The bags contained lobsters at various stages of development; Wickford water was rich in feed and the water in the bags was kept moving 'so they don't settle down and become cannibals'.

Coming out of Wickford, Cotton deliberately made a wrong turn. A few hundred yards past a small pond, he came across a tiny flower shop. By the door was an image of the god Mercury carrying a bunch of flowers. He stopped the car and went in. A young woman told him he could send flowers to his sister. His father in Britain would be more difficult. Indeed, she didn't know whether or not they had the service over there yet. As he listened he saw the black Ford coupé come past. He arranged to have flowers sent to Joan and wrote a note to accompany them.

Then he turned the Buick and started back to Narragansett. A little way on, he pulled into a gas station and filled up. Ten gallons cost him one dollar fifty. He

remembered that was the price Eleanor had said for an adult meal at Rocky Point. Behind the pumps was a low, shingle store. The black Ford coupé drew up. Two men in suits and hats got out and went inside. Cotton looked around. The only two cars there were his and the black Ford. He gave the attendant two dollars.

'Are you sure about this, sir?'

'Yes,' said Cotton.

He waited. It was very hot and there was no breeze. The two men came out holding sodas and snacks. Perhaps they were stocking up before he drove on. Cotton straightened up and walked towards them.

'How can I help you, gentlemen?'

One of the men frowned. 'What are you talking about?'

Cotton nodded. 'So I won't be seeing you again on my meander through Rhode Island? Thank you, that's good to know.'

'Just keeping an eye on you, Mr Cotton,' said the other man. 'It's for your own security.'

'That's very considerate. Thank you. Up to now everyone in your Intelligence Services has called me Colonel. I don't know why. Give me a telephone number and I'll let you know my plans. It'll cut down on inconvenience. You might also be able to help me. For instance, do you know anywhere good for a meal round here? I'd be happy to buy you both lunch.'

'It's not quite like that, Colonel Cotton.'

'I'll say.'

The man frowned. Cotton understood he may have thought he was imitating him.

'You do know I'm here to recuperate?' he said.

The other man spoke up. 'You don't exactly look like you're an invalid.'

'Not any more. I'm getting back to normal. I'm swimming. I am eating a lot of fruit and vegetables. Ah, I imagine you already know that. This trip was just to see if you were following me or not.'

'Why would you want to do that?'

'Two reasons. Life's a little quiet here, let's be honest. And I was also surprised I should be under surveillance.'

'Just doing our job, Colonel.'

'I understand, of course I do.' Cotton shrugged. 'I can assure you I'll be here until Labor Day. But I don't really have anything grand planned. I believe there's a Tuna Tourney in late August. Apart from that, I plan to get fit again and to have a look at the sights. Can you recommend anything? Is Newport worth a look?'

'Do you like boats?'

'Not particularly.'

'Well, they've also got the big mansions there. And an early synagogue.'

One of the men was sweating a great deal. He took out a handkerchief, flipped up his hat and wiped his forehead. The handkerchief smelt of Old Spice aftershave.

'Keeps the bugs off,' he said.

Behind his head a blue and grey butterfly, some sort of fritillary, fluttered towards the gas pumps.

'Anything else, gentlemen?' said Cotton. 'I'm happy to cooperate.'

The man with the handkerchief spoke. 'What's your interest in your neighbour, Mrs Ingram?'

Cotton held up his hand. 'Purely neighbourly. She's taking courses, hopes to become a legal secretary. She's a widow with a child. Her husband died in the war.'

'He overshot the deck.'

Cotton frowned. 'I'm sorry?'

'In his plane. He messed up his landing on an aircraft carrier, bounced over the bows and the carrier went over him.'

'Would she know that?'

The other man made a face. 'Oh, no, Colonel.'

'Good. I'm glad to hear it. Now I'm going to drive back to Narragansett. All right? Are you FBI?' said Cotton. He gave them a couple of seconds, before he shrugged. 'I can find out.'

'No, we're not. But we're not at liberty to say—'

'That's fine, gentlemen.' Cotton smiled. 'I'll be seeing you around, I suppose.'

Cotton drove off. He was confident they were low-level operatives and did not know what he was recuperating from. He wondered, partly because of where he was, if they were Navy men. But, of course, he didn't know if they were or not. Nor who they were reporting to.

Back in the guest-cottage, Cotton got out the notebook and drawing book Dr Sanford had given him. He drew a bird in bright colours, but without a model the thing turned out as what he thought of as vaguely Aztec. Then he drank a beer.

For his second drawing he remembered the shield of Madrid. It shows a she-bear and a tree called *el madroño*. Somebody had told him the English name was *Arbutus* or strawberry tree. He didn't really mind. He doubted his drawing was good enough to invoke Madrid in any case. He wanted a bear and a tree that bore fruit and that, more or less, was what he produced. He thought the fruit was probably red apples. That was a positive sign if the drawings ever got into the hands of someone looking for indications of his personality. He groaned. He thought his bear looked like an oversized porcupine.

A little later he fell asleep and had an unpleasant dream. It involved a tunnel, a rifle barrel and a syringe. He was inspecting rifles, as he had in the army. He looked down and could see a bullet in the barrel. He jumped back and turned to see a bubble going into the needle of the syringe. It was not clear to him how a bubble could stop a bullet except by meeting in him. He woke with a start and saw that a bead of sweat had dropped on to the back of his hand.

'Oh, I'm sorry,' said Eleanor. 'I came to invite you for supper, Peter. I thought we could talk about literature. Would seven o'clock do you?'

Cotton swallowed and nodded. 'Thank you,' he said.

'You're sweating, you know?'

'Yes. Thank you.'

Another drop of sweat trickled down past his eyebrow towards his jaw. He wiped it away.

Cotton had no idea what effects the lack of Dr Sanford's 'stabilizers' was having on him.

*

At dinner, Eleanor did not talk of literature so much as her late Garrett's love of books and reading.

'He died out there, you know, on the porch in his chair. Heart failure. He had a glass of lemonade beside him and his cheroots. He had a kind of routine. When we arrived for the summer, he'd read two Melville stories, *Bartleby* and *Benito Cereno*. He'd top them off with Edmund's first speech in *King Lear*. Then he'd see what was new.' For dessert, Cotton was given Indian pudding. It looked like a lumpy brown porridge.

'I guess it's a kind of baked custard really. It's milk, eggs, molasses, salt and yellow cornmeal.'

'It has cinnamon and nutmeg too,' said Felismina.

'What's nutmeg in Portuguese?' said Eleanor.

'I'm an American Portuguese,' said Felismina. She turned to Cotton. 'You tell her.'

'*Nozmoscada*,' said Cotton.

Felismina shrugged. 'You see?'

The Indian pudding combined the sweetness of crème brûlée with the heaviness of soggy school crumble.

'It's terrific,' said Eleanor. 'Real comfort food.'

Cotton nodded cheerfully. After a couple of mouthfuls he took in some water in an effort to flush the sweetness off his teeth.

As he expected, Cotton was given Garrett's first books of summer to take back to the guest-cottage. *Bartleby* and *Benito Cereno* both deal with types of passivity. Edmund in *Lear* is not passive in the slightest, but gives a skilled rhetorician's treatment to the word 'bastard' until it loses meaning and becomes a sort of dry husk rather than a word.

Cotton was mildly surprised. He took it that Garrett really had read the stories and the play and had been, according to Eleanor at least, a wonderful, quiet man but a dutiful professional. But Cotton wondered why she had given him these books. Was it a comment on his own passivity? Though he couldn't see where he fitted in as a bastard.

He shook his head. He turned off the light in the cottage and sat for a while in the dark with his face turned towards the ceiling fan.

'You're always thinking about something, aren't you?' Emmeline had said to him.

'Is that unusual?'

'Oh, I assure you. It is.' She looked up. They were on a picnic in 1943 on a Surrey hill. 'What are you thinking about?'

'There are two wasps here. They have different faces.'

Emmeline laughed. 'Like miniature tigers?'

'Something like that. Then I saw your legs. You're wearing silk stockings on a picnic.'

'Absolutely my last pair. I got so tired of saving them!'

Now, Cotton felt something like shame. There was also a spasm of self-loathing that had something to do with his past behaviour. There was no reason why he should have survived and she had not. He was not sure whether this was the aftermath of the drugs or just a sense of survivor's displacement and guilt. He thought it was probably the miserable second.

He closed his eyes. He saw a chessboard except that all the squares were black. The white was limited to the

lines between the squares. The chess pieces themselves were made of ice that appeared to be melting.

'Shit!' he said and then laughed. If this was his mind's version of getting lines into things as a way of getting himself to stiffen, it wasn't doing very well. His stomach grumbled. A moment later he retasted the Indian pudding. Whatever this was, it wasn't a proud or refined business.

15

S USAN TURNED five on Saturday, 2 August. Cotton was invited to the party. It turned out to be quite a large affair.

'We've got a clown!' said Susan.

'Good!' said Cotton.

'Just a local clown,' said Sally Ingram.

'What other kind is there?' said Cotton.

But despite her efforts to play the celebration down, it struck Cotton as noisy and full of people. He had no experience of this side of America. There were about twenty children and their parents. Amongst the girls were multiple Susans, Lindas and Marilyns, although he found later one was really MaryLynne. The small boys had names like Bobby and Johnny, though Cotton did notice a child saddled with Eugene Junior and another called Randy. Their parents separated according to gender – the women in a group by the food; the men over towards Eleanor's trees.

He thought the men seemed amiable enough but there was also a decided reserve in their eyes – or perhaps they were just adding some briskness to their caution with an unknown foreigner. Their greetings followed a formula: 'Hi. Bill/Tom/Herschel. Pleased to meet you. I'm in Insurance/Toys/Pens.'

'So you're Pete, right? You're British, is that what they're saying?'

Cotton nodded, smiled when he was quite sure it was appropriate, but couldn't help comparing them with British couples of the same age. The Americans were well past the war, and were frustrated by the time it was taking to accommodate the returned soldiers into the workforce and the 'change-over' in manufacturing. Some blamed 'the unions'; others preferred to blame the President. All agreed that when times were bad in America, they were always worse in Rhode Island.

'Hell, textiles here are down the drain and Walsh-Kaiser shed twenty thousand jobs just as soon as Liberty ships were no longer required.'

Cotton was not particularly sympathetic. The British had spent a lot of money they did not have on war materials, and he already knew outrage sounded the same whether expressed by an American GI complaining about the declining quality of the steaks he was being served or by someone who did not have enough of anything to eat. He was also aware that the British government was caught in a crisis of its own making – squeezed by paying off the war, establishing an unfunded new social welfare system and a determination to maintain Britain as a military power. It had led to bouts of frantic fiddling. As part of the loan negotiated by Lord Keynes when Cotton had been in Washington in 1945, the British were obliged to buy American goods in American dollars. They were now desperately trying to renegotiate at least the payment in dollars. On an anecdotal level, he had just read an item on Lord Inverchapel,

the British Ambassador in Washington, buying ten pounds of butter and eight of bacon in New York to take back on the ship for friends at home.

He did not say anything. He did think some of these youngish men looked almost portly. They also struck him as almost triumphantly dull, their talk all about the cost of things and best deals to be had. Their insistence on their own acumen was the only thing that disturbed their good but decidedly distant manners. It was something Cotton had seen before in Americans, a kind of projected collective decency, thoroughgoing but oddly unrelated to the personality and manners of the speaker. He was relieved when two small boys approached to ask where the bear had been shot.

Cotton showed them.

'Does blood bleach grass?' asked one child.

Cotton thought it more likely that urine did. He pointed.

'The head was here.'

One small boy sniffed. 'Can you smell that stinky old bear?'

The other child frowned. 'No,' he said.

Both laughed and ran off. While one had a go at imitating a charging bear to frighten a small girl, the other little boy yanked down one of her ponytails. The girl shrieked, more in surprise than pain. Cotton could see she was unsure how to react next. This was how Cotton found out her name was MaryLynne and not just Marilyn. He calmed her down and showed her how to swivel her hands from a prayer position and then waggle the two middle fingers.

'Hi there.'

The woman was very drunk but looked happy enough. 'I'm JoBeth Barber,' she said.

'Peter Cotton.'

'Oh, I know.' She gave her glass a quick shake so that the ice cubes rattled. 'How come you're so good with children, Peter?'

'I was brought up in Mexico.'

She parted very red lips and showed very white teeth. 'What does *that* mean?'

'Children are welcome there. In Britain they're not.'

JoBeth frowned. JoBeth was almost as pretty as she was knowing.

'Are you saying we Americans are as cold as the British in that respect?'

'I don't know. I haven't been here long enough.'

'We're like the British, I guess,' she said. She stared at him. 'What are you? Six two, six three maybe?'

'No, I'm barely six one.'

She laughed. 'I'm sorry,' she said and laughed again. 'I've had just a little too much to drink. Are you and Sally—?'

'Eleanor – she's my elderly, distant relative by marriage next door – asked me to keep a neighbourly eye on her and take Susan to the beach. Eleanor said there were a lot of dogs about. I don't quite know what that means but—'

'She means unscrupulous men. Oh, they're around, I can tell you.' She put her free hand between her breasts. 'So you're just watching out for her, is that it?'

'It's not exactly a full-time position,' said Cotton.

JoBeth laughed. 'My. You know how to insinuate.'

Cotton moved his lips into a smile. JoBeth was very fashionably dressed, in a blue cotton summer dress with slightly built-up shoulders, a very low neckline, a cinched waist and full skirt. Her hair was considerably shorter than most of her friends, her lipstick a little thicker.

'Tell me who your husband is.'

She frowned. 'Who?' She shrugged. 'That's A. T. Cross over there.'

'The pen maker? What's his own name?'

'Eugene. He's senior. Junior is over there.'

Junior had been the pretend bear rather than the pigtail yanker.

'He's a good kid,' she said, 'but he's a slow reader.'

'They say Einstein and Picasso were slow too.'

She laughed. 'You really don't have to be gentlemanly, you know.'

'Oh yes, I do.'

She took a sip of her drink and licked her lips. 'Are you married, Peter?'

'Honestly?' said Cotton. 'No.'

She laughed again. 'Quite my least favourite month is August, Peter. It's far too hot. Clothes are almost *de trop*, don't you think?' She allowed a moment for his imagination. 'Summer's the American version of hell,' she said. 'I need to freshen my drink, Peter. Look, the ice is almost all gone.' She leant forward to show him, shaking the liquid and her cleavage. The flesh moved like some wonderful, weighty soufflé. 'I'm in the phone book. Mrs Eugene Barber, just a couple of gear shifts down Ocean Road.'

Cotton smiled politely. When she left, she was playing far less drunk than when she had arrived.

They had of course been seen and Sally Ingram made sure to bring him a slice of birthday cake.

'Was JoBeth bothering you?' The emphasis was all on the first part of 'bothering'.

'No. We talked about children.'

'Yeah?' Sally Ingram looked anxiously around. 'It's just that she has, well, something of a reputation, you know?'

'No, I don't,' he said. 'What's the reputation for?'

Sally dropped her voice. 'We say "fast".'

'Really? All I learnt was that Eugene Junior is not so good at reading. In other words, not fast but slow.'

Sally Ingram tilted her head and opened her eyes at him. 'You're a strange man,' she said.

'No, I'm not. I'm just half foreign and reasonably polite.'

She laughed. 'Half foreign! What's that?'

'We all speak English.'

'Ah! JoBeth said listening to you she could hear a different background music.'

'You see? She's really quite sensible.'

Sally Ingram appeared to be placated. Cotton hid his irritation. Spanish has the word *cursi*. It had once meant showy; had become prissy. He felt this exchange combined the two. It also occurred to him that a spell with JoBeth Barber without her clothes might do him a power of good, but instead of groaning, he managed to smile yet again.

After cake it was time for the clown.

219

The clown was a shy young man who evidently prac-
tised at being a magician but, for this job, had agreed
to put on a clown's outfit as well. Beneath the painted
smile, his lips twitched and sweat broke through the
grease paint where his moustache should have been. The
children were really too young for card tricks and he
made a mistake by using Susan as his subject rather than
as his helper. She did not like the laughter when he produced a coin from her ear and a thin flow of milk from
her outstretched arm.

The men, swaying comfortably by this time, watched
and commented on his abilities with the only real amusement they had shown all afternoon. They weren't entirely
cruel. Some remembered their own stumbling as young
men.

Cotton talked to the clown later. The boy was anxious
to explain that his rabbit had got diarrhoea 'at the last
moment. I couldn't take the chance, you know. I only
did this show because Mrs Ingram asked.' He showed
Cotton the rabbit in its box. It was white with red eyes.
He looked up. 'She's the kind of woman you want to
help, you know, being a widow and all.'

'You have a mild crush on her.'

The clown looked surprised. 'It's not so mild.'

'That's fine.'

'I let her down.'

Cotton shook his head. 'What's your name?'

'Patrick Carpenter, sir.'

Cotton called Susan. 'Hey. Patrick here has something
special for you. But it's only for you. You understand
that? Shh. Look in this box. What's that? A white rabbit!'

Susan frowned and looked up. 'Is this some kind of real secret?' she asked.

Cotton looked at Patrick Carpenter. 'Yes,' said Patrick. 'You see the rabbit wasn't feeling—'

'That he wanted to come out. He just wanted to see you,' said Cotton.

'OK,' said Susan doubtfully. She wrinkled her nose. 'He smells kinda funny.'

'It's the hay and the carrot he's eating. Shh. You keep the secret to yourself.'

'OK,' said Susan. She blinked. And then she ran off.

'I'm just not that good with children,' said the magician. 'My mom says I've forgotten what it was like.' Patrick Carpenter looked at Cotton. 'I'm due for call-up soon.'

'Good luck,' said Cotton.

'Right,' said Patrick Carpenter. 'What's military service like, sir?'

'Dull but demanding,' said Cotton. 'Leave the rabbit out of it.'

'I think she's bound for the pot, sir.'

That night Cotton woke about 3 a.m. He had been dreaming of weighing JoBeth's breasts. There was of course a lack of balance. He didn't know if he was blindfolded but that weight had to be adjusted by touch and a little pressure. Then he found himself shaking talcum powder on to the left breast and blowing very softly, as if on a burn.

16

ON MONDAY, 4 August Cotton received a stack of mail. There were letters from his father and sister – and one unexpected and rerouted from Dr G. S. Aforey. Cotton had met this distinguished sociologist in Washington DC in 1945. He was a professor at Howard University and had remarkably thick glasses, a taste for two-toned shoes and an old-fashioned, sometimes slightly off-key eloquence. The British had wanted him to provide a counterpoint to the Marxist Pan-African Conference in Manchester, England, but Dr Aforey had proved far less biddable than was hoped. Cotton liked him. While prone to sweeping, even grandiose formulations and a certain self-concern, Dr Aforey was also shy, stubbornly diffident and acutely conscious of being an African in the United States.

'In my confusion,' he had once written to Cotton, 'I try to be as decent as patience, humility and caution permit me. It is not a dashing or even very comfortable position but I hope it is careful of others and conforms to the precepts laid down by Our Lord.'

This letter was more to the point.

My dear Cotton,
I am under the distinct impression that you have

been posted to New York City to assist in the British part of setting up the United Nations Organization. My congratulations.

If this indeed be the case, I should be delighted to meet with you to discuss a certain pressing personal matter concerning my own arrangements with that soon to be august institution.

Bluntly put, I am not sure which part of the bacon to slice. I should therefore like to consult you on how to proceed in my quandary. I shall be in Manhattan from August 4 to August 18 and would deem it an honour to meet with you again, at your convenience, of course, during that time. Do let me know at the earliest.

If this finds you late, please feel free to telegraph me. I shall be lodging with an Abyssinian Baptist friend, the Reverend Taylor Caswell, at Number 203 W136th Street but can, of course, sally forth into other parts of the metropolis.

May I suggest the Museum of Modern Art as our venue, since it constitutes the epitome of the liberal arts and provides a suitably decorous meeting place for two persons of different races.

Hoping this finds you well in body and spirit, I remain, sir,

Your old friend
Aforey

There was also, British fashion, as in a schoolbook, a private publication of the British employees in the Consulate and the Rockefeller Center office. He opened

it and found himself listed, with his education, military service and London address. There was also an entry for Hornby. Cotton already knew Hornby had less rank than he did. Now he saw he was some years older. He thought it was interesting in itself that his employers had not sent someone more imposing to see him in the Ogden Clinic.

Then, just above his own name in the alphabetical list, he saw the name Butterworth, Herbert Ashley Roland. Herbert Butterworth had been the archivist in the Chancery in Washington, the person to go to if you wanted information of just about any kind, from the producer's name of an old film to the implications of a recent treaty. Cotton did not know why Herbert had moved to New York and had certainly not known he had an MSc in physics from Imperial College.

Cotton sent him a note about Dr Aforey and Herbert got back at once. 'Your friend has been offered a rather highly paid job. It is not yet quite clear whether he will work in the Area of Development or Decolonization. If I remember, you were rather complimentary about Dr Aforey. The UN is anxious to acquire staff from nations other than the powerful. They want other kinds of power – moral, for example – to allow them at least the look of representing the entire world and its concerns.'

On Thursday Cotton telegraphed Dr Aforey suggesting they meet at 3 p.m. on 12 August at MoMA. He also asked to see Herbert Butterworth at five the same day, and made an appointment to see Dr Sanford the morning after.

224

On the Friday he received replies and purchased his return ticket to New York.

On Tuesday, 12 August Cotton took the train for the short, leafy distance from Narragansett to Kingston, and from there, a larger, faster, sleeker train to New York. He had a slight tilting problem but then understood that it was due to the train rather than him. He found the rush and tremor invigorating. It felt good to get out of Narragansett, to be on the move again.

Cotton had been in Penn Station before. He strode across the marble concourse, but outside he paused, closed his eyes and breathed in. Somebody bumped into him. There was no apology, only a grunt of complaint. Cotton smiled and moved forward to get a cab. He had already seen more people in a few minutes than he had seen in Narragansett in more than a month – including those on the beaches.

From Penn Station he went to his bank. There he withdrew cash to meet his expenses for the rest of the month and for the hotel that night. He checked in at the Waldorf, ate a club sandwich, freshened up and walked the three blocks to the Museum of Modern Art on West 53rd Street.

Dr Aforey was wearing a double-breasted blue suit, a grey homburg and brown and white shoes. He smiled delightedly when Cotton appeared and pointed at him.

'You are looking, if I may say so,' said Dr Aforey, 'a little peaky. You appear to have lost some weight. Or have I built you up in memory, sir?'

'I've lost a little weight,' said Cotton.

'I hope it was not out of illness or vanity, my friend.'

Cotton smiled and shook his head. 'And how are you, sir?'

'Oh. I suppose I am really in no position whatsoever to complain.' Dr Aforey looked up. 'I thought we might consider Vincent Van Gogh's rendition of a starry night sky. Would you be agreeable to that suggestion?'

'Of course,' said Cotton. 'What is it you want to speak to me about?'

Dr Aforey was not tall and Cotton had to stoop to hear his whisper. 'I have, in the most discreet manner imaginable, received the formal offer of a rather high position at the United Nations Organization.'

'Then congratulations,' said Cotton.

'Let us not be too hasty, my friend. I have some doubts as to whether or not I should take up this post. At one level I can appreciate it does credit not only to my own person and career but to my homeland as well. In addition, if I may speak in more mundane terms, the salary and pension arrangements offered are in no way to be sneezed at.'

'What's the problem, then?'

'As you know, I am a scholar. I am not a worldly man. I am not a politician. And I am not at all enamoured of administrative tasks and matters of that ilk.'

'They have plenty of politicians and administrators already,' said Cotton. 'They need other talents, I assure you.'

'Yes, but I also worry that they are, as it were, making me into a mere representative.'

'Of what?'

'A black face, sir, with a doctorate.'

Cotton nodded. 'You don't want to appear a token.'

'You identify my problem exactly.'

'But at this stage, Doctor, isn't that just about everybody's fear? The Secretary General himself knows he's there as a compromise choice and on sufferance. You are really being offered an opportunity to make a mark. You don't think it's unrealistic to expect more at this stage?'

'Oh,' said Dr Aforey. He frowned. 'I do hope you are not suggesting that this new organization will be as ineffective as the League of Nations. That was a mere, mealy-mouthed talking shop, a political eunuch by any other name.'

'Well no, it certainly won't be the same. It will be larger and it will be here in New York. It will also have more agencies to deal with specifics like refugee relief, education, health ... What would be your field of interest?'

'Development,' said Dr Aforey. 'The shift away from traditional societies to those that will have a better chance in the modern world. The problem, as I see it, is that everyone is far too keen to start helter-skelter on whole-scale industrialization in the most unsuitable places. They are looking for quick, even grandiose, solutions that are more suitable to political arrogance and fine photographs than to what is truly needed.'

They were now in front of Van Gogh's famous painting. Dr Aforey gave it a few seconds and then shook his head.

He turned away from the painting. 'Am I right – Van Gogh was something of a mad man? Is there something you wish to see?'

'I believe there's a famous Picasso called *Les Demoiselles d'Avignon* in the museum,' said Cotton.

'Then we shall go there. Let us point ourselves in that direction.'

As they walked, Dr Aforey sighed again. 'You are an economist, my friend. I am not. I mean, what is this thing "the invisible hand" people have started going on about? I hear the phrase everywhere, even at dinner parties. I spoke to a banker in Washington and he sounded quasi-religious about it. '

'Ah,' said Cotton. 'I think Adam Smith's capacious eighteenth-century irony got lost some time ago. I'm not sure your banker's attitude was exactly spiritual, but there may have been elements of hope and faith in his enthusiasm.'

'But are you calling the invisible hand mere juju?'

'I'm suggesting that people tend to use certain texts as lay bibles. Adam Smith's *Wealth of Nations* is one. People refer to it to give weight to their own interpretations and to counterbalance Karl Marx. But most people don't bother to read it. As a result, Smith has had a lot of interpreters. People have started to cite the "invisible hand" to justify their own views, but I can assure you, Adam Smith himself never used the term *laissez-faire*, for example; he certainly never said anything about free markets being self-regulating, and did not mention the "invisible hand" in the context of markets in the first place.'

'Very well. What is your advice in this regard?'

Cotton shrugged. 'Keep away from invisible hands, Dr Aforey. In the banker's case, his self-interest would

be in the money he'd make with less supervision. In a communist's case, the term is used to show up the "pusillanimous superstitions" of capitalists. Smith used it for what we now call hunter-gatherers.'

'Excellent. Then let me try something. Which of your colonies, Colonel, has a tax base large enough to fund grand schemes for progress and employment or pay the interest on the loans required to build them? Is that not a recipe for corruption and neo-colonialism?'

'Dr Aforey, forgive me. Surely these considerations are exactly why you have been offered the job.'

Dr Aforey frowned. 'It is of the very greatest importance that my work be effective, you know. I am determined it shall be.'

Cotton nodded. 'Of course,' he said. Aforey looked up at him.

'The salary would even allow me to marry,' he said.

Cotton was truly surprised. 'Really?' he said. 'Then my congratulations again, sir. Are you talking of an American lady?'

Dr Aforey looked even more surprised. 'I do not follow you,' he said. 'I was talking of the principle only.'

'I see! You mean you could marry should you wish?'

Dr Aforey frowned. 'In any case, I would not marry an American woman. I am not a believer in romantic attachments, Colonel. They are not a good basis for a properly blessed marriage. Romance does not wash socks, you know.'

Cotton smiled. 'I suppose not.'

'And I am not getting any younger,' said Dr Aforey, 'or less set in my ways.'

'I understand.'

'I have another problem. If I take this post, where shall I live?'

'Somewhere convenient surely for Lake Success,' said Cotton.

Dr Aforey did not look comforted.

'I am talking of race here,' he said. 'I am accustomed to race relations in DC. Here I am more at a loss. Presently I am lodging in Harlem, you know. It is a very strange place. And very small. Oh, this painting is very big.'

Cotton understood what Dr Aforey meant. There were far more Negroes proportionally in Washington than in Manhattan. They had arrived in front of Picasso's *Les Demoiselles d'Avignon*. They stood for a moment. There were five female figures in the painting, the two to the right with faces like distorted masks.

'On the whole I do not approve of modern art,' said Dr Aforey. 'This man Picasso is something of a show-off, don't you think?'

Cotton smiled. 'Only incidentally.'

Dr Aforey put a hand on Cotton's forearm. 'My friend,' he said and giggled. 'Have you heard of this writer fellow, Richard Wright?'

'He wrote *Uncle Tom's Children?*'

'That is he. He lives in Greenwich Village, you know. He is married for the second time to another white woman, a Jewess from the Bronx. Their relationship and their children receive sufficient public disapproval from taxi drivers, shopkeepers and neighbours for Mr Wright to have decided to move – to Paris.' Dr Aforey

looked up. 'What worries me is that American Negroes romanticize Africa. As if they had been plucked from a land of milk and honey to toil for American pharaohs.'

'You said Mr Williams is going to Paris?'

'Oh, Paris is just a would-be rational stepping-stone, I assure you. My own countrymen call me a "been to" – because I have been to places, you know, and most of them have not. It is not a compliment. Imagine what they will call Mr Wright, an American-born Negro eager to see the land that saw his forebears enslaved. They will view him as I view admirers of Picasso's work. They will see him as gullible.'

'I don't know,' said Cotton, 'but I read that in this painting Picasso is blowing up some old masters and challenging what could be termed a Renaissance view of perspective. I think this is the energetic beginning of what came to be called cubism rather than any real approximation to Africa. Some think of it as a kind of anti-imperialism.'

Dr Aforey looked suitably sheepish.

'Oh, but I have to confess, Colonel, I have another, more personal doubt that gnaws at my vitals. It is not to my credit; indeed, it makes me something of a sinner. I would not describe it as envy exactly, but I am certainly guilty of fearing invidious comparison. That is something that gives me pause, and causes me more agitation than I want to admit.'

'You're talking about another person?'

'I am indeed, Colonel. A colleague at Howard University and presently, I am sure, very hard at work in the United Nations. He is a very considerable talent and

231

dashed good-looking. But we have profound disagreements, you see.'

'Are you talking of Dr Ralph Bunche?'

'I am. He is an American Negro, but he was in charge of Colonial Affairs for the old Office of Strategic Services until 1943.'

Cotton nodded. 'But you're not saying that because he is American, he was somehow unfit? Just a representative black face?'

Dr Aforey winced. 'Oh, do not misunderstand, I beg you. But I fear a curiously ingratiating, even gung-ho element in him. He has a considerable degree of glamour but also a considerable bent for flashy words and compromise that makes me most uncomfortable.'

'There are lots of ambitious white people like that,' said Cotton. 'Nobody is going to confuse you with him.'

Dr Aforey scrunched up his face. 'At root, you see, I really do doubt his powers of deduction and analysis. Did you know he has suggested class will one day supplant race in world affairs? It makes me think he understands neither concept. It is the kind of smooth political chit-chat that an academic finds meaningless but journalists applaud as somehow profound.'

They had stopped at the museum's latest acquisitions – a trio of paintings by Juan Gris.

Dr Aforey sniffed. 'Would these be fully cubist?'

Cotton laughed.

'I do not know what it is,' said Dr Aforey, 'but this cubism seems to me something of a one-trick pony. Wouldn't you say?'

Cotton, on the other hand, was pleased. The blue in the left-hand painting seemed to him particularly impressive, because he realized that he was now able to register even small shifts in the colour.

Cotton smiled. 'Tell me. What have you been doing in Washington?'

Dr Aforey blinked. 'Oh,' he said. 'My duties. But there have been some nefarious doings in many other fields.'

'Such as?'

'Jim Crow regulations, shabby zoning laws and the like,' said Dr Aforey. 'But I have also been involved in this report the Truman Administration is preparing on rights for Negroes. On the face of it, it is an act of innocence but it also has a certain worldliness to it. The Administration will not of course pursue the recommendations with any fervour but they will be there and they establish precedents for the future.' He looked up. 'In a way, I view my work there as preparatory to the United Nations. This Human Rights business will be the successor to the American Constitution. It is an ideal towards which nations and people can aspire. Does that make sense to you?'

Cotton nodded. 'I don't see why not. It's certainly a more effective method than trusting to an "invisible hand".'

Dr Aforey grinned, and wagged a finger. 'You English realists have no power any more. You are like the boy on the bicycle. No hands, hoping your knees will save what teeth remain to you.' He looked up and smiled again. 'And what can I do for you in return, my friend?'

Cotton nodded. 'I'd be interested in anything you can find about drug experimentation on unwitting people.'

'Ah,' said Dr Aforey. 'I have no doubts at all that it is happening. I recall a case of Negro mental patients undergoing all kinds of outrage. But I will make further enquiries for you, my friend.'

'Thank you.'

At the door to MoMA, just before they shook hands, Dr Aforey asked Cotton directly, 'Do you advise me to accept the offer from the United Nations?'

'I don't know the terms of the contract, Dr Aforey – how long it is for and so on. But the job would provide you with an opportunity at almost the very start before things become truly set in bureaucratic cement. You would be able to talk to those of the highest level involved in dismantling the colonies and influence the debate on development. In your shoes, I'd find it very tempting.'

'Thank you, my friend. I shall consider what you say. I permit myself the hope that we may meet again before too long.'

17

A T 5 p.m. Cotton met Herbert Butterworth, ex-archivist at the British Embassy in Washington, at an agreed place on West 50th Street. Herbert was rather short, very plump of body, but had somehow retained an almost trim thinness of face and neck that, particularly behind a desk, and given his narrow sloping shoulders, was utterly misleading. He was pear-shaped, had one of those bellies that came out under the middle button of his jacket, and very stout legs. Under his hat he had a lot of straw-coloured hair and whenever he scratched his head, which was often, strands of the stuff would stick out. Cotton was not sure he'd ever seen Herbert walk before. He did so with a quick, short, somehow busy-looking step, but they did not have to go far until Herbert found the place he was looking for, an air-conditioned cocktail lounge with a pianist. Herbert was breathing quite heavily.

'This has become my local,' he said. 'I come in here before I go home. A drink and some olives allow me to regain my composure before facing the children. Mine's a gin and French.'

Cotton ordered. 'Do you miss Washington?'

'I much prefer the anonymity here. And of course the theatre's better.'

Cotton smiled. 'I thought you'd be in DC forever.'

Herbert laughed. 'Like a fixture? No, no. Besides, the job here is a tad more interesting.'

'Is it a secret?'

'Of course not. I'm here in charge of listening,' said Herbert. '"Communications security" is the phrase. We're having rather a wrangle about special-purpose machines – that began with something called "bombes", by the way, and went on to "busy beavers" and so on.'

'You're in favour?'

'Oh yes.'

'What do these bombes and busy beavers do?'

'They're basically very good at arithmetic. Add in some algebra and you get something rather quick and thorough and with lots of applications in our line of work.'

'Are you going to get them?'

'I very much doubt it,' said Herbert cheerfully.

'Too expensive?' said Cotton.

'Oh, for pity's sake we're British,' said Herbert. 'Never awfully fond of stuff that's hard to understand so we talk of pragmatism. What Eve calls, with some accuracy, mince.' Cotton knew Eve was Herbert's wife but had never met her. Herbert shook his head. 'One of Churchill's last mistakes was to treat our bombes and busy beavers as if they were the devil's work. Frightened not just of mathematics but of numbers, you see. Cheers.'

'Is the stuff hard to understand?'

'You've obviously never had to explain binary theory to Members of Parliament.'

'They'd be worried about breaking information into

two digits, one of which is zero, and presumably by the word "bombe". I imagine the word "beaver" might also cause them discomfort.'

Herbert smiled. 'Yes. Are you interested?'

Cotton shrugged. 'I'll be back to work in September.'

'All right,' said Herbert. He popped an olive into his mouth. 'Aren't you going to ask me about Ayrtoun?'

'I thought he was in Canada.'

'Who told you that?'

'A very rich old lady I met in Washington. A Mrs Duquesne of Dupont Circle. She wrote me a letter.'

'Such security, eh? Actually, he has just spent three months in the States, at Duke University. That's in Durham, North Carolina. I think he's back in Canada now. Seems to move between Toronto and Ottawa.'

'What are we talking about?'

'Apparently trying to cure his depression.'

'Caused by the death of his wife?'

'Yes. My theory is that people like Ayrtoun hate the idea that they can't control things. An alcoholic wife is quite a test in that regard. You must have met her.'

'I did. We exchanged a few words but not a great deal of communication. I did get to carry her once.'

'Quite,' said Herbert. 'Ayrtoun has embarked, entirely by choice, on a gruesome regime of drugs and electric shocks.'

'He's offered himself up as laboratory rat?'

'Well . . . there's no shortage of doctors eager to accept his offer. The man at Duke is British, you know, fellow called William Sargant. His speciality is narcosis and abreaction.'

Dr Sanford had mentioned these in the Ogden Clinic along with cerebral lavage.

'That's still sedation and shocks.'

'Yes.'

'I thought it was for traumas.'

'Sargant would have no difficulty in accepting a dead wife as a trauma.'

Herbert was eating all the olives. Cotton was not sure why, but he couldn't bear the smell of them.

'Do you believe it?' he asked.

'What do you mean?'

'I never had the impression Ayrtoun felt much guilt about anything at all.'

Herbert shook his head. 'It's not about guilt, it's about control. Ayrtoun got a dreadful initial shock, you see. When she died he found he couldn't function. He tried to speak but something had happened. He couldn't produce any words.'

'As if he'd had a stroke?'

'He was checked. After about a day or so he contrived to come up with the idea of electric shocks. All on his own. He said or rather wrote down that he'd had them before, in the thirties when he had become depressed after his marriage, and that they provided considerable relief.'

'Was he sacked?'

'What? Oh no. He resigned, insisting he was no longer fit for purpose and we should look immediately for a replacement. He went off for his electric shocks as if he was going on an afterlife sort of holiday.'

Cotton frowned. 'Are you suggesting he's become

some sort of connoisseur or addict of electric shock therapy?'

Herbert laughed. 'I have to say that occurred to me as well. Particularly when the man at Duke added barbiturates and kept him in a sort of sleep, enlivened of course by jolts of electricity.'

'Christ,' said Cotton. 'Have you seen him since?'

'No,' said Herbert. 'Eve and I did have an entertaining evening once wondering about their marriage, though. You met Penelope Ayrtoun, you said. What was your impression?'

Cotton shrugged. 'What the Americans call a lush. By the time I met her she was alcoholic thin and not really a clear talker. I once had to collect her when she had passed out and take her home. And at a dinner I went to she retired very early. What was her background? He seemed rather proud that she was a Lady.'

'Really?' Herbert shrugged. 'She was the daughter of an Irish lord she claimed had fiddled with her when young. She managed to kick a cocaine habit when she was about twenty but that was the limit of her life's endeavours. I don't think anyone ever worked out why she accepted Ayrtoun's proposal of marriage. She may have seen something briefly out of the corner of her eye. And she probably wanted to get abroad.'

'They had no children?'

'That would have been tricky. She wasn't, I have it on good authority, the least bit keen on that side of things. But she was exceptional at sucking on a bottle neck, if you know what I mean.'

'Great,' said Cotton.

'What's the matter?'

It had just occurred to Cotton that he had been holding off considering the American suggestion that a man so keen on electric shocks might somehow have suggested him as a likely candidate for experiment, very likely to the Americans.

'I worked for him,' he said.

'Quite,' said Herbert. 'We all have to do that, if you know what I mean.' He smiled. 'I don't think the story of their marriage would be permitted in print, but then I remember my first job. My boss had an ostrich feather and cried when young men didn't laugh when he tickled them. He's still with us. Rather high up, you know.'

'Can you tell me who, on our side, knows of my case?'

'Oh, really not many at all,' said Herbert.

'And are they all within the department here?'

Herbert smiled. 'Well, it's summer; the politicians are on holiday and might get upset to think that an ally was treating one of our own this way.'

Cotton nodded. June, which is when he was taken, did not strike him as being quite summer.

'Thanks, Herbert.'

Herbert glanced at his watch. 'Oh, I could provide a few more minutes. One of our children is hell at bedtime.'

'OK. Would you like another drink?'

'Yes. Good man. This is the only place in New York I have found that does a decent gin and French.'

Cotton ordered. He smiled. 'Herbert,' he said, 'I know you're up on bombes and beavers. How are you on what Dr Sanford calls "truth drugs"?'

'I know bugger all, really. I'd call that an American thing as yet.'

'What do you mean?'

'Well, they're not going to let all that German science go to waste, are they? I mean, they've got the V2 people here. And drugs would be science, wouldn't they?'

'I suppose so.'

Herbert's second drink arrived. 'Lovely,' he said.

'Good,' said Cotton. 'I'm really interested in who, amongst the American agencies, has the lead role on these so-called truth drugs.'

Herbert looked surprised. 'Oh, that's easy. That's always the Navy Department. I know they've recently given the green light to something called Operation or Project Chatter to test the effectiveness of drugs for interrogations. Not, I have to say, that they've done awfully well so far. Apparently they got two volunteers to take a mix of scopolamine and mescaline and the results were disastrous.'

Cotton nodded. Herbert was frequently called 'an absolute sweetie'. Cotton was quite aware that sweeties in Intelligence did not exist and thought it was not by chance that Herbert was identifying two of the drugs Cotton had experienced himself.

'What does "disastrous" mean here?'

Herbert popped the last olive into his mouth. 'Ehm . . . I don't think either volunteer has, as it were, come out on the other side.'

'They're fucked?'

'Oh, totally. But Americans are never daunted. They have been, I think the phrase is, "widening their sample".'

'I see. Thanks,' said Cotton.

'Good. We seem to be a bit short of olives, old man.'

Cotton smiled and signalled to the waiter to bring more olives. 'Was it you who got me sent to the Ogden Clinic, Herbert?'

'I was on duty. As soon as I learnt they had left you your wallet and keys, I thought we'd better get you somewhere discreet and good as fast as we could. You're not really believing this, are you?'

'What do you mean?'

'I suppose your own side letting you hang to this extent.'

'No,' said Cotton wryly. 'I got that.'

'Yes, it's a bit of a bugger,' said Herbert. 'It's difficult to know what to do and perhaps inadvisable to do anything. Are you going to want us to make a formal complaint?'

'Absolutely not.'

Herbert nodded. 'I see that. But Hornby has suggested that if we don't, the Americans may think you have something to hide.'

'Did they send a bill for my treatment in the Ogden Clinic?'

'No. Well, not so far.'

'Thanks, Herbert,' said Cotton.

'For what?'

'Getting me to the clinic.'

'I thought that would be safest. Let's be honest, I also wanted to see if the Americans would cooperate. We knew it wasn't us. We had nothing on the Soviets. After

some initial confusion, the American response was very quick. An allied veteran would go to their top clinic.'

'Right. Did you see me?'

'No. Hornby did. Dr Sanford wasn't then prepared to commit himself as to whether or not you'd survive. After three days he said you would but he didn't know in what mental condition.'

Cotton nodded. 'Yes. Of course.' He looked up. 'I have an additional problem now,' he said.

'What's that?'

'I'm being watched.'

'Not by us.'

'By someone amongst our many American allies. Not the FBI.'

'There are other agencies. But why would they do that?'

'I don't really know. Presumably because they don't know what longer-term effect the drugs may have. Do I remember something that might compromise someone? Am I in my right mind? Am I really "loyal" to the Americans? The HUAC people who came to see me in the clinic of course asked me about my meetings with the Russians.' He shrugged.

Herbert smiled. 'I say,' he said. 'That's quite exciting.'

'It's why I am talking to you, Herbert.'

'I listen, Peter. That's what I do.'

'Yes, but you also record and remember, surely.'

'Very selectively, I assure you. Or to put it another way, there's an element of convenience and survival involved. Certainly as concerns your case. Survival is

personal, as I am sure you understand.' He paused. 'Right now the main reason I'm not on holiday is because of our economic crisis and upcoming Indian independence. We emphasize Indian freedom to the Americans. Potentially millions are going to suffer, but we are here in August to ensure the local press glaze over and have another ice cream in the meantime.'

'So you're speaking as well as listening,' said Cotton. He raised his glass to drink and almost didn't. What was that phrase – someone walking on your grave? He had been very lucky it was Herbert on duty. He remembered to drink a little.

'Don't worry,' he said. 'I'm just keeping you up to date, Herbert. Here, have another olive.'

Herbert took one.

'An American suggested to me that Ayrtoun might be involved.'

Herbert looked doubtful. 'It may simply be that he said you were psychologically robust at some stage and someone kept that in mind when they were looking for suitable, unwitting candidates to test.'

Cotton nodded. 'Would Ayrtoun be in a condition to answer questions now anyway?'

'Haven't the foggiest,' said Herbert. He paused. 'How are you actually feeling?'

'It's taken me a long time to get the right word to describe it. But I think it's "addled".'

Herbert laughed again. 'Do you know the etymology of the word? No? Applied to an egg, it is a mistranslation. The Greeks were saying "wind egg" but the Romans got it wrong and said "urine egg" and we northerners

have followed the Romans. Rather apt for what happened to you, don't you think?'

'Well, if you know who thought it a good idea to get me addled with drugs like scopolamine and mescaline, just tell me.'

'Oh, I can't know that,' said Herbert. 'But I am pretty sure you will. I'd suggest a little bombe or busy beaver work.'

'Logic? Mathematics? But without the machine?'

'It'll be in there, in your head.'

Cotton thought for a moment. 'Not if I've been pass the parcel.'

'Meaning?'

'Let's say Ayrtoun said I was irritatingly self-sufficient to X. X was then contacted by Y and asked for a stable Brit but not given the reason why he was being asked. Y may not have known but passed my name to Z. And so on.'

Herbert smiled. 'I see what you mean. But I think you'll find the trail will be there to follow. I also suspect, without being one hundred per cent confident, that you won't find it as complicated as your X, Y, Z suggestion. You do a little addition; you do a little subtraction . . .'

'Do you think so?'

'I do. And I think you're underestimating how casual and mean people can be. Besides, according to you, whoever instigated this is having you watched. They're available, if you see what I mean.'

Cotton scratched a sudden itch at his neck to the right of his Adam's apple over the carotid artery. He frowned. 'I can't think, offhand, of any American I might have

really offended.' But as soon as he said that he thought of Ed Lowell. He had met Lowell some months before at the Connaught Hotel in Carlos Place in London and had an impression of someone whose Anglophilia had soured. Lowell was very tall, extremely rich, decidedly mannered. He had wanted Cotton to 'liaise' with him by keeping him updated with information on British people who might be considered security risks, Cotton had tried and largely succeeded in not providing the kind of service Lowell wanted. He imagined Lowell would have found that extremely irritating. Perhaps Hoberman was right. This was not so much about stupidity as about power.

'I don't think,' said Herbert, 'you had to seriously offend anyone at all. You're more likely to have been a candidate on a list in a dingy office somewhere. Our lot are a little anxious that what happened to you might be indicative of American attitudes towards us, maybe even a warning, probably contempt.'

'I understand that,' said Cotton. 'Do you know Ed Lowell?'

'Who?' said Herbert. 'Oh, yes. Very cold roast. I'd imagine he's on holiday now. His family have rather a grand Tudor Revival place on Ruggles Avenue.'

'I have no idea where that is.'

Herbert blinked. 'In Newport, old boy. In Rhode Island. Large numbers of the American Administration summer there.'

'Right. Lowell was a Navy man, wasn't he?' said Cotton.

'Yes.' Herbert paused. 'He was. But not, I imagine, often at sea these days.'

Cotton thought for a moment. Lowell might not be directly involved with Project Chatter, but, given that he was part of the operation for tightening security, it was likely that he was close to those who were.

Herbert looked at his watch and stood up. 'I think Florence might have calmed down by now.'

Cotton smiled but something had distracted Herbert's attention over by the door and he suddenly looked alarmed.

'Oh Christ,' said Herbert. 'I've left this too late. I, or rather my wife, organized what the Americans call a blind date for you. A young woman has just come in, just a little bit too early. So either you take her to dinner or I'll have some explaining to do. We thought you'd probably like some company and I understand this young Spanish speaker is on for that. We've told her you're a gentleman, by the way. I hate to spring this on you but Eve is not going to be happy if I'm not home soon to say I've seen you both off on a date.'

Cotton stared at him. 'You say Spanish—?'

'She's South American. From Argentina, where we rather let down her father.'

'Have you left me with any choice, Herbert?'

'I rather hope not. She's coming over.'

Cotton cleared his throat, got up and turned. For the first time in his life, he was hit by an acutely uncomfortable mix of attraction and paranoia. The attraction was because the girl was unbelievably good-looking. The paranoia was because Cotton knew very well he wasn't seeing her accurately. He couldn't find a word to describe her. His confusion must have shown.

'*¿Está usted bien?* Are you all right?' she said in a husky, kind voice.

'*Muy bien señorita.*' He smiled.

'*Don Pedro?*' she said.

'*Sí.*'

'*María de los Angeles Vergara Fratelli.*'

'Peter Cotton. *Mucho gusto*,' said Cotton and continued in Spanish. 'I hope you're hungry. Where would you like to eat?'

'I know a place,' she said. 'It's nearby. Though if you want something more – exotic, then perhaps the Village would be better.'

'No,' said Cotton, 'I am entirely in your hands. I don't know New York. I spent the afternoon at MoMA and that's all.'

The girl looked cheered. 'One thing,' she said, stretching out her hand towards his forearm. 'People here don't like us speaking in Castilian.'

He saw the girl's hand was shaking with nerves. That made him relax a little. She had an emerald ring on what Americans and British but not the Spanish think of as the wedding finger. 'All right,' he said in English. He shook hands with Herbert.

'Give my love to Eve,' said the girl. 'And to the children, of course.'

'We sometimes have a babysitting arrangement with Angeles,' said Herbert.

Cotton nodded. So Maria de los Angeles Vergara Fratelli was, at least according to Herbert's wife, Eve, almost family. There was a certain relief in this. He knew where he was. Then Herbert leant closer.

'Eve considers her to be a very precious refugee,' he said. Cotton blinked. The precious refugee babysitter from Argentina was wearing an outfit in silk that, even if she were an accomplished seamstress, bespoke couturier standards and enough money for expensive shoes. 'But I'm not sure Angeles agrees.'

Herbert waddled off looking like some cupid mole of blind dates.

'Ready?' said the girl.

Cotton was relieved to get outside. The heat was like hot, damp towels. He breathed in.

'It's really not far.'

Seven doors along, Angeles took him down some stairs and into a restaurant that was quiet and dark, with a certain circular theme to the booths and the ceiling.

'I was told you have no desire to be seen,' she said.

Cotton had always liked having his hair washed; he would close his eyes and have a small holiday. Listening to her was a little like that. The warmth and huskiness of her accented English took him back some years.

'Your Spanish has a Mexican touch,' she said.

'Born in Colombia, brought up in Mexico City.'

She smiled. In Cotton's experience, Argentines could be a little patronizing about other South American accents, rather regarded themselves as cosmopolitan Europeans in South America.

'I'm an undergraduate at Columbia University here. But it's so expensive,' she complained. She shook her head. 'Though that's not really the problem.'

'What is?'

She shrugged. 'I have no balls,' she said in Spanish. 'I really wanted to paint.'

Cotton nodded. 'Are you talking about a lack of confidence? Or the difficulty of making a living?'

She thought about this, then shrugged. 'No,' she said. 'I simply don't have the talent.'

'You're quite sure about that?'

She looked surprised. 'Oh yes! My brain sees far more than my hand can produce.' She shrugged. 'I should have studied psychology.'

'Really?'

'Yes. *Eso sí que es muy bonito.*' She meant psychology was, literally, a pretty or nice subject.

The waiter gave them the menus and she looked at hers.

'I'm stuck with art and that doesn't have many prospects,' she said. 'Though I've done a little restoration work. Just the first part. You take a little cotton wool and turpentine and rub as gently as you can. It refreshes the colours of the painting.'

'I see,' said Cotton. He was focusing on her make-up. It looked professionally applied. He realized he was looking for flaws, a lack of symmetry in her face.

Angeles suddenly looked up from the menu as if he were being extraordinarily understanding. She dismissed the starters, ordered filet mignon, rare. It was eight dollars fifty. Before the sommelier could speak she told Cotton the Nuits-Saint-Georges was excellent. The sommelier politely indicated the wine's place and price on the wine list. Cotton was impressed and wondered why on earth she should consider Columbia University so

expensive. Would they have anything to drink before the meal? Angeles said they would open the wine directly. Cotton tasted, Angeles drank. He had to order another bottle when she was halfway through her almost raw filet mignon.

'¿Y usted?' she said. 'What are you doing here?'

'Naciones Unidas,' he replied. 'I start in September.'

She put down her fork and looked at him. 'OK!' It was the first time she had sounded even vaguely North American. 'So you'll be sticking around.'

'That's the idea.'

'Have you found somewhere to live yet?'

'I'll be renting an apartment in September. By East 56th Street.'

Angeles nodded. 'The main thing here to bear in mind is that Americans don't like foreigners,' she said.

'Surely lots of Americans start as foreigners.'

Angeles frowned. 'No, no. I mean they lack all interest in other cultures.'

'It's because they don't have to bother. And the idea is immigrants adapt, isn't it?'

She sighed. 'It's so impersonal,' she said, 'and then it's very personal. Yo, por ejemplo, no agrado. I'm not attractive here.'

'Really?'

'Es que these people think I look like Lupe Vélez. Es totalmente absurdo. Quite crazy. What are they thinking? The fantasy here is brutal.'

Cotton nodded and sighed. Angeles struck him as good-looking – she even looked appetizing, much more so than the rather dry chicken he had been served – but

there was indeed only a very slight resemblance to what Cotton could remember of 'the Mexican spitfire' film star. If not asking for a compliment, Angeles was certainly always drawing attention to her appearance. Perhaps she was also talking of what the Americans called 'Latin looks'. Or maybe she objected to being taken for a Mexican. He suddenly remembered that Lupe Vélez had committed suicide a couple of years before.

'I assure you, you bear no resemblance whatsoever to Lupe Vélez.'

'You see? *Usted sabe*. You know. But these Americans don't really look. So they don't really see.' Angeles did not wait for the waiter. She poured more wine into her glass and frowned. 'I don't remember. I don't think Lupe was married to Gary Cooper. But she was, I think, married to Johnny Weissmuller.'

'Tarzan?'

'Exactly!' Angeles frowned. 'She divorced Tarzan, but then she killed herself because she was – well, you know. She couldn't bear the shame of being an unwed mother.'

Cotton closed his eyes briefly. Oh Herbert, he thought. 'Didn't we agree, you don't look anything like Lupe Vélez?' he said.

'That's true,' she admitted. 'But it's not about what we think. It's how people see us that counts. The Americans still see a resemblance and find it off-putting.'

Cotton tried again. Beyond her dark hair and her complexion, he could not see it. He shook his head. She was saying she was typecast, as if America was trying to be a movie and the Americans had limited her roles.

'Why did you leave Argentina? Was that something to do with your father?'

She blinked. 'He's dead. I'm never going back to Argentina. My mother's there.'

Cotton did not know what to make of this trio. 'I'm sorry. When did your father die?'

'*El Cabronazo*.' The big bastard.

'Perón?'

She nodded. She drank some more wine. 'My father shot himself,' she said. 'Two days after I got on a plane to come here. He gave me five hundred dollars and a kiss. I couldn't go back for the funeral.'

'I'm sorry.'

She blinked and shook her head. 'There's no need to be. He was a man,' she said.

Cotton was unsure whether or not it was just the wine making her sound like old Argentine movies.

'Don't mind me,' she said. 'I get bitter.'

Cotton shook his head. 'How long have you been here?'

'Since October 18, 1946.'

'That's not even a year. Give it time.'

'That's what I do, Peter! All the time,' she said. She frowned, sat back and looked around. '*Estos gringos son algo sositos.*'

Sosito means 'insipid', 'dreary'. Cotton followed her gaze. The restaurant was about half full. He did not think many of the other couples were married and the man at the table nearest them was considerably older than his companion.

'That's her uncle,' said Angeles in Spanish. She

narrowed her eyes judiciously. 'He's a pig. She's just his secretary. Her perfume is horrendous.' She smiled. '*Ay*. August is the cruellest month. The wives and children leave the men to sweat it out.' She laughed and switched to English. 'Do you dance, Peter?'

Cotton smiled. 'Do you want to dance?'

'Agreed.' She was beginning to translate from the Spanish. She swayed a little but then nodded confidently and confidingly. 'I know a place. But first, I don't like to miss dessert.'

Angeles ate a peaches and cream sundae and they drank coffee. He learnt she lived in the Upper West Side, that she had an elder brother in the Argentinian air force and that she had done some work for *ustedes*, meaning the British.

Cotton did not enquire, but she told him anyway. 'I was eighteen. There was a small sports car involved. Do you like cars, too? And there was an old gentleman.' She shrugged. 'It wasn't difficult.'

'May I ask how old you are now?'

'That's no problem. I'm twenty.' Cotton knew she was lying but not by how much. It even occurred to him that she was adding a year.

'*Usted paga*,' she said. '*Quiero bailar*.' You pay. I want to dance.

The bill was amply more than Cotton had ever paid in a restaurant. With tips, it was spectacularly over. It did occur to him that she might be on commission.

'You have money in reserve?' she said.

'Just a little,' Cotton said. She smiled, as if he had said something funny.

'It's not much to get in to the club, a dollar fifty maybe.'

Cotton translated this: ten gallons or a reasonably priced meal at Rocky Point. Again, the place she took him to was not far and down some stairs. A trio of piano, bass and drums was playing, the drummer with brushes. *Ticotico*. They were shown to a table.

'*Güisqui*,' she said. Cotton nodded.

'*¿No es chic?*' said the girl. 'I'll have one sip and then we'll dance.'

Cotton tasted his. He did not know what it was, but it wasn't whisky.

'Do you want more ice?' said Angeles.

'I really don't think it would help. Do you like these places?'

She laughed. 'You see too much. Relax.' She looked at her wristwatch. 'Soon they will play proper Latin.'

She was partly right. The trio was replaced by a quintet with ruffed sleeves but the Latin remained of the cocktail lounge kind, softened and smoothed down.

Cotton could not remember when he had last danced, nor did he recall dancing being quite so physically close. Though it was not a tango, she approached him almost from the side, her hips pressed hard against his right thigh. She was a much better or at least more decided dancer than he was, but was complimentary. Cotton shook his head. He had really begun to feel that he had been up since six. His shoulders and back were beginning to ache and he felt not so much footsore as dull and unresponsive. Against that, he was aware that physically she was extremely toned. She applauded

255

when the music finished. The band then started playing the carioca.

'No, no,' she said at once, 'I don't like this.' There was something of a pout there.

'All right.'

'Are you a gentleman?' she asked as they left the floor.

'Herbert told me I was. Why?'

She smiled. 'Gentlemen in New York don't send their dates home in a taxi.'

'I see. What do they do?'

'They accompany them!'

'Of course.'

She smiled forgivingly. 'You pay,' she said.

Cotton paid and she considered her face in the mirror of her compact.

As they went out up the stairs, she put her arm through his.

'Where are you staying?'

Cotton told her. 'I'm at the Waldorf.'

'OK.' She made a face but then shrugged. 'You may have to slip the porter something,' she said. 'But I'll help you. Is that clear?'

On the brief taxi ride she held his hand. Cotton found this rather touching, as if she did not want him to get away. Were they some sort of team? She behaved that way and he found he did not have to slip the porter anything after she had spoken to him very quietly. He definitely heard the words 'Mr Getty'.

'Who's Mr Getty?' he said in the elevator.

'The owner,' she replied. 'He's mostly oil. *Algo lúgubre.*' Rather lugubrious.

Angeles did not look at all impressed with his room.

'You should have taken a suite,' she said. 'They're better, more spacious.'

'I know. Can I get you anything?'

Angeles considered. 'Yes,' she decided. 'Have them send up some champagne.'

Cotton called room service. While they waited, Angeles looked in on the bathroom and then went to the window and looked out at Park Avenue and New York.

'This is where the world is now,' she said, 'and I have to adapt. I am good at adapting.'

Cotton said nothing. He watched her watching her reflection in the window. She was critical but finally very pleased. She turned. 'You should believe me.'

'All right.'

He poured her champagne when it arrived, and she tasted it.

'You see?' she said. 'It's not too sweet.'

She put down the glass and looked at him. Cotton was feeling not only tired but also dispirited.

'Hey,' she said. 'My underwear is quite as good as anything Dolores del Rio has made by nuns. Do you understand?' She turned her back to him. 'Unfasten me.'

Cotton was unsure why she should compare herself with a second Mexican-born film star whose underwear was presumably not seen in public, but it soon became clear that Maria de los Angeles Vergara Fratelli was wearing no underwear at all. He had said he was addled to Herbert. He should have said fuddled. Without taking off her shoes, she made sure to put her dress on a hanger.

257

'Do you like my shoes?' she said. 'I'm going to keep them on.'

He blinked.

'You make me feel short,' she said. 'I am only five foot three.'

'That's fine.'

She shook her head. 'No, it's not. All women want longer legs. You must know that.' She turned round till she was looking down at her very pert rear.

'*Pedro*!' she said. 'You have to concentrate.'

'You have a good scar on this leg,' she said later.

Cotton laughed. 'It's not pretty.'

'It's much better. Women like damaged men, but nicely damaged. And this is much more intimate than a scar on the face.'

She had a very winning smile. '*Quiero más*,' she said. Cotton remembered this was the Spanish translation of Oliver Twist's famous request for more.

18

WHEN COTTON woke the next morning, Maria de los Angeles Vergara Fratelli had gone but she had left a note. It read: *You are a good man and an absolutely marvellous lover. But I have to say it – ¡olvídame! A.* She had removed all the money from his wallet except enough for a taxi fare.

Despite the expense, Cotton smiled. The expression *olvídame* took him back to his time as a small child at school in Mexico, when it was used to mean 'go away'. But most of all he remembered it from the lachrymose melodramas popular at the time, when the hero or heroine would say 'forget me' in dramatic tones when about to sacrifice themselves to the vicissitudes of fate.

He also remembered back in the war when another officer on a course in 1942 had been asked why he was walking like that. David Durie had replied that he was 'privately sore after a fabulous weekend, sir'. Cotton knew something of how Lieutenant Durie had felt. He closed his eyes for moment. He felt relaxed, rather better than he had for some time.

Cotton made a call to his bank, showered and shaved, had breakfast in his room, dressed and took a taxi to the bank, withdrew more money, returned to the hotel and paid the bill. With the champagne it was nearly thirty

dollars. He did briefly try to calculate the mark-up on the room-service champagne, but settled on a memory of Maria de los Angeles instead. At one point she had used her emerald ring to score the full-length mirror with a capital *A*. She had done this at the lower right-hand corner. Rather than signing it, she had affixed her initial. Cotton smiled. She had left him with, as the Spanish say, 'an act of presence'.

Later that morning, at 11.15, Cotton had an appointment with Dr Sanford at his private consulting rooms on Park Avenue. On August Wednesdays Dr Sanford came in from the Hamptons. He was looking well and very tanned. He was wearing a white linen jacket and yet another bow tie.

'Most of the year I live upstairs,' he said. He smiled. 'How are you getting on, Colonel?'

'Not bad. Although almost everybody seems strange and uncontained,' said Cotton.

Dr Sanford nodded. 'Did you talk to Mr Butterworth?'

'I did. He fixed me up with a blind date.'

'How did that go?'

'You knew about this?'

'Yes,' said Dr Sanford. 'Was it a success?'

'It was very expensive,' said Cotton.

'Well, of course,' said Dr Sanford. 'I understand the young lady has very high-class tastes.'

'I had to go to the bank this morning.'

'It's not about money,' said Dr Sanford. 'May I ask an intimate question? Were you afflicted by any problems?'

'What kind of problems?'

'Impotence, for example.'

Cotton shook his head.

'And the other? A certain over-readiness?'

'No.'

Dr Sanford lowered his head to make a note then raised it, looking very pleased.

'Excellent,' he said.

'In what sense?'

'I don't know what Mr Butterworth told you.'

'He did mention that others who had been given sco-polamine and mescaline had experienced difficulties, though he did not mention any specific difficulties.'

'Yes. In every sense so far, you've been doing remark-ably well.'

'How remarkably?'

'Enough to help us, I assure you. I've written a report, you know, urging extreme caution in the use of these substances in any genuine clinical trials.'

Unimpressed – Dr Sanford's recommendation seemed little enough – Cotton cleared his throat. 'I have had spells of tunnel vision. Sometimes I see things that aren't there. I have had something like flash attacks when things and people turn repulsive. I have considerable dif-ficulty working out what people are saying or doing. It's as if they are melting. Their words lose shape and look liquid. The people sometimes look as if they are mumming or miming.'

'I'm sorry, Colonel. All these things have been recorded. I am not for a moment belittling your experi-ence. But I certainly can't say why you have managed a certain degree of resistance to the drugs. Mr Butterworth

may have told you of some men who, frankly, have lapsed into extended psychotic episodes.'

'He told me.'

'Colonel, you can be confident you have not had a breakdown.'

'Fine, but as I told the Un-American Activities people, I feel as if someone has tried to break me down.'

'I don't understand.'

'It's more personal and more external. As if I'd been picked out for particularly unpleasant treatment by someone I don't know. I suspect they don't particularly know me either.'

Dr Sanford nodded. 'Right,' he said. He made another note. 'I can't pretend this is pleasant or will help you resolve any feeling of utter betrayal. But you may want to take comfort in how you have turned out.'

'Really?'

'Shh,' said Dr Sanford. 'I can't be sure, of course, but I genuinely consider that after another spell in Narragansett you'll be – recovering yourself.' He shook his head. 'By Christmas this year I reckon you'll be pretty much back to normal.'

'I see,' said Cotton. 'Well, that's nice. Tell Mr Butterworth I want Maria de los Angeles on expenses. Full expenses, that is.'

'Colonel—'

'Just tell him. I simply don't have the kind of money that allows for a follow-up test on impotence. As to the quiet of Narragansett, I'm finding it's what Jane Austen called a "neighbourhood of spies". I think of it as furiously genteel. Next door I have a widow who appears to

have reverted to simpering adolescence. And I have an invitation from a lady further along Ocean Road to call in some time.'

'I don't think we need to bring Narragansett into this.'

'But that's where I'm going this afternoon.'

Dr Sanford frowned. 'All right. But may I urge discretion on you? Don't get too involved.'

Cotton sighed. 'No need,' he said. 'I understand.'

'Good!' said Dr Sanford. 'Have you been taking the pills I prescribed?'

'No,' said Cotton. 'The hallucinations have got less since I stopped.'

Dr Sanford looked briefly surprised. 'Right,' he said. 'That's impressive.'

'Is it?' said Cotton. 'I don't know.' He smiled. 'How are we doing, Doctor?'

'I don't think we are doing badly. I'm on call, of course. Do you have my number in the Hamptons?'

'No. But I'd prefer not to have it. Do you understand?'

'In which case we should fix up an appointment in September.'

'Of course,' said Cotton. 'My train's at one. I'd like to get some lunch before I get on it.'

'Of course,' said Dr Sanford. 'This is my card. I know what you said, but I'd prefer you to have it in any case.'

'Fair enough,' said Cotton. 'Thank you, Doctor.'

Dr Sanford shook his head. 'No need,' he said. 'Just one thing, though. If you're not going to take my prescriptions, make sure you get rid of the pills safely.'

'Understood,' said Cotton.

'What else is there troubling you, Colonel?'

'Apart from feeling dense, ungenerous, lacking trust in myself and a very stubborn sense of fatigue . . . I'm beginning to think I'm making excuses.'

'In what way?'

'I'm treating what happened to me as an excuse. It excuses me from respect for others. My problem is . . .'

Cotton remembered that he wanted to continue his break and wanted to return to work in September. He decided to borrow from Picasso and Dr Aforey.

'What?' said Dr Sanford.

'I see people as twisted, displaced within themselves but also disfigured. I'm not sure whether they're disgusting or pitiable, whether I'm punishing them in some way, or I just can't get hold of them.'

'Ah,' said Dr Sanford. He made a note. 'That's interesting. Can you tell me more?'

'I'm afraid it's an unpleasant form of self-pity. Maybe even of self-importance.'

'I'm sorry?'

'I mean, I may be disgusted by myself but I'm shifting it on to other people. I once saw one of my nephews drawing. He was unhappy with what he had done. So he almost attacked the figure he had drawn. Gave it huge ears, a massive nose, and then he scored the thing out, took another piece of paper and started again. It was as if the figure was to blame.'

Dr Sanford sighed. 'Thank you for being so honest.' He looked up and smiled. 'Oh, I could use you, Colonel.

Have you any idea how hard it is to get intelligence, self-awareness and the effects of drugs matched up?'

Cotton shook his head. 'I'm not so sure about that.'

'Let me reassure you, then,' said Dr Sanford. 'What you are experiencing is the continuation of what you woke up to in the Ogden Clinic. People often use the word 'heightened' when they talk of their experience with certain drugs. Let's say they mean a certain suggestibility or openness to the strangeness of the observable world. You are trying to come to terms with that.' The doctor paused. 'You were at Cambridge in England, is that right?'

'Yes.'

'The philosopher David Hume has that wonderful passage in his *Enquiry Concerning Human Understanding* in which he says we think our imaginations are unlimited when the reality is that we are startlingly good at combining very simple building blocks.'

Cotton said nothing. Dr Sanford seemed to be trying to relate to him. He did not remember the passage quite that way. 'You're sorting out your building blocks,' said Dr Sanford with some satisfaction. 'Tell me. When you say you "twist" people, what actually are you seeing?'

'It's a kind of visual smear. Sometimes I have the impression of two people or at least it's as if I'm using my thumb to displace and distort the first person. The second person underneath reduces to something pretty featureless and static and cold.'

'Wonderful,' said Dr Sanford.

Cotton nodded politely.

'You're going to be all right,' said Sanford. 'Do you

265

know why? You have resources of character and education.'

'I lied to my sister,' said Cotton, 'about what happened. I said I'd had a bad reaction to an anaesthetic and adrenalin when getting some stitches.'

'That's not too bad. But I suppose – you want continuity? Try telling her it was lidocaine hydrochloride. Some people react badly – well, enough for your purposes . . .'

'Thank you. I do have another question for you, Doctor,' said Cotton.

'All right. What is it?'

'When I was coming round in the Ogden Clinic I heard another voice. Later I think I saw the owner of that voice. A man called Bob Yeager. He was part of the HUAC visit with a Mr Eric Gaynes and a Navy man called Lockhart.'

'That is very good,' said Sanford. 'Excellent. I didn't think you were in a position to evaluate what was happening. As soon as you came in our Intelligence Services were in touch with me. I'm a doctor, Colonel, I'm not part of national security, but I know when my skills are – well, outranked.'

'He said "That's more like him", or something like that.'

'Mr Hornby was also there and I believe he had briefed Mr Yeager on the kind of person you were.'

Cotton smiled. 'Thanks,' he said. 'All right, Doctor. Give me a date in September.'

Dr Sanford did.

*

266

On the train back to Kingston, Rhode Island, Cotton wrote Herbert Butterworth a note.

Awfully sweet of you to fix me up with the redoubtable Srta A to see whether I had been unmanned or not. She left me just enough money for a taxi to the bank. I don't want to alarm you about the babysitting but there were times she struck me as not all there, at others all there but fairly crazy, and she has a curiously personal but entirely one-sided relationship with female film stars from Mexico.

Cotton put the note in an envelope to post later, then closed his eyes. There was a frizzy-haired young woman on the train, very small and thin, with callipers on her legs. Her problems were more than physical. Cotton knew she was going to Boston because she announced it almost immediately. Cotton looked up and saw she was not accompanied and was speaking to no one in particular. When the ticket inspector came round she spoke to him.

'I'm in a panic. I have got to get off at Boston. You'll tell me, won't you?'

'Yes, ma'am.'

'You don't understand. I can't go past Boston. My sister's meeting me.'

'I'll make sure, ma'am.'

'The ticket man noted down her seat number and the carriage and smiled at her.

But by Stamford the woman was in tears. 'I can't go

past Boston,' she said. 'I just can't. Will nobody help me?'

Another passenger tried to reassure her. But the woman in callipers was not listening. The next time the ticket inspector came round she went through the whole thing again. Cotton watched, impressed, as the inspector found an elastic band in his pocket and put it on her wrist. He then produced a pale blue label and attached it by string to the elastic band. He wrote *BOSTON* on the label.

'I'm not going to forget,' he said. 'And you can see I haven't forgotten when you look at the label. Right?'

The train trundled on. At Old Saybrook the woman got up, got hold of her crutches and wailed.

'I can't miss my station! Don't you see I need help? I can't handle my suitcase!'

The inspector appeared at a run. 'We're not there yet, ma'am. I'll tell you, I really will.'

The little woman refused to sit. 'I want to know that's not my sister on the platform.'

The inspector looked out of the window. 'No,' he said cheerfully. 'I know her. That's Dinah Shore. She gets this train every day.'

'I don't know her,' said the little woman. She was exhausted. She dropped into her seat. She did not sleep but sat there rocking to the movement of the train, any expression gone.

Cotton closed his eyes and allowed himself to be lulled by the sound of the train. Perhaps he should be grateful he had not been more seriously damaged. Then he thought back on Maria de los Angeles keeping

on her shoes in the Waldorf Hotel. Without meaning to, Cotton smiled.

When he next opened his eyes, the little woman across the aisle was frowning as if at something very difficult to understand. Cotton sat up and took off the Ray-Bans. He saw something else had been written on the label: *This lady should be accompanied at all times.*

His eyes were evidently very much better. And then Cotton suddenly remembered something from the passage from Hume that Dr Sanford had referred to: *To form monsters, and join incongruous shapes and appearances, costs the imagination no more trouble than to conceive the most natural and familiar objects.*

Cotton looked around the carriage. For the first time in months he felt a surge of confidence, almost delight.

At Kingston station he got off and posted the note to Herbert Butterworth. The heat was very humid. After the train had gone there were only insect sounds in the silence. As he waited for the connection to Narragansett, he wondered how David Hume – a fat man – would have got on in Rhode Island.

Cotton got back to Narragansett Pier at about 6.45 p.m. He did a little grocery shopping and drove back along Ocean Road.

'Thank God you're here!' said Eleanor.

Cotton said nothing. Eleanor had a dramatic side and he waited to see whether or not it was justified. He got his groceries out of the car.

'Aren't you going to ask me why?'

'Have there been more bears?'

'No! But Joe Samms has had the gall to ask Sally out!'

'What did she say?'

'She didn't know what to say!'

'Why not?'

'What is the matter with you?'

'Nothing as far as I know. Joe asked her out. She says yes or no. We're talking about Sally. She trained as a teacher but is not allowed to teach any more. Joe's got a small building company. And they both live in Narragansett. So it's down to whether they like one another. I don't think Joe is the kind of person to go into this lightly.'

'But Joe's not good enough for her,' said Eleanor. 'He's not an educated man.'

'I'm sorry, Eleanor. I haven't spoken to Sally that much but I have never had the impression she led the intellectual life. She's decent, she's kind, she's rather shy, and maybe Joe thought that because she's a war widow she'd be more understanding of his position as a vet who was wounded but who has a decent future to offer her.'

'Her husband was an officer. Joe wasn't.'

'Eleanor, I met officers who were absolute boobies.'

Eleanor was so surprised by this that she laughed. She frowned.

'Did you *encourage* him?'

'No. But I made sure he knew he wouldn't be treading on my toes.'

'You could've said!'

'No. Because having said that I was out of it, it wasn't my business, Eleanor.'

'She came to me!'

'I don't doubt it,' said Cotton. 'What did Sally say?'

'I think she said she'd think about it. I mean, she looked pretty shocked.'

'Well, let's see what she decides,' said Cotton.

Cotton went back to the guest-cottage, opened all the windows, showered and changed. He then made a pot of coffee, prepared some fruit and sat on the deck.

Around sunset at a quarter to eight he heard a rustle and a second or two later a whisper.

'Peter?'

'Good evening, Sally. Would you like some coffee?'

'No thanks.'

Cotton got up and offered Sally Ingram a chair. She sat.

'Is Susan asleep?'

'Yes. Did you have a good trip?'

'Just some things I had to clear up before I start work in September. New York is hotter than here.'

There was a pause. 'Did Eleanor tell you about Joe Samms?'

'She said something.'

'He asked me out.'

'What did you say?'

'I told him I needed time. To think, you know.'

'That's fair. You're a widow, you have a child, you have a lot to think about.'

'I suppose I do,' she said. 'Do you know him?'

'I only met him a little over a month ago but he looks like a good man. He works hard and he doesn't complain.'

'What do you mean?'

'He has a metal pin in one leg and quite a few reminders every day of what he did in the war. But he's adapted and he's thinking ahead. I admire him. He's practical and he's kind.'

'I don't really remember him,' she said.

'What does that mean?'

'At High School. I guess I knew he was there but he didn't make a big impression, you know?'

'I don't know, Sally. Are you saying he was shy?'

'Maybe.'

'Did he have a girlfriend then?'

'I don't know.'

'Well, if he did, you could talk to her. And if he didn't, well maybe he was very shy.'

'Are you saying he was interested in me then?'

'I don't know, Sally.'

'I hadn't thought of it like that.'

Cotton waited but she did not speak. He wondered if surprise and titillation weren't part of the initial shock of Joe's invitation and how long it would take her to appreciate how positive they could be.

He smiled. 'Come on, it depends on what you think of him, that's all.'

'I hadn't thought of him before,' she said.

'Well, you have a think and decide.'

'OK.'

There was quite a long pause.

'Would you babysit?' she asked.

Cotton raised his eyebrows; not, he thought, that she could see that in the dark.

'I mean that would keep things – kinda discreet.'

'I understand,' said Cotton. 'Yes, of course I'll babysit. You tell me when.'

'Friday? six p.m.?'

'Right,' said Cotton.

'That's when he suggested.'

'Good. I'll look forward to it then.'

He wasn't sure if the sound she made was a small, excited laugh. A moment or two later she fumbled around his head and he realized she may have been trying to kiss his cheek but settled for stroking it instead.

The next day at breakfast a delighted Joe Samms stopped off to see Cotton at the Ocean Café.

'She said yes.'

'Congratulations.'

'Did you know?'

'Last night she asked me to babysit.'

'She didn't tell me till this morning.'

'I think she wanted some discretion.'

'Here?'

Cotton smiled.

'She has some pretty snooty friends.'

'What are they snooty about exactly?'

Joe Samms blinked.

'This isn't Newport,' said Cotton. 'It's not society people here, is it?'

Joe Samms laughed. 'You mean like the Vanderbilts? Right!' He shook his head. 'But I guess the thing is, Narragansett is finer cut about less, if you know what I mean. Less money but they compensate with more

morals, you know. Amongst the people who stay through the winter.'

'Do you know Newport?'

'Way back we did a couple of repairs there but the rich can be kinda leisurely about paying, you know?'

'Exactly.'

'I don't follow.'

'How many friends have you got? Real friends, I mean. People who matter to you.'

'Three. Oh, maybe two. One died in the war.'

'Sally's probably the same. The rest are acquaintances, people you come into contact with for a while. Then you move on.'

Joe Samms looked doubtful. 'Not when you do business here.'

'Can you take on more work now?'

'Not really.' Joe Samms nodded a while. 'What does Mrs Ramsden say?'

Cotton lied. 'I don't know,' he said, 'but I could find out if you want. Does it matter? You should be thinking of where to take Sally.'

'I'm thinking the Dunes Club. It's kinda swank.'

'I don't know it.'

'I don't either, really. My dad's a member.'

When Joe had gone, the waitress came over to Cotton's table.

'He's kinda old and beaten up to be so nervous about a date.'

'She's a widow with a daughter.'

'Right. You brought the little girl here. Then he should go for nostalgia, you know, starting over.'

Cotton looked up. Carla looked at him as if what she was saying was obvious.

'He should go for lobster and walks on the beach, nothing too fancy.'

Cotton told Eleanor of his meeting with Joe. She agreed with the waitress.

'Not the Dunes,' she said. 'He should take her somewhere without swank. Like Aunt Carrie's in Galilee.'

'Does that mean you approve?'

'Does he care?'

'He mentioned you specially, Eleanor.'

'Did he now?' Eleanor looked slightly flustered. She leant forward and whispered. 'Do you know how he eats? With those knuckles of his?'

'I've seen him handle a hammer and nail and he's not bad with a cup of coffee. In a romantic novel he'd be described as adaptable and quick.'

Eleanor flushed. 'You're a terrible man, Peter Cotton.'

'Practical,' said Cotton. 'It would be good if we could get rid of the airs and graces, Eleanor.'

'You're getting to be quite the matchmaker. Except for yourself, of course.'

'I met a girl in New York,' said Cotton.

'You going to marry her?'

'No,' said Cotton. 'I think she'd be as expensive as she is good-looking.'

'Oh, one of those,' said Eleanor. She nodded. 'Sally's a good manager with what she has. She makes her own clothes, you know. You make sure Joe knows that.'

'All right. Are you on side, now?'

'Let's not take our fences too early.'
'But you're prepared to let them try?'
'OK.'
'Thanks, Eleanor.'

On Friday morning at breakfast he told Joe he should go for lobster and sea views.

'That's my impression, anyway. Smooth, calm and relaxed. Nothing too fancy.'

'Swank would be pressure?'

'I'm no expert, Joe, but something like that.'

'I don't want to underestimate her. I mean, she deserves a lot.'

'Maybe later. But I understand this is one step at a time.'

'Did she say this to you?'

'Not directly, Joe. I don't really know, but I'm getting the impression this is like old friends catching up and finding out a bit more about what's happened in the meantime and seeing how they've both changed. Does that make sense to you?'

Joe took some time to reply. 'Yeah,' he said finally. He nodded. 'That makes a kind of sense. She's a responsible woman. And she's a mother.'

After breakfast, Cotton saw the grackle on the mailbox. He had heard back from Herbert Butterworth. The letter was handwritten and not on official paper.

The person you call Srta A owes us – a small sports car was involved. We allow her a certain leeway, however, in her private arrangements to supple-

ment her income. She did, by the way, call you 'not like the others'. You were a man, she said, but gentle, too. You are free to believe that as you wish. From our point of view, we wanted to sharpen you up, get you reading people again.

On babysitting – it's a method of control. Eve is on lots of charities and sometimes takes her along as a lovely refugee. It works pretty well. Though I'm not sure some of those rich, charitable wives like it.

As I am sure you have already surmised, I was landed with checking you out. After all, I knew you before and can spot any differences with now. I have reported that you are perfectly fit and capable of assuming your duties in September. I'd have thought that amply compensated any expense you incurred.

PS. I enclose an article from the magazine *Foreign Affairs*. Look it over and tell me what you think.

Cotton read the letter several times. Instead of 'sweet', he now thought of Herbert as 'cosy but ruthless'. It hadn't occurred to him that the 'babysitting' was Eve babysitting Maria de los Angeles Vergara Fratelli at charity functions. He also wondered how those who read his mail before he got it would interpret this letter. It would, he considered, set them off looking for 'Srta A'. Though they might not think *A* was for Angeles but for her surname. On his own behaviour, he thought Herbert's note would reassure them. He did write back.

277

Herbert, I would be changed if I did not claim for expenses and would hate to give that impression. (See attached.)

Cotton itemized and enclosed those receipts that involved Maria de los Angeles Vergara Fratelli but, of course, did not mention her by name. He added the sentence, *Since I am unable to provide evidence of some expenditure, witting or not, I think this is pretty fair.*

The article Herbert had enclosed was called 'The Sources of Soviet Conduct' and the author was given as 'X'. Herbert had added a note: *X is George F. Kennan, a fluent Russian speaker expert on the Soviet Union. Until recently he was adviser to Ambassador Averell Harriman in Moscow. He's been urging the need for a rethink about how to handle the Soviets for some time – I understand he wrote an enormously long private telegram to the Secretary of State about it last year. He's decided to go public with it. See what you think.*

Cotton looked through the article. It was decidedly belles-lettres for his taste. He thought the style worked against what amounted to a wake-up call. Cotton put it down. He needed to read it several times more before he was confident that Herbert had not sent it simply out of general interest. Presumably this was another part of Herbert's sharpening him up.

19

O N FRIDAY evening, 15 August, Cotton went through the gap in the fence at 5.45 to find Susan already bathed and in her pyjamas waiting for him. Her mother had been trying out perfumes. Chanel No. 5, Ma Griffe, Miss Dior and White Shoulders.

'I can hardly breathe in here,' mouthed the little girl.

Her mother was getting over-anxious. Chanel No. 5 was 'too strong'. Miss Dior was 'too young'. She put those bottles away.

'She's had her hair in rags,' said Susan.

Now down to Ma Griffe or White Shoulders, Sally held up both bottles and Cotton attempted to look as non-committal as possible.

'What does the French one actually mean?' said Sally.

'*Griffe* means "claw", I think, but it also means—'

She did not let him finish.

'Oh, no. I can't wear that.'

'It's a perfume!'

'I know.' She turned away. A few seconds later Cotton smelt another waft of White Shoulders.

'I've got a book for you to read me,' said Susan. 'It's called *Rabbit Hill* by Robert Lawson.'

Cotton nodded. The cover showed a large, smiling

rabbit high in the air. Behind and below it near the crest of a hill was a large house with a red roof.

Just before six Sally appeared. Cotton did not know what kind of blue the dress was. Pale sea-blue? It was slightly shiny. Around her waist she had a wide, dark blue and white belt, on her feet white shoes. Sally never quite got her clothes right.

'Do I look all right?'

'You look great,' said Cotton. 'Doesn't she, Susan?'

'Yes,' said Susan. 'That's pretty, Mommy.'

Sally was looking flushed. 'I haven't done anything like this since – 1940.'

'Breathe in,' said Cotton. 'Go on.'

Sally started breathing in and then there was a toot as Joe Samms' car entered the drive.

'Should I wait for him to ring the doorbell?'

'Yes. And then wait a few seconds.'

Cotton began reading. 'All the hill was boiling with excitement.' The story, in Susan's words was 'kinda cute'. A group of woodland animals was waiting and hoping that the new occupants of the house would be better than the old. They were in luck. The new occupants planted a garden and put food out for the animals on the hill every night. In return, the animals left the garden alone. These generous people had a cook called Sulphronia.

'Sulphronia? That's a funny name,' said Susan.

'Well,' said Cotton, 'maybe the writer made it up, like Wendy in Peter Pan.'

'Wendy's a better name than Sulphronia.'

'Agreed. Shall we read the story?'

Susan was asleep by 7.45, tucked up with a rag doll called Molly.

Sally had left Cotton a glass of milk and a ham sandwich in the kitchen. He'd have preferred a beer, but he drank the milk and ate the sandwich. The house did need improvements. Cotton guessed most of the furniture came from the late husband's grandmother. There was a photograph of him in uniform on the sideboard. Round-jawed and slightly chubby, he had small, soft-looking eyes. Cotton wasn't sure whether or not he was being cruel or overly influenced by the failing-to-hit-the-flight-deck story, but the man in the photograph looked neither quick nor precise.

Then he sat down, picked up the *ProJo* and read about Indian independence. It was an agency report that talked of 'displaced people'. It was difficult to estimate how many had felt obliged to uproot their lives and travel to Pakistan or India. What was called a 'guesstimate' mentioned 'six million souls'. There had been reports of 'sporadic violence'.

Cotton had taken Herbert's note and the X article, 'The Sources of Soviet Conduct', with him. He read both again. This time his reading of the article was a little different. He even began to have some sympathy for George Kennan's position. Kennan seemed to feel he was being ignored and was struggling to understand why the Department of State was being so dense about the Soviet regime's intentions. But, as this was a public article, he seemed anxious not to go too far or be too specific in his argument and had left too many points to develop. He

used the term 'containment' to describe what American policy towards Soviet Russia should be. But he did not spell out what he meant. He had limited his aim to waking up the American establishment with his analysis. He really needed to write another article.

Sally was back by 10.30 sharp. He heard the car draw up, stay a minute or two and then leave. Sally looked calm and pleased.

'Did you have a good time?' said Cotton.

'Thank you, Peter. I most certainly did.'

Cotton smiled. 'Good. Susan is tucked up and asleep. I'll be getting back.'

Sally approached him and kissed his cheek.

'What's that for?'

'Being here. There was nothing awkward at the end because you were here.'

Cotton's eyebrows came up. 'I don't know that that's the reason.'

She smiled. 'Yes. Joe's a gentleman in that way, isn't he?'

Cotton left the house, went through the gap in the hedge and on to the guest-cottage deck. The night was warm because any breeze was from inland, and he caught something – just the slightest whiff of Old Spice aftershave, then hair oil and sweat. He stopped and listened. He could hear nothing. Carefully he opened the guest-cottage door and put on the light. There was nobody there. But there had been. Someone had thought it worthwhile checking the place out while he was next door. They had done this thoroughly. He found even the end of his safety razor had been unscrewed and not quite

tightened up again. The books on his bedside table were not quite aligned.

Cotton sat down. Then he looked at his notebook and drawing pad for Dr Sanford. The contents seemed sparse but he thought they might be convincing enough to show a restrained, even unimaginative response to his predicament.

Then he went over the guest-cottage to check for listening devices. This did not take very long. The place was not large and did not have many hiding places. He found nothing.

He frowned and opened a beer. For the first time he asked himself if his watchers weren't being deliberately clumsy, that this had been less a search than a bully's nudge to remind him he'd been sequestered and drugged only a few weeks before.

Up to now Cotton had become accustomed to thinking his experience had been a mistake, a something gone wrong, and that whoever was responsible was anxious not to be found. Now he wasn't so sure.

On Monday, 18 August Cotton drove down to the beach, swam and then went to the Ocean View Café for breakfast. As he ate he looked at the *Time* magazine story on Indian independence – no mention of Pakistan – that mentioned 'some deaths'. But there was no attack on the British. Instead, the article claimed that virtually the entire British commercial community was staying, since business people preferred having 'dozens of servants and abundant food to the deepening drabness of post-war Britain'. The lead story was a hatchet job on

Soviet Ambassador Gromyko. Portrayed as a bogeyman from 'another planet', Gromyko had a chauffeur with stainless steel teeth and was described as a prototype of a new race of men, 'an almost perfect neo-paleolithic specimen'. The piece was titled 'Negative Neanderthaler'.

Cotton thought Herbert Butterworth would feel relieved by the report on India, but he was more intrigued that the Soviets were being portrayed in the mainstream American press as primitive, pre-humans – but with unfortunate veto powers at the United Nations, where Gromyko had just been employing those powers.

On his return to the guest-cottage, Cotton found the postman had been. In the mail was a formal invitation to a party in honour of a member of the House of Representatives for Massachusetts being held by Mr and Mrs Spencer Lowell on Wednesday, 20 August. It came with a note from Ed Lowell: *Herbert Butterworth tells me you are holed up in Narragansett being something of a hermit. The party should be fun if you feel you can manage it. I know it's awfully short notice, but do give it your best shot.*

Cotton smiled. Herbert had been busy. He went to Eleanor.

'Lowell is a big name in New England. What's the address in Ruggles Avenue?'

Cotton told her.

'Oh, that's got sizeable ocean frontage.' She nodded. 'Yes, big place. Ballroom can seat a hundred kind of thing. Orchid houses, gardeners, you know . . .' She looked up. 'You're going up in the world. Or are you just showing your true colours?'

'No, I'm worried about my dinner jacket.'

'You're joshing me. Are you going to go?'

'I'm thinking. It might be worth the experience.'

'You bet,' said Eleanor.

'Who's the party in honour of?'

'A member of the House of Representatives.' Cotton showed her the invitation.

'That's one of Joe Kennedy's boys.'

'You're talking of the man who was American Ambassador to Britain and who rather misjudged events?'

Eleanor laughed. 'His son. There's a difference.'

'What is it?'

'Joe has done terrible things so his son can be a prince.'

'You don't have princes.'

'We have other things nearly as good. Garrett used to say heredity works differently here. There's a wonderful missing link. A father can be a rapacious scoundrel but his son can be a patrician public servant. I want to know something, though.'

'What?'

'I want to know everybody who is there.'

Cotton smiled. 'I'll do my best.'

Cotton was cheerful and impressed. He was impressed by Herbert Butterworth and his way of working. The cheerfulness came from a sense of relief he had been right to be patient when he had had very little choice. He was hoping that the Americans and in particular Ed Lowell now considered him with contempt. He thought it was Ayrtoun who had said what a desirable state this was.

285

Dear Ed, he wrote, *I'd be delighted to attend your party. I don't know how much Herbert told you, but I recently had a bad reaction to some drugs, was laid rather low. That's why I am here in Narragansett in my sister's husband's cousin's guest-cottage. I am recuperating nicely. I look forward to seeing you again. Yours, Peter.*

Later he found that Eleanor had put a copy of *The Great Gatsby* into his postbox. She had written a note: *I really must buy some more modern books. The only others I could find about money were by Henry James and Edith Wharton.* Cotton smiled. He had been tossed F. Scott Fitzgerald's book to read while waiting to invade Sicily, having been offered a choice of that or another book he had mistaken for Hemingway's *Death in the Afternoon* that had turned out to be by Agatha Christie – *Evil Under the Sun*, or something like that.

Sally visited. Cotton saw that she had been what his sister had once called 'cooking' since her date with Joe. She was trembling when she asked him to babysit again on Wednesday evening.

Because Cotton was slightly slow in answering, she carried on. 'Oh I know it's an awful bother, but you see—'

'That's all right. It's just that I have to go to Newport then, to a party. I'll be happy to babysit any other time. The day after should be fine. If that's convenient.'

Sally sank into a chair. 'I'm sorry.'

'You don't need to be.'

'I'm ashamed. Of course you have your own life.'

'Stop it. You've nothing to be ashamed about. I'll be only too delighted to babysit when I come back. How's that?'

'What party is this?'

'Do you say "high-toned"?'

'No,' she said. 'You mean "high-class".'

'There's a political element in there too, you know.'

Sally sighed. There was a small tremor in it. 'We'll say the evening after.'

'Three days from now?'

'Yes.'

20

C OTTON WAS told it would take an hour and a
quarter to drive round the bay from Narragansett
to Newport. It took him a good half-hour longer. He
arrived in Newport around noon and checked into the
Hotel Viking at 1 Bellevue Avenue on Historic Hill, a
five-storey Georgian colonial red-brick building decorated accordingly. He arranged for his hire car to be
washed, then had a manicure while his hair was trimmed.
For lunch he ate grilled striped bass. After that, he slept
a siesta in a four-poster bed. He woke feeling that the air
conditioning and a soft interweave blanket had done
him good. He ordered a cup of tea and some iced water,
showered, shaved again and then put on evening clothes.
From his hair, tan and clothes he looked, he thought,
almost American.

He was intrigued when the hotel offered to provide
transport to the Lowell party. After a little chat about
parking and convenience, he agreed to pay for the
service. Ten minutes later he was in the back of a black
Lincoln. They went way down Bellevue Avenue and
turned left on to Ruggles Avenue.

As soon as they turned into the drive, Cotton nodded.
It was recognition of mild surprise. In 1945 he had dined
with the very monied Mrs Duquesne in Washington at

her mansion on Dupont Circle. He had taken that as graciously and capaciously American. Newport however, looked nearly as stiff as a reception at the British Embassy on Observatory Hill.

His car door was opened by someone in uniform. He got out, went up the steps, handed his invitation to another uniform and then, in a hall full of cut flowers, chintz and chinoiserie, joined the receiving line. He was welcomed by Mr and Mrs Spencer Lowell – he tall, elderly and courtly; she considerably younger but aged by boredom and her make-up – and shown through the house into the garden.

The lawns leading down to the sea were dotted with elaborate white and black awnings, each over a round table for twelve. They reminded him of the tents in Laurence Olivier's wartime film of *Henry V*. There were even flame torches, but at some distance, presumably to deal with bugs. At the head of the steps down to the lawns, Cotton was handed a glass of champagne. He went down the steps.

He recognized a few faces from newspapers. Some he could put names to – Henry Cabot Lodge Jr, for example – but others he could not. There was a blonde girl he thought might be a film actress but he couldn't recall her name or what she had been in.

'Peter!'

Cotton turned. It was Ed Lowell at his most affected and elegant, wearing evening clothes that looked cut by the Duke of Windsor's tailor. 'So pleased you could make it.' He was wearing a white orchid buttonhole.

'Very kind of you to invite me, Ed.'

Ed Lowell smiled. 'Let me introduce you to my fiancée.'

Though Cotton leant forward he didn't catch the name Lowell murmured. The girl was very slim, very tall and very lovely in a cover-of-*Life*-magazine sort of way. She was wearing a white gown of vaguely Grecian cut with the confidence of someone who'd have been perfectly prepared to carry off being draped in a parachute.

'Congratulations to you both,' said Cotton. 'When is the wedding?'

The fiancée looked bemused and turned towards Ed.

Ed Lowell raised his eyes heavenward, then mouthed 'June next year. We're thinking of having it here.' He smiled and turned to the dark-haired woman in blue on his other side. 'And this is Minty. Now, Peter, Minty is clever. Watch out for her.'

Lowell saw someone else and moved his fiancée on. 'Gerry! Grand you could make it!' The girl called Minty sighed.

'There are times I could absolutely kill him,' she said. About five six, with very dark, straight hair, a small head, high cheekbones and sly, intelligent eyes, her gown looked somehow separate from her body. There was something catlike about her forehead.

'I could kill him any time,' said Cotton.

'My,' she said. 'I like that. You gave that feeling.'

Her mouth sloped a little to one side. It wasn't clear to Cotton whether this was due to a sarcastic tilt or something more natural.

'My name is Peter Cotton . . .'

'I know. You're a colonel. You do something spooky. You don't have a title to inherit.'

'I don't even use colonel. And you?'

'Just a woman lawyer.'

'Why "just"?'

'Women begin in trusts and estates because the clients are dead and everyone is usually too polite to complain that a female is dealing with their estates. And we can all be kept in the basement out of sight.'

'And now?'

'A partner understood that the war would be good for divorces.'

'Was he right?'

'On the button. I do tend to get the modern woman's side. Not always; some women still prefer male lawyers. Again it's very discreetly done. Side entrance, flowers, padded chairs and a supply of disposable tissues.' She smiled and raised her chin. 'Now, you do understand how this works? I am your appointed companion for this evening. If you're as vulgar as to see someone more attractive, you have to tell me. You understand that, don't you?'

'Does the same apply the other way round?'

The girl frowned and looked out over the tents. 'Not really. I suppose I know everyone here – except that fat little actress.' She looked doubtful. 'Have you any money?' she asked.

'No.'

She sighed. 'Me neither. But I've been instructed to marry it.'

'Is that awfully hard?'

She laughed. 'It's tricky, Colonel, when you are looking for unmanned money. That's someone relatively

young but grown-up, who loves the arts and prefers aesthetics to intimacy.'

Cotton nodded. 'You've narrowed your search, then?'

'Don't you believe there are men like that?'

'I know there are. Lots. What's the problem?'

She smiled. 'I do like some men too. I don't know what the expression for my tastes would be. Catholic seems wrong.'

'I see. A generalist, perhaps?'

'That's not bad. The law has its tedious side. I'd like to be a writer too.'

'Is that a very special combination?'

'Haven't you heard of my cousin Louis?'

'No.'

'He's beaten me to it.'

'I'm sorry to hear it.'

'Well, he does use a pseudonym and I only say he's my cousin.'

'He's not?'

'He might be. My mother's been married five times. Always to money. A couple of years ago I met a rather quiet old man. There was something familiar in his eyes. So I asked him if he was my real father. He was awfully sweet. He suggested my mother's first husband's best man had been my father but couldn't swear to it. He then made an absolutely disgusting suggestion.'

Cotton nodded. 'Right. Is this one of your short stories?'

She laughed. 'That's good!' she said. 'Not all of Ed's friends pass.'

'I'm not Ed's friend.'

'A sort of colleague, then.'

She put her arm through his. 'Let me show you around.' But she did not move. 'Look over there. That's a superior crook who wants to do business but also look clean. Do you see how anxious he is about his shirt cuffs?' She made a face. 'That's just a politician.' She shook her head. 'Politicians just want to cause a swirl, like Ed.'

This caught Cotton by surprise. 'Ed has political ambitions?'

'You bet. I think he just wants to get the dirt on everyone else before he starts.'

'Do you think he'll make it?'

'I don't know. My mother always marries money. I haven't. Politics appears to have something of that. You've got it. Or you haven't.'

'What's your surname?

'Auchincloss.'

'Is Minty short for Araminta?'

'No,' she said and smiled. 'Ooh good, your next test is coming over. I'm going to describe him, politely, as a political valet.' She looked up. 'Rutherford! Allow me to introduce Colonel Peter Cotton. He's had me in absolute stitches since we met.'

Rutherford Jennings was a fairly short, extraordinarily neat but anxious-looking man in his mid thirties. He shook hands very firmly and frowned when he spoke.

'I understand, sir, you once had lunch with Cherkesov?'

'Yes,' said Cotton. 'Ed just can't keep his mouth shut, can he?' Minty hit him on the arm.

'You brute! You absolute brute! Why didn't you tell me?'

'It's the kind of thing I usually save until much later in the conversation.'

Rutherford Jennings looked somewhere between alarmed and impatient.

'I'd really like to hear about that, sir,' he said.

'So would I,' said Minty.

'Can't Ed tell you?' said Cotton.

Rutherford Jennings' voice became much deeper. 'Ed's never met Cherkesov,' he said.

'No?' said Cotton. He shrugged. 'We were all in London at that time. What is it you want to know?'

Cotton had eaten lunch with Oleg Cherkesov, a high-ranking Soviet, in February 1947 at Simpson's in the Strand in London. Cherkesov's reputation in the West was one of fabulous brutality and ruthlessness. This reputation helped obscure his extraordinary success in placing agents in the USA between 1931 and 1939, at which point, via a hastily taken train to Canada, he had found it advisable to quit the USA. But he had other talents. Back in Soviet Russia, he was credited with straightening out and improving the production of fighter aircraft and bombers.

'Is he as vulpine as they say?' said Minty.

'Nobody's ever as vulpine as they say. When I saw him he drank an entire bottle of vodka and ate almost raw beef and spoke, with some charm I have to say, of what he considers real politics.'

'Realpolitik?' said Rutherford Jennings.

'Yes,' said Cotton. 'His version, of course.'

Rutherford Jennings made a face. Cotton understood he was asking for more.

'Very well briefed. Knew about me back to childhood in Mexico. He mentioned Ed a few times, usually as having no budget to worry about.' Cotton held up three fingers. 'He made three points. One was to explain how grateful the Soviets were to what he called "idiot intelligents" in the universities and press in the West. Second, he was delighted the way the Committee on Un-American Activities was going – he compared that to a witch-hunt and their own purges in the thirties, though here toned down for the squeamish. Finally, he was delighted by American support for a Jewish state in Palestine. He imagines that will hand the Arabs to the Soviet sphere of influence for a couple of generations.'

'He sounds quite fun,' said Minty. 'Did he disappoint in any way?'

'I wasn't looking,' said Cotton. 'He's tall, very thin, has a cigarette for both hands and a cough that makes a cement mixer sound frivolous. He had two shorter but much wider bodyguards and shrugged off his fur coat for them to catch. I found him – I don't know about aristocratic – but certainly a very autocratic comrade.'

Rutherford Jennings barely bothered to hang around and was soon gone.

'Did I pass that too?' said Cotton.

'Oh yes,' said Minty. 'On the other hand, I think most people pass with Rutherford if he gets something he can pass on.'

Cotton laughed. 'He doesn't edit?'

'Only for his masters and he knows what they want. Did you see that even his hair looked starched? Will you light my cigarette?'

'Of course I will.'

As he lit the cigarette for her, Cotton tried to think of someone in British Intelligence who had political ambitions. He could not think of anyone. Any aspiring British politician would have to keep their intelligence work secret. The American take was novel, rather more bare-faced.

'Are you involved with anyone?' asked Minty. She puffed inexpertly at her cigarette.

'Are you talking of a young woman?'

'Of course. The usual kind of thing?'

'I'm sorry?'

'You know, head, legs, the usual kind of thing.'

'I see. Then definitely no.'

'Good.'

Cotton smiled politely. God, it was hot. A moth landed on Minty's dress. It was, in a powdery brown way, almost orange. He blinked. It had gone without her apparently noticing.

A little later, just after Minty had finished her cigarette, Cotton was summoned. One awning had been folded down to make a kind of tent. Inside, the table had been cleared of place settings. Instead there were ashtrays, glasses and bottles. There he met a Republican senator of about forty-five and a Democrat member of the House of Representatives not much older than Cotton was. The tent was filled with cigar smoke, there were various attendants and the younger politician was, with a certain heavy-lidded look of anticipation, stroking the behind of the compliant young blonde actress Cotton had seen when he arrived.

Cotton was greeted with smiles, affability and a large variety of alcoholic choices. He stuck to champagne but let the glass sit.

'So you're a man that's actually met Cherkesov?' said the senator.

This was not so much a question as a prompt for people to start telling stories about Cherkesov's brutality. These tended to black humour and in some ways sounded almost admiring. There was one Cotton had not heard before, which Rutherford Jennings started off but then Ed Lowell took over. Cotton saw a chubby man from Yale who almost mouthed along with Rutherford Jennings, then became seriously impassive when Ed Lowell started speaking. Cherkesov had reputedly been unhappy with aircraft quality in one factory, so he had loaded workers on to a just finished bomber plane and invited them to take it for a spin themselves. They protested that no one amongst them could pilot the craft. He said he didn't care. Somebody would have to try. They began pleading and weeping. At this point, Ed Lowell took over. Tired of the noise, Cherkesov lost patience and made his point in another way. He rounded up the workers and formed them into a circle on the runway. Two of the foremen were bound with stout rope, taken up in the plane and dropped from the bomb bay. The idea was that the pilot would try to hit the circle of workers with foremen bombs. The bomber had missed. The foremen bombs had landed behind the circle of workers, 'each with a short popping noise'. The bomber had been demoted.

Cotton had not known Cherkesov's reputation had been quite so embellished, but was even more intrigued

by the switch of tellers. Ed Lowell had waited to see if the story was going down well before he took it over.

The younger politician turned to Cotton. 'And what did you think of our Soviet friend, Colonel?' he said.

'Well, he certainly made a couple of lords jump when he came into the restaurant,' said Cotton. He gave the aristocrats' names.

They laughed. This was the kind of thing they wanted in the manner they wanted.

Cotton was there for about an hour. Cotton already knew that they were not particularly interested in Un-American Activities or a Jewish state, but they did want to know how Cherkesov was playing Beria, Stalin's chief of police, and Malenkov, a possible successor. Cotton heard again, this time from the Republican senator, the story of Beria's way with rape, which consisted of having his goons kidnap a woman off the street, raping her 'in the comfort of his own home' and then giving her a bouquet of flowers as a keepsake. Cherkesov was often credited with writing or editing or releasing this story himself.

At the end of his visit the politicians shook Cotton's hand. The elder appeared to think some solemnity was necessary.

'So what's our biggest security problem, Colonel?'

'That Vice-President Truman knew far less about the Manhattan project than Comrade Stalin.'

There was a brief pause and then laughter.

'Droll,' said the younger. 'Colonel, that was droll.' He patted Cotton's shoulder. 'Let's meet again some time.' Cotton saw a man behind him make a note. The politicians had already moved on.

When he got out of the tent he found Minty waiting for him. She kissed him briefly on the lips.

'What's this about?'

'I heard the laughter and just wanted to see how you tasted.'

'Of second-hand Cuban cigars?'

'No. Pretty bland actually.'

Cotton smiled. 'Thank you. You're very kind.'

'I like you, Cotton. You've got no trousers.'

Cotton smiled. 'What does that mean?'

She put her arm in his again. 'Oh, you know. So many men stride around as if the contents of their trousers gave them incontestable privileges. Let's go and eat something. We're in tent three, you know. How did that go?'

'Lots of chummy laughter.'

'Boys will be boys?'

'I'm not sure it was even that.'

'You disapprove?'

'I think I was supposed to watch.'

She smiled. 'From perfidious to voyeuristic Albion? Isn't that a comedown?'

'These days we know we are what you call the help.'

'I really must remember that,' she said. 'May I recommend the lobster?'

A very elegant young man sat sideways on to the table and looked not at his supper companions but out at the waiters criss-crossing the lawn. Whenever someone tried to speak to him, he waved them away and said, 'I'm busy ogling.'

Cotton leant towards Minty. 'Would he be unmanned, from your point of view?'

'No, he's a purist,' said Minty. 'And something of a muscular socialist, I suppose. He likes young men with big biceps from poor backgrounds.'

Cotton nodded but was beginning to feel tired. He wondered, but not very hard, what the difference between English and American aristocrats was. He could only think the British kind was lying low, at least in 1947.

'Do you sail, Peter?'

'No.'

'Good! I don't like that weather-beaten look. How about golf?'

Cotton shook his head. 'I haven't played for years.'

'I sometimes think I should take it up,' said Minty. 'I like the idea of it but it takes so long to get round the course. Peter—'

'What?'

'You're not being fun any more.'

They were interrupted. Ed Lowell was looking very pleased. He smiled and bent down.

'Peter, I forgot to ask. You had that bad reaction to something.'

'Yes,' said Cotton. He paused. 'I found out I was allergic to lidocaine hydrochloride.'

'Really? What is that exactly?'

'It's a local anaesthetic. It is supposed to go well with adrenalin.'

'Why were you having it?' asked Minty.

'I was having a scar stitched up again.'

'The man's a hero. I'd much rather see a man's scar than his thing.'

Already straightening up, Ed laughed. 'Isn't she shocking?' He didn't sound as if he meant it in the slightest and moved on.

'He's practising his technique,' said Minty. 'I think it's called "dipping". After supper, why don't we make a quick getaway?'

'You have plans?'

'I thought we'd wing it. These people are awfully stuffy, don't you think? Come on, don't be mean. It'll do wonders for my reputation as someone urgently looking for a husband. It might even do something remarkable for yours.'

Cotton glanced at her watch. It still wasn't 9 p.m. It felt very much later.

'What time can we go?'

'Ten thirty would do.'

'Then you let me rest till then. Have a chat with some nice people.'

'You do drive a hard bargain,' said Minty. 'I'm not sure I can do that. There's a marked shortage of nice people. Would you accept very slow dancing instead?'

Cotton did dance with her. She grabbed hold of his thumb, apparently not aware that she did not have his hand. He looked down at her.

'Are you trying to look down my gown?'

He smiled. 'No,' he said. She brought her head to his chest.

He had the strange image that she might flee, wriggle

301

out of her clothes and leave him holding them. He shut his eyes. He tried to rest.

After 'Moonlight Serenade', Minty went over to say something to Ed Lowell's fiancée, who, she had seen, was on her own. Cotton watched them for a moment, then found a chair in a corner and sat down. It took him a couple of minutes to notice he had nearby company. There was an old lady in the shadows fanning herself against the heat. She told him she had been akin to a Gibson girl – 'that's even before flappers' – and that things 'this post-war' were some way short of the last post-war and not a patch on the turn of the century. 'It was fairly brutal, I suppose,' she said, 'but somehow more obviously fun.' She looked over at Minty. 'People disguise their appetites a lot more these days.'

The actress Cotton had seen in the tent sat down.

'Hi there.' She had a breathy, almost childish voice. 'I hope you don't mind. I'm trying to give my rump a little break.' The actress opened her eyes wide and pouted.

It took Cotton a couple of seconds to understand she was performing. He smiled and nodded.

The girl laughed. 'You have nice eyes, you know. You've seen some things but you're still pretty nice. It's unmistakable. It's something we share – a little like kindred souls. Do you photograph well?'

'I've really never thought about it.'

The actress looked surprised. 'Oh, I do. All the time. But I take care. Some angles are just plain unflattering.'

'I'm not an actor.'

'Me barely. So far I've been a secretary and a maid. You really have to perspire to get better roles. My agent sent me here.'

'I see!' said the old lady suddenly. 'How does that work?'

'I'm not sure yet. It's a kind of positioning. Personal and otherwise. You learn to pout. You've got to pout, like you really know what a blow-job is. You've got to know the camera angles. But you've got to have the bones, too. What I do is imagine I'm wrapped in cellophane. The gleam gets them.'

'Who? The audience?' said the old lady.

'My agent uses the word "Maecenas" – you know, the patrons – but yeah, I guess the audience needs positive titillation too.' She looked round. A flunky was frowning at her. She sighed. 'You know what the worst thing is? If you gleam, they keep pestering till the cellophane rubs off.' She stood up. Cotton got up too.

Cotton bowed. 'It's been lovely to meet you.'

She smiled and gave him a wink. 'Yeah. Hasn't it?'

Cotton sat down. The old quasi-Gibson girl nodded. 'I really liked her. She's got all the goods,' she said. Cotton looked round. The old lady shrugged. 'Goods get damaged.' She lowered her head and Cotton wasn't sure she hadn't dropped off. But her head came up again. 'Bustles weren't a bad idea, you know.'

Minty had come back to get him on his feet again. Cotton bowed to the old lady.

'What bustles?' she said, as they walked away.

'Protection, I think, from grabby hands.'

'Ah. What did the actress say to you?'

303

'Something about my having eyes like hers,' said Cotton.

'You fell for that?'

'No.'

'So you're not that gallant?'

'I'm not gallant at all, Minty.'

'I believe you.' She laughed. 'Come on, there are enough people looking the worse for wear for us to slip away. What do you say?'

'I should say goodbye to Ed.'

'Really? As you wish.'

Ed Lowell was talking earnestly to the chubby little man from Yale Cotton had seen in the political tent. Ed's fiancée appeared to be sleeping with her eyes open.

'Lovely party, Ed. Thank you.'

'You're off?'

'Yes. Thank you for everything.'

'Have you met Professor Walter Resnick?'

Cotton nodded. 'No, but I saw the professor when everyone was talking about Cherkesov.'

He shook hands with the academic. For such a short man, the professor had a remarkably deep voice.

'Entirely my pleasure,' he said. His German accent was strong, as if he had a bad cold.

'Fine, Peter,' said Ed Lowell. 'You'll be in New York in September, is that right? Good. I might see you then.'

Ed Lowell turned away. Cotton nodded at the fiancée.

'Good evening,' he said. 'I didn't quite catch your name, but I'm delighted to have met you.'

Ed Lowell turned back. 'Rosemary Tyler,' he said.

'Miss Tyler,' said Cotton.

'Ooh, Ed tried to dismiss you,' said Minty as they walked away. 'And you said no.'

'Mm,' said Cotton. 'Tell me about your plans now.'

'They're secret.'

'Of course they are.'

Minty looked at him. 'I am talking fun, you know.'

'Thank God for that,' said Cotton.

Minty had what she called 'a runabout' – a Frazer automobile.

'Well, it's a Kaiser-Frazer. I like the body. The mechanics are nothing special. Where are you staying?'

'Hotel Viking.'

'I think we need something much less formal.'

Cotton wondered if she'd be a fast driver. She wasn't. She was a slow, rather nervous driver. But perhaps that's because she was in town. She drove along to the end of Ruggles Avenue, turned along Spring Street, then towards Newport Harbor at Ann Street and parked.

They walked down towards the port past a couple of bars and a restaurant, then went up some narrow wooden steps, opened the door on a small bar, walked through that and another room and came out on a wooden balcony. It took Cotton a second to understand the thing jutted out over the water. He sat in a creaky wicker chair. Through the cracks in the soggy-feeling planks he made out some flotsam. It included a length of orange peel in a corkscrew shape and some sodden sacking. It was a warm night and Cotton had experienced fresher seas.

'This is absolutely my favourite place in Newport,'

Minty said. 'Look at the lights on the boats. Go ahead. Just look at them.' She was squinting.

The lights on moored craft were blurred, any sharpness taken away by a mix of brighter town lights, the moon and thin mist from the sea.

Cotton knew a lot of people could find sights poetic. What he enjoyed was the silence. He heard laughter, a slap of water against a wall. The silence returned. It felt thick or clogged.

'I like the . . . closeness,' she said. 'Would you like a drink?'

'Iced water.'

'Good.' She pressed a bell on the wall. A glum waitress shuffled through. 'I'll have bourbon. He'll just have really cold water.'

The waitress went.

'Isn't this heaven?' she said. She slipped off her shoes. 'Being alone, I mean. I've even got you to myself.' Minty smiled. 'I meant without you or me looking around all the time.' She lit a cigarette. 'Do you have to be awfully clever to do what you do?'

'You're confusing brain and intelligence work.'

'No, I don't think I am. But I was really wondering after your session in that fancy tent whether your kind of work doesn't have aspects of a higher kind of gossip.'

Cotton smiled. 'I'm not sure there's such a thing as higher gossip.'

'How about heightened gossip?'

The waitress brought their drinks. Cotton sipped his water. It was so cold it made his throat ache. He looked

at Minty and smiled. 'Might your heightened gossip have something to do with a young lady?'

Minty laughed. 'And who do you imagine that would be?'

'Let me think. She's getting married next year. Yes, her name is Rosemary Tyler. I saw you talking to her.'

Minty Auchincloss smiled, then shook her head. 'Do you really think she'll go through with it?'

Cotton shrugged. 'I have no idea.'

'Ed is a wonderfully civilized but highly compartmentalized being.' She laughed. 'You know. I don't think he tweaked her clothes or tidied her hair all evening.'

Cotton raised his eyebrows. 'He does that?'

'Well,' she said, 'how can I put this? For some men, it's the pleasure of the formalities rather than the person herself. Oh, he's perfectly respectful towards her, but even that's part-time, if you know what I mean. He brings her out when it's convenient for him, but she's not wrapped in tissue paper when he's not there.'

'Why are you being so indiscreet? Isn't Ed your friend?'

Minty snorted. 'You can observe your friends!' she said. 'It's just that you don't get everything in love, certainly when you pick someone decorative from an old family. She's pretty stupid, you know. But that's how it goes. She looks elegant but it's all on the surface. Underneath she has the mind and motives of a sulky eight-year-old.'

Cotton looked at her. 'She's coming, isn't she? I can go now if you want,' he said.

Minty shrugged. 'I don't know when she'll arrive. But I'd like her to see you.'

'So that she can say she has?'

'She won't. But she might be jealous.'

For a time they sat in silence. She lit another cigarette.

'Do you really have a scar?' she said.

'Right leg. I won't offer to show it.'

'You're not going to tell me how long it is?'

'I'm not that unmanned.'

A moment later Ed Lowell's fiancée stumbled on to the balcony. She stared at Cotton as if he were unutterably strange. Cotton thought that was probably how he had looked the first days after coming out of sedation.

Minty was looking at her. 'The poor lamb thinks she can drink but she can't.'

'Do you need help?'

'No, Colonel. You get some beauty sleep. If she doesn't improve, I'll throw some of your cold water on her.'

'It's been lovely, Miss Auchincloss,' said Cotton. 'Thanks for everything.'

'Did you say you'd be in New York?'

'I did.'

She smiled and turned her attention to Ed Lowell's fiancée, Rosemary Tyler. 'Are you feeling very bad, baby?'

'Why don't you just fuck off,' said the lovely girl.

Cotton got out and into Ann Street. At the corner, he saw a chauffeur standing by a Cadillac smoking a cigarette. He trudged back up the hill to the Hotel Viking.

He was relieved to get to his room, put on the air conditioning, drink cold water and sleep.

He did wake around three in the morning. He had been dreaming of Minty Auchincloss. But the entire scene involved a tea party on children's furniture.

'I don't have any milk but you can have blueberry juice instead,' said Minty.

'I'd prefer just to have the tea.'

'Then I'll put in *lots* of sugar!'

Cotton sat up. He was not so much disgusted as drowsily disappointed in his abilities in dream. He drank some water, turned and tried to get back to a deeper sleep. For just a moment, he saw a black spot. He wasn't sure whether that was a mole he had seen on someone during the evening, or something to do with R. L. Stevenson's *Treasure Island* – an image and suggestion that a large full stop on a scrap of paper was meant as a death sentence. That had troubled him at age eight. He suddenly realized the actress at Ed's party had been wearing a beauty spot. And then he remembered something else. Someone had once told him that more women should be employed in intelligence work 'in the field'.

'They have advantages. Get the leering out of the way and they can indulge in behaviour that your average manly man can at best patronize and at worst shrink from.'

Who had said that? Jim Gowar in Washington in October 1945. Poor Jim had been obliged to resign by Geoffrey Ayrtoun for choosing the wrong girl. Cotton decided to find out more about Minty Auchincloss. As for himself, he accepted he was still not up to late nights.

21

O N   T H E   morning of 21 August Cotton wrote and
posted a thank-you note to Mr and Mrs Lowell
and then took the car ferry from Newport to Conanicut
Island before driving over the Jamestown Bridge and
back to Ocean Road in Narragansett.

As soon as he pulled up, Eleanor came out.

'Well?' she said.

'Sorry, Eleanor. It was pretty humdrum – the political
class trying to play.'

'Who was there?'

Cotton gave her politicians' names.

'Nobody glamorous?'

'There was an actress. She picked up one politician's
fingerprints all over her rear.'

Eleanor laughed, then shook her head. 'Are you being
discreet or just plain forgetful?'

'Probably just ignorant,' said Cotton.

'Did you meet any nice girls?'

'I met a girl,' said Cotton, 'but it wasn't about being
more than amiable. She's looking for a rich husband.'

'What was her surname?'

'Auchincloss, I think.'

'Oh, I'll take that! Did she say who her mother
was?'

'No.'

Eleanor smiled. 'OK. That'll do,' she said. 'For now. Your sister called.'

'What about?'

'She didn't say. She did ask how you were.'

'How am I?'

'I said you were doing pretty good and had moved on up to Newport. Do you want to call her?'

'I'll do that later,' said Cotton.

He went back to the guest-cottage, unpacked, checked what groceries he needed, and drove into Narragansett. He looked around for the black Ford coupé, but it wasn't there. He made a telephone call to his sister from the office behind the Towers.

'Hello, Joan. I got a message from Eleanor that you had called . . .'

'Yes. We got a telegram yesterday morning that Pop had been taken to hospital the day before. His heartbeat was irregular and he was complaining about pain in his left arm. In the event, they only kept him in overnight. By the time we got the telegram, his heartbeat had settled down and the pain had gone and they had sent him home in an ambulance. The tests they ran didn't show anything serious.'

'Then we are not talking about an actual heart attack?'

'They don't seem to think so. I talked to a Dr Powell.'

'That's the local doctor.'

'He didn't inspire much confidence.'

'No, he doesn't. He's a bluff old party.'

'He suggested a course of rest, mostly. We got in an

311

agency nurse. Dr Powell told us we were wasting our money.'

'All right. Have you learnt anything else?'

'Not really. I had a very brief conversation with a grumpy but rather chastened-sounding old man.'

'All right. I'll telephone him too, then. It's noon here. Five p.m. there, right?'

'Yes. Tell me how you get on. How are you getting on?'

'Pretty well. I'm getting back to normal.'

'Eleanor said you were in Newport.'

'My first and probably last Newport function. How are the children?'

'Fine. Oh, Foster broke his arm. Fell out of a tree.'

'Is he in pain?'

'No, darling. His arm's in plaster that's becoming filthier by the minute.'

Cotton laughed. 'Send them all my love.'

Cotton booked a transatlantic call and about an hour later he spoke to a Nurse Dimmond and then to his father. James Cotton sounded uncomfortable and disapproving, like a bank manager who could not understand an overdraft request.

'There's no need for all this fuss, you know.'

'What happened?'

'I got a bit breathless, that's all. I noticed my heartbeat was jumping about. I could hear it in my head. And then my left arm went numb. I don't know. As if I had been sleeping on it. When I moved it . . . well, it hurt rather a lot.'

'So they took you to hospital.'

'Yes,' said James Cotton. 'In an ambulance.' He did not sound as if he approved.

'They did tests and kept you in overnight is what Joan said.'

'Yes,' said James Cotton. 'It was all quite unnecessary.'

'Well we don't quite know that, do we?'

There was a long pause, enough to make Cotton think the call had been dropped.

'Hello. Are you there?'

'Yes, yes, I'm here.' James Cotton cleared his throat. 'It was just bowel stuff, you know.'

'I'm sorry?'

'I've been a bit constipated, you see. Well, rather badly. It's been taken care of now.'

'I see,' said Cotton. 'Well, that's good in itself, isn't it?'

'Oh,' his father said. 'Yes, I suppose it is.'

Nurse Dimmond later described his father as having had 'a trying time', meaning he was being trying. She said she was making sure Mr Cotton was getting plenty of roughage but he was having 'problems with his appetite'.

After that, Cotton paused before telephoning his sister.

'Ouch!' said Joan. 'Of course, he is Victorian, you know.'

'Yes. Perhaps we should have a word with Mrs Douglas about his diet.'

'You can't. I'm sorry. I probably forgot to tell you. She gave in her notice. Off to Australia. Adelaide, I think.'

313

'This was when?'

'June. It wasn't what came to mind when I saw you.'

'I understand. So what we really need is a replacement for her, right?'

'Yes.'

'Otherwise he'll go back to cooking for himself, or whatever he does.'

'Actually, now you've told me what the problem is, I'm thinking we should ask him to come over again.'

Cotton did not think his father would move. 'OK,' he said. 'We'll try to squeeze him out.'

'Peter!'

'It's that or we get another housekeeper. I am not sure how easy that will be when we're both here.'

'Exactly!'

Cotton shrugged. 'Lots of dignity, then.'

'Rely on me. I've known him for longer than you.'

Carla, the waitress at the Ocean View Café, looked delighted to see him. 'Hope you've been somewhere nice.'

'Newport.'

'So you've been slumming it? What can I get you today, sir?'

'Could you just bring me a fruit salad and some coffee?'

The waitress looked disappointed. 'Oh, I know that look,' she said. 'You've had enough.'

'Of what?'

'Here.'

Cotton smiled. 'It's been a long holiday,' he said. 'Aren't you looking forward to going on to college?'

She shook her head. 'It's not been that good a summer. You know. My dad always says the only thing where you don't have to decide between quality and quantity is money.'

'I'll see how I go,' said Cotton. 'OK?'

'Yes, sir.'

She brought him his fruit salad and coffee. The fruit salad contained peaches, melon, cherries, oranges and strawberries.

Joe Samms appeared when he had nearly finished the bowl.

'Are you having dessert or what?' he asked.

'I'm seeing how I go. Have you eaten? How about some crab cakes? Will you join me?'

'OK. If they're quick.'

'Let's see.'

Cotton called the waitress. 'Can we have some crab cakes, please? Joe's in a hurry.'

Joe growled. 'Oh, it's OK.'

'Drink?'

Joe paused. 'Beer,' he said. When the waitress had gone, he smiled. 'Do you know why I'm here?'

'I can guess.'

'Yeah? OK. Well, we're pretty sure they'll be here on the 23rd. Yeah? I'm inviting you. We'll watch, drink a few beers. OK, the boat's not big, so I'm kinda worried.'

By this time Cotton knew Joe was talking about tuna or footballs and not Sally. 'About what?'

'You know, I'm thinking maybe Susan doesn't have her sea legs.'

'If there's any problem, I'll go ashore with her.'

'What about Eleanor? Should I invite her?'

'She'd love it.'

'You're saying I should get her on my side?'

Cotton made a face. 'Nice but not a necessity. She'd love this, though.'

'OK. Do I have to invite her in person?'

'Wouldn't a phone call do? Ask her if she'd like to see – you said "footballs", didn't you?'

'Yes.'

Joe Samms ate his crab cakes in four or five mouthfuls. He used a fork, catching it between the two surviving fingers of his right hand and using the stub of his thumb as a clamp.

'I have to get back.'

'I know. I'll see you.'

'Is that affair going well?' asked the waitress.

That evening even Cotton was surprised by how well. After Susan had fallen asleep, he read a little but found he had dropped off himself. He was woken around ten twenty. For a moment he thought there was another black bear outside. Then the sounds rearranged. Sally was making a lot of noise in what was a springs, gasp and hush episode. Cotton blinked. He wondered whether or not he could just go home. No. About eleven, Joe's car drove off and Sally came in. Her face was flushed.

Cotton got up and smiled. 'No problems at all,' he said. 'Susan went straight to sleep and hasn't stirred.'

She put out a hand nowhere near him but meant to

stop him. 'Don't go,' she said. 'Do you think I'm a bad person?'

He shook his head. 'No,' he said. He was not sure she was listening.

'Can I be honest?' she said. She looked up at him. 'I've never felt that before – with anyone.'

'I'm glad,' said Cotton. He wanted to say go ahead, go public and get off the porch. 'Sally?'

'Yes?'

'I'm going to go now. All right?'

She nodded. 'Thank you, Peter,' she said. 'You're a real friend.'

Cotton got out, ducked through the gap and went back to the guest-cottage. He sniffed. Nobody had visited. He was frantic to get out of Narragansett. He had nothing against the place. He just didn't want to be there any more.

22

E ARLY ON 23 August Cotton drove Eleanor, Sally and Susan to Point Judith. Joe was there, looking excited, but behind him, out to sea, there was enough wind to show white tops.

'I'm not going out there,' said Eleanor.

'Of course not,' said Joe. 'We'll just see the boats leave.'

There were over a hundred boats taking part in the Tuna Derby and many smaller boats had come to get a view. As they walked to Joe's boat, a wide-beamed little craft with a cabin barely wider than an English telephone box, Cotton saw small boys chopping up fish and dropping the bits into trash cans.

'That's butterfish,' said Joe. 'You understand? They make a slick first and then they start fishing. Get them encouraged.' He pointed. 'And that's squid. My dad believes in squid.'

Cotton nodded.

'After all, squid's what they come for. Water's at its warmest – the Gulf Stream's just due south and the tuna gang up on the squid. And we kinda gang up on the bluefin.'

Joe's father had a share of Joe's uncle's 45-footer, and Cotton was introduced to them. More importantly,

Sally and Susan were. It was all very demure and a little agitated – the older men wanted to get going. Joe wished them luck and they turned back to his boat.

'My uncle says my dad gives him luck. In '43, he caught a 700-pounder and came second.'

Joe had a photograph. It showed the two men he had just seen on either side of a fish about seven feet long hanging from a weighing hook.

'How do you hold on to something like that?' asked Cotton.

'Yes, they really struggle. It took forty-five minutes to get that one on deck. They put a nine-inch hook inside a thirteen-inch squid.'

Cotton looked out to sea. 'Where does this happen?'

'Oh, you've gotta read the sea, the wind, the currents. I mean, you can go maybe ninety miles south if you have to.'

'You're not thinking of doing that.'

'No! They'll be back tomorrow.' He pointed at his own boat. 'This is just a pleasure boat.'

Eleanor was not impressed. In the end it was only Joe Samms and Cotton who took to the boat and chugged out with the others to watch the competing teams leave. It was very noisy with whoops and beeps and somebody yelling through a megaphone from the lead boat with the big cans of slick. They had barely broached land cover when Joe cut the engine and settled them down.

'You must miss it,' said Cotton.

'Yup. This – and my fingertips.'

Cotton smiled. 'You do well.'

'I did think of tying the line round my forearm, you

319

know. But that's tricky if you get a big one. I've had enough cut off. There's a beer in that box.'

Cotton opened two bottles of beer.

'Only time I drink this early,' Joe said.

Cotton watched him. With the movement of the boat Joe was testing himself. He drank.

'OK,' he said, with satisfaction. 'We have a buyer for one of the houses. Guy from Boston.'

'That's good.'

'He's being a little picky about the price.' Joe belched. 'Sally and I—'

'I know.'

'Did she speak about it?'

'Just enough.'

'I didn't know it would go this fast.' Joe looked up. 'What do you think? I want to marry her . . . but I don't know about the timetable.'

Cotton nodded but then saw Joe expected a reply. 'There's a lot to work out,' he said.

Joe sat and nodded and finished his beer. He tossed the bottle overboard and watched it sink.

'You know what I really miss? The snap! When that big bluefin hits. It's electric. The line goes tight and you find yourself almost like coughing, you know, your back hunches and your legs fight back against the jolt.'

Joe had closed his eyes. He opened them and smiled.

'We should get back and see the girls.'

Joe Samms turned the boat and they chugged back to the berth to find Eleanor, Sally and Susan had been joined by JoBeth, Mrs Eugene Barber, the lady who'd rattled her ice cubes at Susan's party, and Eugene Junior.

'Do they club those bluefin?' said Eugene Jr.

'You don't want them to suffer,' said Joe.

'Is there blood?'

'JoBeth's invited us all to a tuna bake,' said Eleanor at her most impassive. She was wearing a grey hat pinned to her grey hair and a grey dress. JoBeth was wearing wide pants and a blue and white spotted halter-top and a wide hat. Sally had tried a pale buttercup sort of colour. Cotton thought she had probably made her dress herself.

'That's swell,' said Joe.

Cotton had barely one ear on the conversation. It was mostly about fashion: the merits or otherwise of rayon, the New Look as an extravagance, and the American tempering of the New Look. He heard that Eugene Sr often brought JoBeth a Sophie's Original from Gimbels when he visited New York – 'he has to go about once a month, you know?' – and that these only began at $49.50.

Bored, he concentrated on the food. JoBeth had also been keen to show she could cook. The tuna was fine. Baked with a little garlic and olive oil and overlaid with yellow, green and red peppers. Cotton would have been happy without the dill. He would have been even happier without the black grape salad. It had black grapes but was dominated by pineapple juice in gelatine. Eugene Jr and Susan ate this as dessert with some ice cream.

'Are they an item?' JoBeth asked him when they were clearing up.

'I'm not involved,' said Cotton. 'I like Joe. He's served his country and he's making a life for himself.'

321

'What are you saying? They're both casualties?'

'Please don't do that,' said Cotton.

'Do what?'

'Be mean.'

JoBeth took offence. Cotton did not mind.

Back in Ocean Road he learnt that JoBeth had helped Eleanor choose sides.

'What a woman that is!' she said. 'And those points!'

'What points?'

'On her chest! Who wears underthings like that?'

'She's anxious to be fashionable.'

Eleanor shook her head. 'Desperate, more like. That son of hers is *very* peculiar.'

'That's one of the reasons she's anxious,' said Cotton. 'I thought the tuna was good.'

'You think? You've got to stroke the olive oil on the fish, not just dribble it. Ask Felismina.'

Later, Joe Samms came through the gap.

'I expected a bigger guest-cottage,' he said.

'No, it's like a railway carriage without wheels. Do you want a beer?'

'No,' said Joe. 'I've just been talking to Sally.' He paused. 'She found that hard.'

'Because of JoBeth?'

'That woman can really preen, right?'

Cotton nodded. 'Eleanor and I have agreed she's unhappy.'

Joe thought about it. 'I don't know that that helps, you know? Sally thinks it might be best for us to stop.'

'Because of an unhappy woman?'

'She called it indicative.'

'Of what?'

'Attitudes,' said Joe.

There was a silence.

'My dad didn't do so well,' said Joe.

'He did fine,' said Cotton.

'Yes,' said Joe. He sighed. 'Sally says she shouldn't have, you know – with me.'

'I'm sorry.'

'Do you think I have a chance?'

'That depends on Sally. Why don't you give her a little time? Certainly tonight.'

'Right,' said Joe. 'I've been looking round next door. It's not in the best condition. But I was kinda working on possibilities, you know? About repairs; freshening the place up . . .' He sighed. 'Or maybe it would be better just to tear it down and start afresh.'

On Sunday morning Cotton drove to the Ocean View Café.

'How are the lovebirds doing?' said Carla.

Cotton shrugged. 'Would you have mushrooms? For an omelette?'

'Nope,' said Carla. She made a face. 'Who's got the problem?'

'I don't know. Really, it's their business, Carla.'

'Sure,' she said. She gave him the newspaper and took his order.

Cotton looked at the foreign news. A polio epidemic as severe as that of the US in 1946 was currently

sweeping the British Isles. The government was doing what it could and had closed public swimming baths.

Carla put his food down. 'I don't know,' she said, 'but there's another girl who really likes Joe. Laura Verrier?'

'I don't know who she is.'

'Yes, you do! She's the cute waitress at the coastguard place.'

Cotton had a vague memory of a short, smiley, top-heavy girl.

'You know it's the girl who chooses, right?'

Cotton looked up.

'Don't be like that. If he needs to, Joe'll get over it.'

After he had eaten eggs Benedict with smoked salmon, Cotton drove back.

'What's going on?' said Eleanor.

'I think they've run into a problem.'

Eleanor frowned again. 'That's disappointing. I thought Sally was a whole lot tougher than that. I mean, he's going to have less of a problem finding someone else than she is. He's got a job. He hasn't got a child to take on. She's not making sense.'

Cotton nodded. He didn't disagree but knew Eleanor was going to insist on explaining what she thought. He sometimes thought people were keener on occupying time than getting anywhere with their thoughts. The grackle was standing on his mailbox. He opened the box. It was another drawing from Susan. It showed a sea with a lot of fish in it.

*

Around 3 p.m. Joe Samms called by.

'Ready?'

'For what?'

'The footballs!'

Joe drove them to Point Judith to see the boats come back and the tuna the rodmen had caught.

'I talked to Sally,' said Joe. 'On the telephone.' He shook his head. 'She's slept on it and it hasn't made a whole lot of difference. She's just kinda shut down and closed up, you know.'

'I'm sorry, Joe.'

'No. I didn't handle it well. I'm cursing myself, you know.'

Cotton looked around. 'Will JoBeth be here today?'

Joe Samms shook his head. 'No. It's not her fault anyway. She wasn't being deliberate, you know.'

'What are you going to do?'

'Mope, I guess. Well, in private.' He smiled. 'Hey, I came for the bluefin.'

'Have you heard of Laura Verrier?'

Joe Samms frowned. 'Yeah,' he said. 'She's kinda cute and dopey and fills her uniform pretty well.'

'Apparently she likes you.'

'Who said?'

'The waitress at the Ocean View Café, Carla.'

Joe Samms laughed uncomfortably. 'Why are you listening to waitresses?'

'Because she talks a lot.'

'OK,' said Joe. 'I guess that makes sense. What would you do in my shoes?'

'I'd probably write Sally a letter. Tell her how I feel, of course. In a kind of way tell her what I'm offering.'

'Yes. I don't write so good,' said Joe. 'It's not just the fingers, you know.'

'Right,' said Cotton.

'Thanks,' said Joe. 'Let's enjoy this now. OK?'

The boats had started coming in. With over a hundred boats and four fishermen to a boat there were a lot of tuna fish to unload, ranging from forty-five pounds in weight to one colossus just over a thousand. There was whooping and cheering and a cup awarded. Cotton thought Eugene Jr should have been there. So many guts went into the water that a sizeable patch of sea turned pink and red.

He and Joe both drank too much beer. By the time he got back to the guest-cottage, after a weaving drive, he was, as Joe put it, 'just plain out of Narragansett'. After the beers, Joe himself had decided against writing Sally a letter.

'There comes a time,' he announced, 'when people want to see things. Or they don't.'

Cotton woke late next morning, squinting more because of a hangover than anything else. He drank water, made some coffee and went out on the deck. It was too late for Susan and too early for the grackle. He went to the mailbox. There was an envelope inside.

Lovely to see you the other evening, looking well. I'm not due to return to London until September 14, Ed Lowell wrote. *Would really like to talk before that.*

What do you say to luncheon at the Waldorf, 1 p.m.
Thursday 11th?

Cotton drank some coffee. He liked 'looking well' and wondered, but not very hard, just how arrogant Lowell was. He looked up and listened. He closed his left eye, then opened that and closed his right eye. He thought the left eye was just a fraction clearer than the right. He focused on the last tree before the shore. In his mind, he replaced the tree with Ed Lowell and lined up a shot. When Cotton was quite sure, he squeezed the trigger. He thought from the puff of red he had hit him around the right eye socket.

It was 25 August. He had a week to go. Cotton didn't think of it as sleepwalking exactly, but did recognize a certain zombie quality to his polite behaviour as he worked through a list. He took Susan to the beach and gave in to her requests for an 'Awful Awful', drove her some way to eat a concoction called 'Awful Big, Awful Good' made of syrup and ice milk, and bought her the nurse's uniform she asked for. He saw little of Sally and when he did, she was less willing to engage.

'You've never been married,' she said, the first time she saw him after ending her affair with Joe Samms.

'It's really not for want of trying,' said Cotton.

Sally wasn't listening; she had already turned her attention towards being a legal secretary. He arranged to have flowers and a leather cover for legal pads sent to her on the day he was due to leave. He put in a note: *With very best wishes for success in the career you have chosen.*

*

On Saturday, 30 August he saw Joe at Marty's on the Kingston Road. There were other people there and they drank beer and ate fried squid in semi-darkness. The mood was mellow if not elegiac. Another summer was nearly over.

A girl spoke to Cotton. 'Fall's best. You'll miss that. Winter's tough. But spring! That's just miserable, you know.' Almost immediately her face cleared. Tex Williams' 'Smoke Smoke Smoke that Cigarette' started playing on the jukebox. 'I like this one,' she said.

A man leant over. 'Somebody told me you were a colonel or something like that.'

'It's only because I'm British,' said Cotton. 'Whenever I meet a Hungarian, someone always says he's a baron or a count.'

Joe laughed. 'Leave him alone,' he said. 'He's paid his dues. When are you leaving?'

'Tomorrow. I'll take Eleanor to lunch and go after that.'

Joe nodded. 'Have you seen Sally?'

'Only briefly.'

'Yeah,' said Joe. He smiled with some bitterness. 'It's always like that, you know. She wants to marry a lawyer . . . well, somebody who doesn't use a hammer.' He looked up. 'So I took your advice. I asked Laura Verrier here. She'll come after her shift is done.'

Cotton started. Joe Samms smiled.

'She asked me what had taken me so long. I said I'd been waiting till now. Her season ends tomorrow.'

Cotton didn't wait to meet Laura Verrier again. His parting with Joe Samms was a slightly subdued, slightly

awkward 'take care now' affair. Eleanor actually shed a tear after he took her to lunch on Sunday and asked not to see him off. For her, he had arranged a very large basket of flowers and chocolates that arrived by the time they got back. Cotton took one last look around the guest-cottage and then carried his stuff to the Buick. Felismina was waiting for him. She was holding two wrapped presents – one obviously a canvas, the other a book.

'I accept money,' said Felismina.

'Of course.'

About 3 p.m. on Sunday, 31 August, Cotton pulled out on to Ocean Road and turned the Buick towards New York.

23

BACK IN New York City at his apartment in Sutton Place, Cotton found his sister Joan had been busy. One bedroom had been made into an austere but perfectly functional study with an empty bookcase, a desk, a rather overstuffed partner's chair in dark green leather and the kind of lamp Cotton always thought of as Napoleonic – or was it Empire? It had a dark green shade and three small light bulbs where real candles should have been. She had even provided silver-framed photographs of their parents at her wedding in 1936 and rather more recent studio shots of her own family. In one desk drawer he found paper, a bottle of ink and a packet of pencils. In another was writing paper, envelopes and a small stack of cards with his name, New York address and telephone number printed on them.

Cotton knew his sister had always liked things just so.

But there was more. In the bedroom he found a stack of six white shirts, more underwear, six pairs of socks and two ties. Hanging up was a grey lightweight suit with a barely visible check. A matching grey silk tie had been draped over one shoulder, matching grey socks over the other.

Cotton was used to making do, and knew he could not presently afford what Joan had provided. In the

kitchen he found two boxes containing drinks – gin, brandy, two types of whisky – malt and grain – liqueurs and even a bottle of Angostura bitters. In the cupboards she had provided him with three types of salt, a pepper mill and black peppercorns, olive oil, vinegar and a selection of herbs. In the dining room he found a variety of glasses and a set of very small coffee cups. In the so-called 'great room' were two vases of cut flowers, one with a note.

Welcome back, darling, it read. *Hope you're feeling better. Don't be a twit. The idea is to make a home, you see – and get comfortable as soon as possible. Love J.*

There was a PS. *You'll find a steak in the Frigidaire. It's GOOD that it's been there for a couple of days. Put a little olive oil in the pan and flip the steak every fifteen to twenty seconds. Add pepper AFTER you've cooked it and let it rest for at least four minutes.*

Cotton sat down on the window seat and looked out at the East River. He wondered what Joan was doing for their father in England. He'd be rather more difficult and touchy, certainly about such generous gifts. That reminded him to look at Eleanor's present. He got it and took off the wrapping paper. It was a book, of course, with a plain, faded sea-blue cover. There was no illustration. At the top in black was the title, *Ulysses*, and at the bottom the name James Joyce. There was a note.

I'm not sure this book is legal tender, if you know what I mean. Garrett bought it in 1922 from the publisher Sylvia Beach at Shakespeare & Company in Paris.

I've never read it – Garrett suggested I did not – but in a way I have been waiting for someone to give it to. I can't pretend I wasn't hoping for more company during your visit but I really do understand you had concerns of your own.

The bad thing about getting old is that a recuperative summer break for a young man means much more to an old woman. I was thinking of myself and companionship. It's made me aware of just how much I carry on existing and how selfish and useless I am.

I won't see you again. That's the kind of thing I think. I've been a widow for a long time and I miss someone to talk to. I hope you find someone.

Read the book and give me your opinion.

The second present was one of Eleanor's paintings. It was a portrait of her house above the profile outline of a seagull with mid-blue trees and a battleship grey sky. He put it on the mantelshelf and did not think it looked too bad.

Cotton wrote back to Eleanor as generously as he could. He thanked her for her splendid presents.

I'm sorry if I came over as selfish or withdrawn. Perhaps I misread your remark about 'valetudinarians' at our first meal together. I had just had one of those experiences that shock and shake you up when you are twenty-eight and in peacetime. It made me stupid and, I'm pretty sure, unobservant and very economical with imagination. But it's

clear my time with you set me to rights. I am very grateful.

He put the book as the first on his bookcase. Then he obeyed his sister's cooking instructions on the steak. While the meat was resting, he walked through to his study and transferred the book to his bedside table. He then opened a bottle of wine, poured himself a glass and sat down to eat. The steak was a lot better than the steak he had eaten in the Ogden Clinic.

On VJ Day Cotton put on the new suit and everything else and crossed town to see Joan and her family. The first person he met was his brother-in-law Todd. Todd sounded shocked.

'Good God,' he said, 'you look fit. And damnably slim.'

Todd was fourteen years older than Cotton and, plump in 1945, was heading towards heavy now.

Joan took one look at him and raised her hands Mexican style, before hugging him. 'Oh, I'm so glad that's all over!' she said. She held him away. 'You so look well!'

'Don't cry, Mommy,' said Halliday. 'You'll embarrass us.'

The three children crowded round and he heard of their summer and their plans for the new school year. He examined Foster's filthy plaster. Joan was thrilled.

'You know, I'm going to get us all here. Watch. Pop will come.'

*

On Wednesday, 3 September Cotton arrived at International Tower North, the north-east corner of the Rockefeller Center, to start work. It was the same building that had been used by the BSC, or British Security Coordination, in 1940–41. When the USA entered the war after Pearl Harbor, the American OSS, or Office of Strategic Services, had simply taken over the BSC offices and were still there.

The British had moved down the building – they were now a few floors above the dentists – and had taken the old nameplate with them. Cotton went up in the elevator and entered the British Passport Control Office.

He looked round. He had hoped that his return would spark off something, but he had no recollection of having been in this office before.

'Good holiday?' said Herbert Butterworth.

'Yes, thank you,' said Cotton. 'Did you manage to get any time off?'

'No. They always say August is a good time to get to know New York without all the people. Here. You've some forms to sign. We're all diplomats now.'

'What does that mean?'

Herbert smiled. 'Well, in theory, they could send you to Persia. We've had some trouble with that, some resignations.'

'Persia? Are you saying that's some sort of—'

'Hint, exactly,' said Herbert. 'Did you ever meet Ivan Sanderson? No? He was posted to Persia and took it very badly. He's decided he's no longer prepared to work for a socialist government. He resigned – and has applied for American citizenship.'

334

'Is he going to work for them?'

'No. Apparently he's thinking of starting a zoo and writing books.' He looked up. 'There's been a lot of that about. The great thing about being a diplomat, of course, is that we have immunity, always given that we behave, I suppose.'

'And would that have helped me in June, Herbert?'

Herbert smiled again but moved on. 'No. The good thing, though, is that this office is not really going to be hurt by our financial crisis. It may take a couple of months, but our salaries will be adjusted so that our representation here is not diminished or made to look poor. The Americans can read about it but it's important they don't *see* we're diminished. You'll be getting a tax-free allowance, a sort of representational expenses payment. As far as I know, that should handle your apartment. I think someone has even wangled a clothes allowance. Apparently we don't really need to mention this to people back home.'

'I see,' said Cotton. 'We're all special cases, almost like the UN.'

'They don't pay tax at all,' said Herbert.

Cotton nodded. He signed the forms.

'Right,' said Herbert. 'Now I've had a phone call with Dr Sanford. He suggests you might look for what he calls "triggers". That's sights, maybe smells and sounds that would bring memories back.'

'Did he have anywhere in mind?'

'No. But I do. Perhaps you'd like a stroll down Broome Street. It's in Lower Manhattan. I wouldn't call it the most salubrious of areas, but then you're not

looking for anything too salubrious in any case. It's the kind of thing you might want to do at the weekend as part of an unremarkable stroll, say, as you get to know New York.'

Cotton got up and looked at the map on the wall. Broome Street was long, went across Manhattan from West Broadway to the East River.

'You might try the stretch near the Bowery,' said Herbert.

Cotton raised his eyebrows. 'Why there?'

'Well, my information is imprecise – but the ambulance that picked you up came from that area. See if anything triggers your memory.'

Cotton shrugged. 'All right.' He turned round and looked at Herbert. 'Ed Lowell has asked me to lunch on the eleventh.'

'Really?'

'I understand he has political ambitions.'

'Who did you get this from?' asked Herbert.

'A young woman called Minty Auchincloss. He appointed her as my companion in Newport.'

Herbert nodded. 'I'll get Hornby to look into her.'

'Also check out Lowell's fiancée. She's called Rosemary Tyler. She's the kind of girl who might wake up and wonder why she is on a magazine cover. I mean, she looks slightly pickled in glamour or as if somebody has put chloroform on her corsage.'

Herbert smiled. 'All right. I didn't even know Ed was engaged. Did you ever meet his father?'

'Shook hands with him in Newport. Courtly-looking old gentleman.'

336

Herbert shook his head. 'That may be now. He was, possibly still is, a chronic womanizer. Class hotels, class girls.'

'Is he the one who made the money?'

'No, but he's vastly improved it. It started with Grandpa – a mean, mummified-looking gentleman whose rapine was limited to business and brutality. His sensual tastes concentrated entirely on gilt furniture. Ed's father is a much more polished operator. Cleaned up in the depression when cash was king. That house you visited he got for a song in about 1932.'

'What about Ed Lowell's mother?'

'Ah, that's sad. She died in a mental-home fire in '31. Began as awfully clever, if you know what I mean, but after Ed's birth went somewhere between frenetic and schizophrenic. She was given electroshock therapy. I don't think little Ed had been allowed to see her for some time.' Herbert looked up. 'I'm saying Mummy was crazy and Daddy enjoys his reputation as a cocksman and nobody's fool.'

Cotton nodded. Herbert had been doing his homework. 'So Hornby only has to look into Minty and Rosemary. And perhaps into Ed's finances.'

Herbert sat back and frowned. 'Do you really think his political ambitions are serious?'

'I don't know. Why?'

'If they are, then he must have been tapped, marked out as a possibility. The American system is radically different from ours. All kinds of alliances have to be made or at least squared. If you're running for president and you're a Democrat, you have to get the South on

board and you have to get organized labour with you as well. I wonder what Ed's alliances are.'

'Is Ed a Democrat?'

Herbert shook his head. 'It's hard to tell in this country what someone is politically. But I'll tell you what I'm thinking. Our former OSS neighbours upstairs have finally been transformed into the CIA. Their chief in Washington is Rear Admiral Roscoe H. Hillenkoetter. He has, understandably, expressed doubts about whether the agency can handle both intelligence analysis and covert action. The head of covert is a subject called Frank Wisner. Our psychological report suggests he's a manic depressive. That means he veers from a sort of schoolboy excitement to utter gloom. He's currently sounding out people from his old law firm, Carter Ledyard.'

'You mean he's gone for amateurs?'

'God, yes. He's after adult schoolboys – energetic and privileged young men. That fits better with his "up" moods. But the other name to bear in mind is Allen Dulles. Dulles was OSS in this very building. A powerful player. He's an extrovert and also a womanizer. Have you heard of a woman called Wally Toscanani?'

'Arturo Toscanini's daughter?'

'The elder. Dulles has been having an affair with her on and off for years. The younger daughter is called Wanda and is married to Vladimir Horowitz. He's another one who's been having a spot of electroshock therapy.'

'With barbiturates?'

'I don't know,' said Herbert. 'It's true electricity keeps

338

us together – it's become quite the fashion – but Horowitz is presently trying this to save his marriage. He's hoping electricity will, if it doesn't quite make him positively keen on women, at least deaden his desires for members of his own sex.'

Cotton nodded. He saw Herbert was looking at him.

'What?' he said.

'Tell me about Allen Dulles.'

Herbert nodded. 'Like so many of the people we meet, he flits in and out of law firms, banks and politics. He has quite some background in parts of intelligence. He's working not just for the CIA but also for Thomas Dewey's campaign to become president next year.'

'Are you suggesting Ed leans towards Allen Dulles?'

'It's certainly worth a ponder,' said Herbert. 'Dulles is one of those we call "Wall Streeters" – supremely confident men from very similar backgrounds.'

'Ed's not quite that, is he?'

Herbert shrugged. 'His father certainly is. He'd have had the introduction there, if he wanted it.'

'Is Allen Dulles good?'

'He's clever; he's resolute. But he may try to do too much. A little cavalier, perhaps.'

'Thanks Herbert.'

Cotton tried for a 'trigger' on Saturday, 6 September. He first took a cab to Delancey Street, walked down Allen Street and turned on to Broome Street. Two blocks on, there was a park; a block later, he crossed Bowery. It was a long way from the Ogden Clinic. There were warehouses and crowded tenements. Washing hung out

339

limp in the airless heat. There were large bands of children playing in the chalk-marked street, adults sitting on steps, some winos in hats propped against a wall and smoking, and something called a 'salvage sale' he translated as a rag-and-bone-man. A horse and a cart piled with old pots and pans, kettles and rags. In one stretch he could smell tripe being cooked. In another, the smell of beer from a warehouse was strong, almost sticky. But there was nothing that triggered any memory of any kind.

As he walked, what did impress him was how crowded, raucous and poor this part New York was. There was a brown colour in New York he had not seen anywhere else in the world. It was somewhere between dried oxtail soup and anthracite. Downtown, it stood out against the more frequent crumbling red brick. He paused several times and looked around him. Was it difficult to believe the people who had drugged him would have been able to drive briskly or not be seen? Cotton didn't think it was. There was a lot of commercial traffic, trucks unloading, men shifting goods in sacks and boxes and a lot of warehouses. He was struck by a generational shift in clothes. Some winos he saw wore hats and jackets, but the adolescents around favoured T-shirts and bare arms. As if to emphasize this, two formally dressed young Chinese walked past. At first the T-shirts belonged to Italians; then to mixed-race people. The girls wore thin blouses, wide skirts and had their hair piled up on top of their heads, but with a certain straggle at the neck and in front of their ears.

He walked as far as the corner of Centre Street. He

knew he had been found there in a doorway. He turned and looked back down Broome Street. He understood why Herbert had suggested trying this route. It made sense or at least would have been convenient for the people who had held him and drugged him not to have had to go too far. But he had no memory of anything. He shut his eyes a moment and suddenly felt a chill. Absurd. It was still warm and humid. He opened his eyes. Staring at him was a short old man with a white beard wearing a broken straw hat and a white linen suit jacket several layers cleaner than his once white, now filthy linen trousers. The old man held up a finger and laughed.

'Salvatore's!' he said. 'The best eats in town!'

Cotton hailed a cab. As soon as he got in he understood that he should not have walked; he would surely have been taken from Waverly Place in a vehicle. He should have gone there first and then followed the route to Broome Street. Why hadn't he done that? Why hadn't it occurred to him? He slapped his forehead.

'You OK?' said the cab driver.

'I just realized I made a mistake.'

The driver shrugged. 'It happens.'

But as Cotton sat looking out of the car window, he began to realize that his mistake was much more basic. He had been trying to recall anything, even the smallest scrap, of the circumstances of his kidnapping. But he already knew his mind had been shut down. The effort to remember was now taking up too much time and energy. It was too late. He had to concentrate on his present circumstances and what they might bring. Think ahead.

He shook his head. 'Preposterous,' he said.

The driver looked at him in the rear-view mirror but let it pass. The cab went over a bump. Cotton blinked. In his mind, something dislodged and he had the vaguest glimpse of stone drums, of something rounded and massive. What was that? It reminded him of military or castellated architecture, and he associated that with Scotland, not here. With something of the idiot clock-work response of a toy being nudged, the pipe tune 'Black Bear' filled his head. The sound somehow managed to be fast and a dirge at the same time. It grew louder as they passed the Centre Street police headquarters. A massive piece of civic architecture, it looked overweening and flabby. Then the pipes in his head began to fade and Cotton felt certain that it was here, somewhere very near here, where he had once been huddled, convulsed. He breathed in and closed his eyes – and caught another glimpse of curved stone. The stone drums were quite low – two floors, perhaps.

On Monday, 8 September Herbert Butterworth came to see him.

'Anything in Broome Street?'

'No.'

Herbert shrugged. 'It was what the Americans call a long shot, anyway.'

Cotton nodded. 'I did have a very brief image of stone drums or towers. I don't know that the image means anything.'

Herbert looked at him for a moment. 'OK,' he said.

Cotton winced. It suddenly occurred to him that

he might have merely transferred the towers from Narragansett to New York. But then he thought not. The towers his mind had produced were lower and not of granite. Yet, would he bet on it? He let it go.

'I have to go to Canada,' said Herbert, 'in about half an hour. Anything you want me to do?'

'No,' said Cotton. 'I don't think so.'

'You've lost interest in Geoffrey Ayrtoun?'

Cotton shrugged. 'I have considerable doubts about my own memory. Do you think his would be more trustworthy?'

Herbert shook his head. 'No idea. Unless, of course, we're talking of something specific, perhaps.'

Cotton frowned. 'I keep picking up strange nonsense about the shock of truth, electricity and drugs as the way to specific information and general life enlightenment.'

'You suspect it's not about that?'

'Let's just say I suspect it, Herbert.'

Herbert cleared his throat. 'I understood from Dr Sanford that progress wouldn't be consistent or constant. He said you might have some difficulty getting back to it.'

'Yes,' said Cotton. 'I've got that. Thanks.'

On 9 September Hornby drove Cotton out to the temporary headquarters of the United Nations at Lake Success on Long Island, 'to be introduced'. Part of the old Sperry plant had been adapted rather than converted. Outside, it was a white, nondescript office building, identified by a circle of member nations' flags in front of the entrance. Once inside, however, it soon became clear why, as their

guide told them, it was generally referred to as the 'rabbit warren'. There were some grand, formal offices for the secretary general, Trygve Lie, and a few others, but there were also about three thousand people working there, many in small rooms, many without windows. Cotton felt something airless and ill-fitting about the place, and it was not just because of the cramped conditions. Then a loudspeaker boomed. Apparently, Mr Lie liked to be in touch with everybody.

Their guide was boyish and British, an economics graduate from Glasgow University called Spiller. He came from Huddersfield and had been picked by the head of the Economics Area, the also British David Owen. Cotton could not help but notice that the Economics Area had a disproportionate number of British and Americans amongst its employees. He did not really have to ask. Each of the eight area heads was contracting people they knew or had been recommended to them by people they knew.

Spiller said there had been no choice. 'There's nothing sinister about it. Our chiefs had to get people in they knew would be able to do the job. We've had some awful mistakes when they didn't. The plan is to contract locals in the field and those that are good will work their way up. It'll take time, that's all.'

'Do you enjoy it?'

'Love it. Who wouldn't, eh? Is there anything you want to say to my chief?'

Cotton nodded. 'I spoke recently to Dr Aforey of Howard University. I understand there's some possibility of him working here.'

'This is not HMG speaking, is it?'

'No. It's me. Dr Aforey has some interesting analyses of the imbalances of colonial structures and has thought a lot about how they could be counteracted.'

'Did he say how?'

'I wouldn't want to gainsay him,' said Cotton. 'But I'd certainly listen.'

'I'll make a note of the name,' said Spiller, and he did.

As they were being taken through the warren to their next appointment by a person in a guide's jacket, Hornby looked unhappy.

'You'd think they were all bloody heroes,' he said.

Cotton looked round at him.

'On tax-free salaries and perks,' said Hornby.

'What are you saying?'

'It's as if their world's all here – and the outside's a sort of poor bloody relation.'

Cotton was surprised by Hornby's vehemence. But they were about to be shown into another office.

They were seen briefly by Benjamin Cohen, the Chilean head of Public Information, and were then passed on to one of his assistants, Solomon Baez.

'You're a diplomat, is that it, Mr Cotton?'

'I'm an economist in the Colonial Office,' said Cotton. 'With a special interest in decolonization.'

'In that case, welcome. What's struck you so far about our organization?'

'That everyone's planning for far fewer countries than there will be, surely?'

Baez smiled. 'You're an optimist, Mr Cotton. And like a good economist, you're a counter. But right now it's

the intellectual, legal and moral framework of our organization that is our prime concern. We have an overriding interest in human rights. We are preparing a charter, one that will, we hope, be mentioned along with your own Magna Carta as a milestone in the progress of humankind towards mutual respect and justice. It will set the terms of reference for our member states now and, as you say, in the future.'

Dr Aforey had said something similar. 'Excellent, Sr Baez.'

'Do you think those self-righteous do-gooders ever do anything?' said Hornby in the car back to Manhattan.

Cotton looked round. 'They'll survive,' he said.

A moment after, Hornby touched his comb-over as if Cotton was trying to see through it.

24

O N 10 September Cotton had a full medical at Dr Sanford's town house and consulting rooms on Park Avenue. He began with the old military ophthalmologist he had seen at the Ogden Clinic. The ophthalmologist had a book for him. It contained prints of coloured dots, each a sort of Seurat painting and basically in two colours. They 'hid' images – a letter, a cat, a number, a yacht and so on. Cotton had no difficulty with red and blue. As they worked through variations of the spectrum, he sometimes had to peer, for example with yellow and orange, but it wasn't until they reached orange and green that he had real problems.

The static image took on something of the movement of simple living organisms under a microscope. He began to see specks of red. He paused and tried again. An image appeared that reminded him of the shifting kaleidoscopic things he had seen after recovering consciousness in the Ogden Clinic. The orange had turned into tangerine and that colour was plagued by circles or bubbles as green as mint. He could not tell whether the circles were invading the green or the bubbles were bursting.

'What can you see in there?' said the ophthalmologist.

Cotton closed his eyes again. On his inner lids appeared

347

something as regular as a snowman made of circles. He raised his eyebrows and opened his eyes. The circles were melting in a kerosene sort of pink and his eyes were reacting as if he could smell the fuel.

He had never thought of himself as being so sensitive to colour that his eyes stung. He wiped them. He tried again. Cotton was aware it were as if he was trying to grip the image with his eyes. The figure eight came towards him and vanished into blotches. Once again he closed his eyes but this time opened only the left eye.

'That's a three,' he said.

'Good!' said the ophthalmologist. 'You took a little time. But three is three.' He slapped the book shut. 'Hey, not too many people can do that at the best of times, you know, have that kind of discrimination.'

'Really?'

The ophthalmologist laughed. 'You bet. If patients see anything they usually go for an eight.'

'I can vouch for that,' said Cotton.

The ophthalmologist smiled and clapped him on the shoulder.

'You ask for a lot,' he said. 'I guess that's OK. I'll let Dr Sanford check out the rest.'

Dr Sanford did.

Cotton's pulse rate was a beat or two higher than sixty and his blood pressure was very slightly down. He had put on some weight but was still ten pounds lighter than he had been in May.

'That's not such a bad thing,' said Dr Sanford. 'Now I'm going to test your reflexes and sense of balance.'

He judged Cotton's reflexes as still 'slightly slow', particularly on the right side of his body.

'How old are you again?'

'Twenty-eight.'

'In the Air Force they say reactions start to slow after twenty-seven. Maybe you're OK.'

Dr Sanford tested Cotton's sense of balance.

'That is a lot better than I expected. Any tilt?'

'Slight.'

'Get dressed and we'll talk.'

Cotton did and went through to Dr Sanford's study.

'Now how about your mental life?'

Cotton laughed. 'Well, I'm not aware I'm dreaming at all. I mean, I don't seem to go through that preparatory stuff prior to waking up.'

'I don't quite know how to say this,' said Dr Sanford. 'Our minds are very adaptable, sometimes almost too adaptable. They adjust to things that happen to them. The brain, however, is easier to alter, for a time anyway.'

'When given truth drugs?'

'Yes. Usually it takes us time to build up a pattern of response.'

'Are you suggesting I got other patterns in a very short time?'

Dr Sanford made a face. 'I don't know that I am. I'm only suggesting you might want to go back to school, as it were, for a couple of weeks. I mean, how's your math?'

'I barely use any.'

'You see? I'm trying to get you to use parts of your brain again. Do some geometry. Try learning a poem

349

like you used to at school. Study a map. You understand what I'm saying?'

'You want me to move stuff around again. Yes, I see. All right.'

'You say you aren't aware of dreaming, but are you sleeping OK?'

'Yes. But differently. I get tired in a way I don't remember. But then I don't sleep long. Four hours, perhaps. Then I wake. I read for an hour or so, then doze for a couple more.'

'Do you feel bad on this regime?'

'No.'

'How about mental discomfort? Fear?'

'No.'

'Hallucinations of any sort. You mentioned—'

'No, none of those for a while. Everything stays still. Or at least things close to me do. Outside that—'

'That's just New York,' said Dr Sanford. 'What would you say if I scheduled to see you in December?'

They agreed on the 3rd.

Dr Sanford shook Cotton's hand. 'Of course, if you have any problems in the meantime, don't hesitate to call me. You do understand that you are not so much react-ing to the drugs themselves any more? Your problems are more likely to involve resentment, fatigue, despair, the emotional reactions to what you've undergone.'

For the first time, Dr Sanford gave him what Cotton thought of as a soulful stare.

'You're not a why me, poor me kind of person, are you?'

Cotton smiled and shook his head. 'My attitude to

this now is that some bodies are anxious to investigate the relationship between temporary mental incapacity and a desire to tell the truth. And they really do imagine that by inflicting violence on the mind they might unlock valuable secrets.'

Dr Sanford frowned. 'Is that contempt for them?'

'No. We're all capable of very great stupidity, Doctor.'

Sanford closed one eye. 'But you're not too grown-up to think justice doesn't exist?'

Cotton smiled politely. 'Violence is a short cut anyway,' he said. 'Thank you, Doctor, for all you've done. I'm most grateful.'

Herbert Butterworth, back from Canada, came to see Cotton late in the afternoon.

'I met Ayrtoun,' he said. 'He's living in a rather bare apartment in Ottawa.'

Cotton looked up. 'All right.'

'He really is very much changed.'

Cotton nodded. He found it difficult to imagine. The last time he had seen his ex-boss, Ayrtoun had resembled a sharp-nosed but spiteful and aggressive Buddha. His habitual double-breasted blue suit needed to be let out to accommodate his new weight. 'No old school tie?'

Herbert laughed. 'No, no. He was dressed in sort of nondescript tweeds. I have never seen him so much at ease. Oh, he's positively evangelical about electroshock therapy. I mean that. He says he's been writing articles and talking to what he calls ladies' groups in Canada. It seems there are people who are attracted to the notion of shock before the calm. I think the ladies he mentioned

351

were thinking that their husbands should have the therapy.'

'You're serious?'

'Oh yes. The main thing is, he says, he knows where he is now, that he has a purpose in life. He said he didn't want to die the way he was.'

'I see.' Cotton frowned. 'Is he dying?'

'I have no reason to believe he is. He was talking about being at peace now with himself – and his late wife.'

'All right,' said Cotton.

'I didn't actually ask him about you,' said Herbert, 'but he did offer something. He said that you were something of a rock but that you lacked "the spiritual plane".'

'I see,' said Cotton. He shrugged. 'Using electric shocks to treat depression doesn't sound all that spiritual to me.'

'It opens things up, apparently. Something about access and portals. What do you think of Hornby, by the way?'

'He's a muffin . . .' Cotton started. He had meant to think before speaking.

Herbert smiled. 'I think I know what you mean. But he's rather good at it. He handled you rather well in the clinic, I thought.'

'All right. I'll bear that in mind. Do you think Ayrtoun's opinion on my lack of spirituality led to my status as a lab rat?'

Herbert smiled. 'I really don't know. But if Lowell did have anything to do with this, well, he was in London and had some contact with Ayrtoun before his

resignation. He might have picked something up and decided to use it later. Don't you think?'

'I have no idea,' said Cotton.

Herbert sat back in his chair, scratched at his hair and sighed.

'What do you think of our ambassador in Washington, Lord Inverchapel?'

'I have very little to go on. I believe he can be quite witty.'

'No, no. He can be *very* witty. When he was ambassador in Moscow he's supposed to have nagged and nagged until he got a directive out of Churchill on how to handle Stalin – "I don't mind kissing Stalin's bum, but I'm damned if I'll lick his arse."'

Cotton raised his eyebrows. 'Succinct, generally accurate but not perhaps very clear cut in terms of diplomacy.'

'Actually, Inverchapel's one of the reasons I decided to leave DC. I have nothing against him. He's urbane, perceptive and tough. But this posting is a reward for having been ambassador in Moscow during the war.'

'Surely that acts in his favour. Doesn't that mean he brings experience of the Soviets?'

'Absolutely, but the American mood is not going his way. That's becoming a problem. There are some Americans who believe you can't sup with the devil and not become an apologist.'

'How long do you think he's got?'

'Till next year, I imagine.' Cotton nodded. There was anecdotal chat and there was anecdotal chat in the Intelligence Services. He was beginning to realize that

Herbert was a stopgap. He knew there would be staff changes. What he did not know yet was whether or not there would be policy changes to go with them.

On 11 September Cotton went to the Waldorf and was surprised to find that Ed Lowell had a companion in the Peacock Alley. Maria de los Angeles Vergara Fratelli welcomed him quietly, like an old friend at a funeral for whom large displays of affection on such a solemn occasion were not necessary. She was wearing a very expensive black suit and a small black hat with a black spotted veil that came down low enough for her to adopt a small tilt and an upward look.

Ed Lowell looked delighted. 'Angeles and I are fairly recent chums,' he said.

He was enjoying himself. He beckoned the waiter.

'You two can always talk in Spanish, you know.'

'You're right, Ed,' said Cotton. So he did. '¿Pero qué haces aquí con este cabrón? Me dicen que es medio marica en cualquier caso.' What are you doing with this bastard? They tell me he's half queer, in any case.

Lowell's eyes opened and he smiled.

'Please join in,' said Cotton.

Ed Lowell smiled. 'There's no need,' he said.

Cotton looked at Angeles. 'What can I say?'

She inclined her head as if accepting an apology. Cotton smiled at her.

'I'm not going to London, after all,' said Ed Lowell.

'Are you very disappointed?'

'Frankly? Not at all.'

'Good!'

Cotton looked around him. The decoration of Peacock Alley was decidedly rich for his taste, but he thought that was probably the point. Ed Lowell had eschewed subtlety and presumably had his reasons. On his right hand, Cotton checked off Mari-Angeles, the Waldorf and her recent realignment of her own interests. Ed Lowell's people had been impressively quick in getting hold of her. He licked his teeth.

Angeles ordered steak, of course. Cotton chose salmon. He was a little surprised that Ed Lowell chose the same. He had a peculiar sensation as if Lowell was shadowing his movements. He had seen a man do that with a woman, but not to another man. When his salmon arrived, Ed Lowell told the waiter to 'have it cooked some more'.

'How are your studies going?' Cotton asked Angeles.

Ed Lowell laughed out loud. 'I'm sorry to butt in, but I haven't come to talk about our charming companion. She kindly agreed to come for the food. She's no Dolores del Rio.'

'Why should she be?'

'Dolores is a commie, you know.'

'I didn't,' said Cotton. 'I only knew she was an actress.'

Ed Lowell shrugged. 'I thought you had met the HUAC people.'

Cotton considered this. So Ed knew who had visited him in the clinic. 'Yes. A lawyer called Gaynes. He was accompanied by two others. A Navy man called Lockhart – do you know him? – and someone who looked to me like an interrogator. He was called Yeager.'

Ed Lowell smiled. 'You're quite right,' he said. 'The

355

HUAC are turning their attention to Hollywood now, you know.'

'So they said.'

'They have quite a list of people already.' Lowell smiled again. 'Popular culture,' he murmured, as if forgiving something. 'The thing is, Peter, I really want to talk to you about liaison work. But you didn't show much taste for it in London.'

'No, Ed. That's right. I didn't let you in.'

'I could have helped.'

'No. You were anxious for us to tighten security. But that business in London had nothing to do with a real security leak. It was a witch-hunt by a particularly nasty part of our intelligence services. As Angeles knows, my right thigh met a cut-throat razor. The whole thing was an expensive distraction.'

'My dear Peter! We all have our departments and agencies. They are, certainly at a humdrum level, far closer to us than our real enemies. They squabble and, like those who are presently going after Dolores del Rio and others, they seek publicity. But it's the enemies that really count.' He frowned. 'You like Hoberman from the FBI, don't you?'

'I appreciate him, Ed. He's competent, professional, plays fair and he gets to the point.'

Ed Lowell did not immediately answer. Instead he cocked his head and peered at Cotton.

'Is that because you're both middle class?'

Cotton raised his eyebrows, then laughed. 'In any case, it wouldn't be quite the same middle class, would it?'

'What exactly are you?'

356

'I was an infant ex-pat, Ed. It's not the imperial swell but it's got certain advantages, even privileges.'

Ed Lowell narrowed his eyes. 'You'll have to explain that.'

'From all over the Empire and beyond, small British boys are sent home to be educated. It gives a lot of us more than one viewpoint. It can even make us a little dismissive of what we see of the country we have to learn to call ours.'

'But you don't hate your own country, Peter.'

'No, Ed. It's no stronger than occasional dislike.'

There was a tiny pause before Ed Lowell laughed.

'Your background has lent you a certain . . . independence of mind.'

'I don't like the word "lent",' said Cotton. I think we're stuck with it. And independence of mind is almost always relative. I went from a colourful country and privileged life to a chilly, poor place that was very proud but that had hollow, miserable patches.'

'That's fine. I can see that.'

Angeles excused herself. Cotton got up to help her and for a moment Lowell watched them before barely rising from his seat.

'What else do you do?' said Ed Lowell.

'I'm sorry?'

'You have other interests?'

'Yes,' said Cotton.

'Are you a collector?'

'No, not really. I did have some jazz records but they got broken.' A girl called Anna had stamped on them in London. 'Art Tatum.'

'Jazz,' said Ed Lowell. 'You like American culture.'

'I like Fred Astaire, too,' said Cotton. 'Are you a collector?'

Ed Lowell nodded. 'Meissen,' he murmured. 'Do you read?'

'For pleasure? Yes.'

'What are you reading now?'

'Somebody from Rhode Island gave me a book as a going-away present. I'm not sure it's freely available. *Ulysses* by James Joyce.'

Lowell smiled. 'Not, as I understand, the kind of writer who uses euphemism, like "powder one's nose", for example.'

'I've been reading of the role of Jews in Irish society,' said Cotton.

'Is there one?'

'I think that was the writer's point.'

Lowell smiled. 'What is it you get from reading?'

'It helps a certain flexibility of mind, I think.'

'Good,' said Lowell. He paused. 'You know I could arrange for Angeles to see you again. Only if you're interested, of course.'

Cotton looked at him. Ed was always telling him what he had the power to do.

'I have a bet with Minty,' he said. 'It's not much. Ten dollars, I think. She says you won't marry next year. I have bet you will.'

'You'll win,' said Ed Lowell. 'Minty is much less clever than she thinks. Good lawyer for detail, though. You know she specializes in divorce?'

'She said something about usually representing modern women.'

'She's been very busy post war. I think it has made her cynical. She's all day in the bitterness of broken lives, you see.'

Cotton got up again as Angeles came back. 'What have they got you on?' he said to her. 'Residence?'

Angeles raised her veil slightly. She leant towards him and kissed him. She nodded and sat down again.

Ed Lowell nodded and applauded so softly there was no sound.

'Peter. I really do think we can do business.'

'Good,' said Cotton. He allowed a brief pause in case Ed Lowell was about to say what it was. 'I look forward to it.'

'Do I have your home number?'

Cotton knew very well he did. But he handed his card over in what he thought of as a very demure version of snap.

'We'll call this a hostage to fortune, shall we?'

Ed Lowell smiled rather distractedly and summoned a waiter. 'The lady will have dessert. Just coffee for us?'

Cotton had never seen Herbert Butterworth look quite so taken aback before.

'But why on earth would he bring Angeles along?' said Herbert.

'To show me what I already knew – that they were reading my mail, that they had found and got hold of "Srta A" very quickly, and that she now has a new employer.'

359

Herbert frowned. 'But he's just entirely wasted his use of her! Would you have done the same?' Something else occurred to him. 'Oh, dear, Eve is going to be rather annoyed. I think she liked watching Angeles in action.'

Cotton said nothing.

'What does he want, do you think?' Herbert was still frowning.

'It's not clear yet. He talked of working together in the future and asked for his salmon to be cooked some more.'

'Really?' Herbert sighed. 'Ed's a classicist, you know. Started learning ancient Greek at the age of five sort of thing.'

Cotton raised his eyebrows.

'Nothing new under the sun – how men really behave, their types, their flaws, their deficiencies . . . it does tend to hubris, though.'

'He suggested that Sam Hoberman of the FBI and I had something in common: we're both middle class.'

Herbert winced. 'I don't understand. Does he mean you're bourgeois? He can't mean you're acquisitive? Hypocritical? Is he calling you second rate?'

Cotton shrugged. 'Hoberman certainly knows who he works for. He's a lot more realistic than Ed Lowell appears to think. But within that he has a job to do with American security and he does it well.'

'Perhaps Lowell thinks both of you lack the overview.'

'Then that's his problem. J. Edgar Hoover has power and an organization and is extremely jealous about maintaining both. Sam Hoberman works for him. What do you think Lowell has?'

360

It had been a serious question. Herbert didn't answer at once. He was thinking.

'The academics and theorists are getting a lot of work these days,' he said.

'Lowell's not an academic.'

'No, but academics play a larger role in political life here. They're part of Lowell's network of advice.'

Cotton sat back. He had listened to this kind of stuff very often; flustered British attempts to work out what was going on. He was aware that his sense of detachment had nothing to do with any drugs. Sitting here, high up in a building in New York, he waited. He wondered if the Americans would have killed him in Narragansett if he had looked unreliable or crazy – a summer drowning? A hunting accident? Probably just an overdose. That would have fit better with depression and suicide. He also remembered that he had spent a lot of time exercising his eyes and drawing up target lines. Possibly, he was looking for a shot but without a rifle or ammunition. He grunted. He must have confused himself with the hunter.

'Peter.'

'What?'

'Are you depressed?'

'No. Or if it is depression, it's a very calm sort.'

'Right. Well, we don't have their money, of course, but we do have some people in place.'

Cotton sat up. Herbert had been thinking through 'need to know'. He had not been in a hurry and had taken some care.

'Last year, Lowell was sent to London to write a

report on British Intelligence; an analysis of how our various services work, their strengths and weaknesses. He came to the conclusion that the whole operation was damagingly class-ridden.'

'He's right about that,' said Cotton.

'He has quite a good phrase. "Their social prejudices make them blinder than the moles they are meant to be hunting." He suggests that the prime loyalty of the British intelligence services is not to king, country or government; but to their own small group, at one level, a kind of club. This makes it inconceivable for us to question the behaviour of people we consider not just colleagues and friends but who make up part of our own identity.' Herbert looked up. 'Of course, he was talking of the top people. But he also made the point that our services had its own internal class system. He didn't think Ayrtoun, for example, was regarded as quite "top drawer". What do you think?'

'Well,' said Cotton, 'I can see how he came to that conclusion. I'd probably have said something similar. From the American point of view, we're a loyal if touchy ally with not much energy or flexibility but quite a few leaks. I don't know about you, but I've never been asked to find a traitor. I imagine that's so as not to cause friction among fellow workers. But we're also ridden with fatuous hierarchies and so compartmentalized that we mislay information.' Cotton paused. 'But isn't Lowell the American equivalent of our own version of a small, clubbable group?'

Herbert laughed. 'Yes, but America has its virtues. One of them is that I don't think Lowell would actually

trust anyone in that group of his. I don't think he has a natural talent for friendship – but he does make mutually beneficial alliances. There's a professor at Yale—'

Cotton looked up. 'You mean Resnick?'

'Yes. You know him?'

'I met him in Newport. Briefly.'

'Ah. Well, Resnick looked over Lowell's London report and was impressed. He also asked the kind of basic questions ambitious academics with an interest in strategy and international relations do. They can be quite astute when dealing with the Administration. He asked why, if the Soviets can provide a potential haven for British traitors, the US could not. Yes, there are Soviets who defect directly to the US. But why do British traitors choose the Soviets? Resnick calls this intellectual self-righteousness. He thinks it's due to the tendency of scientists to choose what he calls a closed structure of belief. It's how they're trained. They are deluded in thinking Stalin has any interest in justice for the workers or in world peace. Their anti-Americanism trumps that.'

'Not all traitors are scientists,' said Cotton.

'That's true,' said Herbert. 'The non-scientists are the ones who don't get caught.' He paused. 'You know, I'm wondering if you may be a new development. Lowell has identified you as a potential outsider. After all, he knows that you almost left Intelligence to move here and marry an American citizen at the end of 1945. Do you think he may, by offering you Angeles, be underestimating your choosiness in women? He has his own father for reference and of course Allen Dulles upstairs, for example,

works hard but is fond of an evening of play that involves feminine company.'

'Angeles is very pretty.'

'But outside the sex thing, she is unbearably provincial and snobby.'

Cotton had not seen Herbert quite this unsettled before. He had the impression of a ball rattling about a roulette wheel.

'I'm sure Ed is not the kind of man to judge another's tastes, if he can get use out of him.'

Herbert sighed. 'Oh, Ed Lowell's above quite a lot,' he said. 'On the drugs thing, I imagine he suspects that their own volunteers failed precisely because they were volunteers.'

Cotton sighed. 'So he'd favour practising on the unwitting?'

'He would see you as a challenge. You were more flexible. It's the stiff that crack. And to some extent, I suppose, the not too sensitive survive better.'

Cotton laughed. 'That's demented, Herbert.'

'Whoever said it wasn't? The thing is, Lowell believes in special people. He believes he is one, for example. But he looks for others remarkable in their own, doubtless lesser way. Your biggest problem may be in understanding that he both really admires you as being as tough as old boots and also despises you. There might be some fear in there, too. Perhaps a little envy.'

Cotton smiled. 'I think I've got that,' he said. 'It's quite common with competitive people.'

'Do you think he's competing with you?'

'Absolutely not.'

'Are you competing with him?'

'That only depends on how disposable he considers me to be. For now, he's critical of the other American agencies. I don't know to what extent he sees me as part of a chance or opening to develop something beneficial to him, but I imagine I'm not his only possibility.'

Herbert sighed. 'Look,' he said, 'I don't want to press you, but I need some idea of how you're thinking of playing this.'

'Well, honestly, I still don't know for sure who thought it worthwhile having me drugged, or why. I do know, however, that after my recovery, Lowell has stepped up his interest in me. If he was responsible, his approach now might seem surprising, to say the least, but I'm taking it as to do with who he wants to be.'

'What do you mean?'

'I don't know whether this is Intelligence-related or has do with his political career. But from my point of view that doesn't really matter. I mean, I think Ed's playing to an audience. That was my impression of him in Newport. I think he's showing he can be resolute and daring and is prepared to take things on. I don't really think he's hoping that I, an outsider as you said, can keep them on the inside track in British Intelligence.'

Herbert smiled. 'Put like that, it does seem a little lame.' He sucked on his teeth. 'Did you know that when Lowell was in London, he spent quite some time with the people who set up the Tavistock Institute?'

'I didn't know that,' said Cotton.

'That's partly funded by the Rockefeller Foundation here.'

Cotton nodded. 'Group behaviours. Organizational dynamics.'

'Exactly,' said Herbert. 'A lot of people from politicians to marketing departments are very interested in their findings and theories.'

Cotton shrugged. 'Yes.' He remembered Ayrtoun's Rikki-Tikki-Tavi nickname. 'Ayrtoun worked with the Tavistock Institute when he was in advertising, selling sausages and soap. That was before he went on to misdirection during the war.'

Herbert sighed. 'Dear God,' he said, 'sometimes I think we're all becoming Dr Goebbels' heirs. The Nazis certainly crystallized things.'

Cotton tried again. 'Herbert, do you have any idea what Lowell wants from me?' he asked.

'Not yet.'

'Then I think I should I see Dr Resnick.'

Herbert thought about this. 'Very well,' he said. 'See if you can arrange that. Is there anything else you want?'

'Could we call Hornby in?'

Cotton saw that Hornby was carrying an unlit pipe with his files.

'Did you manage to get anything on Minty Auchincloss?'

'Yes, I did.' Hornby put the pipe in a side pocket and opened a file. 'She was actually born Edith Millicent Petrie in 1921. At ten, she took her mother's third husband's name and stuck with it, even though that marriage lasted a bare eighteen months. She had four half-siblings, three of whom survive. Her mother's maiden name was

366

Blackwell – a tobacco family. She got cut off because of her behaviour and there's some doubt whether this man Petrie was actually Miss Auchincloss's father. He went off to Paris and rather forgot to come back, but he did set up home with a young Italian count. His money came from soft drinks. She was a good student but rather stroppy in a quiet sort of way. She made an elaborate plan to ridicule Harvard Law School, because they don't accept women. I don't think that went down well. She went to Columbia Law School instead – that's very liberal.'

'What does that mean?' said Cotton.

'Oh, they've got Negro women there as well. She lives on one floor of her great-aunt's house on East 70th Street and is rather a light at the Cosmopolitan Club on East 68th.'

'That's women only,' said Herbert.

'I've got her down as a rather sassy child of the suffragettes,' said Hornby.

'Have you?' said Herbert. 'Anything else?'

'Everybody says she's smitten with Ed Lowell.'

'But it's not reciprocated?'

'Well, she's hardly the decorative rose type. And I imagine her chosen name is a problem.'

'Why?'

Hornby paused. 'Isn't it Jewish?'

Herbert looked up. 'The original Auchincloss was a grocer from Paisley in Scotland. The name Auchincleck, sometimes pronounced Affleck, is from the same root. Perhaps they should say Affloss.'

'Interesting,' said Hornby. He looked round at Cotton.

'She told me she had lesbian interests,' he said.

Hornby shook his head. 'I don't know about that.'

'You said she lived with her great-aunt,' said Herbert.

'Maternal. I don't know what the arrangement is, if there's rent or companionship or what. The old lady is a spinster, Miss Amy Blackwell.'

'Any suggestion Minty Auchincloss is in Intelligence?' said Cotton.

'Not directly,' said Hornby. 'She knows a lot of people who are, of course. Wait a minute. I know what it was. The reason I thought her name was Jewish was because her best friend at Columbia was Adele Rothstein, now Resnick. In fact, I think she's godmother to the girl Adele had in 1944.'

Cotton smiled. So Minty was a friend of Resnick's wife.

'What have I said?'

'It's all right. I'm remembering something she said. Something about higher or heightened gossip. How do I get in touch with her?'

Hornby already had a list of what he called 'her haunts'.

'Tell me when you want to see her and I'll find out where she is for you.'

25

COTTON'S BLOCK had a white-gloved Negro porter called Rodney. About seven on Friday evening, Rodney buzzed up on the internal telephone.

'There's a young lady to see you, sir. A Miss Vergara.'

'Thank you, Rodney. I'm expecting her.'

'Will you be coming down, sir?'

'No,' said Cotton. 'She'll be coming up. Could you see her to the elevator?'

Cotton put on a jacket and retied his tie. He lived on the fourteenth floor and timed opening the door to his apartment just right. He was slightly surprised that Rodney had come up with her.

'That's very kind,' he said.

'No need, sir. Just doing my job.'

'Miss Vergara and I will be going out later,' he said, 'on diplomatic business.'

He pressed, Rodney accepted the gratuity and took the elevator down.

'He didn't trust me,' said Angeles. She handed him a card. It was the one he had given Ed Lowell at lunch in the Waldorf.

However grim her personal circumstances, Angeles paid a great deal of attention to her appearance and clothes. She offered her cheek.

'This way. Can I get you something to drink?'

Angeles thought about it. 'A gin and tonic,' she decided. She walked into the hall and turned into the 'great room'. Cotton went directly to the refrigerator and got out a bottle of tonic.

'Who picked this apartment?' she said.

'I did,' he said as he walked via the glass cupboard to the dining room. 'With some help from my sister.'

'Ah.'

Cotton poured some gin into the glass. 'Meaning?'

Angeles gave in to her aesthetic opinion. 'Really, it's not very chic. The colours are faux colonial. Pasty. This furniture's not yours, is it?'

'No,' said Cotton.

'Don't you care?'

'Not particularly. A comfortable chair's always nice, but quite hard to get.'

'*Ay*,' said Angeles. She pointed at Eleanor's still unframed gift. 'That painting is almost Mexican.' She did not sound approving.

He gave her the gin and tonic. '*Cuéntame*.' Tell me.

Angeles sighed, then tried the drink. 'I have problems.'

Cotton nodded. 'Have you been offered any solutions?'

'I think one is you. Do you have lemon?'

'No. In what sense me?'

Angeles shrugged. She looked around, put down her drink and sat on the sofa. She made a face. 'Do you want me or not?' She smiled. 'And before you reply, think. I don't know what other options he'll give me.' She looked

up. 'I don't understand. He must really want you,' she said.

'I don't really know what Ed wants. But it's miserably unpleasant for you.'

'Why?'

'Presumably you're talking about me or deportation? That's not a choice, Angeles. It's a threat.'

Angeles shook her head. 'Sometimes,' she said sadly, 'choices are not my friends.' She recovered almost instantly with a very husky, very brief laugh.

'*¡Y yo con este cuerpo!*'

'It's a wonderful body. But no choice at all hardly constitutes a friend.'

'I don't know if that's true. I told you, I am very adaptable. I don't know what other choices there will be if I make this one. I don't know what choices you would give me.'

'Would it solve your problems?'

She shrugged. 'I'd have permission to stay. I could pursue my studies.'

'Angeles. Be practical. I don't have the kind of money that even keeps you in shoes.'

'He said that would be taken care of.'

Cotton frowned. 'Really? Then our problem would simply be that we would have to provide whatever Mr Lowell wanted or you'd find yourself on a plane to Argentina and I'd find myself even more compromised than I already am.'

Angeles shook her head. 'No, no, no. You don't understand. He assured me the offer came without strings for you.'

'Are you offended?'

'I wasn't offended the first time we met.' She smiled. 'I once met a very rich old man. He called me his "beautiful mistake". I have that effect.'

Cotton nodded. 'I see. What happened to the rich old man?'

'Oh, he had a heart attack. It was a very difficult situation.'

'I can imagine,' said Cotton. 'May I offer you supper?'

Angeles thought. 'Yes,' she said. 'In the Village. I know a place.'

'Quiet?'

She frowned. 'But why do you like quiet so much?'

'It means I can hear what you say,' said Cotton.

Cotton took her to the small restaurant she chose. It was called La Estrella Azul, the Blue Star, and had star-shaped glass shades over the tables. They emitted very little, almost oily gold light. The loudest sounds were the shuffle of an elderly waiter's feet and the occasional sizzle of steak landing on a grill.

'*Carne. Dos*,' said Angeles. Meat, two.

'When are you due to talk to Mr Lowell?'

'When I've seen you.'

'All right,' said Cotton. 'Tell him I think he has things in the wrong order.'

'What does that mean?'

'He'll know.'

'*Yo no.*'

Cotton smiled. 'Sorry. We both need more time and

more information. By saying he has things in the wrong order, I am opening negotiations, through you. At this stage – and tell him this – what I am doing is as significant as saying you come without strings. There is a small risk here, of course, mostly for you. He could, I suppose, decide you are not worth the trouble.'

'I'd prefer to keep that risk away.'

'Then let's say I want you as the go-between for just now. What do you think?'

'Do you know what you're doing?'

'I'm negotiating. I'm saying his offer of you is not serious but I don't want you to—'

'Pay the price,' said Angeles.

Cotton nodded. 'Has Mr Lowell shown any personal interest in you?'

Angeles shook her head. '*Pero nada*,' she said. 'His sense of hygiene is – *tremendo*.'

'He has a fiancée, you know.'

'Truly?'

'I've met her.'

Angeles looked suspicious. 'What is she?'

'I don't know that she's a model, professional, I mean. She's from a well-off family and certainly she knows when she's being photographed.'

'You see?' Angeles shook her head. 'It's pure appearance.'

Cotton shrugged. 'I don't know, Angeles.'

'*¡Yayaya!* He's threatening me. Who cares that he's *formalito*, that his language has the appearance of respect? He has none. His fiancée and I are just different degrees of female commodity.'

'Maybe,' said Cotton. Though he thought that she had that about right.

'You're not going to sleep with me tonight, are you?'

'No. You have to talk to Ed Lowell.'

Angeles sighed. 'That's why I like old men.'

'Why?'

'They get excited and grateful and make me feel needed. Someone tried to tell me once sex and love were different.' She shook her head. 'There are just expectations.'

Cotton smiled. 'Isn't love supposed to last a little longer?'

She laughed. 'You're just talking of selfishness and dreams and a repetition of need. I'm talking about – more sensory things.' She shrugged.

'Angeles, I also want you to tell Mr Lowell I'd like to talk to Professor Walter Resnick.' Cotton spelt out the surname. 'That's important. Have you got that?'

Angeles nodded. From her bag she took out a small bottle of perfume and dabbed at her wrists and behind her ears.

'Meat clings,' she said.

The perfume struck Cotton like horribly sweet smelling salts.

'What is that?'

'Chanel No. 5,' she said. She shrugged. '*Sirve*' – it does.

Cotton saw Angeles into a taxi. Before she got in he checked that she remembered what to say.

'Wrong order, no strings, Resnick,' she said and kissed him.

374

When her taxi had gone he suddenly felt as exhausted as he had in the Ogden Clinic just after he had come out of sedation. He was absolutely out of energy. As soon as he got home, he dropped into a chair. His sister was probably right. He should get out of this. The reasons were simple. He no longer had the mental or physical stamina required. Simplest of all, he wanted nothing to do with people who thought drugs could substitute torture, and nothing to do with arrogant American aristocrats who indulged in stratagems that involved lovely if slightly crazy refugees from Argentina as currency.

When he woke up the next morning he felt the sleep had done him some good and that he would have some responses to Lowell. He immediately tried to squash this and tell himself it wasn't worth it. But he had what he thought of as a lump of stubbornness running in his veins.

He spoke to Herbert. By the time he finished, Herbert's hair was all over the place.

'Angeles as an earnest of intent? Do you really buy that? What's the matter with him? Does he think you're some sort of sex maniac or something?'

'I don't know. I suspect he thinks I have more interest in sex than he does. I took it as an opening gambit by a theoretician.'

'Trying to get your trust? Demonstrating his power?'

'I see him as one of those men who feels rather superior to other men; who doesn't actually understand other men's tastes but understands he has to pretend that he

knows what they're talking about. He needs to pretend so that he's supported and accepted.'

'Like an intellectual who tries to swear like a navvy?'

'Lowell doesn't swear. He treats women and language very formally. Of course, behind any offer he comes to me with now, I have my experience as a lab rat as a warning. And of course, the airport for Angeles isn't very far.'

Herbert made a face. 'I'm going to invite Hornby in on this. If you don't mind, that is.'

'As you wish.'

Herbert rang through for Hornby. Cotton was pleased, when Hornby had been brought up to date, to see him frown.

'This doesn't, offhand, make a lot of sense. You're saying this Argentine tart used to work for us but now Mr Lowell is offering her back to Cotton here. Would that be a sort of payment?'

'We surmise Mr Lowell is trying to find out what kind of payment would please or at least unlock the door to cooperation.'

Hornby turned towards Cotton. 'Do you have any idea of what this cooperation would entail?'

Cotton shook his head. 'No, I don't. Ed Lowell has mentioned words like "liaison" but hasn't been specific. He appears to be concentrating on getting his sticks and carrots lined up before he gets to that part.'

'But we cooperate with the Americans,' said Hornby. 'We always have.'

'The Americans don't think we cooperate well or enough or when they want,' said Herbert.

Hornby nodded. 'I see,' he said. 'Mr Lowell must know what risks he's taking. I know he was in London. For some Americans, with our socialist government, that's almost Moscow.'

'I hadn't been thinking of the Soviets,' said Cotton. 'I had thought of checking in with Hoberman in the FBI but decided to hold off.'

'I wouldn't give up on the Soviet angle just yet,' said Hornby. He looked at Cotton. 'Remember. You're supposed to have met Cherkesov.'

'I did.'

Hornby nodded. 'Well, how about insinuating other American agencies?'

'I don't think it's necessary yet,' said Cotton. 'And I think he'd take that in a way we don't want.'

'Quite,' said Herbert. 'But we do want to know what he's after, wouldn't you say?'

Hornby frowned. 'Do you think Mr Lowell is sincere?' he asked.

'About the cooperation? No, I don't,' said Cotton. 'I think he may be trying to undermine my position, intro- duce doubts about my loyalty, but whatever he's doing, his aim is to drive me towards the Americans because I'll have nowhere else to go.'

'What do you think his long-term aim is?'

'I'm not sure,' said Cotton. 'But he may be practising.'

'On what?'

'People like me. You mentioned Cherkesov; he told me you practise on your own first. I think Lowell is doing something similar. He can't practise on unwitting Americans yet, but an ally will do. A hint that I wasn't

377

cooperating, that I had had two high-level meetings with the Russians, might have been enough to make some people think themselves justified in trying out their latest techniques on me in the guise of a security check. Ed was in the Navy, wasn't he? He's now in security. Even if he's not directly part of Operation Chatter, he's close to those who are.'

Hornby looked almost happy. 'Right,' he said. 'Under the circumstances, I think we're perfectly able to consider a bit of tit for tat; you know, slip him a Mickey Finn – chloral hydrate – and take a few compromising photographs. Would this woman cooperate?'

'No,' said Cotton.

'Right. I'll give it some more thought.'

'I'm impressed,' said Herbert when Hornby had gone. 'You were right. He is a bit of a muffin.'

But it was Hornby that gave Cotton the information on where to find Minty Auchincloss after work. It was a rather grand place with beige marble columns and a lot of lawyers. She was sitting alone at a small corner table reading a document.

'Hello, Miss Auchincloss. How are you?'

'Well, Colonel. Look at you!'

'I ate with Ed the other day. And missed you.'

She laughed. 'I think I'll have a dry Martini,' she said. 'I don't always accompany his guests, you know.'

'Yes, but you're close.'

'Why Colonel, is this an interview?'

'Not really. I thought I'd ask you for some information.'

She laughed again. 'Well, you're up front. Not subtle. But up front.'

Cotton ordered the drink and turned to her again. 'It's about Ed.'

'Ask him yourself.'

Cotton smiled. 'It's a little delicate.'

'Do you mean awkward?'

'Ed told me he collected Meissen porcelain.'

'Oh, you're not going to be mean, are you?'

'No, just discreet. What I really want to know was how possessive he is. You talked to me in Newport of civilized men. And you claimed an interest yourself, of course.'

'What are you talking about?'

'Come on, Minty. The girl is absolutely gorgeous.'

Minty frowned, then opened her eyes wide. 'You can't really be saying you're interested in Rosemary? But I told you! She's vile. She's stupid and she's mean.'

'Ed has feelings for her.'

'He's in love with what she represents.'

'And what or who is she in love with?'

'She's in love with what she's used to. Money! You don't have it.'

She paused. 'You're not really interested in Rosemary, are you? You're asking me to be indiscreet about people I know.'

'OK. That's fair.'

She shook her head and smiled. 'I'm trying to remember if I really ever thought you were altogether nicer.'

'Probably not.'

She looked at him. 'Tell me what you really want.'

'Ed and I have entered negotiations about something that would involve collaboration. I'm trying to understand him. I wondered whether his choice of Rosemary was a mistake or not.'

'It's a mutually beneficial deal. At least, that's what I've always thought it was.' Minty frowned. 'He might be rather annoyed you're asking me.'

Cotton shrugged. 'He asked me to collaborate. I'm looking at his references. You'd be one, wouldn't you?'

'Would he find your interest flattering?'

'He might. Though my sister says flattery is bad for men.'

Minty Auchincloss laughed. 'I like the sound of her.'

'I think I'm asking you to be my translator on American mores and so on.'

Minty smiled. 'For example?'

'In Newport, when you did Ed so much service in accompanying me, nobody apparently thought he might have met Cherkesov in London. Was this discretion?'

'What do you mean?'

'I mean do people know Ed's in intelligence but don't admit it?'

'I shouldn't have thought so. After all, you got taken into the main tent because you'd met him. That would be more flaunting, what he's been doing, wouldn't it? It makes politicians feel they're a little nearer the action.'

'All right. Why does Ed wait till next year to get married?'

'Because it'll be a society wedding. Big Splash. Big names. Perhaps a mention or two that he is planning a career in politics or public service.'

'Right. That's another of my doubts. Is this political stuff genuine?'

'Of course. Why do you think he was sucking up with a party to people he can't stand?'

'Who's paying? Sorry. I'll rephrase that. Where does his money come from?'

'Not movies and bootleg liquor, I assure you. But there's been a lot of mingling of interests. Some mining, some oil, some shipping. Ed has a trust fund of about a hundred thousand a year. I believe he remits his actual salary to charity. By the way, that wasn't his mother at the party. That was wife number three, I think.'

'How much has Ed thought about the future?'

She laughed. 'A lot! Ed's thinking 1960 onwards. He thinks by that time a man with security experience in what he calls the Cold War with the Soviets will be a popular choice. May even look a lot better than the pure politicians.'

'What? For president?'

'Joe Kennedy's second boy is heading that way too. Though Ed says he won't make it. He's a Catholic. He's stuck with being a turncoat or being under orders from the Pope.'

Cotton laughed. 'That's certainly planning ahead.'

'Somebody has to. Ed says it's usually the eventual winner.'

'How will he get known to the public?'

'I think they're starting with a book. You know Professor Resnick? He has an ambitious doctoral student on the research and I think there's a professional ghostwriter lined up too.'

'Do you know the subject?'

'Metternich, Talleyrand, that kind of thing.'

'The Congress of Vienna?'

'If you say so. But I think it's really supposed to be about the Iron Curtain.'

She looked up around the bar.

'You don't understand something,' she said. 'Most of the men in this room want to be president. Half of them think they have a pretty good chance. Ten per cent really think they will get to the White House.'

'You're a very ambitious people. I admire that. Or are presidential ambitions some rite of passage for youngish men here?'

Minty smiled. 'Didn't you ever want to be whatever it is you have?'

'Prime minister? God, no. How long have you known Ed?'

'Since I was about thirteen. We're not family but we're in the herd.'

'Do I get a story?'

'Oh, actually you do. I really got to know Ed after I met a man who looked very old to me in the orchid house. It was just a peremptory, possibly even polite massage, you might say.'

'But at the time it felt more than gruesome.'

'Invasive to horrifying.'

'And nobody was interested to hear about the incident?'

'I was never that naïve, I assure you.'

'And Ed was sweet.'

'He was, actually. At least, not a shit, like most men.'

'Good. I'm pleased to hear it. And in return you've done things for him.'

'Not those things, Colonel. I was in love with him, naturally, when I was about thirteen. But even I knew nothing was going to happen.'

'Why not?'

'All kinds of reasons. I didn't have money, I was not thought of as one of the beautiful girls, and I thought I'd probably become too dependent on him. Will that do?'

Cotton smiled. 'It will indeed. Thank you very much. I'd like to see you again, if I may, Miss Auchincloss. Perhaps dinner sometime soon? There'd be other people there, of course. But you might find it interesting. Even novel.'

Minty Auchincloss raised one eyebrow. 'I might just take you up on that, you know?'

Cotton gave her his private card and got one back.

'Light me a cigarette before you go.'

'Of course.'

Cotton lit the cigarette and left her puffing away inexpertly as she went back to her document.

26

'P RESIDENT?' SAID Herbert Butterworth. 'Are we supposed to take that seriously?'

'My information is that Ed Lowell does.'

'He's keeping his nose clean.'

'I'm sorry?'

'He's hiding in the intelligence services because he knows no one will challenge his patriotism when he comes out. Security considerations, you see.' Herbert wrinkled his nose. 'It's all becoming a tad Roman emperor, don't you think?'

'Which one?'

Herbert wasn't listening. 'Thomas Dewey did rather well, you know, against Roosevelt in 1944. By far the closest result Roosevelt had to endure. At one time during the campaign Dewey wanted to accuse Roosevelt of prior knowledge of Pearl Harbor.'

'Why didn't he?'

'Security. He was told this would indicate to the Japanese that the Americans had broken Code Purple, were able to decipher what the Japanese military were saying. As a loyal American, he obeyed, of course.'

'Dewey's running again next year, isn't he?'

'Yes. But he still might not win, you know. He

hates mud-slinging and likes to think of himself as principled.'

'In what sense?'

'He's against Red baiting and is on record as saying "You can't kill an idea with a gun." You can't have that many scruples if you are running for president.'

'Perhaps Ed Lowell's learnt from that,' said Cotton. 'Can you tell me what we really had against Angeles?'

Herbert shrugged. 'Frankly? She's not ours any more.'

Cotton nodded.

'What do you want to do with her?' said Herbert.

'Let her become a picture restorer in New York.'

Herbert laughed. 'I don't have your intimate knowledge, but I'm not sure that's really an option. You're not a sentimentalist, are you?'

'No, but I think it's time to react to Ed's offer of her.'

'What have you got in mind?'

'Find her protection. Do you think Eve could give me the names of wealthy gentlemen unhappy with their wives or feeling lonely in New York? Is that too simple?'

'No,' said Herbert. 'I don't think it is, really. Eve's rather good at this sort of thing.'

Two days later Cotton was dining at the Plaza with Minty Auchincloss, Herbert and Eve Butterworth, Angeles and a gentleman of about fifty 'in town' for a few days from Wilmington, Delaware. Angeles took half a second to look at Minty, saw no threat and concentrated entirely on Robert A. Culver.

'She's wonderful,' murmured Minty. 'Positively oozes

sex. And that attention she pays the florid gentlemen. Do men fall for that?'

'I hope you're joking,' said Cotton.

The American pronounced Angeles' name like the city in California.

Cotton had never met Eve before. He had heard her described as 'an earth mother', but she turned out to be slight and very small, perhaps not even five feet. He watched her skilfully guide the conversation on to colours and link Angeles' history of art with Robert A. Culver's profession – he was a director of Dupont. After the first course, Angeles persuaded Mr Culver to dance. Cotton was interested to see how she approached this. Angeles was, certainly from the position of her body, going for the long, slow term.

'She asked me how far Wilmington, Delaware was from New York City,' said Eve.

'How far is it?' asked Cotton.

'I don't know. A hundred miles. A little more, perhaps.'

'Is he married?'

'Of course. But his wife is what Americans call a dreadful sourpuss. A number of people have told me that Bob's business success is based on a reluctance to return home from the office that's even more powerful than his ambition. I know him through his favourite charity. He really is rather a sweet man, you know.'

Cotton looked at the dance floor. Bob was looking a little flushed but, in a bemused sort of way, delighted.

'He's also heavily involved in the development of certain extraordinary new fabrics,' said Herbert. 'He's a

real chemist, you know. I say, don't you think we should dance, too?'

Eve and Herbert got up and took to the floor. To Cotton's surprise, Herbert was something of a tyro, or at least he flung out his arms, swivelled his head and proceeded to twirl Eve about.

'No, don't ask me to dance,' said Minty. 'I've always been a very willing wallflower.'

'We danced in Newport.'

'I was being nice!' Minty smiled. 'I must say, I'm enjoying this.' She leant forward and spoke quietly. 'Now, is she a *real* professional, Colonel?'

'That would depend on how you define reality and professional. She's very fond of the movies and she likes to dress very well.'

Minty Auchincloss laughed and sat back. 'What were you like as an adolescent, Cotton?' she asked.

'Reasonably polite, I think; not all that sullen but probably somewhere between shy and stunned. I was at boarding-school. And during the holidays my late aunt did not live in a place with many temptations. And you?'

'Also boarding-school. I was taught to be sociable, or at least to drink and not to cough when smoking. When left alone, I curled up and read a lot. I had to wear gloves all the time, was made to attend hops, sometimes wearing a corsage, and was warned against allowing fumbles that could be punctuated by intercourse with the male sex.'

Cotton smiled. 'Was this the Dorothy Parker school?'

'If only! No.' Minty shook her head. 'Mine was

more Emily Dickinson but with breaks, sometimes aggressively sentimental, to celebrate brave suffragettes like Susan B. Anthony – oh, and to feel for the poor in China. It was Emily's "blameless mystery" for women-folk, but it came with the right way to lay a dinner table and give instructions to the cook.' She shrugged. 'My mother had usually passed out by dinner. But she was a great beauty, even when unconscious.' She paused. 'Have you ever thought of suicide, Cotton?'

'I don't think I have,' said Cotton.

Minty smiled and put her hand on his. Cotton felt a slight tingle. 'From thirteen to fifteen, I thought about it a lot. Or at least I imagined a mix of Ophelia and biers and flowers. There might have been a bit of Minnehaha in there as well.'

'And now?'

She removed her hand and shook her head. 'I'm twenty-six. On the shelf, as they say. I'm rather looking forward to being twenty-seven.'

'Do you want children?'

'Am I supposed to say yes?'

'No obligation.'

'Then no. I used to think I could be a better mother than my own, of course, but I'm no longer sure about that. At my age children are beginning to look very painful and slippery.' She leant forward. 'Quite what are we doing here?'

'Angeles over there has a problem staying in this country. I don't know that she wants a husband exactly, but certainly a respected protector.'

'So we're on a charity mission! That's nice.' She took

out a cigarette but shook her head when Cotton reached for the matches on the table. 'Is her predicament why you visited me the other day?'

Cotton smiled. 'Only incidentally. But you were helpful and I thought you might enjoy this dinner and watching her in action.'

Minty Auchincloss put the cigarette back in its case and looked at him.

'Tell me something. If I were to ask you how you'd spent your summer, what would you say?'

'That I chose the Ogden Clinic over the Hamptons and Narragansett over Newport, except for the evening I saw you, of course.'

'I'm a lawyer, you know,' she said.

'Quite,' said Cotton. 'So you know what confidentiality is.'

She nodded. 'I wouldn't have advised you to take those choices.'

Minty Auchincloss frowned. 'Damn it,' she said. She got the cigarette out of her case again and let him light it. 'Tell me this. Was your experience in any way related to the girl currently persuading Mr Culver that he is more charming and attractive than he previously knew?'

'Not the experience, just the fallout.'

Herbert and Eve came back to the table, Eve thought the dinner party had gone very well. 'He's very keen to see her again,' she said. 'I understand they'll be meeting *à deux* tomorrow.'

'I say, do you think this is going to work?' said Herbert.

Eve got quite sharp. 'You don't know how lonely he

is! I've told her to let me bring up the residence business with Bob when things have moved on a little.'

Minty Auchincloss smiled. 'Wow,' she said to Cotton when Herbert and Eve had left. 'She's an organizer.'

Cotton nodded.

'You've made use of me,' she said. 'So I'm going to make use of you. Fair?'

'Of course. Do I get a clue?'

'I want to introduce you to someone.'

'Very well.'

They took a cab to East 70th Street. Minty Auchincloss let them into a tall, narrow-looking brick house. It had an elegant self-supporting spiral staircase. They climbed one floor and entered a library. Just for a moment, Cotton remembered the old lady in Newport, the quasi-Gibson girl, and was relieved to find a diminutive but elegantly tucked-up old lady sitting amongst a clutter of books – there were too many for the shelves – and Chinese vases. There was a modern print – a bright Matisse – on top of the mirror over the mantelpiece.

'Aunt Amy,' said Minty Auchincloss, 'this is Peter Cotton.'

Aunt Amy may have been intrigued but behaved as if pretty well blind. She beckoned Cotton to come closer and closer and then pulled down on his hand till his face was about six inches from hers. Dressed in a kind of silk Chinese jacket, embroidered with colourful birds, in one hand she held a large magnifying glass. For a moment, Cotton thought she was going to use it to look at him, but she limited herself to peering at his face. She

frowned. She made a few noises, possibly to do with her dentures, but then nodded and looked at Minty. 'He's got a good, steady hand,' she said. And then, as if she had to explain, 'Some men have weak hands. Hopeless hands, I call them.' She had not given up his. 'You sit here,' she said.

Cotton sat on what looked like a porcelain drum.

'Minty,' said Miss Amy Blackwell.

Her great-niece walked round and put on a scratchy recording of the first part of the first movement of Beethoven's Piano Sonata No. 14, the 'Moonlight'. Minty stood; Miss Blackwell held on to Cotton's hand. Though he could smell lanolin ointment, her hand felt slightly rough, as if flaking. He looked at the Matisse but could not think what the word was. It wasn't 'Ottoman'. It wasn't 'Arabesque'. And despite the pants and embroidered vest on the model, it wasn't 'Harem'. Cotton relaxed and let his mind go blank. 'Odalisque'. That was it. Matisse had painted many odalisques.

When the music finished, Amy Blackwell nodded. 'Good,' she said. 'Order refreshments for your guest, dear. I'll take myself off to bed.'

They helped her up and Miss Blackwell's maid came to assist her to the elevator.

'She believes,' said her niece when the elevator had started groaning, 'that she can tell what people are like by their reaction to that music.'

'Right,' said Cotton. 'So that was the hand business.'

'That's our deal, really,' said Minty. 'She wants me to hold hers when she dies. And just to make this perfectly

clear, I have nothing to inherit. Aunt Amy's trust fund is not mine. OK?'

'OK.'

'I'm on the sixth floor and my rent is exactly the maid's wages.'

'Why are you telling me this?'

'Because I want to.'

Cotton nodded. 'My rent is now met by the British government.'

Minty Auchincloss shook her head at him. 'I'm serious,' she said. 'My great-aunt is helping me. She wants me to be independent after she's gone, not have to rely on anyone.'

'That's good,' said Cotton.

'It is, isn't it?' She smiled. 'Do you really want any refreshment?'

'No, thanks,' said Cotton.

He wondered if Ed Lowell had passed Aunt Amy's hand test.

Herbert Butterworth was looking bleary the next morning.

'Do you think Miss Auchincloss will report your evening to Lowell?'

'I imagine she'll edit.'

'What do you think he'll do?'

'Adjust his approach.'

'And how do you think he'll do that?'

'Oh, I imagine he'll demonstrate how powerful he is. He'll show me who he can call on. Or he might try to move against Angeles.'

'I don't like this,' said Herbert.

'I think this is just a little social jockeying, Herbert. In Narragansett, I had a dream that I killed him.'

Herbert groaned. 'You do know we are not allowed to do that?'

'It helped me clear my mind, that's all. I don't want to kill him in life, but it's what Americans call touching base. I was able to kill him in the dream. Twice, actually. Once I picked out one of his eyes from about four hundred yards with a rifle shot. Oh, in the other he may have been dead already; I was using a boat hook. I saw that in New England with very large tuna. Look, at one level, I'm showing him I'm not taking the Angeles proposal that seriously. On another, it shows I'm prepared to help her on, perhaps a little more nobly than he's doing.'

'You don't think you've had too many conversations with Dr Sanford.'

Cotton laughed. 'Far too many. But he's not a psychologist.'

'What really worries you?'

'I don't know that my opinion of Lowell is right.'

'And what's that?'

'That he's clever enough, can certainly be dangerous, but that he's also arrogant and foolish.'

'You're still trying to see his view of you.'

'Not any more, Herbert. I'm over the drugs. And getting back to more down-to-earth stuff.'

Herbert nodded. 'Have you made a connection with Miss Auchincloss?'

Cotton shrugged. 'An understanding, perhaps. She's

393

fairly insistent that she may look like a poor little rich girl – but she has no money. I could be wrong, of course, but I'm betting she's much tougher and more flexible than she might appear. She told me she wanted independence and I think I believe her.'

Herbert sighed. 'Eve said she was rather intense. "Tight-strung", I think she said. How do you know she isn't working for the Americans?'

'I think she's too clever. And I'm pretty sure she knows how women get treated in the intelligence world.'

Herbert looked doubtful. 'Have we got this properly focused, do you think?'

'I don't think we have. But look at it this way. Lowell is in security. Now he has other ambitions. At one simple level, this makes him exposed. He's trying to move from one activity to another very different, much more public one that requires cooperation from people who are a lot more self-interested. He is certainly ruthless but has no natural, easy talent for people.'

'You can't kill him.'

'I have no intention of touching him, Herbert! All I'm remembering is that old business of political careers always ending in failure.'

'What are you talking about?'

'In politics, there are so many things that can go wrong. At this stage, Lowell's ambition is a bud.' Cotton paused. 'We help nip it.'

Herbert looked at him. 'Are you seeking revenge?'

'Of course not,' said Cotton. 'And I certainly don't believe in poetic justice. But I'm beginning to believe in typecasting and I do have a personal issue here. What I

really don't want, Herbert, is to become a wretched anecdote.'

Herbert frowned. 'What do you mean, anecdote?'

'When I was in Newport, there was a little boozy business in the political tent. A person Miss Auchincloss called a "political valet" started telling an overblown story about Cherkesov, and about halfway through, when he saw it was going down well, Ed Lowell actually took it over. Cherkesov has become something to bring out at parties.'

'But what would your anecdote be?'

'To be the person who simply walked through drugs. Let's leave hallucinations out of it. I'm drugged. This bloody Englishman barely notices.'

'I see! You become a sort of Rasputin.'

'He died in the end, didn't he?'

'After many efforts to kill him.'

Cotton shrugged. 'I would be reduced to being a name for an ally untroubled by what has felled some Americans who volunteered to be experimented on. And it shows that the practice of injecting the unwitting with a concoction of drugs isn't as bad as some claim. It even suggests that a real sort of man doesn't have problems, doesn't whinge and still likes his women. It's absurd, of course, but it's the way things go, especially after a couple of whiskies. I saw this, with all the differences, in Newport when they were talking about Cherkesov. Cherkesov, of course, couldn't care less. He might even be flattered if he knew. I'm not. I really don't want to be reduced to a name and a single thing. It would be hard to continue if that happened.'

A secretary came in. 'There's a Dr Aforey on the phone for you, Mr Cotton.'

Dr Aforey asked for a meeting and suggested the Cesnola Collection at the Metropolitan Museum of Art. Cotton took a cab. Dr Aforey was already there staring at a pot.

'I like the modesty and perspective these ancient artefacts provide,' he said. 'Oh, you will think I am quite the culture vulture. But it is the serenity and comfort I enjoy. This pot has become great because it has survived for so long; it reconnects us to a sense of proportion about our own agitated concerns.'

'Have you accepted the United Nations offer?'

'I have,' said Dr Aforey. 'Even now, I am on my way to sign the necessary forms and so on and so forth. My university has proved most receptive to the plan.'

'Dr Aforey,' said Cotton, holding out his hand. 'Congratulations.'

Dr Aforey smiled modestly, but enough to show his new gold tooth, and they shook hands.

He lifted his briefcase in front of him with both hands.

'I have made enquiries, my friend, on your question. The matter is exceedingly grave. Behind a cloak of science, American doctors – men who would be deeply shocked to be described as brethren to the Nazis – have indulged in an orgy of abuse on the weak, the mentally ill and the defenceless. I am talking of decades, Colonel, not something recent or fly-by-night.'

'I believe you.'

'The most vexing thing is that a lot of this information

396

is in the public domain. But it is not common know-ledge, if you follow me. It would appear that neither the general populace nor, more dispiritingly, the press can stir themselves to insist on disseminating the infor-mation or to make further enquiry.'

Dr Aforey shook his head. 'It is particularly galling because some of the so-called experiments are of dubious scientific value. Take the case of untreated syphilis, for example. This terrible disease was given to unwitting and disenfranchised people in the southern states of this country, mostly to poor black sharecroppers. It was then judged expedient to move the study abroad; to start again in Guatemala, where the peasants are even poorer and less protected. The justification for this programme is extraordinary. On the one hand we are told that this country needs to protect itself against the possibility of biological warfare. On the other, they are making efforts to speed up the syphilis, as it were, for potential use as a weapon. I was invited to consider the devastating and demoralizing effects on an enemy when it found out that many of its troops were too sick to fight. It is a horrible prospect only made quite absurd by the present impos-sibility of infecting many men quickly with a disease that can take years to manifest itself. We fear and are con-vinced by the possibilities of evil imaginations, often our own, and react in kind.'

They had arrived in front of a bronze waterspout in the shape of a lion mask.

'This is very exquisite workmanship,' said Dr Aforey. He peered at the card with the likely date and place of origin of the piece. 'Were there lions in Cyprus?'

'I don't know. Probably not naturally. What else do you have on drugs?'

'A great deal, Colonel. For instance, persons associated with the Navy have been conducting experiments on inmates, to look no further, in at least one asylum in Washington DC. There is talk of mind-altering drugs and suchlike.'

'Yes,' said Cotton. 'Dr Aforey, thank you for all your trouble.'

'I have much more, should you wish.'

'I've made some enquiries too,' said Cotton.

Dr Aforey clutched his briefcase. 'What do you think? Will science produce drugs that will control free will?'

'There are people who think so,' said Cotton. 'I don't think it is an immediate possibility.'

'Like accelerating syphilis?'

Cotton smiled. 'Along those lines.'

Dr Aforey smiled. 'I am glad to see you looking calmer, my old friend. I may need to see you again.'

'Please do.'

'I have something here cooking,' said Dr Aforey. He tapped his head.

27

W HEN HE got back to his office, Cotton found a 'schedule' for the next day. It came from The American Foundation for Foreign Affairs and International Relations. Item one was a train journey to New Haven, where he would be picked up by a 'chauffeur-driven limousine'. A return ticket had been provided and was enclosed.

Dr Resnick lived on Oenoke Ridge in New Canaan, Connecticut, in a house that looked to Cotton the size of a small prep school in England, the kind of gloomy country place adapted to take 80–100 boys between the ages of eight and thirteen. It even appeared to have an attached chapel and, away from the main house, a couple of Tudor-style classrooms. The professor told Cotton the place was convenient for Yale and for 'the train service' to New York – or to Harvard. The interior was formal and rather bare-looking, and in a rather stark hall Cotton was introduced to the professor's wife, Adele and two small children, a girl of three and a boy of eighteen months. The children were called Lillian and Louis and Cotton noted the boy was dressed as a miniature adult, in a suit and tie, and suspected this formality was not all that unusual. He could not remember when he had ever been welcomed by an

eighteen-month-old in his mother's arms with the words 'Hello, sir.'

Ushering Cotton towards the area Cotton had thought of as a chapel, Dr Resnick displayed impressive degrees of confidence and caution. He explained that he preferred to film interviews 'with foreign agents'. Cotton glanced down to see whether this had any sign of a joke about it. It did not. Resnick was short and had a solid to portly figure for a man of thirty-one. His height and shape reminded Cotton of the much older Dr Aforey. One difference was in the voice. Dr Resnick's voice was deep, very slow and, away from the politicians who provided patronage, used to command. Another difference was in the hands. Dr Aforey gave the impression that he always carried a briefcase so as to avoid wringing his. Dr Resnick kept his close to his body and did not spread his fingers. Instead, he tended to two gestures: hands flat and parallel, or hands curved but still parallel. Cotton did wonder how a man who was considered exceptionally intelligent, and who certainly considered himself quite as intelligent as others thought, bore the kowtowing necessary to obtain the patronage.

One reason was power, of course. Dr Resnick was ambitious and at some stage would want a position. Ed Lowell might dream of being president, but Walter Resnick was probably aiming to be secretary of state. Being appointed rather than elected is always an advantage. What interested Cotton was how much of a power broker this made him. In Resnick's position, Cotton thought, he'd definitely have more than one possible presidential runner and treat them all with consideration.

'I have two reasons for filming these interviews,' he explained in his heavily accented but decidedly inexpressive English. 'One is to check what I say, possibly in the heat of exposition or argument. The second is to improve my English-language abilities. I arrived here too late. I arrived as an adolescent. By that stage the mind has lost its adaptability in terms of language acquisition. That is because we move on physically to prepare for reproduction. As I am sure you are aware, this is not the flexible condition required by language.'

Cotton realized he was on the receiving end of a ponderous, academic joke that was slightly risqué perhaps. He smiled politely, but also understood that Dr Resnick was merely filling in time while his assistants set up. Cotton had been taught by some distinguished and sometimes very rich academics in the UK, but he had never seen an academic with the use of a staff and organization anything like this. There were uniformed members of the domestic servants, and also seven young men in suits and two young women in suits, one with a notepad.

'The Foundation provides this,' said the professor. 'I am merely the present incumbent.'

Cotton nodded. Dr Resnick did not expand on what 'incumbent' meant.

They sat.

'I admire you,' said Dr Resnick.

It was the bluntest but also the most inexpressive admiration Cotton had ever received. He made no response.

Professor Resnick looked slightly surprised. 'You have

brownie points with me,' he said, as if Cotton might not have understood.

'What *are* brownie points exactly?' said Cotton.

Resnick smiled. 'I'm in an excellent position to inform you on this. I worked for Curtis Publishing when I first arrived in this great country. There were greenies, five, to every brownie. I delivered the *Saturday Evening Post* and *Ladies' Home Journal*. Do a good job – and I mean by that sell subscriptions – and you got points. These points made up green and brown vouchers that could be traded in for items from the company catalogue. During the day I worked in a factory. I went to night school. I won three scholarships.'

'Impressive. I've never done anything remotely similar.'

Resnick shook his head. 'On the contrary, Mr Cotton. I understand you had a pretty hard time and yet came out on the other side with an exemplary and I'd say manly sense of containment. You recognize the realities of power.' He smiled. 'And you have also kept all your options open.'

Cotton nodded. 'Have you ever had hallucinations, Professor?'

Dr Resnick showed slight boredom or disappointment. 'No,' he said. 'I'll tell you what we are doing. I have coined the term "interlocutor" as most apt for a certain role I want to talk to you about. I'm talking internationally. Nobody is asking you to betray your country, Mr Cotton. Far from it. But if you are agreeable – and I can give you every assurance that you have a choice – you could be one of these people I call interlocutors. It's entirely – and freely – up to you.'

'What are we talking about?'

Resnick smiled. 'It is in no way a formal position. It does not come with a salary or office. But let's say it corresponds to a certain status, Mr Cotton. Call and you'll get straight through. Do you understand?'

'Does it depend on what I say?'

'And that is exactly my point! You see, we need intelligent voices. And not just intelligent American voices. It's not about reinforcing the status quo. It's about considerations we should take on board when facing the new realities.'

'No matter how uncomfortable?'

'Mr Cotton! You're in Intelligence. You know intelligence is power!' Dr Resnick laughed. 'I am not, by the way, saying that we'll treat what you say as gospel. The truth, alas, is not always the uppermost concern. There are a lot of other considerations. Sometimes stupidity wins.'

'What would we talk about?'

'As I say, the new realities, Mr Cotton. You'll note I say "interlocutors" – I don't use emotive words. We don't think of ourselves as being in an emotional business. But let's say we want tried and tested men – men of integrity, resilience, insight and discretion. Let me ask you a specific question. What is your opinion of Oleg Cherkesov?'

Cotton was always slightly taken aback by the direct quality of American flattery.

'That's not specific enough,' he said.

'Is he a survivor?'

Cotton shrugged. 'That's always a question of

timescale,' he said. 'But he's clever, agile and tough. In the end, when the dark really starts and the paranoia squeezes, when Stalin dies for example, I think he might be seen as too eccentric by some. But that would depend on who he had backed. I certainly wouldn't bet against him.'

Dr Resnick nodded as if Cotton had just amply demonstrated something. 'Excellent. Quite excellent.' He leant forward. 'One of our most valued sources tells us Cherkesov was arrested a couple of days ago and says he may already be dead.'

Apart from flattering him, Dr Resnick was also indicating to Cotton he was privy to the very latest intelligence at the very highest level.

Cotton weighed this information for a second. 'I'd be surprised if that were true. I'd certainly check with your other sources,' he said. 'Cherkesov lost his wife and children in the war, you know.'

'Yes. Terrible thing. You're saying he is extraordinarily resilient. Our source said he had fallen foul of Zhdanov.'

Andrei Zhdanov, considered by some a likely heir to Stalin, was now responsible for culture. 'The only conflict that is possible in Soviet culture is the conflict between good and best' was his chief dictum.

Cotton shook his head. 'I forgot to say that both Zhdanov and Cherkesov may beat everyone else to it by killing themselves with alcohol.'

Cotton was pleased that Dr Resnick looked a little discomfited.

'You're saying Zhdanov isn't up to it?'

'Not with Cherkesov.'

The academic looked up and round at the camera. 'Aren't you ready yet?' Dr Resnick could express his displeasure with quite a rasp.

'On reflection, I'm not sure I'm allowed to be filmed,' said Cotton.

Walter Resnick laughed as if Cotton had said something truly funny, even put out an appreciative arm.

A uniformed maid arrived with coffee.

What Cotton had taken for a chapel might have started as such. It was a double-height space about forty-five feet long and twenty wide with exposed beams and pointed windows in the walls. Cotton couldn't remember what the expression for arrow-headed windows was. Were they 'punched' into the walls? There was no altar or lectern; there were no pews. There was a shallow stage, however, with a framework of lighting around it, and a cloth background. The windows had cinema-type curtains.

One of the lights exploded.

'Those are unreliable,' said Professor Resnick.

On the platform were two armchairs. At the back were bookcases. In front of it was a camera that looked pretty professional to Cotton. There was also a man with a microphone on a boom.

'I think we're pretty well there,' said Walter Resnick.

Cotton and the professor moved towards the shallow stage and the representation of a library.

'I'm a historian but I'm looking towards the future,' he said. 'Can you imagine what it would be like if we

had film of Julius Caesar or George Washington? But that's what's going to happen. And TV, you know, is going to change everything. Within a few years, politicians will be able to appeal to the electorate in their own homes. Against that, they will have to undergo an examination by millions of people looking into their eyes.'

Cotton stepped up. Walter Resnick put him stage right. It made Cotton conscious he would have preferred the other side, but he had no time to think why.

'Sit on your jacket,' said the academic. 'And you may want a little powder on your face. It cuts gleam.'

Cotton submitted to make-up. It wasn't an extensive or long-drawn-out business, but a girl used first a sponge on his face and then a brush with a powder between nude and orange. It was slightly uncomfortable. The girl pulled on the lapels of his suit as with a safety harness on an aeroplane during the war. Cotton had the feeling he should not move his face too much in case the crust on it cracked.

'Try not to shy from the lights,' said the professor. 'It makes people look shifty.' He smiled. 'I do these interviews for my students.'

There was a clapboard. 'Resnick Archives.' There was a clack and they started.

'I'm talking today with Mr Peter Cotton, presently in the United States for His Majesty's Government to examine the progress made in the establishment of the United Nations Organization. Mr Cotton is a high-ranking official in the British Civil Service. We may talk later on this because, as you all should know, the

British have chosen an administrative system that deals with politics in an apolitical or at least non-partisan way. That is to say, the UK employs a body of career administrators who serve whichever party wins their elections.

'Mr Cotton himself studied economics at Cambridge in England and served with great distinction in the recent war, rising to the rank of lieutenant colonel. I am sure he won't object to my mentioning – you won't, will you? – that he was wounded and decorated on the invasion of Sicily and was at one time in the British Economic Warfare Unit, with particular responsibility for tracking down Nazi efforts to regroup funds and then for hunting down certain metal plates used to print money in occupied Germany that turned up in Soviet hands.'

As Resnick rumbled on Cotton realized he had no idea whether or not he was presently in camera frame. On reflection, he did not particularly mind. In fact, he was finding this experience invigorating.

'Peter? You don't mind if I call you Peter?'

'Not at all.'

'Good! Shall we begin with Operation Paperclip?'

'That's an American operation, Walter, but I'll certainly do my best.'

'Would you agree that President Truman was correct and well advised in affirming that the US would have absolutely no truck with those German scientists who had been Nazi Party members?'

'Most certainly. And I'd imagine the American public expected no less.' Cotton paused briefly but Dr Resnick was letting him speak. 'The President's statement was an

act of reassurance for an electorate that had been through the travail and heartache of a world war. And it was also a restatement of the principle enshrined in the US Constitution that the three branches of government take precedence over administrative problems and difficulties. From this practical, organizational and secondary point of view, that of the American public servants dealing with the scientists in Operation Paperclip, one problem was working out which scientists had been active Nazis and which had, for their own survival, found it necessary at least to carry a party card. Given the state of Germany at the end of the war, this may appear a serious difficulty and a difficulty as much practical as moral. Many records had been lost or destroyed. The public servants then had to rely heavily on personal interviews with the scientists, often through translators. Did each and every scientist answer questions in good faith? Probably not. And there were other considerations to weigh up, one being that morality has nothing or little to do with scientific or technological advances. Whether we liked it or not, the German scientists working on, for example, rocket fuel were ahead of those in our own countries.'

Operation Paperclip was one of the few operations that had a name that alluded to what the operation actually did. Paperclip referred to real paperclips. In effect, about sixteen hundred German scientists had been offered immunity from war crimes in return for a new life of research in the USA as US citizens. In inconvenient cases, the paperclip had been made to hold invented or cleaned-up reports of the scientists' wartime activities

and the old, grimmer reports destroyed and official records changed. In a number of cases everything, from the paperclip down, was new.

'Excellent,' said Dr Resnick. 'Of course, democracies loathe the idea of learning from regimes such as the Third Reich, but the fact is that if democratic governments don't learn they lose out, they become vulnerable, particularly when one wartime ally simply scooped up as many German scientists as it could and set them to work for post-war enmity. I refer, of course, to Soviet Russia. Matters that are now past justice have invaded a present and future competition that may be vital to the survival of the democracy we all champion.'

Cotton had waited patiently. He now thought he should react. He hoped it was an unreasonable moment to do so.

'When do I get to speak about the JIOA?'

'Stop filming,' said Dr Resnick.

There was a short pause. The JIOA or Joint Intelligence Objective Agency had been in charge of Paperclip and circumventing President Truman's affirmation that no one associated with the Nazi Party would receive US citizenship.

'I understand Mr Churchill is presently writing his own history of the recent war. I don't have to tell you, Peter, that history and editing go hand in hand.'

'Of course not,' said Cotton. 'Snip away.'

There was quite a pause. Cotton had not seen Resnick smile quite so genuinely before.

'OK. Start the film again.' He waited till the whirr started.

'In terms of realpolitik, Colonel, what do you think history can teach us?'

'History is a form of shaped experience, Walter. We have Marcus Aurelius, for example, and we can contrast his account of power with that of Machiavelli's advice to his prince. But most of the lessons are in our own reactions and actions to what we face. We make reference to the past but the future is our own to distort.'

'Cut,' said Resnick cheerfully. 'You now exist as two snippets, Colonel, for ever and ever.'

Cotton nodded. He realized he had just had a sort of casting session. The film of him would be examined and he would be judged.

He was given lunch with Dr Resnick's family. His children were extraordinarily well behaved. The food was on the bland side. Adele Resnick was polite and charming. 'I understand you know my friend Minty Auchincloss,' she said.

'I do,' said Cotton.

'Too high strung,' said Walter Resnick.

'She's a very sweet girl, Walter,' said Adele Resnick, 'but men tend to find her lacking certain submissive qualities.'

As Resnick saw Cotton to the Lincoln to go back to New Haven, he said, 'Ah, what happened to Geoffrey Ayrtoun in the end?'

'I really don't know. I was told he was in Canada.'

Dr Resnick smiled. 'The son of a bitch wasn't as tough an ally as we thought,' he said. 'Pity.'

*

'How did it go?' said Herbert.

'Fabulous meeting. Dr Resnick filmed some of it.'

'He did what?'

'They're not as depressed as we are. Quite a lesson. I'd give them thirty years as top dog, not much more. And then a lot of confusion and bitterness. But for now they are wonderful, full of energy. Resnick loves the trappings and apparatus of power.'

Herbert frowned. 'You haven't been drinking, have you?'

'No. And I didn't say the British would ever come back. We're being left way behind. Walter Resnick is an energetic ideologue, a believer, a tremendous positivist.'

'You're impressed?'

'Yes. But they have nothing to test themselves against except a fairy-tale by Comrade Grim.'

'Peter, I'm not following you.'

'Well, it's evident that the Americans are intent on building up the Soviet threat – even though they are a chronically corrupt and inefficient enemy. They need to do this because the Americans' problem now is that they really have no competition, and when you don't have any competition, your aim becomes confused. They managed to bring everything together to crush the Japanese and the Nazis because they were reacting to them as direct, violent competition. The situation now is different. The Soviets don't have the Germans' discipline, skills or drive to expand. They're also broke, chronically inefficient and paranoid. But they do have something extremely powerful – an ideology to export.'

'What are you suggesting?'

'Dr Resnick kept mentioning the new realities. The problem is really cultural. The Americans are the only people in the world with vast supplies of money and industry. But Resnick believes, I think, that they'll get soft and self-indulgent. He's not going to object to the Un-American Activities people and their communist witch-hunt because that might stiffen the fear quotient. They're trying to compete with the Soviets on the level of arms trading and influence, but the real competition, when it comes, won't come from Moscow. The American way of life is not an ideology – that's its great power. But they're going to try to crank up a bit of ideology of their own to compete with the Soviets' failed model.'

'Do you think Resnick is dangerous?'

'That would depend on who you are. For us, there's no change. If we are biddable, good; if not, tough. We get to cosy up but there's little in the way of pay-off unless they let us buy arms we can't afford so we can pretend we matter.'

'You don't sound depressed.'

Cotton laughed. 'Let's have a drink to Dr Goebbels. Resnick is in the business of propaganda. He might say "presentation of the salient facts". He's convinced that television will change the way politics works.'

'What did he say about Ed Lowell?'

'Nothing direct.'

'Did he talk about drugs?'

Cotton shook his head. 'We talked piously and in general terms about Operation Paperclip on film. But that was about the Soviet threat, not the methods used to

combat it. I imagine Resnick would be surprised, possibly delighted to learn that some drugs worked, made people cooperate precisely and accurately when they didn't want to, but he is not holding his breath. I'd imagine he thinks a substitute for torture a pipe dream, but he's prepared to read about how drugs can be developed in other ways.'

Herbert smiled. 'Not a man who minds casualties?'

'He described me as "manly".'

Herbert groaned. 'As a sentimental man said, "One death is a tragedy, a thousand deaths are a statistic."'

Cotton raised his eyebrows. 'Who was that?'

'Stalin.'

'All right,' said Cotton. He shrugged. 'Now I want something from you.'

'What kind of thing?'

'Resnick told me that Oleg Cherkesov had been arrested and was possibly already dead.'

'We haven't heard that. Is he letting us know? Is this the kind of information you'll get if you collaborate?'

'I think this is another test, Herbert. And I need to pass it as soon as I can. I need to know if it's true. I met a Kremlin watcher earlier this year. He wore a deerstalker. May I have access to him? His name is Allen Beresford.'

Herbert paused but did not scratch his hair. 'Could you leave it with me?'

'All right,' said Cotton. He got up but did not move away.

'Anything else?' said Herbert.

'Yes. When I was in Newport in August a pompous

413

politician asked me what our greatest security problem was. I replied that it was often a failure to communicate with our own when others, including our enemies, already knew.'

'What are you suggesting?'

'Every single American in Intelligence that I have met has asked me how Ayrtoun is. I really don't know, but let's say they are really quite remarkably kind in remembering a man who had a breakdown more than six months ago.'

Herbert nodded. 'I'm afraid I'm not in a position to enlighten you on that.'

'Strict instructions?'

Herbert Butterworth did not reply.

'Thanks, Herbert.'

That evening at home, Cotton received a phone call from Herbert.

'You'll have the information you asked for tomorrow first thing. It'll be in the secure room. All right?'

'Thank you, Herbert.'

The grandly named secure room was not at all big. Along one wall it had a metal counter visitors used as a desk. On the other side, two operators handled incoming and outgoing communications. Cotton was given a coded message and a codebook. It did not take him long to transcribe the message. He read it twice, then handed what he had written to the operator. Cotton signed a sheet of paper on a clipboard to show that he had received and understood the numbered communication. The operator shredded the paper Cotton had given him

and pressed a button. There was a wait of a few seconds before the door opened.

Cotton returned to his office and wrote to Professor Walter Resnick. He did not, of course, name Oleg Cherkesov.

Our own source suggests that the subject of our recent conversation was out of sight because he was acting as a more or less honest broker at a meeting between two warring factions. The meeting was at a warehouse at an address duly noted.

One of these factions was the Jewish Anti-Fascist Committee or JAC. The other represented the Party. As I am sure you are aware, JAC was highly successful in raising funds for the Soviets in the USA when they were allies in the recent war. Likewise, you will know that the JAC's *Black Book*, amongst other things documenting some of the atrocities perpetrated at Nazi concentration camps like Treblinka, was published in New York last year. Indeed, some of their documents were used as evidence at the Nuremberg trials.

You will also be aware that no Soviet edition of the book has yet appeared since official Soviet policy is 'inclusive'; that is to say, the official line insists the atrocities were committed against Soviet citizens and not specifically against Jews.

Our subject may have been introduced as an honest broker but our source and our analysts agree that the meeting was less a consultation than a secret but formal warning to JAC. The book will

not be published in the USSR. JAC itself was placed under caution.

There is some disagreement here as to whether JAC will comply but none that the person we talked about is alive and busy.

Cotton then called Walter Resnick's office in New Canaan and was informed his letter would be collected by private courier. Dr Resnick had his own security arrangements and Cotton complied with them at about 11 a.m., when the courier arrived.

28

OTTON MET Dr Aforey at the American Museum of Natural History, in the Akeley Hall of African mammals, conscious that he was using the doctor as a kind of holiday, in part just to hear other concerns.

'I am considering these exhibits with some ruefulness, my friend.' Dr Aforey looked round and up at Cotton. 'I have never seen most of these animals that God put on our continent. I understand they have been stuffed most accurately, not using straw and stuff like that, but wood and clay to construct an internal scaffolding. And all these little tableaux are, I understand, scrupulous representations of the habitat in which the creatures were found.'

Cotton nodded politely. He knew nothing about taxidermy.

Dr Aforey laughed. 'Shall we look at that fine gorilla?'

They walked over.

'I have addressed myself to your present employers,' said Dr Aforey. 'Indeed, I have made a request. It concerns you, my old friend.'

'In what way?'

'I have suggested to your employers that you join the area of development at the United Nations. If you are

agreeable, of course.' Dr Aforey cleared his throat and leant closer.

'I have also attached a private note to my formal letter suggesting that having someone I know and think to understand alongside me in the United Nations would be advantageous to all concerned. I am also conscious, sir, that I need a quick and worldly mind beside me.'

'May I ask why you didn't consult with me beforehand?'

'Oh. I have no doubt you would have discouraged me.'

Cotton closed his eyes briefly. He certainly was in demand, but never in what he would have chosen. He opened his eyes, unsure what to say, but Dr Aforey was already speaking.

'Look at that splendid gorilla . . .'

And indeed the gorilla was splendid, fixed in a replica of its habitat, quite near the final resting place of Carl Akeley in the continent he loved.

'The tableau is called a diorama, you see,' said Dr Aforey. 'But note the stance of the animal, rearing on its hind legs, showing that immense chest. Forgive me, but it is a realist's version of King Kong. Only Tarzan is missing. Or rather, perhaps we become Tarzan looking through a sort of window.'

Dr Aforey made a snuffling noise, pleased by what he had said. 'Mr Akeley was most anxious to save African wildlife and so he slaughtered this magnificent creature and brought it here to make his point that such creatures were worth saving.'

'No,' said Cotton.

'I'm sorry?'

'Your offer is very kind, Dr Aforey, well thought out – but my reply is no.'

'Oh, you have quite taken me aback, sir. That is a very great disappointment, my friend. Are you entirely sure?'

'Yes, I am, Doctor.'

'May I ask why?'

'Because I don't think my personality and temperament are suited to the United Nations Organization. And my background might cause problems. To you, for instance.'

Dr Aforey lifted his chin and looked away. 'Does the word "pristine" mean anything to you?'

'Yes. Though I can't think when I last used it,' said Cotton.

Dr Aforey nodded. 'You see, my friend? You have not had any reason to do so. My very first interview in the Area of Development was with some white people urging me to consider the promotion of national parks or some such in the future of Africa. Mr Akeley's heirs, if you understand me. They are big-game hunters turned conservationists. They call natives poachers for killing to eat. They love the word "pristine".'

'I appreciate what you say, sir,' said Cotton. 'But I assure you I will probably be more useful and valuable to you outside the UN.'

'I am quite downcast,' said Dr Aforey. But he suddenly grinned. 'I am looking for a person who is much better than I am at dealing with persistent people. Will you keep an eye out for such a person?'

419

'Of course,' said Cotton. 'Have you found somewhere to live?'

'Oh yes,' said Dr Aforey. 'I have found comfortable lodgings in Queens with a widow. I live upstairs and take meals with her downstairs.'

As they walked out, Dr Aforey pointed at some stuffed colobus monkeys and giggled again.

'Some of my countrymen call that bush meat,' he said.

On Friday, 26 September at about 9.30 in the morning, Cotton received a telephone call. The speaker was female and spoke very softly.

'Marjorie Simon, sir, Dr Resnick's personal assistant, with a request. Do I have your permission to proceed?'

'You do.'

'Colonel, Dr Resnick would be grateful if you could be outside the *Youth Leading Industry* door on Fifth Avenue at two thirty this afternoon. Would you be able to fit that into your schedule? Dr Resnick suggests the meeting would take no more than thirty minutes of your time. Could you work with that, sir?'

'I think so. What's this about?'

'I'm allowed to say it's pursuant to a recent conversation you had here in New Canaan, sir. Dr Resnick will pick you up, sir. He'll be in a Cadillac, sir, a recent gift. For ease of identification, may I say the colour is described as honey beige?'

'You may,' said Cotton. 'Tell Dr Resnick I'll be downstairs at two thirty.'

Cotton put down the telephone and laughed. He was intrigued by the language but wondered what a honey

beige Cadillac meant. A rich benefactor? Or was he meant to infer that the business community, in the shape of the makers of Cadillac and Lincoln automobiles, was showing just how seriously it took foreign affairs and America's place in the world?

He told Herbert that Walter Resnick had asked for a half-hour interview.

'What do you think it's about?' said Herbert.

'Let's see. Where's Hornby?'

'He's at a dentist on the eighteenth floor. Poor devil's having an impacted wisdom tooth pulled.'

Cotton spent some time drafting a note to Dr Aforey. It was not a serious draft but more akin to a doodle while he waited and thought. He had lunch in his office. It was a salad that combined alfalfa, walnuts, radishes and what was described as smoked duck. He wasn't sure whether the red on the duck was from the radishes. At 2.15 he scrunched up his note to Dr Aforey, threw it in the waste-paper basket, went to relieve himself and comb his hair and then took the elevator downstairs.

At 2.30 exactly a large vehicle the colour of a honey-comb pulled up to the kerb. The back door swung open and Cotton got in.

'I'd be grateful for your advice,' said Walter Resnick.

'I'll do my best,' said Cotton.

'Tell me what you think of Ed Lowell.'

'I never answer questions like that,' said Cotton. 'I've only met him a few times, first in London, last year. He mentioned that he'd have preferred more liaison then – well, he did when we ate together earlier this month. But my decision in London wasn't personal.'

'Would you trust his judgement?'

Cotton had spent time imagining his response to this question or something very like it, but it wasn't until Resnick asked that he decided how to answer.

'I think he has a tendency to be premature,' he said.

Resnick glanced at him briefly but then stayed silent for a while before nodding and raising an index finger and hitting an invisible bell twice. He sighed.

'That's it. You have it exactly. Do you think judgement can be learnt, Mr Cotton?'

'Of course I do. You're the historian, Dr Resnick. The English example given me as a schoolboy was Oliver Cromwell, but there are many others.'

'Cromwell was extremely cautious. He was observant, secretive and gradually moved up as he understood he was better than the other generals.'

'Isn't that what General Eisenhower did?' said Cotton.

Resnick laughed. 'Not quite the same circumstances.'

'Exactly,' said Cotton. 'But he certainly showed an ability to learn how power works. I don't know that you can tell Ed won't learn.'

'Sure,' said Walter Resnick. 'Sure.'

'I think you Americans, despite your differences, may be doing what we have done, choosing people from what we call "the right background". Someone once told me it was like choosing a wife of the right class who'd understand her husband's "affairs of the heart".'

'Heart has nothing to do with it.'

'Exactly my point. In Intelligence, there's background but there's also the psychology and the character. And

that's much more about the individual than the group he comes from.'

'Would you describe yourself as cautious, Mr Cotton?'

'I'd prefer patient,' said Cotton. 'I once met an agent who had come to the conclusion that almost everything in his life had been a reaction against his miserable father. I don't know if that was accurate or even reasonable. What matters is that he believed it. A degree of accurate self-knowledge is necessary in our work, otherwise you end up believing what you want to believe and then reporting it or acting on it. Without self-knowledge, you become poor at reacting to surprises and things going wrong.'

Resnick said nothing for a while. Then he cleared his throat and began to speak in a gruff monotone. 'I told you in New Canaan. This is a two-way relationship. And I owe you this, Mr Cotton. Your experience of certain drugs began just outside a pharmacy on the Avenue of the Americas. You were snatched as you turned to close the door, bundled into a car and from there taken to Fort Clinton and put into a Navy ambulance and more thoroughly sedated. You were then taken to a secret place – I am not at liberty to say where – and there administered the drugs you know about by someone who took advantage of Operation Paperclip.'

'A Nazi?'

'Ex,' said Resnick. 'You did not, however, respond usefully to interrogation. When the name Cherkesov was mentioned, you talked of Guadalajara in Mexico. Does that make sense to you?'

'Yes. When I had lunch with Cherkesov in London, he

said Guadalajara was where he would have liked to have lived, a kind of dream he had when he thought the USSR was about to collapse about ten years ago. I went there once as a child.'

'The dose was increased,' Resnick went on. 'You still did not respond in any useful or informative manner. And you vomited. By this stage your coherence was compromised, although after vomiting you sometimes had reasonably coherent spells. You talked of someone called Emmeline and the play *Uncle Vanya.*'

'I was going to marry a girl called Emmeline Gilbert. She was killed in a bomb attack, a V1, I think, in November 1943. We saw the play, very badly acted by amateurs, in a village hall. Ah. I'm forgetting. That performance was to raise funds for the Soviets – they were then our allies.'

Resnick nodded briefly and continued. 'The decision was made to increase the dose again. And I believe a variation was made to the proportions of the various drugs. Unfortunately, you began having convulsions. Your heart rate went over two hundred. At some stage and under circumstances still not made clear to me, a decision was reached to remove you from the facility and dump you in Centre Street. Your people received an anonymous call. I think you know the rest.'

'More or less,' said Cotton. 'Thank you.'

'It's not a good story,' said Dr Resnick.

'No.'

'It shows, if I may say so, incompetence and a lack of decision. Or ruthlessness, if you prefer. Do you understand me?'

424

'Of course. Dumping me was bad. If secrecy was important, they should not have let me go.'

'Exactly!' said Dr Resnick. He nodded. 'Do you have any questions?'

'First let me thank you for filling me in.' Cotton shrugged. 'As for questions, I have some doubts about whether you'd tell me who the source was for the Cherkesov death story.'

Walter Resnick half turned towards Cotton. There might have been a very quick smile.

'My guess,' said Cotton, 'is that if you had been less enthusiastic about building up Cherkesov as a bogeyman, things might have been different. I imagine that Ed was obliged to go lower in the Soviet Embassy for information, and found someone who perhaps resented Cherkesov's treatment of him. From what I saw, our Soviet comrade did not treat underlings with much consideration.'

Cotton paused. What had not occurred to him before was that Lowell may have been jealous of him because he had had lunch with Cherkesov in Simpson's on the Strand. Was that crazy? He glanced at Resnick before continuing.

'Being ambitious, Ed then chose to think of his source as reliable. I suspect Ed's biggest mistake was being taken in by a low-level sting. He became too anxious to show how well he had done.'

Resnick said nothing. Cotton thought of him as looking replete.

'Isn't this a small victory for the Soviets?'

Resnick cleared his throat. 'You mentioned "questions",' he said.

'Yes. In a more general way, I suspect my employers could be worried that my experience may indicate a change in the special relationship between our two countries.'

Resnick blinked. 'No,' he said. 'Similar techniques have been employed on American intelligence personnel.'

'Unwitting, you mean? Have you tried on women?'

Resnick did not reply.

'Your man Ayrtoun is coming back,' he said. 'What's he like?'

'Aggressive and very tough. I don't know what he'll be like now.'

Walter Resnick looked very serious. 'That will depend, you see, on how permanent the effects of the electroshock treatment are. Our information suggests results vary, even in the short term. He might need to top up, as it were, from time to time.'

'I know nothing about electroshock therapy,' said Cotton.

Resnick nodded.

The automobile had come round to his office again. It pulled up and, after a nod to Resnick, Cotton began getting out.

'I'm eternally grateful for your discretion,' said Resnick in his most rumbling voice.

Cotton smiled but did not pause. He closed the Cadillac door and a moment later the car swung away from the kerb.

He went up to his office and looked at a map: the Avenue of the Americas – Waverly Place – Fort Clinton.

'How did that go?' said Herbert.

'Far too early to say,' said Cotton. 'But useful. I learnt some things.'

Hornby put his head round the door. His cheek was still swollen from the dentist.

'I've just heard Sir Geoffrey won't be in until next Wednesday, 1 October,' he said.

'Thanks,' said Herbert.

Hornby closed the door and left. In 1945, when Cotton's original boss D told him who he would be working for in Washington, he had added that Geoffrey Ayrtoun was the kind of name that begged a Sir in front of it.

Cotton didn't know what Ayrtoun's return might mean to Herbert.

'Are you going to be staying, Herbert?' he asked.

'Oh yes. I told you about the bombes and the busy beavers, didn't I? I'm really in charge of technical matters.'

'How long have you known?'

'I knew I was temporary from the off, only accepted it because of that. What I wasn't told was that it would be Ayrtoun redux and knighted, also moving from DC to New York. I didn't learn that until this morning.'

'Resnick just told me. I think he was intrigued by the breakdown and then the knighthood, as a pairing, you understand. You saw Ayrtoun in Canada.'

'Yes, but he said absolutely damn all about coming back.' Herbert scratched at his hair. 'I have a daughter called Florence. She's a demanding child; the kind that in the school nativity play, given the part of an angel,

moves up stage in front of the crib and leans forward to peer at the audience. Having ascertained they are there, she waves and looks pleased they've turned out to see her. It's not theatre but, by God, it's convincing. She has a marvellous ability to concentrate on herself and ignore others.'

Cotton smiled. 'Who's better? Florence or Sir Geoffrey?'

'Florence. But then, she's not really aware of what she's doing.'

At the weekend Cotton put in a call to his father across the Atlantic in Peaslake in Surrey. James Cotton was in put-upon mood.

'I really don't like this new housekeeper, Peter. Her name is Wilmot. She talks too much *and* she jollies me along. You all *know* I don't like change.' His father paused slightly.

'I imagine she's trying to get to know you.'

'What? Do you really believe that?'

'You may not recognize that's what she's doing or think she's particularly good at it, but that's what's going on. Don't you think?'

'You must be spending a fortune on this call. There's no need, you know.'

'Of course there's a need! Both Joan and I are in New York and you're thousands of miles away.'

Cotton heard a sniff on the line. 'Your mother was a very *contained* sort of woman. It's one of the reasons I so respected her. She had dignity.'

'But she wasn't a housekeeper, was she?'

Cotton had to wait a little before his father responded.

'I'm depressed,' said James Cotton.

'Then come over here,' said Cotton. 'Joan would love to have you stay. You don't even know your own grandchildren. What have you got against having a holiday and unrationed comfort? Come on now.'

'You don't understand. I wonder what it's all been for. I've been thinking quite a lot.'

'Then give yourself a chance. At least come to meet your grandchildren.'

'I'm talking about the world. It's doomed, you know.'

'We've just come out of a war.'

'But why did we get into it? We were told we were going to war for Poland. After six years and millions dead, what's happened there? The Soviets have got it instead of the Nazis. At my age you do wonder what the difference is. Don't you think we British were guilty of absolute cynicism and humbug? We were caught by our own bombast. If we had had the guts to prepare and therefore been prepared to stand up to Hitler before, there wouldn't have been that ghastly war.'

'I understand. But that doesn't stop you coming here, does it?'

'No,' admitted James Cotton. 'But I'm at the age when I really don't want to be bothered by having to take decisions.'

'It's no more than accepting your daughter's invitation.'

'But I can't even take any money out of the country! There are all kinds of rules and regulations. And who'd

429

look after the house? I can't help feeling, you know, it would all be a lot easier if they came to see me.'

'But Todd has a job and the children are at school. They can't just get up and travel. You are in a much better position to do so.'

'I'm perfectly comfortable here.'

'With rationing and a new, talkative housekeeper?'

After a while they managed to agree that perhaps Mrs Wilmot wasn't so bad. Cotton then called his sister Joan and she admitted their father was not going to move. Joan said she'd think about 'getting over' in summer '48.

'It'll be better then, won't it? Britain, I mean.'

'I hope so,' said Cotton. He did not sound very convincing, even to himself.

29

O N Saturday evening Cotton put on his dinner jacket and went to the theatre. Minty Auchincloss told him that *All My Sons* had received 'rave' reviews. They had a drink, they sat down, the curtain went up, but almost at once Cotton was surprised by the strength of his reactions. He didn't know what it was – whether the actors were over-anxious to draw attention to their skills as actors, or that the characters they played were overblown. Cotton had never jeered or booed at any function. Here he almost started to his feet. He felt Minty's breath on his ear.

'Problem?' she whispered.

He breathed out. 'Wrong mood. Sorry.'

'Don't be.'

They left.

'It's only very recently I've allowed myself the luxury of walking out of plays,' she said.

'First time for me, too. Sorry.' He was still shaking.

'Film's so much less personal, don't you think?'

He kissed her on the cheek.

'What was that for?'

'For allowing me to leave. Thanks.'

She smiled and tucked her arm through his. 'We're

becoming friends, aren't we? Are you OK? You looked in some kind of distress in there.'

He smiled. 'Yes. I'm fine now.'

'What didn't you like?'

'That would be unfair,' said Cotton. He shook his head. 'I'm sure it's a very fine play.' He breathed in again to calm himself.

Minty smiled. 'Do you believe the Great American Novel already exists?'

'Isn't it *Moby Dick*?'

She laughed. 'OK. How about the Great American play?'

'You've got me there. I can't think of one. Do you have a candidate?'

'No.' Minty Auchincloss almost closed one eye on him. 'My aunt liked you, you know. She said you were polite and admirably self-contained.'

'But she didn't approve.'

'No, she approved too much. She may have said you were manly.'

Cotton smiled. 'I see. You're wondering if my behaviour just now in the theatre was quite manly.'

'Panic?'

'More rage.'

'Red mist?'

'It's a black shape. It has nothing to do with you.'

'Do you really hate actors?'

Cotton shook his head. 'Not in theory.'

'Good! Now why don't we move on and eat something? I'm famished.'

*

On Wednesday, 1 October 1947 Cotton walked from Sutton Place to his office. The news-stands were all about Dodgers 3, Yankees 5 in the first game of the World Series the day before: 'Game 2 tonite'. The office was fairly hushed. Cotton went to his desk and read through the reports he received every morning. The Islamic Republic of Pakistan and the Yemen had joined the United Nations the day before, raising the number of member states to fifty-seven.

At ten he was called through. He put on his Ray-Bans. A secretary showed him into what had acted as a kind of boardroom. At the other end of a long table sat a figure he did not recognize. He did not think the sunglasses were the problem. Nor, indeed, the amount of smoke in the room. The person behind the desk looked nothing like Ayrtoun and Cotton had to concentrate on that long nose with the pea-shaped bump on it to make sure it was him.

'I've been expecting you,' he said. 'Sir.'

'Really?' Ayrtoun shook his head forgivingly. 'We didn't want to compromise you, you see. I assure you, that is the only reason you were kept out. Do sit.'

Ayrtoun's transformation was more than remarkable. In a period of about seven months, he had attempted to recast himself entirely. He had lost many pounds of weight, the double-breasted blue suit had gone for something single-breasted in dark grey, and the old school tie had been replaced by one in black, presumably as a sign of mourning for his late wife Penelope. He had changed his hairstyle, now looked much more honestly balding, but most striking were his eyes and manner. The old

433

aggression and sneer had gone, his treacle-coloured eyes had softened and there was almost a kind of wistfulness in his face. He had given up his fight to stop smoking and was surrounded by clouds of surrender. His voice had changed, was slower and much less abrasive. Perhaps instead of his old snort, he had developed a nasal sound, mostly air, as if he had been very delicately punched or had just – so as not to disturb the person listening – made an effort to lift something large and precious.

'That's our problem,' said Cotton.

'What do you mean?'

'What our allies upstairs would call bullshit.'

Ayrtoun smiled. 'You've changed.'

'I've changed?'

Ayrtoun nodded and made an expansive rounding gesture with his right, cigarette hand. 'Take your time.'

'No, I'm ready,' said Cotton.

'Good. Do you mind having a look at this?' said Ayrtoun. He slid a slip of paper across the table. Cotton picked it up and read.

The simple truth is, the United States is inhabited by people of many conflicting races, interests and creeds. These people, though fully conscious of their wealth and power in the aggregate, are still unsure of themselves individually, still basically on the defensive.

'What do you think?' said Ayrtoun.

Cotton shrugged. 'Does somebody think this is true?'

Ayrtoun pointed to the paper. 'That's what we thought in 1940.'

'And now, seven years on?'

'We're actively considering it. This was the basis for

434

Sir William Stephenson's British Security Cooperation in this very building. His use of the media to sway US public opinion in favour of supporting Britain in the war was so successful that we're thinking of reviving it for our present needs.' Aytoun smiled. 'What were you doing in May 1940?'

Cotton thought. 'Sitting my finals,' he said. He looked at the words about America and Americans again. 'My tutor would probably have struck out "simple truth" for being peremptory and weak. He might also have given me a bollocking for making hopeless and snide general-izations. And probably dismissed it as journalism.'

Ayrtoun raised his hands as if impressed by a gift.

'Then he wouldn't have been much cop at misinfor-mation, would he? The point is, you see, that the electorate, whether American or British, hasn't been to Cambridge in either country. "Simple truths" are what people vote on. You can talk about prejudice, gut feel-ings, aspirations, even stupidity, but in 1940 we needed to persuade the American voters just as much as their elected government because we wanted them on our side during the war. In a sense, we had to help do the US government's job for them.'

'All right,' said Cotton. 'But surely in 1940 we had a clear, specific aim. For us to survive we needed to get the US into the war. Our targets here, the pro-German press, Irish and anti-imperial resentment and an understand-able desire not to send men to war, were also clear.'

'Absolutely. Stephenson was even Churchill's link with President Roosevelt and very close to the founder of the OSS. His main triumph was getting stories printed

435

in the US press as if they had come from proper news agencies. We have no evidence the American authorities are aware of this, even now. Do you see?'

'Yes, I do.'

'And?'

'Sir William Stephenson had a clear task and a direct link to FDR in a way I don't think anybody has with President Truman. Even so, the Japanese still had to attack Pearl Harbor before they would act. And as soon as America entered the war, Stephenson's task was over. The Americans were not only on our side, they took over the office upstairs. And since they won the war, I'd imagine some of those individuals have acquired a little more confidence in themselves.'

For the first time Ayrtoun looked to be in some sort of pain. 'But, confidence is one matter. Getting things right is another, don't you think?'

He picked up a fat file and handed it to Cotton.

'Take a look at this. It's the original list of journalists that assisted us in 1940 and 1941. Give or take a casualty or two, there are three thousand names there, from Alvin Allen to Walter Winchell.'

Cotton glanced through the pages. 'Are you saying we're going to crank up some journalists again?'

Ayrtoun smiled. 'We're thinking a little more defensively now. We've been getting a kicking from the Yanks about our security. It's fair to say we're thinking of kicking back, as loyal allies, of course. I've even used what happened to you to bolster my case. Our masters like the idea of dusting down an old successful plan.'

'Who are we trying to get into a real war now?'

Ayrtoun ignored this. 'I've been in Canada, you know. Bill Stephenson is Canadian.'

'Are you saying you have consulted him?'

'No. I'm saying that little Bill had a lot of his organization in Ottawa – upwards of two thousand Canadians who know the ropes. I've picked about fifty, most of them women.'

Cotton put the file down on the desk. 'The Americans may not know the specifics of what Sir William Stephenson did, but they certainly want to plant news stories themselves in the US press to influence public opinion. That's part of what they're gearing up to upstairs, surely, in the CIA as it is now called?'

'Yes, but they've started late and they're rather ensuring that they're poor and ineffective at it. You see, from our point of view, we don't have to be better than the Soviets. But we sometimes have to be a bit better than the Yanks.' Ayrtoun smiled. To Cotton's alarm he looked somewhere between wistful and whimsical. 'Of course, the Soviets always think they're playing chess. The Americans can't go along with that. They appear to be leaning towards dominos.'

Cotton's eyebrows went up. 'And we're supposed to play both? Or are we to play something else, like draughts or checkers?'

Ayrtoun laughed. 'That would be the same board as chess.' He smiled. 'You know, I helped you take Ed Lowell down.'

'I'm not sure I've done anything to Ed Lowell.'

Ayrtoun smiled. 'Well, you could thank Cherkesov too, of course.'

'For being alive?'

'Yes, and me for getting that information to you.'

Cotton nodded. 'I passed it on to Dr Walter Resnick.'

'Lowell thought his source was good. These mistakes add up. How did you play it with Walter Resnick?'

'Brief and clear,' said Cotton.

'You've been an absolute pro-American lamb, is that it?' He shrugged. 'Lowell has been dropped, by the way – well, moved back to the Navy. He's been half saved by Allen Dulles and some people who grow bananas. He's being sent to Guatemala for more hands-on experience. What do you say to that?'

Cotton shrugged. 'Poor Guatemalans, probably. Is he taking his Paperclip Nazi doctor with him? Dr Aforey told me the Americans have been injecting peasants there with stuff like syphilis for some years.'

'Quite dreadful,' said Ayrtoun. It was the nearest to his old drawl that Cotton had heard.

'Ed Lowell dreamt of being president,' said Cotton.

'Oh so many do, old boy. It's such a crowded field. But then they learn or at least settle for less – diplomatic rank, that kind of thing. There's also a business career. The banana people are getting a little anxious about how things are going in Guatemala. Something about democratic pressures. Perhaps you could mention that to Dr Aforey?'

'He suggested I join him at the United Nations.'

Ayrtoun nodded. 'You turned him down. We already have some people there.'

'In the economics area?'

'Yes.'

438

'You'll give me their names?'

Ayrtoun smiled. 'Yes. And you'll collaborate with Dr Resnick too.'

'Is that a good idea?'

'Why not?'

'My impression is of someone as ambitious as Lowell but considerably tougher and more calculating. He needs good information to impress those he works for. Getting it right once may have earned me more brownie points and helped remove Lowell, but for me to do more would require better briefing than I've been getting.'

Ayrtoun smiled again. 'Yes, yes, yes. Whoever said you wouldn't?'

'And the aim?'

'You'd be a very useful observer of the American process. A relationship with a man who has very close ties to three members of the National Security Council. He's the push; they're the older mouthpieces. You appear, however unwittingly and however unpleasant the experience, to have passed some sort of test. We should take advantage of it. You could, after all, provide a corrective to some of the more outlandish schemes that will crop up.'

'I doubt that,' said Cotton. 'Didn't you say Allen Dulles had half saved Lowell? Resnick is far too clever to be part of the CIA. And people return, even from Guatemala.'

Ayrtoun looked at him. 'You're sounding jaundiced.'

'No, I think I'm recognizing what you meant by "simple truths", Sir Geoffrey. The Americans – and us too, mostly by default and a bit of deference to the ally

we depend on – have granted the Soviets the inability to make mistakes. The Soviets always have an ulterior motive, sometimes of extreme and even invisible cunning. The fact is that the Soviets do not see themselves as being in a debate, or in a position to compromise and lose face. It leaves us open to over-valuing daft, dangerous and intemperate reactions. It's not quite politics and it's not quite war.'

'Quite so. I call it poxy politics and proxy war. I'm not sure we're really giving Clausewitz one in the eye.' Ayrtoun smiled. 'We still want you in on Soviet business, Peter.'

Cotton shook his head. 'I have a number of doubts about that,' he said. 'First, if it's true that we're riddled with Soviet agents, they're all waiting for the chance to betray us. Second, I suspect that the British position will be mostly geared towards showing we're trying hard to help the Americans.'

Ayrtoun smiled. 'You do know the alternative candidate is Hornby? He'd leapfrog you on the career ladder.'

'I'm not responsible for appointing Hornby.'

Ayrtoun looked delighted. He sat back and lit yet another cigarette.

'Let me tell you something. During the war our people here imported an astrologer from Hungary. Well, that's what they said. He was sent out on tour to tell American audiences, newspapers and radio stations that Hitler's astrological chart did not have a good ending. Look, he had the chart with him. Hitler was doomed by the stars. Hornby thought it worthwhile suggesting we resurrect the idea.'

Cotton frowned. 'He can't be serious. Who for? Stalin?'

Ayrtoun smiled and blew out some more smoke. 'Quite. Look, last February, in an aeroplane over the Atlantic, I was woken by a spell of very bumpy conditions. It was also quite incredibly cold. And I suddenly realized I had made a bad mistake. I had not wanted to see something, had held it off because we're the junior ally and our senior ally was giving us such stick on security. I understood – I *knew* that the Americans were about to make the most awful strategic and organizational mistake in their Intelligence Services. '

Ayrtoun looked up.

'But I needed to think. And there was poor Penny, of course.'

Ayrtoun paused, very briefly, after mentioning his dead wife's name.

'I thought I needed time, to think things out. Time away.'

Cotton nodded and waited. But Ayrtoun said nothing more about his dead wife, abrupt resignation or electric shocks in Canada or Duke University. Cotton had once thought of Ayrtoun as a spiteful Buddha lookalike with a long nose. Now any Buddhism was in his capacious, soft manner.

'I wrote a paper,' Ayrtoun went on. 'I argued that the Americans have condemned themselves to repeated failures of intelligence. Despite their own experience during the war, they have committed a basic error they should have learnt to avoid. They've mixed covert operations and propaganda. They're looking into the possibilities

441

of assassination when they really should have people blending in abroad. Without any official domestic remit, the CIA has to deal with domestic political or intelligence issues all the time. Paying radio stations and parts of the press abroad doesn't actually get you much information. Their organization is confused.'

Cotton nodded. 'I agree. That's why I've been thinking about the colonial side.'

'You're not being sentimental about the developing world, are you? You've heard of the Camel Corps, I take it?'

'The Arabists.'

'And now you're telling me you want to be part of the Machete Mob?'

Cotton said nothing.

'Shit! You *have* changed,' said Ayrtoun. He sat back and lit a new cigarette from his old one. 'We needed to stand back,' he said. 'Don't be innocent, Peter. These days many of our allies confuse it with sentimentality or a lack of commitment.'

Ayrtoun had never called Cotton by his first name before. It did not make Cotton feel particularly favoured.

'I'm not sentimental, but I'm not convinced, Sir Geoffrey. Our closest allies want to think that there may eventually be drugs that will alter minds when and as desired, but they're nowhere near getting to whatever they're after. I suspect they don't actually know what that is, but they are prepared to see what turns up. They like having the funds and the authority to fiddle with lives.' Cotton shrugged. 'As a response to the Soviet threat, it's not only ineffective, it's harmful and

confusing to the perpetrators as well as to their subjects, and it doesn't meet the case.'

He paused.

'Go on,' said Ayrtoun.

'When Stalin dies there will be a long period of small reforms and then clampdowns, because the Soviets are even more frightened of ideological infection than the Americans are. The Soviet thing will grind on, but it will eventually crumble because it's incapable of change. When I met Cherkesov in London, he told me that we British and the Americans both pursue a sort of mirror image of them. He suggested it was a belated, distorted and weaker version. I think I agree. The Soviets control their people very closely. Our governments react by worrying about the weak-mindedness of their electorates and how easily they might be swayed or misled. While I was in Narragansett, Herbert gave me George Kennan's X article, 'The Sources of Soviet Conduct', to read. Kennan says pretty much the same thing about the Soviets' present inferiority complex or defensiveness as we did about the Yanks in 1940. It's what my father would call "cultural bombast".'

Ayrtoun smiled. 'Is this what you've taken from your experience? I can't agree, of course, but I accept some of what you say. He paused. On the drugs thing, it may not be much of a comfort, but you're not alone, you know.'

Cotton shrugged.

'In fact, I'd say you were something of a pioneer. But you're right. These experiments are only the beginning. Wittingly and unwittingly, all kinds of stuff is being

prepared, sometimes by very strange people. I think we're getting a couple ourselves to join the biological warfare boys.'

Ayrtoun sat back. 'When I was in Canada, I read about a psychiatrist, called Friedman I think, who gave an eighteen-year-old girl, a survivor of Dachau, sodium amytal. He wanted to unlock what was distressing her and causing her crippling headaches. He decided that her problems adjusting to the post-war world in a different country were due to her failure to form strong attachments in childhood. He was, of course, an invincible Freudian. Some of us wondered why Dr Friedman did not consider the possibility that it might have something to do with the girl's concentration camp experiences and the fact that she was the only member of her entire family to survive. I did actually mention this to another professional or two. They appeared baffled, partly at my impertinence in asking such a question.'

Ayrtoun positively beamed. 'Dachau is quite interesting, actually. The liberating troops – Americans – reacted with horror and a considerable degree of violence towards the German guards, but their superiors found notes on the use of mescaline on the inmates and came to the conclusion that America was frighteningly behind Nazi scientists when it came to the properties of mind-altering drugs. That was because of the volume rather than the content of the notes.' Ayrtoun raised his eyebrows. Cotton had the impression of some sort of invitation.

'And that sparked off Paperclip,' said Cotton.

Ayrtoun nodded. 'Exactly. But the thing is, when

something awful happens, people often don't know how to react. They will look around for clues from other people to see how they themselves should respond. In Dachau, it took one GI hitting out at a guard with his rifle butt to set the others off.' He held up the piece of paper on his desk. 'You didn't like this description from 1940 of individual insecurities in a powerful collective. But think about it. Insecure people loathe indecision and a lack of response. They take comfort in a strong reaction, however irrational. They despise weakness but don't want to admit their own. It's our old friend corruption being preferable to anarchy – or non-response.'

He put the paper down and sat back. 'Right now, the US Air Force has some distinguished scientists from concentration camps continuing their experiments into the effects of high altitude. A lack of oxygen; matters to do with pressure. People die without oxygen. It's well known.' He looked up. 'Who has taken the place of the concentration camp inmates in the experiments going on now?'

'Recruits?'

'A lot are volunteers. Patriotism tends to be so trusting. The Army's doing other stuff, mescaline for example, mostly at Edgewood Arsenal in Maryland.'

'More recruits?'

'Exactly. The point I'm making, Peter, is that Intelligence has to take the world as it is, with all its mess and confusion, or we don't take it at all. Let's face it. People want to believe that this was a just war. One result is that nothing we do can ever be as bad as Dachau or Belsen. Do you see? Places like that have set the

yardstick for evil and in one way rather absolved us. We can do pretty much anything as long as we stop just short of Belsen.'

He paused. 'Did you know that when the 51st Highland Division got near Belsen they could actually smell it at distance? Those soldiers who hadn't gone in didn't believe what they were hearing from those who had. Some actually thought it was a put-up job; a monstrously overdone olfactory trick to convince them their own sacrifices had been worthwhile. They were decent enough men, though perhaps from a society less mobile and insecure than the American. But they were most anxious not to know the horror behind the ghastly smell. People still don't. They don't want to be disturbed. And I don't blame them. Do you? That's why they elect governments – to take responsibility for them.'

Ayrtoun stubbed out his cigarette.

'Have you worked out yet what Lowell meant by "middle class"?'

Herbert had obviously been keeping Ayrtoun informed. Cotton shook his head and shrugged. 'Didn't you say Ed was off to Guatemala?'

Ayrtoun beamed like a vicar happy after a successful sermon.

'Yes. He might have thought you were too moral. Or that you shared some of Kennan's idealism. Or innocence. Didn't Kennan in his famous X article mention the need for a supple, prompt response? That's just not realistic. It can never actually happen. Governments can't be supple in their reactions. Too large. Too bureaucratic. And Kennan is saying this to people who have just

won a war! You know the old line "Man proposes, God disposes"?' Ayrtoun shrugged. 'Now God is on the back burner and we're being holy about human rights.' He smiled. 'But from our own point of view, we're back to "a few men dispose of the rest", or at least of how they'll live.'

'Surely Kennan was right about something else,' said Cotton. 'The Soviets have their own insecurities. They're desperate not to lose face. That's what makes Gromyko behave as he does. The Americans are far richer and more powerful. Kennan was right. They should be firm but confident. The farther the Soviets get from the kind of control they have at home, or can impose on their buffer states, the more they have to depend on influence. Is that what you meant by dusting down the 1940 approach? Surely there's a difference. In 1940 the Americans had to be persuaded they were at risk. Now they only have to keep up American alarm. Getting some German scientists did that.'

Ayrtoun shook his head. 'The problem is, your view is not truly security-conscious. Something may go wrong. The Soviets may change tack and become active belligerents rather than suppliers of arms to others. We're only the British. We didn't win the war. We were on the winning side. The difference is immense. Now, as before, we bind ourselves to the Yanks. They protect us. We'll get some play out of our loyalty and previous experience of power. We'll also be helped by their acute paranoia and their consequent capacity to be unfavourably surprised and alarmed. And you know they really will be awfully surprised when their intelligence fails, as it

447

undoubtedly will. That's the American dream. It's such a *hopeful* business, but it does lead to dreadful surprises and furious reactions.' Ayrtoun looked up.

Cotton nodded. 'That's probably why I don't want to be part of the Russian business. No, the Soviets aren't quite the Nazis in several respects. They're not nearly as efficient or as talented. And they're not expansionist in the same way. But the war is simply being called "cold". That's not accurate. The main parties are not fighting – they're facing off, but in sometimes grotesque ways. I'd much prefer something more down to earth and less fantastic.'

Ayrtoun considered. 'I see,' he said. 'I hope you're not making your own experience into something general. That doesn't work.'

'No,' said Cotton. 'I'm not doing that.'

There was a long pause.

'Tell me what you're thinking.'

'Well, if this is going to be war by proxy, we're directly involved because of our Empire. Indeed, all the European nations with colonies will become involved as the colonies get some kind of independence. There's enormous scope there for influence from the US – and the Soviets.'

'All right,' said Ayrtoun. 'Not South Africa, but what if I were to give you the rest of our colonies in Africa. What are the problems you see?'

'Bad borders, poor post-imperial infrastructure, and those colonies with white settlers like North and South Rhodesia and Kenya. That will cause real problems.'

Ayrtoun did not so much sigh as leak smoke. 'I see,'

he said. 'I wouldn't give you South America – we barely have any colonies there – but I might give you a watching brief on the Far East.'

'I don't know anything about the Far East,' said Cotton.

'But it has the potential to be a shambles. The Dutch have abandoned Indonesia. The French, judging by their behaviour with the Japanese, will rationalize themselves into giving up Indo-China. The Chinese themselves are in the middle of a civil war. The Japanese have got a constitution from MacArthur and we ourselves demonstrated conclusively with the fall of Singapore that we are both incompetent and untrustworthy masters.' Ayrtoun looked up. 'Not India,' he said. He shrugged. 'With Mr Gandhi's spiritual superiority and Mr Nehru's socialistic claptrap, they're condemning themselves to a couple of generations of poverty. That's one of the more depressing aspects of Empire. Those who get out of it want to believe they were always better and that some sort of Eden was raped by the Imperialists.'

'Dr Aforey uses the word "pristine" *for that*.'

'Good for him,' said Ayrtoun. 'He's going up in my estimation. Do you think he'll be of any use?'

'That depends on how he manages to adapt to the UN.'

Ayrtoun grinned. It was the first time Cotton had seen anyone as enthusiastic and excited as Walter Resnick about the future, certainly on the British side.

'Yes, I think that will do for now,' said Ayrtoun. 'You write a report of this meeting and we'll see where we've got to.' He leant forward and clasped his hands in a

vaguely prayerful position. 'I'd call that a very valuable beginning. Thank you.'

As soon as Cotton had sat down in his office, Herbert put his head round the door.

'It appears our friend from Wilmington, Delaware is busy arranging rather spiffing lodgings for our Latin courtesan.'

Cotton looked up. 'He's not leaving his wife, then?'

'Angeles is considerably relieved.' Herbert frowned. 'She must be awfully clever at it.'

'At what?'

'Making men feel good.'

Cotton smiled. 'I'm not sure I was paying that much attention,' he said, 'but I don't think I'd have said clever. She doesn't really have to be, does she?'

Herbert sighed. 'I'm going back to listening. Sir Geoffrey tells me I should write a report on bombes and busy beavers. He says it won't be any use but will be something for me to do. He's quite . . .'

'What?'

'Ascetic and polite in his contempt, don't you think?'

'I haven't got the words right yet,' said Cotton. 'I felt oily when I came out, as if I had just been working on a motor engine, not something I know anything about.'

'Right,' said Herbert. 'We'll have to see what he does, I suppose.'

Cotton smiled. When Herbert had gone, he wrote down as much of his conversation with Ayrtoun as he could remember. This was partly bureaucratic reflex – Ayrtoun would get a copy and a record would be agreed.

It was also an effort to see through the smoke. Whatever the causes and motives of Ayrtoun's new guise, it didn't make him any clearer to read. The previous sarcasm and aggression seemed almost simple by comparison. Perhaps that was the point. Cotton certainly did not trust Ayrtoun's confidence in British abilities over American difficulties in any way whatsoever.

Cotton had not finished his summary of his interview when someone rapped on the glass of his office door. A middle-aged man, dressed as a tweedy English country-man in New York and with checked shirt and bow tie, had used his pipe to tap. Cotton did not know who he was and had no interest in finding out. He shook his head and returned to his report. The man opened the door.

'Mr Cotton?'

Cotton glanced at him. 'I'm rather busy just now. See a secretary and ask for an appointment.'

'Sir Geoffrey thought I should see you.'

'Did he? Sir Geoffrey failed to mention that to me.'

'I assure you, it won't take long.'

Cotton put down his pen. 'Really? The last time someone thought he had the kind of priority you want, he wore a dog collar.'

The man smiled. 'Oh, I'm not a man of the cloth, I assure you. I'm a psychiatrist. I'm here to help.'

'I don't mind whether you wear a dog collar or a bow tie. Both priests and psychiatrists lay claim to a superior overview, one based on an appointment as God's conduit and the other on what they feel are superior perceptions of what really motivates us all. Both *always* want to help

451

and both always feel justified in interrupting whatever else I may be doing.'

'I'm not here to talk about salvation. I'm here to talk about adjustment after a traumatic experience.'

'I see,' said Cotton. 'All right. Well, if you want to know how I feel about someone who had a breakdown earlier this year becoming everyone's boss again, I'm not saying it's a comfortable position, but I have enough experience to take it step by step. To say more at this stage would, I think, be unfair.'

'That wasn't what I came for.'

'Really? Why on earth not?' Cotton was beginning to enjoy himself. 'All right, you explain to me why you've interrupted me during work and I'll tell you what I think of your reason.'

'I say, you're being quite extraordinarily combative, you know. Almost aggressive.'

Cotton smiled briefly. 'Have I been ordered to listen to you?'

'It was regarded as a useful exercise—'

'By whom?'

The man paused. 'My name is Dr Roberts.'

'Have you had grants from the Rockefeller Foundation?'

'I'm sorry?'

'I believe the Rockefeller Foundation has provided funds for the Tavistock Institute.'

'To help investigations into the very serious effects of stress and trauma.'

Cotton nodded. 'I didn't say philanthropy couldn't be innocent when it wanted to be.' He looked up. 'Is

this the arrangement? You get to ask questions, but I don't?'

'This isn't very helpful, you know.'

'I have no intention whatsoever of collaborating, Dr Roberts. Is that clear to you?'

'I really don't understand.'

'You feel entitled to ask me questions because you imagine yourself to be part of a hierarchy. You think you're acting on behalf of my superiors. You're mistaken. They have left you on your own to deal with people like me. I don't accept your authority. I'm also aware that Sir Geoffrey may have sent you along to test my resolve.'

'I assure you—'

'But he's also testing you, man! That's how he works. I'm helping you now. Do you understand?'

'No, I don't. And I really must object to your tone.'

'Then you're free to leave and find out just how much support you have. Or you can start negotiating.'

The man frowned. 'I have nothing to do with negotiations!'

'Then I have nothing more to say to you.'

There was a pause.

'What is it you want?' said Roberts.

'I want all the papers on mass psychology and group behaviour we're passing to the Americans. Give me that stuff and I'll answer your questions.'

'I'm not sure I can do that without clearance.'

'You see? Ask Sir Geoffrey and see what he says. If I don't hear from you again, I'll know he said no. If I do hear from you, I'll know we're making progress.'

*

'Are you all right?' said Herbert.

'Mostly,' said Cotton.

'What was going on?'

'Just a little loud unpleasantness with the psychiatrist on duty. He came with Ayrtoun. Apparently they're letting these Tavistock people follow us around the office.' Cotton shook his head. 'Dr Sanford once asked me if I felt like someone else. I thought he meant Jesus or Napoleon or someone like that. But I think I may just have found out I'm turning into Ayrtoun.'

Herbert laughed. 'Not the new version.'

'Quite, I'm lacking that holy tone,' said Cotton. 'Damn! I think I've just used a psychiatrist as a punch-bag.'

'Good for you! I'm sure the bugger deserved it.'

'Wrong punch-bag, Herbert.'

'I don't think you should think Ayrtoun picked on you.'

'Oh no. But he may have picked me out.' Cotton shrugged. 'I've had difficulty reacting to the word "betrayal". I never really understood it.'

'And now?'

'It's a sort of one-way bond. Like one of those similes that doesn't come back. An actress I met at the Lowells' party in Newport told me we shared something in the eyes. She'd seen something of herself in mine but was not saying my eyes were like hers.'

'I don't have the necessary ruthlessness,' said Herbert. 'But I'm pretty sure Ayrtoun thinks it's about getting results.'

Cotton couldn't help it. He laughed out loud. 'Herbert!

454

It's always about keeping things uncertain. Dramatic flux, grand words and lending cock-ups some sense.'

Herbert looked uncomfortable. 'I'm not sure I'd say that.'

'No? I told him I'd rather be on the colonial side – in what he calls the Machete Mob.'

'But what about the Soviets?'

'He said Hornby would take over if I didn't.'

'Christ Almighty!' Herbert was appalled. 'Peter! Ayrtoun looks to me like he's making you an offer. Don't you see? It's right in front of you. A big step in your career!'

'I don't think he's sweating on my reply.'

'What are you saying?'

'At the very least, I'm going to take my time, Herbert.'

30

WHEN HE came out of the International Tower North that evening, Cotton saw a couple. The man he did not know, but the girl he recognized. It took him a second to place her and then he strode forward, smiling broadly.

'Rosemary!' he said. 'How lovely to see you again!'

She frowned but not nearly as much as her male companion.

'In Newport,' said Cotton.

Never fast, Rosemary Tyler's features paused but then stirred.

'You're a British colonel, or something?'

'How's Ed?'

'I'd rather not say,' she replied.

'Oh! I'm so sorry to hear that,' said Cotton. 'But are *you* all right, Rosemary?'

'Well, Minty's helped. This is Judd. He's at Carter Ledyard.'

Cotton promptly offered his hand and Judd, whether still at Carter Ledyard or with the CIA, shook it.

'Nice to meet you, Judd. Look, I won't keep you two. You have fun.'

Judd looked quite pleased. Cotton smiled.

'Look after yourself,' he said to Rosemary and turned away and began walking.

The bagpipes – Cotton had never liked them – have drones. The drones provide the dirge. When a tune starts up, a fraction before the chanters of the notionally melodic part come in, the whole can sound as an initial bray, like a donkey furious at the prospect of castration. Add in the rhythmic rolling of wooden sticks on taut animal skins and you have a military pipe band.

As he strode along Fifth Avenue, Cotton's head was filled by the deafening skirl of 'Black Bear', a raucous melody, a barely musical 'fuck you'. Dressed now as a sedate professional man, he could recall the swing of the kilt he had worn on parade during the war. There was lead shot at the base of the pleats to help keep mishaps at bay. For the wearer, it added a weighted swing to the swagger. His head came up, his eyelids lowered and without emitting a sound he felt his entire body stiffen up to yell 'Hey!'

But once he turned towards the East River, New York crowded back – the honk and roar of traffic noise and the jostle of a lot of querulous-looking people pushing on sidewalks in an overbuilt small island. For a few steps, the low sun coming through the mass of tall buildings warmed his back. Then he stepped into the shade and continued walking towards his apartment in Sutton Place. There was a slight chill that evening.

He knew he wasn't thinking. But it had nothing to do with drugs. The last time he had felt anything like that was on a beach in Sicily; that had begun with recovering

457

consciousness, then pain and adrenalin and finally a dull, but very great, determination to keep going.

'Mr Cotton.'

Cotton slowed his pace but did not look back. 'Mr Hoberman.'

Sam Hoberman fell in step.

'I've advised my superiors that I consider you, within the proprieties, of course, as someone we can work with.'

Cotton took several paces to reply.

'Yes, Mr Hoberman?' he said.

Afterword

As CUSTOMARY, I have introduced real people and events into this novel. These touches of recorded reality range from quotes to physical fact – British Intelligence and the CIA in New York really did find themselves in the same building at this time.

Rear Admiral Roscoe H. Hillenkoetter was the first head of the CIA until 1950, when he resigned. He was ultimately responsible for the failure of American Intelligence to foresee the North Korean invasion of South Korea.

Frank Wisner became well known for the 'Mighty Wurlitzer' – campaigns to orchestrate press coverage and comment along particular lines. The Wurlitzer was originally a pipe organ. In its electric form, it is often used at baseball games. The name may also allude to Dr Goebbels' famous 'Think of the press as a great keyboard on which the government can play'. Wisner's aim was to influence and support pro-American stories in the foreign press, but he needed and acquired domestic support in the US media, both to report what was being said abroad and to influence the reports published there. A number of foreign organs were financed, wittingly and unwittingly, by the CIA.

Frank Wisner was also involved in covert actions for

the CIA, including regime change in Guatemala and Iran in the 1950s. Anyone who doubts that Ayrtoun could have returned to a position of power after his 'breakdown' has a number of cases to consult. One is Frank Wisner. After a failure of intelligence on the Soviet invasion of Hungary in 1956 and subsequent failures of communication with those waiting for American help, he spent six months at the Sheppard and Enoch Pratts Hospital in Baltimore, where he received electroshock therapy. Later, however, he was appointed bureau chief at the CIA office in London, from which he agreed to resign in 1962. A working colleague of his in British Intelligence, Kim Philby, defected to the Soviets in January 1963. Frank Wisner committed suicide in 1965.

Allen Dulles was the younger brother of John Foster Dulles, secretary of state for President Eisenhower and head of the CIA from 1953. He and others were fired by President J. F. Kennedy after the Bay of Pigs incident in 1961.

Operation Paperclip was the name given to the transfer of German scientists to the USA after World War Two. It continued for some years, well into the 1950s, and its influence was very considerable, from rocket science to the alkaline battery.

Cotton himself is caught by a subset of the US Navy department's Project Chatter. The purported aim of this was to find chemical agents that would assist in obtaining information from people without the use of torture. The results were judged 'disappointing' and the project ended in 1953. In the same year, however, under Allen Dulles, the CIA started their own version, called Project

MKULTRA, to investigate the possibility of 'mind-control' drugs as well as other methods of obtaining information. Most of the records of this project were destroyed in 1973 on the direct orders of the then head of the CIA, Richard Helms.

Neither Herbert nor of course Cotton would have known the background to the 'bombes' and 'busy beavers' (early computers) mentioned. Bletchley Park remained highly secret in 1947.

The FBI suspected Rex Stout of being a communist or communist sympathizer from early in his career and particularly after his work with Friends of Democracy and his chairmanship of the Writers' War Board during World War Two. The distaste was mutual. In 1965, Stout published *The Doorbell Rang*, in which Nero Wolfe is hired to stop the FBI from harassing, following and phone-tapping a woman.

All My Sons with Ed Begley, Beth Miller, Arthur Kennedy and Karl Malden ran for 328 performances between January and November 1947 at the Coronet Theatre (now Eugene O'Neill Theatre) at 230 West 49th Street in Manhattan. *All My Sons* beat Eugene O'Neill's *The Iceman Cometh* as best play of 1947 for the New York Drama Critics Circle Award.

I owe the identity of the drugs used on Cotton to a conversation with an elderly Englishman that took place near Guadalajara in Spain in 2005. He also gave me specific information on their effects on him.

'Black Bear', the traditional pipe tune played for Highland Regiments marching back to barracks, is variously but not ideally available online. For the shout,

probably the best example is in a very short clip of the Canadian Black Watch marching off. Though there is a voice-over, the shouts are clear. For those who haven't heard a pipe band, the sheer din of the drums and the skirl of the pipes in the clip of the 12 May 1945 Victory March of the 51st Highland Division at Bremerhaven is worth watching. The 51st HD is mentioned in the book in the context of Belsen. Quite a number of those marching had been prisoners of war until shortly before, having been left as a rearguard in France in 1940.

Finally, black bears that stray into built-up areas are no longer killed as they were in 1947. Instead, they are sedated or drugged and returned to the wild.

Acknowledgements

T HANKS AS always to my agent Maggie McKernan, my editor Kate Parkin and all the team at John Murray for their support and encouragement.

Particular thanks to all those, still living and now dead, who were generous enough to share their memories and experiences of this period with me, which have been invaluable for understanding the background to this story.

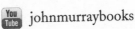
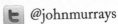
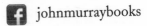

Praise for the *Peter Cotton* series

'Confirms Aly Monroe's genius for creating such tension that, while nothing much happens, you don't want things to stop *not* happening. She's commercial writing's rarest beast – a gloriously defiant individualist' *Daily Telegraph*

'Monroe is terrific at evoking this world' *Guardian*

'Monroe creates the atmosphere of the time brilliantly . . . an original novel and its people and places are so well described that I was gripped from start to finish' *Literary Review*

'Riveting stuff' *The Times*

'The Peter Cotton series by Aly Monroe is proving to be absolutely unmissable and her protagonist a truly fascinating creation' *Good Book Guide*

'Monroe's research is spot on and she paints her supporting cast with so many shades of grey that it makes a John le Carré novel look positively straightforward. This is wonderfully atmospheric' *Shots Magazine*

'The Peter Cotton series is getting better and better, and in *Icelight* the internecine squabbling of the security services is a prequel to the real-life problems during the Cold War. I'm really looking forward to the next book' *Crime Scraps*

'A wonderfully atmospheric book' *Euro Crime*

'Dodgy underhand dealings, political manipulations as well as a labyrinth of twists and turns . . . Definitely an author to watch' *Falcata Times*